'No God for a Warrior'

Jan Turk Petrie

Volume Two of the Eldísvík Novels

All names, characters, places and events in this book are fictitious and, except in the face of historical fact, any resemblance to actual events, locations, or persons living or dead, is purely coincidental.

Printed in the United Kingdom
First Printing, 2018

Pintail Press
Pintailpress.com

Author's website: JanTurkPetrie.com

ALSO BY JAN TURK PETRIE

Until the Ice Cracks:
Volume One of the Eldísvík trilogy.

Within Each Other's Shadow:
Volume three of the Eldísvík trilogy

The Story So Far

Bruno Mastriano, a young man hiding his extra-sensory abilities, is discharged from hospital to wander alone in a blizzard on the border of the city's Orange Zone – a rundown area plagued by criminals and subject to nightly curfews. He stumbles into a derelict building and a group of militant rebels who coerce him into helping them.

Meanwhile, a police 'decoy' agent contravenes orders to enter the Double Red exclusion zone, slaughtering members of the cartel operating with impunity within it. Decoy agents normally pose as regular citizens to lure the Orange Zone's criminals, switching the tables to overpower them with the help of a pack of genetically altered vixens – animals trained to assist their 'pack leader' – the decoy. There is shock and outrage when this decoy's foxes drag the body-parts of the dead cartel members away, dumping them in more affluent areas of the city.

Homicide Inspector, Nero Cavallo, needs to hunt down this rogue agent, along with her pack of foxes, before she threatens the fragile equilibrium between the legitimate and criminal worlds of the city.

Student protesters and sections of the media, believe this rogue decoy's survival against all odds is showing them the way forward and they begin to make demands on State Governor Leifsson to reunite Eldísvík.

Nero finds himself irresistibly drawn to his team's mysterious trainee – Acting Constable Chan though he begins to suspect this exotically beautiful woman isn't all she seems.

Unknown to each other, Bruno and Nero are both refugee survivors of a tiny minority of Italian, telepathic visionaries who were oppressed and hunted down in their native land by those determined to exploit or destroy their extraordinary abilities.

With the body count steadily rising, Nero uncovers evidence that blurs the line between perpetrator and victim, the guilty and the innocent. The status quo is under threat and Eldísvík's many fault lines are beginning to open up. Things reach crisis point when the homicide team is ambushed and Nero's friend and colleague, Lúter, is killed.

Though seriously injured, Nero survives. An earthquake wakes him just as his would-be assassin enters his hospital room. Male nurse, Nelson, tries to save him, but is killed by the deadly injection meant for Nero. The turmoil caused by the quake then forces his unknown attacker to flee the scene.

Having finally escaped his captors, Bruno uses his extraordinary abilities to locate Nero – the only other telepatico he has ever encountered. Knowing more about the deadly forces ranged against them both, he encourages Nero to escape from the hospital before the assassin can strike again.

'Let me remind you folks sitting up there on the moral high ground that, just as bad people can occasionally, maybe by accident or a sudden attack of conscience, do the right thing; good people can sometimes act in ways that turn out to be not so good.'

Former Chief Inspector Gautur Rafnkelsson
– sworn evidence to Eldísvík Police Corruption Tribunal
(October 2066)

'Everything has its limitations, even hindsight. It can't stop that speeding bullet heading straight towards you.'

Dr Jóra Bjarnadóttir (2088)
'*Memoire of my life in Crime*'

One

Eldísvík City State – Winter 2068

The floor beneath Nero begins to shake; every object around him is rattling. He hopes this is just an aftershock. Laid out on the hard floor beneath flickering lights, he's as helpless as a beetle on its back.

The world steadies itself. He turns his head to see one of Nelson's enormous hands is now pointing towards him like an appeal, or an accusation. With so much life in him only minutes ago, it's hard to accept the medic is really dead. Closing his eyes, Nero can still hear the poisonous hiss of the epijet the woman had jabbed into Nelson's throat. By all that's right, he should be the one lying motionless over there.

'I'm sorry,' he says aloud, hating the inadequacy of words, 'è stata colpa mia.' No, not Italian – he spoke English, for Christ's sake. 'I swear to you,' despite the searing pain, he raises his head to look directly at Nelson, 'if it takes me a lifetime I'll hunt her down. I'll make sure she pays for what she's done to you.' Though he long ago lost his faith, for a moment he almost fools himself a spread-eagled, lifeless man might still be able to hear his vow.

The building shudders, and it feels like he's lying on the back of some beast; he hopes it's about to settle down for a snooze.

Nero hauls himself up into a seated position. Face prickling with sweat, it's hard to draw in enough air through his cracked and battered ribcage. Once again he's escaped death by a hair's breadth. His luck – for want of a better word – must be all used up.

The lights above him blink a few more times and then stay on. Everything in the room is harshly illuminated. Nelson's feet are still stubbornly pointing up to the ceiling. Bruno should have let the poor man rest in peace instead of leaving him like that with his arms and legs splayed out, robbed of his overalls, his identity badge and most of his dignity.

His would-be assassin had taken a big risk coming here tonight. During their struggle he'd made contact with her naked wrist for a split second – enough to learn that she's found out his secret. She'd seen the boy as a potential asset but a police inspector with his abilities is too wild a card in the game she's playing. He remains a potential threat that must be extinguished. She's damn right about the threat part. Interesting that she'd chosen not to wear the suit. It seems the woman likes the chase – invincibility would have spoiled tonight's fun for her.

He hears voices on the other side of the door followed by hurried footsteps in the corridor, only exhales when they've passed on by.

Bruno's plan, such as it is, involves the two of them strolling past security and out through the main exit. Just getting that far would seem to require some kind of minor miracle. Shouldn't he stay here to help with the investigation into Nelson's murder? On the other hand, logic would suggest that she'll be furious not to have succeeded tonight; she's bound to have another go – and soon. Next time, she'll make certain no one will see her coming. In this weakened state, if he stays here he'll be nothing but a sitting duck.

There's an odd taint to the air like something is burning or melting. Nero makes a grab for the bed's side rail. On the third attempt, his hand closes on the cold metal. He tries to breathe his way through the pain as he pulls himself up into a standing position.

The sole of his bare foot is pressed into something jagged. Looking down, he can see it's fragments of that mug – the last drink Nelson had brought him. *Tastes a bit better in a proper cup*, the nurse had declared with a broad smile.

Still no sign of Bruno. It's too much to hope that the boy has at last come to his senses and left the building. No point in them both being caught in the crosshairs.

Though the room's stopped moving, Nero can't seem to maintain his balance. In the end he has little choice but to sit down on the bed and rest.

There's a noise from outside. The door opens and Bruno rushes in pushing a disability chair. 'It's me,' he says, somewhat unnecessarily. 'Sorry it took so long. You wouldn't believe the chaos down there – people being brought in on stretchers, broken glass and stuff all over the place. There was even a fire but I think they've put that out now.' He stops to catch his breath. 'I hope you're impressed; it wasn't easy to find an all-terrain model.'

Bruno pulls back the blanket on the chair. 'Ta-daa!' he says, thrusting a pile of clothes at Nero. 'Put those on, you'll need them. In the end, I had to force open some medic's locker. Fa un freddo atroce! My Italian's pretty rubbish but I believe that's what you say when it's cold enough to freeze your balls off out there.'

He reads Nero's mind. 'Yeah, course I'll help. Don't worry – I'll try not to look.'

The clothing belongs to a shorter, fatter man but it does the job. The boots, on the other hand, are huge. The boy shrugs. 'I figured too big would be better than too small. Besides, in your state you're not going to be walking very far.'

It hurts to shake his head. 'Tact's really not your thing, is it?'

Once he's dressed, Bruno throws a pack of something at

Nero and it lands in his lap. 'Painkillers,' he says. 'Stole them from a trolley. You got to hand it to precognition – it really helps with the details.'

It's clear the boy is more than a little pleased with himself. 'Oh, and I even got this for your face.' He holds up a burn mask. 'Yeah, I knew you'd hate the idea.'

Reluctantly, Nero takes it from him. It's a disquieting though not unpleasant sensation to be covering up his whole face. In his borrowed clothes and with his features so blanked out, he's more like a mannequin than a man.

Bruno walks across to where Nelson is lying. 'Thanks for the loan,' he says, taking off the nurse's overall and feeding those great floppy arms through the sleeves one at a time. It's quite a struggle with such a dead weight. Finally, he lifts Nelson's head and hangs his ID back round his neck.

Standing there in just his street clothes, Bruno looks a lot younger and skinnier. *Should I put a sheet over him or something?* the boy asks, without speaking.

No. Leave him like that – anything else will confuse things further.

Refusing his help, Nero pulls himself across into the wheelchair's seat. Overwhelmed by the resulting pain, he swallows two of the pills and then decides on a third. It's hard to get them down without a drink.

Nero takes off his stud and tosses it under the bed. He hears it skitter and then hit the wall. Like him, it's been through a lot, but its location tracking will still be working and might buy them some valuable time.

Bruno goes to the door and cracks it open a fraction. Outside, the corridor appears to be deserted again. The boy gives him the thumbs-up.

'You go ahead. Keep your distance,' Nero tells him. 'If someone challenges me, just keep walking. You got that?'

Bruno nods and then saunters out as casual as a regular visitor might. Nero waits thirty seconds before steering himself out of the room.

Further along the corridor, two people are busy clearing up scattered debris and broken glass. Like all modern, high-rises in the city, the main structure of this hospital will have been designed to withstand seismic activity as high as a 7.5 magnitude quake; loose objects, including people, are a different matter.

Neither of the workmen looks up as Nero passes. The disability chair is quite a revelation – despite its all-terrain wheels, it glides along soundlessly navigating any obstacles and potential trips using its built-in sensors.

It's impossible not to pass by the nurses' station on the way to the lifts – there's no other route. Getting closer, Nero can see the console monitors are lit up but all the medics are absent – no doubt busy elsewhere. Everyone around them is in a hurry, too preoccupied with their own urgent problems to give either the boy or him a second glance.

Out in front, Bruno is already calling a lift. The doors open and he holds out his hand to Nero like an impresario 'After you, sir.' Given the circumstances, his smile is way too assured.

See what I mean – troppo facile!

Don't go getting too cocky. Nero pushes the button for the ground floor. *That's exactly when you make mistakes.*

The doors open onto the entrance hall. The noise level is quite a shock. People are coming and going in every direction, many of them the walking wounded. Trailing some twenty metres or so behind the boy, Nero weaves a path through to the main exit.

Off to one side of the doors, two uniformed security guards are embroiled in a rowdy argument with a group of drunks. Bruno walks straight on past them.

'You seem a bit lost.' The voice came from behind him. Nero swivels round to find the speaker is yet another security guard. 'Can I help you, sir?'

'Couldn't get back to sleep after all the excitement,' Nero tells him. 'You know how it is? Thought a bit of fresh air might help – it's always so damned stuffy in here.'

The guard looks skeptical. 'Not sure that's wise, sir; it's dropped to minus six out there.'

Damnit – despite their agreement, the boy seems to be loitering half in and half out of the building.

'Look, I'm only popping out for a minute or two,' Nero narrows his eyes on the guard. 'Are you suggesting that, because I'm in this wheelchair, I don't have the right to do exactly as I please – foolish or otherwise – just like any able-bodied citizen of this city?'

The security man's posture changes – he literally backs off, wisely deciding against the alternative of physically restraining a disabled person for no good reason. The row with the drunks has, in any case, escalated into pushing and shoving. After a moment's hesitation, the nosey guard piles into the affray.

Nero gives the whole altercation a wide berth as he glides through the exit doors.

Outside, a powdery snow is being blown in every direction. Bruno is loitering a few metres from the entrance waiting for him. 'Didn't I tell you to keep on walking?'

The boy strides off down the street without a word. His thoughts are another matter. The bitter wind is already infiltrating Nero's ill-fitting clothes. Up ahead, Bruno is hood up, hunched down into his coat, both hands stuffed into his pockets. There's more debris here and there but mostly small stuff, easy enough to manoeuvre around.

Bruno, you need to turn left at the end. At the first junction, go right. The boy is still in a strop and in two minds whether to take any instruction from him. Nonetheless, he slows down. *Why should I?*

We should try to avoid the principle surveillance points.

Once they're a few more blocks from the hospital, Bruno comes to a halt beneath a streetlight. He turns to face Nero. 'It's time to wake up your friend,' he says. 'Yeah, that's right – the only person you completely trust at this precise moment.'

'What? No. I'm not prepared to risk anything happening to her.'

'It won't – she's much too careful.' It's still the early hours. The boy looks around at the deserted streets. 'We can't do this by ourselves.'

Nero's not sure he likes the sound of that "we".

Ice particles are clinging to Bruno's fringe. 'I promise you it'll be okay,' the boy says. 'She'll pick us up a few more blocks from here in her partner's pet ambulance.' *Who knew there were such wondrous things in the world?* 'In any case, what's our alternative?' He holds up both hands in appeal.

'Okay, genius – so tell me where to after that?'

'Old hunting lodge up in the western foothills.' *Yes – you've heard her talk about the place. Belongs to her dad but since his stroke, he never goes there. No one except Kass ever uses it.*

'Christ!' Nero says aloud. 'How come you're always so fokking precise with these predictions of yours?'

Bruno laughs, head back, snowflakes landing on his face. 'Your powers are weak, old man.' *What? Don't tell me you haven't seen Star Wars? Shame on you.*

'So, what's going to happen after that?'

'That's as much as I have right now.' The boy shrugs – a favourite gesture it seems. 'You of all people must know it's not a precise thing – stuff comes and other stuff, well, goes. Can't say I'm always one hundred per cent right.'

'That's not exactly reassuring.'

Bruno detaches the stud from his ear and holds it out to him. His hand is shaking. 'You'll need this. It's quite a piece of kit – signal's triple encrypted.' Between his words, the boy's teeth are chattering. 'Can't be tracked unless you allow it – not even by the military.' God alone knows how this boy acquired one of the new AVRs. Bruno gives him a knowing look. *If you concentrate really hard, you might even notice its other benefits.*

Like a true native, the quake doesn't seem to have woken Kass. '*Ha*?!' Her voice is still thick with sleep. 'What is it?'

'Go secure,' Nero tells her. 'No – you mustn't use my name. Someone just tried to kill me.'

'Fokk!'

'Look, I need your help. I wouldn't be asking if there was any other way.'

'Forget all that,' she says. 'What exactly do you need me to do?'

Two

They wait. Bruno keeps looking around, half expecting a patrol vehicle to emerge at the end of the street. The low rumble of wheels tells him something is approaching. Nero tucks himself into the shadow of a dumpster. As it draws nearer, Bruno shrinks back into the nearest doorway, stays there until he sees the words PET AMBULANCE emblazoned across the front of the vehicle and, below that, *Thought for Paws*.

The introductions are awkward. 'This is Sergeant Kassöndrudóttir,' Nero says.

'Just call me Kass.' Bruno can't see the woman's eyes with the streetlight bouncing off those old-fashioned, heavy framed spectacles.

'This is Bruno,' Nero tells her.

'And?' she says.

'He's Italian,' Nero says. 'Or should I say his family are – were.'

'Yeah, I guessed as much – what with me being a detective and all.'

Leaning heavily on the chair's arms, Nero pulls himself upright. 'He's a sort of relative – the distant kind.'

'Really?' Though the woman's not really buying it, she nods in his direction. 'Well then, it's nice to meet you, Bruno – at last.'

'Likewise,' he says. There doesn't seem much point in him adding anything else.

'First things first,' she says, 'let's get you off the streets.'

Refusing her help, Nero struggles up into the passenger seat – the more comfortable option. Bruno feels his pain.

'I'm afraid you're in the cheap seats, young man,' the sergeant says, opening the back doors of the ambulance.

Ignoring the ramp, Bruno climbs inside. There's only a narrow pull-down bench to sit on. The whole thing smells of cat piss and, worst of all, wet dog – one of his *pet* hates. He's surprised when Kass climbs in right behind him. She manoeuvres the folded-up wheelchair and secures it inside one of the cages. 'Don't want this thing flying around,' she says, before jumping down. She slams both doors shut and locks them into place. Bruno feels like a prisoner about to be transported.

'I want you to find a way to take that back to the hospital,' Nero says from up front. 'I'll be able to manage without it once I get the strength back in my legs.' Though it's clear she's less than convinced, Kass says nothing.

They pull away and it's such a relief when the heating finally kicks in. Despite the vehicle's bulk, the ride is as smooth as anything. The engine is almost silent – guaranteed not to spook all those pampered pets.

Nero begins by telling her about Nelson and how he's convinced their attacker is a woman. He doesn't elaborate much, doesn't adequately explain his decision to 'go to ground' as he puts it. She doesn't challenge anything he says though Bruno knows she has a head full of questions.

Nero falls silent. Bruno checks to see he's still awake.

Kass gets tired of waiting. 'Go on, sir,' she says.

'That's about all I know,' Nero tells her.

'I see.' Her sigh makes it clear she's seriously pissed at him for refusing to divulge any more.

One arm of the wheelchair is sticking out through the cage; when they change direction it keeps nudging Bruno in the ribs like the stupid thing's trying to remind him of something.

Nero cracks. 'Look, Kass, I know that you know I'm deliberately holding back certain information, but you're going to have to trust me on this – it's for your own protection.'

Still she says nothing, just carries on steering the ambulance.

'You must see that, by making you a party to all this, I've already put you in a compromised position,' Nero says. 'I'd rather not compound the situation. As you well know, some knowledge can be dangerous.'

'Whatever you say, sir – after all, you're the one calling the shots.' Her tone is anything but subservient. Bruno is beginning to really like this woman.

Once they reach the fringes of the built-up area, the roadway turns to dirt. The ambulance begins a steep climb. Bruno has to hang on to the bars of the nearest cages to stop himself sliding off the bench. It's not long before all the lights of the city are left behind them and they're heading into complete darkness. Bruno follows the arc of the headlights as they run along the sides of the hewn-out rock. 'These old tracks are a bit rough and ready,' Kass says, glancing over at Nero. 'I'll do my best to avoid the bigger potholes.'

'Don't worry about that,' he tells her. 'Right now, thanks to my young friend in the back, I'm more than a little high on painkillers.'

Bruno chuckles. *If this is you when you're stoned, I haven't got great hopes for what you're like sober.*

The three of them fall silent. Rounding another bend, Bruno puts his eye to a ventilation slit. He catches a glimpse of the Central Business District lit up far below them – already a whole other world away.

It takes a further half hour to reach the cabin. Caught in the vehicle's headlights, the place looks dilapidated and spooky – a thrown together collection of corrugated tin and wood on rough stone foundations. In Bruno's mind it was a lot more inviting. If you didn't know, you'd imagine the place had been abandoned long ago.

Kass kills the lights then gets out holding a small flashlight. Bent over, clutching onto whatever he can for support, Nero hobbles along behind her.

There's a large pile of logs sheltering under the eves next to the door. Kass reaches up to fish an old-fashioned key from the gutter. 'As you can see, the security features of the place are particularly impressive,' she says.

Inside it gets better. For further insulation, the outside walls have been lined with mismatched pallet boards. There's a central stove, two bunks piled high with furs and a basic kitchen. The air is really musty and bitterly cold. Bruno's eyes are drawn to the polar bear pelt lying on the floor between the two bunks.

'When my dad bought this place, it had been abandoned for years but most of the furniture you see had been left here,' Kass says, her breath misting the air. 'The old way was to leave everything in place for the hidden people – the invisible folk they believed were living here alongside them. They themselves might be moving away but the elves would be staying put and they would need all these things.'

Kass closes the makeshift shutters so no telltale light can escape. 'I'll get the stove going in a minute,' she says. 'It should soon warm the place up. You can even cook on the top.'

'The smoke will be quite a give-away,' Nero says, 'in daylight, at least.'

'Up to you,' Kass says. 'I wouldn't have thought it's much of a risk; there isn't another house for two kilometres or more in any direction.'

She turns to Bruno. 'There's no grid connection this far out but, if you're brave enough to climb up to the ledge when it's light, you'll be able to fix up the windmill and get some power out of it.'

The quake must have dislodged the tin plates and books that are strewn across the floor. Bruno helps Kass to put them back where they belong.

'Help yourself to whatever you fancy,' she says, opening a cupboard stuffed with tins, bottles and dried food. 'There's several flashlights and there's even some candles in the bottom drawer here just in case. They're not easy to get these days, so try to go easy on them.'

Nero sits down heavily on one of the bunks. They both stare at the cabinet above his head, which is protected by metal bars and a stout combination lock. 'What do we have here?' he asks.

Bruno follows the sequence as Kass punches in the code. 'Let's hope you won't need these,' she says, opening both doors out.

Nero whistles. 'That's quite some arsenal.'

'My dad is, or should I say *was*, what you'd call an old-school hunter. As you can see, he has a thing for antique guns and hunting knives. I offered to take them to his house in the city but he wants them to stay here just in case he miraculously recovers.'

Bruno laughs. 'Maybe he thinks the hidden folk might be planning a battle.' The other two remain stony-faced.

'What sort of things did he shoot?' Nero asks, though the furs on the bed speak for themselves.

'Mostly he went in for pest control – non-natives like rats and rabbits mostly. Then there were the escapees: mostly mink and – ' She nods at the furs. 'As you can see, he particularly hated the red foxes for displacing the rightful artic fox.'

Bruno gives her a wry smile. 'So, your old man's a bit of a white supremacist.'

'Only when it comes to animals.' Kass looks from Nero to

Bruno. 'I wouldn't say my dad is the most liberal-minded of men, but, like they say, we don't get to choose our relatives.'

'Touché.' Nero laughs out loud.

'And the polar bear skin?' Bruno asks. 'What's that all about?'

'He helped to track that bear down. Poor thing had floated over here on the ice. Dad was the one who finally shot it, so he got to keep the carcass.'

'But why would someone kill such a magnificent, endangered creature?' Bruno demands. 'Couldn't they have darted it and sent it back to wherever it came from?'

'Endangered or not,' she says, 'no one will accept them back; they're worried about possible contamination once they've been in contact with other species and their potential diseases. My dad, along with the other hunters, had strict orders he was to shoot to kill and so he did just that. But the next time it happened, he was on his own when he tracked down a female bear with her cub. Dad always tells the story of how they looked each other in the eyes and then she turned away and lumbered on with her cub scampering along behind.'

'Don't tell me he shot them anyway,' Nero says, a look of disgust on his face.

'No – he couldn't do it,' Bruno says. 'He lowered his gun and watched the two of them until they disappeared around a bend in the fjord. He never did hear what happened to them after that.'

Kass is staring at him.

Nero coughs. 'I should have warned you, Sergeant, this kid's got quite an imagination.'

Three

Governor Leifsson is up and dressed much earlier than usual. Despite the shower and the fresh set of clothes, he feels unprepared, half-awake. He can't stop rubbing at his eyes – as if that could help.

The bathroom he's in was built to impress by its sheer size. He hates how every tiny sound echoes off the hard surfaces. Whenever he moves, a lowlight comes on in anticipation of his next action. As he reaches up, a mirrored door soundlessly opens, its interior shelves softly illuminated. There's no way to outwit this fokking room.

He extracts the eyewash and goes through the usual ritual. After he's done, his eyeballs still look like they belong to a dead fish.

The governor peers down at his hands, holds them straight out in front of him. These days, they're never as steady as they ought to be, particularly the right one. On the opposite hand, the flesh is raised around his wedding ring making it hard to remove. How can his fingers have swollen so much? He makes a mental note to get a replacement in a larger size.

It's little wonder he feels like shit; during the night, he'd been shaken awake time and again by those tremors. Like some primitive torture, no sooner had he drifted off to sleep when another one would rouse him.

Leifsson recalls his mother's weird old grandfather – his own great-grandfather. Whenever there was talk of earthquakes, the old man would mutter some story about Loki, the shape-shifting god who was tied up somewhere underneath the earth with a venomous snake hanging directly above his head. Even though Leifsson was a small, frightened boy at the time, the old man would stare right at him with those ancient, clouded eyes and describe how, each time the snake's venom drips onto Loki's face, he shudders with excruciating pain causing the earth to shake.

That's enough, Afi, his mother would scold. *Don't fill the poor boy's head with such nonsense.* Still the image has stuck fast.

All his friends would shrink away whenever the old man visited. Back then, there were some in his home village who claimed, in all seriousness, that his langafi was some kind of sorcerer.

Though the old man is long dead, a shiver runs through Leifsson at the thought of him and all his terrifying stories.

He takes a swig of mouthwash, swirls it around. Ever since that damned decoy started her killing spree there's been no let up. Leifsson spits out the chemical masquerading as mint.

He's more than a little tempted to pour himself a bit of a stiffener – just a small, odourless vodka to help him get through what promises to be another trying day.

No. He's promised his wife, Liljan, he'll stay sober until the sun is over the yardarm – as the British used to put it. Fortunately for him, at this time of the year that's not so late.

To distract himself, Leifsson decides to run through his routine of stretches, beginning with his shoulders. Though he's hardly dressed for it, he gets down on the floor – the marble cold and hard against his arse – and sits there with his knees bent. Following his personal trainer's advice to the letter, he clasps his hands behind his back and straightens his arms while squeezing his shoulder blades together.

It's no wonder his joints are stiff. What did he expect from lying on that damned hard couch all night? It's got to end; holing himself up in his office all day and night is unseemly – unbecoming of a man in his position. Now they've beefed up security at the mansion and doubled the patrols around the perimeter fence, there's no reason why he and his whole family shouldn't feel completely secure sleeping there.

'I'm really sorry to disturb you, sir.' Kassöndrudóttir says in his ear. Amie, his assistant, must have green-lighted this interruption; must have judged it to be important. She'd better be right.

'What is it, Sergeant?' Leifsson holds the pose again, counts to three before releasing it. He's never understood why this woman prefers to be called Kass instead of Arnfríður or Kassöndrudóttir – both perfectly good names.

She clears her throat. 'I'm afraid there's been another murder, sir.'

'You've got to be kidding me.'

'Believe me, sir, I wish I was.'

Heart already racing, Leifsson scrambles to his feet. 'Don't tell me that fokking decoy's been at it again.'

'They found the body in Inspector Cavallo's hospital room. So far we've been able to ascertain that the victim is a 35-year-old male nurse called Nelson Tarone Wood. There are signs of a struggle – though some of the damage could have been caused by last night's tremors. Preliminaries on cause of death are inconclusive at this stage. There are only superficial injuries to the man's body; everything suggests he was forcibly given a lethal dose of something.'

'Are you sure it was murder? What does Nero have to say about it?'

'Nothing, sir.' Kassöndrudóttir pauses. 'I'm afraid Inspector Cavallo is missing.'

'Missing?' He starts to pace the room. 'How can a severely injured man go missing from a busy hospital, Sergeant? I should have thought it's blindingly obvious Cavallo must have been taken by force.'

Again, he has to wait for a response. What's the matter with this bloody woman? 'Well, Sergeant?'

'I think it might be best if we keep an open mind, try not to jump to any conclusions at this stage, Governor.'

'Well excuse me, Kassöndrudóttir, if *I* think it's best we make the blindingly obvious deduction that the man's been kidnapped.'

'If you say so, sir.' He hears her intake of breath. 'However, so far we've received no ransom demand. There's no reason why anyone would target the inspector if it's money they're after.'

Leifsson goes over to the decanter and pours himself two finger. Better make that three. 'As you know, Sergeant, this administration's position is that, whatever the circumstances, we will never give in to kidnappers.'

He gulps down a mouthful and it stings the back of his throat. 'If the state were to pay up even just once, it would open the floodgates to a hundred more hijackings. Who knows where it would end?'

'Yes sir,' she says. 'I'm fully aware of the protocols and procedures in a kidnapping situation.'

'I'm glad you're up to speed on something,' he tells her.

Four

Rashid strides into Cavallo's office. The man's personal effects, including his log, remain exactly where he left them before their disastrous raid on the bank. With Nero officially missing for the last twelve hours, Rashid's determined to sit anywhere but in the man's empty chair.

The department's cleaning operatives must have seen but refused to clear away the half-drunk cup of coffee from the centre of the man's desk – no doubt it contravenes some regulation concerning the disposal of unconsumed foodstuff. It's now acquired a thick skin with lichen-green mould around the edges.

Rashid remains standing with his hands on his hips while he awaits the governor's imminent arrival.

A sound makes him spin round. Sandra Maxwell hesitates in the doorway. 'Yes – what is it, Maxwell?'

'Governor Leifsson asked me to meet him here – in Inspector Cavallo's office,' she adds unnecessarily. Aside from being particularly smartly dressed – and he has to admit those colours look good against her pale brown skin – there's something different about her today. He has it – her hair has been straightened and strained back into a loose bun and now her nervous hand keeps checking for any mutinous strands.

Maxwell glances over to the desktop. 'Yuck, who left that

there to fester? That's just disgusting.' She picks up the cup and lobs it into the regular bin. 'No one's going to want to reuse that.'

Rashid catches sight of Governor Leifsson lumbering down the corridor. The man's grey trousers are too tight for his muscle-swollen legs causing them to rise up around his ankles.

The governor careers into the small office like he might just crash right on through the partition to the other side. 'Good morning, Governor,' Rashid and Maxwell say in unison.

'You're not in fokking primary school,' Leifsson says, eyeing each of them in turn. The governor runs a weary hand over his forehead before pinching the bridge of his nose like a man with a nosebleed. 'I'm sure you can both guess why we're all here.'

Frowning, Rashid decides to say nothing.

'Now that Cavallo's disappeared into thin air, we need to decide how to restructure the homicide department.' Rashid notes he's not specific about who is to do the deciding.

'First things first.' The governor finally looks him in the eye. 'I'm pleased to say congratulations are in order, Ashram; from now on you'll be assuming the rank of Acting Inspector.' Leifsson holds out his hand, smiling expectantly at him. 'Well done, man.'

Shaking his head, Rashid turns away from the governor and his offer. 'You're seriously proposing to promote me for failing to catch the bastard who killed Lúter? Right there when I had the chance, I failed to keep up with the fleeing suspect. This– ' He struggles to contain his temper. 'This sham of a promotion isn't right and nor is it just.'

'Well, boo hoo! Don't be so naïve, man.' Leifsson's face reddens. 'You can stand there telling yourself you're a miserable failure for not catching the bitch but where does that get any of us? You had a go and you failed – so now it's time to have another go.'

'Had a go? She – and I'm still not at all convinced it was a she – ambushed us. We were set up and, by some sheer fluke, I survived the whole thing relatively unscathed.' His jabbing finger is close to the governor's face. 'Out of the four of us, I was the only one not left lying on the floor in a pool of my own fokking blood. Does that make me some kind of hero?'

'No, of course it doesn't.' Leifsson bats away Rashid's hand. His face has gone from simmer to boil. 'But it does mean you're one of only two able-bodied and experienced officers left in the Homicide Department.'

'What about Kass? She's fit for duty now. In fact, while I've been here waiting for you, she's gone back to the hospital to take statements from the staff who were on duty last night. Why not make *her* Inspector?'

'Oh now I see what this is about.' Leifsson laughs into his face. 'This fuss is all about some boy-scout code of honour. Well then, rest assured, Ashram, I'm also planning to promote Kassöndrudóttir to the rank of Acting Inspector.'

'What, for losing three pints of blood? I can think of better reasons.'

'Oh for fokk sake grow up, Serg – Inspector. You've both been recommended for promotion several times in the past; we just couldn't handle the budget implications.'

Leifsson's face is close enough for Rashid to smell how stale the man's breath is. He can see the spidery broken veins that make his nose that angry shade of purple.

'With Lúter lying in his grave and the inspector now missing, do you seriously expect either me or Kass to be happy with the idea of stealing Cavallo's rank and divvying up our dead colleague's salary between us – isn't that the deal on the table here?'

Leifsson turns his back on Rashid. 'I'm going to leave you to calm down, Inspector Ashram.'

The governor steps away and then spins on his heel. 'In the meantime, I expect you as a senior and professional officer, to concentrate your energy, along with all that righteous anger, on the task in hand. Forget this self-indulgent, guilt-fest and move on. Do you think these murdering decoys are going to give any of us time out for injury?'

'As far as I'm concerned we need to concentrate all our resources on finding Cavallo,' Rashid says. 'Whoever killed that nurse must have taken him hostage.'

'Leave all of that to Kassöndrudóttir. I'll make sure she gets the necessary assistance. I'm sure you're anxious to nail the bitch who killed your buddy.' He points a finger into Rashid's chest. 'I'm relying on *you*, Ashram, to find these decoy murderers. I'm giving you my personal authorisation to do whatever it takes to hunt them both down and neutralise them.' He gives Rashid a knowing look. 'Whatever it takes. Is that understood?'

When Rashid nods, Leifsson exhales before clearing his face and turning his attention to Maxwell. 'Constable Maxwell; almost forgot you were there. I trust *you* won't object if we offer you promotion to the rank of Senior Constable?'

The woman fails to hide her delight.

'Good, that's settled then. Don't get too excited, Maxwell,' Leifsson tells her. 'You'll hardly notice the raise.'

'Thank you for your confidence in me, sir,' she says to the governor's back as he walks out the door.

Once he's gone, Rashid turns to the wall and hits it hard several times. 'That piece of shit –'

When Maxwell grabs his arm to stop him, he shrugs her away. 'Shh – or he'll hear you,' she says.

She's right – he can see Leifsson just along the corridor talking to Chan. 'I expect he's just promoted her to Sergeant,' Rashid says, massaging the pain in his hand. 'No doubt he'll want you both to show your gratitude in a tangible way.'

'Is that so, *Acting* Inspector?' Maxwell narrows her eyes on him. 'I've been working my butt off for the last four years – so as far as I'm concerned I've bloody well earned this promotion.'

Rashid sees Leifsson press a hand to Chan's shoulder

before he walks away. 'In any case,' Maxwell says, 'from what I've heard, if the governor is the type to demand sexual favours in return for advancement, he'd be more likely to ask you to do the honours.'

Rashid frowns. 'Are you're saying Leifsson's gay? No way. I mean he's got a stunning wife, a load of kids – all that stuff.'

'He also claims to be a devout Christian but does he strike you as a man of God?'

Is she winding him up? 'So how do you know this?'

'One of his minders is an old friend of one of my friends. Those security officers get to know every last thing about the people they work for and they're not always discreet.'

'But why would Leifsson bother to hide the fact that he's gay? Nobody cares about that anymore. Hell, it would increase his appeal to the pink vote.'

'Yes, but then there's the conservative right to consider. Think about it.' Her smile is conspiratorial. 'What's more, Liljan Leifsson is hugely popular with the voters. The woman's approval ratings are way ahead of her husband's. She comes across as an exemplary wife and mother – all part of the fairy-tale the electorate are so keen to lap up.'

Rashid winces at the woman's mix of metaphors. Chan slips into the room. 'The governor's just made my assignment to homicide permanent. I'm officially part of the team.'

While Rashid's grin is forced, Maxwell shows enough enthusiasm for both of them. 'That's great, Jie Ning.' She hugs her then waits a beat. 'Before you came in, *Acting Inspector* Ashram here was suggesting that Leifsson might be expecting certain personal favours from us both in return.'

Rashid's hands go up in surrender. 'Look, it was just a throwaway remark – a bad joke, okay? Don't make me out as a sexist bastard.' This is a minefield. He takes a breath. 'I fully concede it was an inappropriate comment and I offer my sincere apologies if I've caused either of you junior officers any offence.'

Chan frowns. 'Isn't Leifsson – I mean I've heard, you know–'

'I think you should leave it there, Constable,' Rashid says. 'Right now, with Nero missing and who knows how many would-be serial killers running around this city, whatever our differences, all of us need to be playing for the home team.'

Five

Nero wakes to the mournful cries of gulls. Daylight is filtering in through the gaps in the shutters. The wooden bunk he's lying on is almost as narrow as a coffin. The last thing he remembers is waking to complete and utter darkness as he groped around on the table for that pack of painkillers. Everything after that is unnaturally blank.

His head heavy from sleep and all those pills, he pushes back the furs he'd piled over himself. 'Ahi!' Nero screws up his eyes and waits for the stabbing pains in his chest to subside a little. Slowing down every movement, he sits up and then tries massaging his aching ribcage. It doesn't help.

The air inside the cabin is stuffy but not nearly as cold as he anticipated. His legs take his weight more readily than before as he hobbles across to the nearest window. It's a small triumph when he gets all the way over without needing to lean on anything for support.

He opens up the shutters and a blast of cold air comes in through the ill-fitting frame. All around the cabin, skeins of seabirds are wheeling and calling in the bright morning air.

Bruno's long legs are dangling out of his bunk but the boy is still out for the count, fully dressed and gently snoring with his mouth half open. The sight of that polar bear's pelt on the floor by the boy's bunk unnerves Nero. Kass's dad had obviously dabbled in taxidermy – he'd stuffed its head and even sewn a pair of glass eyes in the damned thing. The animal is staring straight at him with its false eyes glinting.

A few red embers remain in the stove – a couple of fresh logs ought to get the fire going again. He just needs to summon up the energy required.

Turning back to the view, Nero sees a movement outside in the bushes. Thankfully, it's only a gyrfalcon in its pale winter plumage. The bird flies off to perch on a pinnacle of rock, pulling apart what looks like a duck. With its bloodied talons clamped to the duck's body, the gyr's head comes up to study him, a sliver of fresh meat dangling almost comically from its beak.

The snoring has stopped and Bruno is holding a hand up in front of his eyes like a believer encountering his god. 'Did you have to open that?'

'It's almost noon,' Nero says.

'So what?' A matter of seconds later the boy declares, 'I'm starving. What d'you fancy for breakfast?' *Coffee's not enough – you need to build up your strength.*

What, are you my mother now? Nero tries not to chuckle – it hurts too much.

The boy is straight out of bed and walking towards the door, his dark hair sticking up in several places. 'Once I've had a piss, I'll fix us some breakfast.' *You've got to be kidding – we're miles from anywhere and you expect me to carry a gun every time I venture outside.*

Nero stumbles over to the stove and opens it up. He throws in a couple of sticks for kindling and waits for fresh flames to appear.

The log he picks up seems to be twice the weight it should be. It takes all his strength to feed a couple more of them on top. After a moment, a bright flame is leaping up between the logs.

'I could easily have done that,' Bruno says from the doorway. 'Are you always this stubborn?'

The boy goes over to the supply cupboard. 'So – what's it to be? Beans? More beans? Tinned spaghetti in tomato sauce with meatballs? Some sort of cereal that looks very good for your digestion but probably tastes like cardboard?'

'Aside from my urgent need for a coffee, I'm not sure I care.'

'In that case, I'll rustle up one of my specials. Being a student, I'm pretty ace at this. You could say it's my forte.'

The boy holds out his hands like he always does when he's about to venture into Italian. 'Or, should I say: È il mio cavallo di battaglia.' His laugh is long and loud. 'No pun intended. However, now I think about it, battle horse seems quite a good description for you. Seriously – you should call yourself Inspector Nero Cavallo di Battaglia.'

'Christ, are you always this upbeat in the morning?' Nero slumps into the nearest chair. 'I can already feel a bad case of cabin fever coming on.'

Bruno stares at him. 'Joking apart, it's not too warm in here but you look a bit red in the face. I'm no doctor, but if I had to guess I'd say you have a temperature.'

Due to the pain in his ribs, Nero had forgotten about his other injuries. Now he thinks about it, the burn on his arm is a lot sorer than it was. It's hard to tell if the infection has gotten worse without taking the bandage off and he'd rather not do that right now.

'In any case,' Bruno says, 'if you want coffee, I'm going to have to turn on the water supply.' *Yeah, I remember her instructions. Even if I didn't, I can touch pretty much any object and get that sort of information from it.*

Nero raises an eyebrow. 'Well now, aren't you the cocky one?'

Bruno disappears outside, whistling a tune. Whatever his other abilities, the boy's not much of a whistler.

Nero looks through the food cupboard. Tinned new

potatoes; dehydrated mashed potato, instant noodles – all to accompany the meat the old man had just shot.

The boy comes back too quickly. 'I was just turning on the water when I looked across and there was a fox, just watching me.' All his bravado has gone. 'It stood its ground and just stared at me.'

'So – what do you expect? We're out in the wild.'

'Well, for a start it was a vixen. I've been up close and personal to those damned things so I can assure you I know the difference.'

'Did you see more than one?'

'No. But that murdering bitch could be out there right now.'

Nero frowns at him. 'Look, I'm not so good at predicting things, but you – you're different. Wouldn't you know, wouldn't your instincts have warned you if Ása was really that close?'

'Maybe. Maybe not. Hell, I don't know.' The boy keeps shaking his head. *Like I told you before – it's not what you'd call an exact science.*

Nero can feel how scared the boy is. 'There has to be dozens – possibly even hundreds of foxes up here in these foothills – they retreat up here during the day. It's highly unlikely, in fact I'd say virtually impossible, that she could have tracked us down so fast.'

He puts a hand on the boy's shoulder. 'So come on – how about that coffee you promised.'

Bruno manages a grin. 'Yeah, okay.'

'Don't worry, I can't do much these days but I can keep look out.' He stumbles over to the other window and opens the shutters. More light streams in, showing up thick layers of cobwebs and a trail of mouse droppings near the stove. Nero peers out through the grimy glass. 'Far as I can tell, right now there's nothing but rocks and birds out there.'

The boy turns on the water tap, there's a loud belch followed by gurgling and then the water starts to flow. Hands still a little unsteady, Bruno fills the blackened kettle and puts it on top of the stove.

'You know my nonna taught me to shoot when I was a kid,' Nero says. 'After you've rustled up that breakfast you promised me, I'll show you how to use some of those guns.'

'How d'you fancy beans and spaghetti in tomato sauce with a touch of chilli powder?' The boy starts opening cans.

Not sure about the chilli.

Go on – let's live a little. I might even add a dash of fish sauce.

Nero pulls a face. *I thought you were trying to encourage me to eat.* Smiling at the boy, he decides not to mention hearing the screams of foxes when he woke in the night.

The boy turns from the stove. *You keep forgetting, Nero – I know everything you know.*

Six

Leifsson walks into his office to find his deputy, Hagalín, already in there. 'Good afternoon, Governor,' the man says with a look in his eyes that's nothing short of furtive.

Attempting a slight of hand, Hagalín replaces something he must have picked up off the desk then walks towards Leifsson with a broad smile that tries to shake off any suspicion that he might have been snooping.

'I trust you're well,' the little snake adds, like he's suggesting the opposite. Why the hell had Amie let him in here unsupervised? He makes a mental note to reprimand the woman.

'I thought we should discuss the latest development,' Hagalín says, in that too-knowing voice of his. The man's suit looks brand new and more expensive than his salary can justify.

'Which development are you talking about?' Leifsson walks over to his desk and quickly scans the surface to see if he can spot what Hagalín was looking at a moment ago. Nothing stands out.

'Well, I assume you got the report about that woman.' Though the room's at its usual temperature, Hagalín appears to be trying to loosen his collar.

'Which woman?'

'The one who was clubbed to death in the Orange Zone last night – Andrea North.'

Leifsson tries to disguise his surprise. 'Yes, I've got the intel on that here somewhere.' Why hasn't he been briefed on this?

'Well, as you're no doubt aware, the incident occurred in District Fourteen – close to the scene of the second decoy murders.'

'I imagine it might have been some sort of retaliatory act.'

'Quite possibly,' Hagalín says. 'Although, as you might expect, no one wants to stick their neck out at this stage. Our main problem is the surveillance footage that captured the whole thing.'

'How is that a problem? I would have thought it was a distinct advantage.'

'You're right, it wouldn't be if it hadn't been leaked. The whole damned thing is out there for anyone to see.'

'*Sjit*!' Leifsson goes to his console, unlocks it with his thumbprint and then concentrates on entering the series of new passcodes the security department had insisted on. Talk about belts and fokking braces.

A few more clicks and then, sure enough, he can see all social and news platforms have been showing the same grainy images from a fixed surveillance point. A flashed up message tells him this is not yet available in holo.

Though the angle's awkward, he sees a screaming woman being dragged away from her open front door and up a walkway towards the camera position. 'The numeric signature on this is from a military streetcam,' he tells Hagalín. 'How in the hell's name did this stuff get out there?'

'Exactly.'

The woman is blonde, slim, mid to late thirties at a guess. She's only dressed for indoors. The sound quality is less than sharp but it's possible to hear snippets of what's being said.

'Get yours …'

'How does it feel now, eh?'

' … had it coming, decoy bitch.'

There's whooping and chanting from an unseen crowd. 'Do it! Do it!' More whooping, a barrage of curses and threats.

At first he sees only the backs of the gang members but then they move in to surround the poor woman. She desperately tries running at them and pleading but she can't escape the circle. They close in to form a human wall. A few missiles are thrown; what looks like rocks and stones. One hits the woman smack in the face. Blood starts running into her eyes and all down her face, staining her pale top.

A hooded figure – surely too big and broad to be female – steps forward. The human wall seals itself behind him. He hesitates before approaching the woman. At his side, he's carrying a length of something that could be metal but might be timber. A bat? Maybe an oar of some kind?

Up close, the man towers over his victim. He has to be two metres tall or more – a giant of a man. He raises his weapon and then, with both hands, swings it right down on top of the woman's head.

'Djöfulsins helvíti!' Leifsson winces at the sickening whack as it connects with her skull. 'Fokking barbarian!'

Though they have their hoods pulled up, the faces of the perpetrators are unmasked. Leifsson peers into the screen. They all look to be Caucasians although that one on the right might not be. Late teens? Early twenties? All appear to be men.

The woman ought to have been instantly poleaxed by such a blow but instead she flops forward before slowly sinking to the ground.

Now the whole gang moves in. She isn't even stirring by now, but they kick her anyway; just keep laying into her with their boots and then their bare fists.

'Red in tooth and claw,' Leifsson says as he looks away. He wants to retch, has to take several steadying breaths.

'This has had a record number of hits and shares.' Leifsson winces at the man's choice of words.

'Patrolmen took a statement from the husband – Lazlo North – an American by birth,' Hagalín tells him. 'Seems

Andrea North never hurt a fly. She was a strict vegan. Worked here in the city, as a cleaner. No known enemies. However, she had a habit of putting scraps out to feed various wild animals – mostly rabbits but sometimes foxes. The husband thought some of the neighbours might have noticed her doing it.'

The picture on the screen shows the attackers running off and then just the woman's twisted and abandoned body. He waits to see if anyone rushes to her aid. They don't. After a minute, he turns the monitor off.

'So her coward of a husband watched it all?' He's furious not just at such an act of brutality but also at having to be briefed about it by his deputy. Looking down, Leifsson sees his own fists are tightly curled.

'Lazlo stayed behind the curtain – too terrified to intervene,' Hagalín says. 'Kept repeating to anyone who would listen that he'd be just as dead if he'd tried to help her.'

'What about the identity of these murdering thugs? Shouldn't be too difficult to track them down. We've got facials and the sound on that footage can surely be boosted.'

Hagalín is already nodding. 'Lazlo was able to identify most of them. It seems they're well-known locally. He claims to recognise the hooded guy by his voice. They're being brought in for questioning right now. Unharmed – unfortunately, none of them chose to resist arrest.'

Still shaking his head, Leifsson walks over to the window. He'd like to retreat into the majesty of the view. Despite the many layers of glass, there are shades of pink and grey up there in the sky. He tries to admire what he's seeing – the timeless splendour of the snow-encased mountain ranges wrapped around the bustling city. How fresh the air must be way up there away from everything else.

Right in front of him, a scrofulous looking starling walks back and forth along the ledge outside as if it can't make up its mind what to do next. 'You and me both,' he mutters into the glass.

He turns back to Hagalín. 'We need to make sure the prosecutors throw everything they've got at this. The release of this footage may compromise its value as evidence when this comes to trial. I don't want a single one of those bastards to walk free.'

Leifsson regains the centre of the room. 'This leak is the last thing we needed on top of everything else. I'm going to throw the book and then whole fokking desk at whoever was responsible.'

'Is the response analysis in yet?' He badly needs a drink, wishes Hagalín would piss off.

'Can't be long.' Hagalín gives him a long look.

'Well, we've both got work to do,' Leifsson says, 'Don't let me detain you.'

'Yes, of course,'

Finally, the man moves towards he exit. 'I don't have to tell you, this puts a whole new perspective on this decoy business.' Hagalín can be relied on to state the obvious. Nonetheless, looking down at the image of those retreating assailants frozen in motion on his console screen, Leifsson sees the man's point only too well.

Seven

Through the glass door of the incident room, Rashid has a view of Maxwell and Chan at the other end of the corridor. As they approach, he hears Maxwell say, 'I can't understand why anyone would behave like that.'

He doesn't catch Chan's reply.

They come into the room one after the other and he smells perfume – the scent of blossoms with a deeper note of spice. The women are too close together to identify the wearer.

'Okay, we're all here. Good,' he says, taking charge. Rashid looks at each of the women in turn. Chan and Maxwell have chosen to sit close like new best friends while Kass remains opposite him, resting her injured arm on the edge of the table. He's alone on his side of the room.

'I think we need to begin by taking stock of these various investigations,' he says, 'where we are with each of them, at this point in time.' He focuses on the two constables. 'Inspector Kassöndrudóttir and I will decide between us where we go from here.'

Kass has an odd expression on her face. 'Actually, my rank is Acting Inspector, but as you all know, I prefer plain old Kass.' The light on her spectacles obscures her eyes as she looks directly at him. 'If you're keen on being formally addressed, we should call you Acting Inspector Ashram.'

'You're right – whole thing's too much of a mouthful.' He shrugs it off, won't rise to the bait. 'So let's drop all the acting stuff, shall we? You can call me Rashid.'

'Good, because the rest of it is certainly hard to swallow,' Kass says. She re-crosses her legs so that her body is turned well away from him. 'Leifsson has asked me to concentrate on locating Nero,' she says. 'As far as I'm concerned, that investigation has to involve finding the person who murdered the nurse found in his hospital room. The governor wants me to make Nero's disappearance my priority, while you and the others try to track down those two decoys.'

Rashid sighs with exasperation. 'We need to remember that Leifsson may be State Governor but what he most definitely *is not* is the man – or should I say the person – in charge of the homicide department.'

Kass is ready to say something but he stops her with a raised hand. 'We'll get to Nero and the rest of it in a minute. First off, I thought we should make a start on where we've got to in our hunt for these decoys.'

Kass is still stony-faced. It isn't going to be easy sharing command with her if she doesn't let up a bit. 'Okay then,' she says, 'let's begin by looking at precisely what happened at the Lime Street Bank.'

She steadies herself on the table as she gets to her feet. Using her good hand, she sets about adjusting this and that as she sets up the holo-pro. 'The tech boys have finally put together a full reconstruction from every available source,' she says, 'including the infra-red images from inside the building.' She makes a few final adjustments. '*Play Point Two*.'

Rashid recognises the front of the bank, its façade only partly illuminated by streetlight while the bulk of the building remains in darkness.

As they watch, four shadowy figures approach its pillared portico. 'So here we all are. That's Lúter going off to the right,' Kass says, her finger piercing the projection. 'And here's me, peeling off to the left.'

Two miniaturised, grey-scale figures disappear from the light then re-emerge like a new life-form in glowing purple and red thermographics.

'Here's where we're testing the grids on the windows. As you can see, they're all securely in place.' The images of Kass and Lúter come together at the back of the building. Rashid sees them check every external door before they begin to circle back towards the front elevation.

He can hardly bear to look at that multi-coloured rendition of Lúter in his final few minutes of life.

'Okay, now the two of us are nearing the front of the bank. At the entrance, we can see Nero is retreating, taking cover before he blows the charge on the front door.'

A searing white flash obscures the whole of the front elevation. As it dies down, Nero is on his feet and running right through it into the building. Rashid looks at the man that was him back then – how he's still lingering there on the steps.

Kass and Lúter arrive at the front of the building, transformed once more into monotone. Without any hesitation, the two of them run into the bank while he hardly moves.

Rashid's heart is pumping; his back and armpits run with sweat. He wants to grab hold of his other self and shake him. Roused from its torpor, his doppelganger finally runs into the bank behind all the others.

'Okay,' Kass says, 'so here we are in the main body of the bank.'

The angle has changed. The bank's interior is a cavernous dark blue. Their former selves move in procession, like priests, in glowing purples and reds.

'We're sweeping the building now. Nero's here at the front,' Kass says, once again pointing through the projection. 'Rashid is bringing up the rear.' Her finger looms over his tiny head like the hand of an accusing god.

'Okay, this is the critical part. *Slow, Point Zero Five.*'

One at a time, the four of them mount the stairs and make their way, step by step, up to the first-floor landing.

'I got the techies to alter the colouring here for identification purposes.' Everyone leans in towards the projection. 'As you can see, Nero is a bit greener – there he is out in front. Lúter is the yellowish figure right behind him. I'm in purple, just behind Lúter.' She turns to look at him. 'Rashid, you're in red right at the back.'

They watch Nero lead his team along the landing. His arm rises as a signal to wait. Looking rapidly left and right, he goes through the first doorway on the left. The yellow rendition of Lúter continues on along the corridor and then disappears into the next room on the left.

Rashid sees his own small manikin still loitering like it's freeze-framed at the top of the stairs.

'That's me going past both of the left-hand rooms before I go into the room at the far end,' Kass says, her voice matter-of-fact, apparently unaffected. 'Okay – now watch carefully. Someone comes out of this door here – the second one on the *right*.

'*Freeze.* See how the door has opened but whatever they're wearing blocks their infrared signature. At first, surveillance didn't pick them up. If you concentrate hard, you might just make them out.' Her finger penetrates the shadow of a shadow before it disappears like a puff of smoke.

'*Point Zero Five.* Here's where Nero turns to leave the first room – you can see him right there, immediately behind the door.'

An orange flash envelops the whole landing.

'That's the first blast. Now watch this. Lúter comes out of the room here and begins to run directly towards our technically enhanced assailant.'

'The next the blast is way more powerful.' The second flash lights up the entire building. He sees Lúter runs straight into it, his peace-of-crap visor immediately flies off.

Kass looks at Rashid; her eyes brimming but defiant. She points to her own hologram. 'Here I am – I've heard the noise and I've run out onto the landing and– '

She clasps her hand to her mouth while her other self looks down on Lúter's torn-apart body. Dust is raining down. Mercilessly, the projection highlights the smaller pieces of Lúter scattered along the landing.

Rashid tries to look away but can't. He prays it will stop but Kass is determined the scene will play out.

She masters her voice. 'This is where I try to tackle the assailant from the side. I can't see a thing but I manage to knock their weapon to the ground and there – that's where I get stabbed in the arm.'

Kass forces herself on. 'If you look for how the light is altered around the suit, the ripples you can see, you should be able to just make out our assailant. Here they are running straight past Rashid and on down the stairs.'

'*Point Zero Two Five.*' She clears her throat. 'The assailant is nearing the bottom of the stairs and now Rashid begins his pursuit.'

He's become an abstraction, a human only in theory.

'Here we see him at the first half landing,' she says, 'and then he's almost down the main flight before he trips just short of the bottom step.'

The room is silent. Rashid knows all three women are avoiding his eye.

Another change of angle, and the streetlights reveal an enhanced silhouette emerging from the entrance before dissolving into the darkness beyond.

'Surveillance have trolled through every bit of coverage from the satellites and all ground level surveillance,' Kass says. 'So far they've drawn a blank. The assailant literally disappeared into thin air.'

There's a heavy silence.

Rashid can guess all too well what they're all thinking. Lúter had paid the ultimate price for his bravery – the other two had been severely injured in the line of duty; whilst he had shown himself to be a coward.

How can he bear to sit here masquerading as joint head of the new homicide team? Kass might as well have ended with: 'I rest my case, your honour'.

Chan is the first to speak. 'Do we have any physical stats on the assailant?'

'Um – yes we do,' Kass says, remembering herself. 'The analysis suggests an approximate height of 1.72 metres. The all-angle analysis of body shape suggests the individual we're looking for is around eighty-three kilos and almost certainly a man.'

'Not a woman, this time,' Chan says. 'Yet he's wearing the same sort of suit.'

'That nark – Sams, wasn't it?' Maxwell asks. 'Do you think he set you up or did someone else use him to do it?'

'I'm waiting to get a "Permitted Methods" order from Leifsson before we can interrogate Sams,' Kass tells her. 'He has to be the key here.'

Rashid's aware that everyone is still avoiding his gaze. Kass is de-facto taking charge of the whole operation and he's powerless to do anything but acquiesce.

'If you'll excuse me, I have to look into a certain matter,' he says. His chair rocks backwards as he gets to his feet and leaves the incident room and that awful, damning projection behind.

Just for once, Leifsson had been absolutely right about something.

Eight

'We haven't talked about Ása,' Bruno says, scraping the remnants of the meal from his plate. 'I know you made contact with her.'

'Only for a second or two.'

'So, did you notice it?' *You must know what I'm talking about.*

Nero shakes his head. 'No, I didn't.' *I was a little preoccupied at the time, fighting for my life.*

'Well I noticed something different. Every time.' He waves his fork at Nero. 'Know what it reminded me of? My foster parents – the first ones – had one of those native sheepdogs called Týr.'

He smiles at the memory. 'She was such a great character. I used to sometimes touch her nose to try to find out what sort of things a dog might be thinking about. The trouble was, her mind was wired so weirdly. It's hard to describe. The closest analogy I can think of is that it was a bit like listening to someone speaking an unknown language. It might seem really cool and fascinating but you've no idea what any of it means.'

Pushing back his plate, Nero laughs. 'I could never get a thing from animals. I found their thoughts were more or less impenetrable. When I was a kid, I so wanted to be like Dr Dolittle – you know, talking to the animals and all that.' *What, you've never read that book nor seen the film?*

Before my time.

Bloody cheek – it was before my time too. The book was written way back in the nineteen twenties.

'I could understand Ása's thoughts,' Bruno says aloud, 'though I'd have preferred not to. There was something I couldn't put my finger on – something really odd to do with the way she thinks.'

'Her brain is probably wired-up all wrong? Hardly surprising – the woman's a psychopath, after all.'

Taking a swig of water, Nero washes the next two painkillers down. 'Have you heard of something that's been dubbed the warrior gene? And no, before you say it, it's not someone who worries a lot.'

'Maybe – sort of.'

'The suggestion is that this so-called warrior gene is a variant of an X chromosome gene that produces monoamine oxidase or MAOA-L or possibly a mutant version of another gene called CDH13.'

Bruno feigns a yawn.

'Anyway, bottom line is, the minority who carry these genes are predisposed to violent, possibly murderous criminality given the right, or I should more accurately say the *wrong* kind of upbringing. All comes down to parenting.' He shrugs. 'Or so the theory goes.'

'Maybe that explains it.'

'I've always felt the whole theory was a bit suspect,' Nero says. 'Besides, when the Vikings settled these lands, being a fearless, godless warrior would have been considered a desirable attribute.'

'In actual fact, it was the Christians who accused them of having no god. The Vikings weren't godless – if anything they had too many gods. Later on, many of them just sort of bolted on the Christian one. The rest must have decided that a pacifist martyr was no god for a warrior.'

It hurts when Nero laughs. 'We both know you got all that from plundering the brain of your History teacher.'

Once the breakfast things are cleared and washed up, it's hard to know what to do. Nero is damned if he's going to spend yet another day just resting and eating. After so much inactivity, his body is annoyingly uncoordinated. He doesn't so much need to stretch his legs – it's more about reminding them how to take him more precisely to where he wants to go. In any case, it's clear the boy needs a distraction.

Nero goes over to the old man's gun cabinet, unlocks it and takes down one of the rifles. Exactly as his grandmother taught him, he lifts the bolt and pulls it back to check it isn't loaded. He turns the empty gun over in his hands, admiring the ornate metalwork, the polished and grained wood used for the stock. He can smell the remnants of all that lovingly applied oil.

The boy has been watching him with growing curiosity. 'I thought I'd teach you how to shoot. Think we'll start with this one,' Nero tells him. 'It's a classic make with all the add-ons any hunter could need.'

Bruno comes to stand beside him. 'What about that other one?' he says, 'That bad boy looks like it really means business.'

When Bruno reaches for the firearm, Nero pushes his hand away. 'There's an art to these things. This one here may look a lot less flashy but it's straightforward to use and is just as powerful.' *Are you ready to try it?*

Sure – why not. The boy does a bad job of hiding his excitement.

Once they're outside, the bitter wind comes whistling around their ears. The sudden change in temperature is quite a shock though not an unpleasant one. Now it's daylight, he can see that the shack is simply what's left of a larger farmhouse and its outbuildings. The outline of the walls is still just visible beneath the lying snow. Kass's dad must have scavenged the materials needed to make the shack weatherproof.

Bruno walks over to the edge of the plot. 'That's a hell of a way to fall,' he says.

Nero has to shout over the howl of the wind. 'Let's make it fifty metres to start with.'

The boy weighs down the empty cans from breakfast before he sets them up in a line on rocks that are more like eighty metres away.

'So, first of all,' Nero says, 'do up all the buttons on your coat; accuracy will be difficult in this wind. If you're shivering, that's also going to affect your aim.'

He waits for the boy to oblige. 'Hunters are all too fond of shooting themselves in the foot due to their own carelessness. I'm going to show you how to load this thing the right way.'

Nero daren't shoot the gun himself – the subsequent recoil would only add to the pain in his chest. Although he worries about the noise, he spends an hour showing the boy exactly how to lock, load and fire the rifle.

Turns out, the boy is a natural marksman. 'I'm imagining this is Asa's head,' he says, hitting the can dead square at 300 metres.

They move on to one of the handguns. Oddly, there's a silencer in the old man's collection. Bruno knows without being told how to fix the device to the barrel. 'He used this more than once,' the boy says, weighing it in his hands. 'And it wasn't for animals.'

'You could argue it was self-defence,' Nero says, declaring a statute of limitations. 'That was all a very long time ago. Things had gotten out of hand around here – he wasn't the first or the last. Besides, the stroke means he's been rendered harmless.' *I don't see any point in enlightening Kass about her father's past.*

'You're the homicide detective,' Bruno says. 'Who am I to argue?'

The boy is quick to get the hang of the handgun. He hits the first few cans with ease. They gradually increase the distance and, before it's fully dark, Bruno is regularly hitting targets more than twenty-five metres away.

'You seem to be a natural,' Nero tells him, a little unnerved by the dormant force he appears to have awoken.

Over in his bunk the boy is fast asleep and snoring gently. Despite his physical tiredness, Nero is unable to relax his guard. In the dim light of that wind-up torch he's been trying to read one of the old man's books but instead he must have traced every plank along the ceiling above him. The slightest noise from outside is enough to alert him afresh.

It doesn't help that he's now rationing himself with the painkillers – the damned things are far too easy to get hooked on. His head feels odd and the burn on his arm is hurting more than it was. Bruno might be right about him running a fever.

Nine

Amie buzzes the governor: 'I have a Dr Silas Young out here wanting to see you. He doesn't have an appointment but he says he'd really like to have a word with you in person – if you can spare him a few minutes.'

Leifsson doesn't recognise the man's name for a second, then he remembers he's one of two interrogators on loan from the Training Department. 'Sure, send him in.'

Young shakes his hand with a grip that suggests he's trying to prove something by it. He takes a seat without waiting for an invitation. Deference clearly isn't a strong part of his personality. The guy looks about forty, and could be mistaken for an academic with his brown cords and mouse-grey jumper.

'I take it you're here to discuss the interviews you conducted with my personal staff and security detail,' Leifsson says.

'Yes, exactly that, sir. We – that's to say Dr Davis and myself – we've now completed all the interviews. These of course included ABA – advanced bio-feedback analysis.'

'I know what ABA stands for.' Leifsson knows he's already sounding too defensive.

Young clears his throat. 'As you can imagine, Governor, we would have already drawn your attention to any clear leads on who broke into your bedroom and left that threat.'

'So, I assume you're just here to tell me that you've learnt nothing – that each and every one of my staff has come up smelling of roses?' Leifsson feels his blood pressure rising.

'Not entirely, no, what –'

'Maybe that plastic duck just dropped out of some cleaner's apron pocket, eh?'

When Young doesn't answer, the governor continues: 'I have to tell you that, despite the delicacy of the situation, thanks to your interrogation techniques and all that ABA junk you wired her up to, I've just lost a damn fine cook. In fact, she was the best we ever had. The poor woman was utterly shaken by what you put her through. She told me, in no uncertain terms, that she hadn't escaped from a fascist state to be treated in that way.'

He leans into the man. 'My kids are really pissed at me. They're already giving me a hard time about how they're going to miss her fajitas. What's more, my driver's barely said a word to me since you put him through the wringer. I really can't think why anyone would give a shit about his little habit – it's not like he didn't have it under control.'

Leifsson walks over to the window, tries to take a few of those long, controlling breaths his doctors keep telling him to practice.

When he turns around, Young is still sitting there as calm as anything. 'Excuse me, Governor Leifsson,' he says, his voice maddeningly level. 'The main reason I'm here is because I think we may actually have uncovered something of concern to you – and possibly to others.'

Leifsson returns to his chair. 'Okay, you've got my attention, now spit it out, man.'

'I suppose you could say it's a little indirect.' Young chooses to inspect his fingernails before he finally looks up. 'I wouldn't mention it at all if I didn't believe it could be crucial.'

'I've no idea what you mean by *indirect*. Speak plainly man, for Christ's sake.'

'As you wish, Governor.' He crosses his legs like he's

defending his fokking genitalia. 'We've obtained some interesting information from a member of your staff. A very new employee by the name of Salvatore Machelotti. The boy who was recently taken on at the mansion to do general yard work, outside maintenance and such like. I'm told he hasn't shown up for work since I spoke to him. It would seem he's done a runner. I assume you know the person I'm talking about?'

Leifsson frowns. 'You don't mean the old guy who cleans the cars?'

'No, not Bernard. I'm talking about a young man who calls himself Salvo – tall, Italian extraction.'

Leifsson shakes his head vigorously.

'Slim, dark hair; good-looking. The idea was that he'd help Bernard with some of the heavier work that's becoming too much for him. I'm told Machelotti also doubled as a waiter once or twice when you were entertaining.'

'Yes, now you mention the waiting, I might have noticed him.'

'I'd be very surprised if you hadn't.'

Leifsson doesn't much like what this man seems to be implying. 'Would you mind getting to the point?'

'Certainly, Governor. My point will be clear in a moment. I understand that, although Machelotti was allowed to sleep in the pool house, he had no way of getting through security to access the mansion itself. Our bio-tests concluded that he appeared to pose no security threat.'

'Sounds like a dead end to me.'

Young holds up a finger. 'However, he told us something of a sensitive nature during the interview. Something we felt you personally needed to know.'

Maddeningly, the man takes out his log and spends a moment scrolling through it. 'We understand from young Machelotti and others that you have a close friend who is a surgeon at the central hospital – a Professor Martin Chester.'

'Yes, Marty and I are close, and have been for several years now.' Leifsson's heartbeat is on the rise again. 'What of it?'

'Machelotti told us that he'd seen and spoken to your friend Marty several times in a club he also frequents.' Young looks down at his notes. 'The Jolly Roger in St Thomas's Road. The boy tells us that, in that establishment, your friend Marty goes by the name Dave James.'

The Jolly Roger – that awful dive. 'Go on,' Leifsson demands. 'I might as well hear the rest of it.'

'Salvatore told us that he'd seen your *friend* talking to a group of men who are known to be suppliers of recreational drugs. He said that he'd heard a rumour that the man they called Dave – Professor Chester – is in business with these men.'

'And you believed him?'

Leifsson gets to his feet. 'Isn't it obvious that this drulludeli – this Machelotti – is some bitter little piece of ass with a score to settle. And now he's done so, guess what – he's pissed off.'

'Very possibly, sir. However, the ABA strongly suggests he was telling the truth.'

'What – your fokking machine is sentient now, is it?' Leifsson is sorely tempted to punch this odious man right in his smug, supercilious face. 'It's mistaken. The boy is mistaken – the little piece of shit.'

Dr Young puts his log away in his pocket. 'We've included all this information in our report. It is not our job to take the investigation any further.'

He stands up. 'It is entirely up to you now, Governor, to decide what to do with the information I've given you today and whether you order DSD officers to investigate this particular evidence or not.'

Young steps forward, invading Leifsson's personal space. The man's breath smells of mint. 'Our own conclusion is that your friend the professor is very likely a security risk. If he's had, or continues to have, dealings with these sorts of people, he could be open to coercion or blackmail.'

Leifsson's heard enough. It's an effort to hold out his hand. 'Thank you for your efforts, Dr Young. I feel sure that there's some perfectly innocent explanation and this is simply a misunderstanding.' This time he barely touches the fellow's hand before he walks over to open the door.

He keeps his eye on the man, watches the arrogant way he strides through the outer office. As Young goes by, Annie looks up with curiosity, or possibly a touch of lust.

Once he's sure the man is out of earshot, he turns to her. 'Cancel the rest of this morning's meetings.'

'But, sir, what about your meeting with Commander Rockingham at eleven-thirty?'

'Okay, not that one, just the others. Oh, and Amie, from now until I tell you otherwise, I don't want to be disturbed unless there's a bomb in the building. Not by anyone. You got that?'

'Yes of course, Governor.' She doesn't hide her curiosity.

Leifsson can feel himself beginning to tremble now. He goes back into his office, crosses the room and enters his private bathroom where he punches a code into the lock on a small cabinet. With an unsteady hand, he takes out the green pills his doctor prescribed to help him cope with stress.

He stares at that other capsule of pills alongside them – the ones Marty had given him. 'They can be addictive so use them sparingly', he'd said. 'Reserve them for those moments when you're really struggling to stay on top of things'.

For a second Marty had held them away from his grasp like you might tease a child with sweets. 'Between you and me, it's completely illegal for me to supply them to anyone who isn't registered as my patient'. It had been said with a lover's smile never far from his lips.

Leifsson himself knows only too well how, once you start to break the rules, it gets easier each time, until finally, you stop noticing or caring.

Ten

Kass can't stop worrying about Nero. Her instinct tells her something's not right. It's maddening not to be able to speak to him and find out if he's holding up okay.

And then there's Bruno. Odd that she's never heard of the boy before and Nero seemed confused about whether he was even a relative or not. Now she thinks about it, they do look quite alike. But then again, most of the Italians she knows have those same dark and soulful eyes.

A draughty old cabin is hardly the right place for a convalescing man. What if he needs medical help? Just how long is she expected to keep this secret?

Damnit – she needs answers. If only they hadn't insisted she stay away. She'd promised him not to make contact in any way. She'd made Bruno promise he'd contact her directly in an emergency. Could the boy be trusted to make that judgement?

Kass is trying to get her head round the situation but it's impossible when Maxwell keeps pacing about in her eyeline.

'First they insist on no electronic transfer,' Maxwell tells the ceiling. 'Then they say the missing data entries will arrive under guard, *first thing* this morning.' Her brown boots stalk back and forth. 'I even got them to repeat it,' she says, throwing her hands up. 'Well, so much for their fokking promises.'

'The Secretariat has a reputation for working to its own

time and in its own way,' Chan says, looking at a stream of data on her console. It surprises Kass that Chan should have her ear to the ground on these matters when the woman is only just out of training.

'I expect the file will be here soon,' Kass tells Maxwell, hoping she'll just give up and sit down. The legs aren't convinced.

They come to a halt right in front of her, forcing her to look up into the woman's face. 'It's probably a power thing,' she tells her. 'They like to keep us lower lifeforms waiting.' It's the best explanation she can come up with.

Maxwell's brow seems to be glued into a frown. What does this fokking woman expect from her? Just because she's been promoted to Inspector, doesn't mean she can guess what might be going on over there.

Maxwell is unwilling to budge. 'I expect Rockingham or one of the other commanders must have to sign it off or out, or whatever,' Kass tells her. 'Then they'll have to wait for the official escorts, do a full risk analysis and so on. All those things take time.' She's not sure about the rest, but that last part is definitely true.

Putting both hands to her head, Maxwell utters a strangled 'Ahhh!' This time at least she goes and sits down, scraping the chair on the floor deliberately to create a sound effect. 'We're so damn close to getting that last bit of vital information and yet no one seems to give a shit.'

It's obvious that last remark was partly aimed at her. She stares over at Maxwell until at last the woman picks up her log stylus, holding it like a dart then turning it over and over as if weighing it before a throw. 'I'm not buying all that shit about how their system must have *erroneously* deleted those entries.' Maxwell does air quotes for emphasis. 'They could have sent it to us electronically – fully encrypted and all that, but no, it has to be escorted over here like some HS prisoner.'

The stylus begins to jab at the remains of Maxwell's

cupcake. The woman obviously needs to eat under stress.

Kass looks away. She knows that, as the senior officer, she should be doing something to expedite these matters – anything would be better than just sitting here staring at her log worrying about Nero and waiting for Rashid to finally arrive.

It's almost eleven o'clock and the man is never late. Kass has already checked for any signs that he might have been in earlier and then gone off somewhere else. She'd drawn a blank. There are no new messages scrawled on the incident board; this morning's new batch of plug-ins appear not to have been disturbed; Rashid's coat isn't hung up to dry on the back of his chair – or anywhere else.

All evidence suggests he hasn't returned since she played that holo to the team. Christ – what has she done?

She checks this morning's staff log and it only confirms he hasn't entered the building. Hadn't she expected this – known in her heart or by intuition that Rashid wouldn't be coming in today? What did that tell her? What is it she somehow already knows?

Maxwell is again scraping those damned chair legs across the floor – the bloody woman has such an annoying habit.

'Fokk this!' Maxwell says, this time heading for the door. 'I'm going to see Leifsson. See if I can't get him to put some kind of rocket up their arses.' She doesn't bother to glance across at Kass, doesn't even bother to shut the door behind her.

'I think I should go too,' Chan says. 'Better make sure she doesn't start swinging punches. Is that alright with you, ma'am?' She's being either tactful or tactical – the polite new recruit talking to a senior ranking officer.

'Yes, good idea.' Kass is happy to concede if it means being left alone. She watches Chan hurry to the door – can guess exactly what she's thinking. Nero would know exactly what to do.

The walls close in, Kass finds she's trembling, sweating. She won't give in, won't shut her eyes. In daylight, she's learnt how to banish the sight of Lúter's dismembered, blackened body; it's a different matter every night.

Staring across at her inactive console, she concentrates on the default image of that day they took the children rock climbing, the look of triumph on their upturned, sunburnt faces.

She puts a finger to her wrist. As she feels her pulse-rate slow, it occurs to her that Rashid might have called in somewhere on his way to work. Yes, she should stop worrying about him – he's bound to show up sooner or later.

'You did the right thing coming to me,' the governor says. 'I'll see to it they pull their fokking fingers out over there.' It always surprises Chan that a man so abrasive in person, can switch on the politician's gracious manner in an instant.

The governor buzzes Amie. 'Give me five minutes, then get me the Secretariat – by that I mean the Chief Officer. Raynott? Ragnott is it? Anyway, make sure it's the man himself and not one of his band of dancing monkeys.'

Amie's voice echoes around the ornate room. 'His full title is Chief Administrator Ragno.' They hear her laugh. 'Nero once told me it's the Italian word for spider, which is – '

Leifsson cuts her off. 'Just put him through to my stud when you get him.'

'I hope you don't mind us coming here like this,' Maxwell says. 'Neither of us wants to speak out of turn.' Chan knows this is nonsense – they all do. 'I just wanted you to understand what we're really up against.'

'Given the present situation, it's very worrying that two junior officers should have to bring this delay to my attention.' Leifsson waves a hand at the two chairs in front of his desk. 'Why don't you both sit down?'

The governor waits for them to comply. 'So tell me,' he says, leaning forward, 'How is everything over at Homicide?' Since she's been doing all the talking, he looks directly at Maxwell and all but ignores Chan. Maybe it's just as well.

Maxwell had clearly wanted this when she stalked in here. Now she has his full attention, her hands are unsteady; she seems less sure of herself.

Chan decides to say nothing. It's doubtful whether Maxwell would back her up if she said anything to the governor about Kass being distracted and Rashid being absent.

Leifsson leans back at last. 'I appreciate it's early days but tell me, Senior Constable Maxwell, would you say the department is functioning well under its new joint heads?' Chan reminds herself not to underestimate Leifsson – the man's instincts are razor sharp.

The walls of the governor's swanky office seem to be moving in towards them. Having engineered the situation, Maxwell continues to hesitate. She must sense this whole thing could backfire. The woman had waited so long for this promotion, willing them to notice her efficiency. Now Governor Leifsson himself is asking for her opinions she must be weighing things up, asking herself if this is an opportunity or could it be something else? Maxwell really should have thought this through before insisting on seeing the governor.

A look of irritation crosses the governor's face. 'I should remind you both that it was *you* who came to see *me*. You obviously felt it was necessary. Why don't you make the most of the opportunity?'

His voice has an almost imperceptible undertone – Chan can only describe it as predatory. To satisfy the governor, one of them will have to throw him something.

Eleven

Rashid tries to think back to that moment before he tripped and fell. Lúter's killer was, in all probability, a man and therefore couldn't be either of the decoys they're hunting. Although it's possible it's already become just a memory of a memory, he was convinced at the time it was a man he was chasing. Men and women run very differently. Yet he can't have seen him clearly enough to make that judgment.

He gets to the office by midday. After the initial warmth of her greeting, Kass becomes distant. See seems preoccupied. The woman never smiles these days; Rashid notices how, behind those glasses, a deep weariness is etched into her face.

At least the incident room seems to have sprung into life since they moved everything from Nero's office.

Rashid had insisted it was too small for the two of them to share – though Kass had probably guessed at the real reason. Neither of them relished the thought of occupying the boss's old room.

The inspector liked to start any investigation with one of those old-fashioned schematics to help focus their minds. Rashid keeps looking up at the incomplete whiteboard with the two columns Nero had labeled DECOY 1 and DECOY 2. Each one has arrows with numerous questions leading to and from them.

Nero had added a separate third column to the right. He'd drawn a box and labelled it LIME STREET BANK. The arrow entering the box from above is labelled JACOBS, NARCOTICS. Leading to it, another arrow is labelled INFORMANT- NATHAN SAMS. Another arrow leads from SAMS, which Rashid remembers Nero hesitating over before he'd finally written: SOURCE of INFORMATION?

'I think we should approach this whole investigation the way the inspector would,' Kass says, breaking the heavy silence.

He doesn't contradict her. It seems only right to try it his way.

Picking up a black marker, she draws another arrow going into the BANK box, which she labels ASSAILANT. ENTRY ROUTE? TIME? Next, an arrow leaving the bank on the left reads: ASSAILANT, EXIT TIME? ROUTE?

She squeezes in a final section to the left of the DECOY 1 column, draws a box and labels it GOVERNOR'S MANSION. Then she draws an arrow leading to it marked DECOY 1 OR 2? ROUTE & TIME? Next, she adds two arrows leaving the box. One she labels: STAFF? The other: FRIENDS & FAMILY. Below these she writes: "Check reports from Young & Davis."

Finally, she changes to a red marker and circles all the ends that need to be followed up.

Stepping back, she seems pleased enough with her work though all those unanswered questions have the opposite effect on Rashid. He looks at the board again noticing the distinctive change of style between Nero's original schematic and the new additions. Kass's writing is more compact and seems way more tentative. Her contribution seems to lack any conviction or authority.

Room IR10 is at maximum depth – three floors below the main Homicide offices. The unforgiving lighting gives Rashid's eyes something close to snow-blindness. Sensory recording equipment is built seamlessly into every surface. This room is restless for the truth.

They bring in Nathan Sams and push him down him into the sturdy interview chair. Even the warders have no time for a snitch. The chair he's in is the new type with built-in biofeedback transmitters.

Sams is short – a wiry, strung-out body attached to a worn-out face. They've hung a PainBoy around his neck. Any attempt to escape and the P.B. would do its cruel work.

Rashid signals for the guards to leave them. They'll remain just outside, screened by the one-way panels.

'For the record, please state your name,' Rashid says.

'Nathan Sams; prisoner 3155647.'

Rashid's stud informs him: *bio-feedback operating correctly. Subject registering normal ranges.*

'You remember Sergeant Jacobs from Narcotics, Mr Sams?' he asks.

'Yeah, only too well.' Sams grins. 'Why? Been doing a bit of business on the side, has he? I always thought he might be up for a bit of that.' The man's British accent seems phoney – perhaps an affectation he's picked up from movies.

'Mr Sams – might I suggest you think carefully before making allegations of that nature against a police officer.'

'Only kidding. No offence meant, Sergeant.'

'It's Inspector now, actually.'

The man smirks at him. 'Who's a clever boy, then?'

Rashid draws himself up. 'You've been brought here at my request to answer questions on the information you supplied to Sergeant Jacobs about a former bank premises in Lime Street.'

'Oh, God. It's that fruit tart decoy, isn't it? What's happened now?'

'Please allow *me* to ask the questions, Mr Sams.'

Rashid goes to stand behind the prisoner. He looks down on the man's thinning brown hair and waits.

'Sorry, *Inspector.*'

'Look, Nathan, you informed Sergeant Jacobs that you'd heard from someone that this bank was the decoy's base. Is that right?'

Rashid walks around to stand in front of him again. One side of the prisoner's face has started to twitch intermittently. His eyes seek out Rashid's. 'I told him. I said I weren't responsible if she burned your butts. My exact words, them were.'

Rashid leans in close, into the stench of stale sweat and tobacco. 'What makes you think she's burned anyone's butt?'

'Something must have happened. I'm not stupid – I can tell by the way you're giving me the eyeball. You don't get very far in my business without recognising when someone wanting to –.' The man's tic is becoming almost debilitating. 'To even a score.'

'And why would I want to even a score?' Rashid's smile is deadly serious.

'Look – I – I just told him what someone had told me, that's all.'

Rashid leans closer still. 'And who exactly was that someone?'

'This geezer called Quentin something. Look, I'm not being cute here, the bloke never told me his second name.'

'Where did you meet this Quentin?'

'In a bar in the Orange Zone. Skemmtun.' Through stained teeth, Sams tries a smile. 'A right laugh that is an all. Ironic, I think the word is. That place is hardly what you'd call festive these days.'

Bio-feedback shows no elevations. Rashid begins pacing in front of him.

'Look, I'll admit it,' Sams raises both hands mea culpa style, 'we'd just done a spot of business. Someone in the bar happened to mention them killings. And Quentin – well, he says something like, "I heard someone saw that decoy going into a boarded-up bank in Lime Street". Then he turns to me and gives me this wink and says: "You'd do well not to do any business in that area, mate. It's best none of us upset that particular lady". Then Charley Khan, he says something like: "No doubt she'll be getting a return visit".'

'What did he mean by that?'

Sams shrugs. 'Stands to reason – you don't cross them in a Double Red and get away with it. That lot are hardly likely to take it lying down.'

'What was the name of this bar?'

'King of Spain. Like I said, it's in Skemmtun about halfway between the two expressway stops.'

'And what do these two gentlemen – Quentin and Charlie Khan look like?'

'Charlie, well, he's tall, fat, about forty; mix of all sorts so he's a smidge darker than you are. Wears nice shoes. Real leather, not something you see much these days.'

'And Quentin?'

'He's shorter and thinner. White hair, white face that's not as old as his hair, if you follow. Hard to tell how old he is – but he's got a killer habit – likes to partake of anything that's going.'

Consistent peaks, all within normal range.

'Do you know where either of them lives?'

'Do me a favour! It's not like they're my mates or anything. Just business associates.'

'Business associates!' Rashid looks into the man's washed-up blue eyes and has to put his fist behind his back to stop himself. 'If I find out you've lied to me– ' No point in finishing the sentence – he leaves the rest to Sam's imagination.

The prisoner's head gestures towards the processing monitor: 'This little lot must be telling you what I'm saying is the honest truth.' Sams shakes his head. 'Like I say, *Inspector*, don't go blaming me if you decide to go looking for trouble.'

'I'm a policeman, my business is to look for trouble.'

'If you ask me, you'd do well to give Skemmtun a wide berth.'

Rashid turns away. 'The prisoner can go now,' he says. Two guards come in to lead the prisoner away. Over his shoulder, Sams says: 'Just remember I warned you. If you take no notice, it's not down to me.'

'Get this piece of scum out of here,' Rashid tells them.

Left alone in the room, he projects the bios and asks for summary. *Bio-feedback consistent with 97.5% improbability of fabrication.*

Sams had fooled the chair at least. The interview has given him a new lead. Rashid concedes it has the hallmarks of another setup. That's the thing with leads – they can lead you to places or lead you away. If your luck runs out, they can choke you.

Twelve

At this hour, Rashid assumes most of his fellow passengers are cleaners or maintenance staff. They're all silently focusing on the front of the pod where an anchorman for the state news smiles benignly down at them.

Most are looking into the luminous, giant face and nodding their understanding. If you didn't realise they were listening on their studs, you'd think the newsreader had hypnotised the entire group.

He turns away to the window. Looking into the darkness of the tunnel he can just make out the edges of the monorail and its ever-receding vanishing point. He'd jumped the gun, broken regulations, so how much of the interview should he repeat to Kass? There's plenty he should leave out. Although they're joint heads of the department, he has no intention of allowing anyone to accompany him to the King of Spain bar. Festival Street isn't somewhere a policeman would normally venture alone but it had to be that way. Nothing else for it.

Rashid gets off at his regular station a short distance from DSD headquarters. Above him the sky's still as black as Hades. The angled sleet forces him to weave around pedestrians hugging to the concrete overhangs. On his route, he can't avoid the espresso bar Nero likes to frequent.

Despite the weather, Gianni himself is outside cleaning the

front window. Rashid tries to duck into the crowd, but too late, Gianni calls after him: 'Hey, Rashid!'

'I'm getting a hand from God,' Gianni says, looking up at the sky. 'He likes to do the rinsing.' Chuckling, he straightens up. 'Tell Nero to take a break sometime, eh.'

Rashid hesitates, his tongue tied.

Gianni shrugs. 'Louisa thinks it's that Chinese girl keeping him busy. Who can blame him, eh?' He whistles, eyebrows raised. 'Such a fine-looking lady.'

Several bodies bump into Rashid and yet he's the one raising his hand to apologise. Should he tell Nero's friend he's been kidnapped?

His body decides for him. 'Sorry, Gianni,' he calls over his shoulder, 'I'm really late already.' A brief wave and he's safely round the corner and out of sight.

Was that another wrong decision? Gianni will be hopping mad when he finds out. Icy rivulets from a leaking gutter find the back of Rashid's neck. He's about to embark on a course of action that will be dangerous. There's no denying it but right now he doesn't care. Let things happen how they will for good or bad. Hasn't he already forfeited the right to choose?

The facade of the DSD building is towering above him. It's too early for the usual queues inside. The retinal scan bleaches the scene in the lobby as he passes a group of inattentive security staff. They don't even challenge him with a look.

He rakes back his damp hair and steadies himself in the downward lift. It'll be more than an hour before Kass has seen her kids off to school and made it into work – enough time to summarise the Sams interview and leave the plug in on the desk with all the others.

With none of the usual interim stops, the lift drops six levels before it brakes. Rashid feels his stomach recover as the doors open.

Overhead lights flare up and precede him into the incident room. For the next half hour, he dictates then stalks the room as he plans his solo trip into the Orange Zone. Then it's time to leave.

The echo of his footsteps travels ahead of him along the network of empty corridors.

Thirteen

Patrol officers have already arrested, charged and processed the men accused of killing Andrea North. However, as acting joint head of Homicide, and in Rashid's absence, Kass has a duty to go and see them. The department needs to officially verify that they haven't been put under unreasonable duress, have received adequate physical care in custody, and have each, in addition, been offered appropriate legal representation.

Given all the evidence against the prisoners, it's highly likely they'll be found guilty. With any luck, the judge will insist on long custodial sentences in order to make an example of them for mindlessly beating to death an innocent woman. It comes to something that a person can be murdered by a mob simply for feeding a few wild foxes.

Before her scheduled visit, Kass requests the Orange Fourteen surveillance footage. She forces herself to sit through every gruesome minute. Watching the evidence through one more time – Nero set high standards on thoroughness – the oddest thing is that even during the height of the attack, the eyes of the unmasked attackers seem to be dead – as if they're all operating on autopilot, oblivious to what their boots and fists are doing.

Contrary to what she would have expected, all their subsequent drug tests are negative.

Looking at that baying mob attacking that poor defenceless woman you could easily mistake them for medieval witch-hunters who've accidentally time-travelled into the later half of the twenty-first century.

Kass plays it by the book until she's satisfied that point by point comparisons have been meticulously carried out on the faces of each prisoner and these perfectly match their police mugshots.

In the flesh, each of the prisoners looks a little different. They are brought in one at a time to sit silently before her in their pale blue prison uniforms. To a man, their manner seems casual, off-hand even, as they slump down into the chair in front of her.

'Is there anything else you'd like to tell me?' she asks at the end of every short interview. They shrug, or shake their heads. Not one of them seems to look Kass directly in the eye. She's sure it's not from shame – their bland faces suggest a total lack of remorse.

Despite evidence to the contrary, each of them is determined to stick to a dogged belief that their victim had been one of the wanted decoys and therefore a legitimate target. Kass imagines their defence lawyers will try to argue the same thing.

On social media, the North murder is being defended by a prize group of halfwits calling themselves the Citizen's Defence League or CDL. Available intelligence on this group confirms that, though they have less than twenty-odd members, these are drawn from all sides of the Orange and Free Zone. It doesn't help that so far they've failed to arrest either of the decoys.

Kass is satisfied that each of the accused is in good health and has been allocated a competent defence attorney. The trial itself ought to be perfunctory. However, the widespread distribution of the leaked surveillance footage just might get them off on a technicality.

Looking into their dull, young faces, Kass had had to fight a strong desire to punch each of them. She feels her muscles tighten as she pictures her fist smashing that look of complacency off every one of those stupid faces.

Walking away from the confinement wing, Kass reflects with uncomfortable irony the fact that this visit had incited in her the same, crude desire to extract physical vengeance.

Back in DSD's clean-up room, she splashes water onto her face and then around the back of her neck. It's hard to get those images of Andrea North's dying moments out of her head. Like anyone with a family, her worst fear is that one day such an act of random and senseless violence might befall her partner Wifrith or one of their children. Despite all her training, the likelihood is that, just like everyone else, she'd be powerless to prevent it.

That thought stays with Kass as she walks back to the incident room. It's empty. Maxwell and Chan have apparently been called away.

Leifsson had told her she must concentrate on finding Nero. Knowing exactly where he is, what is she supposed to do with her time? Given the unfolding situation, she'll make damned sure Maxwell and Chan continue their analysis now they've finally received that missing data. It might just provide the final pieces of the puzzle that will lead them to arresting one or both of the decoys.

The central table in the incident room is stacked high with the plug-ins that both she and Rashid have been trying their best to ignore. Kass can see why Nero always cursed these confidential briefings sent to all heads of departments. Nonetheless, he would conscientiously work his way through each one in turn, anxious not to miss a rumour or development that might later prove vital.

She now sets her sights on getting through the bulk of them before the end of the day. Thankfully, most are elaborations and speculations that amount to thinly disguised, arse-covering exercises.

Several reports give voice to what she regards as unfounded suspicions. Some half dozen or more are concerned about the deeper motivations of the individual students arrested for daubing pro-decoy slogans across public buildings – it would seem the conspiracy theorists are having themselves quite a jamboree.

Halfway down the pile, she comes across an in-depth description of a drug-bust, which includes a dramatic pod-to-pod chase on the subway. The report's author, a senior constable by the name of Pétursdóttir, goes on to give a surprising amount of credence to one arrested man's insistence that a vast, pan-cartel alliance lies behind every unlawful activity in the entire city. Kass wonders whether the woman who drafted this is wasting her creativity in the police force.

She's sickened by further accounts of photon-fried foxes being dumped in public places around the city. The boneheads responsible now seem to be targeting the more exclusive areas. One patrol sergeant suggests this might herald a pattern of anti-wealth attacks. In a related report, a clean-up team leader tells of his operatives being harassed by members of the public for showing alleged social preference. In his place, Kass would have been tempted to throw a dead carcass at them.

Sipping a coffee, she listened to a detailed report of two minor demonstrations that had taken place the previous day. Both had been easily contained. Again, the patrolman feels the need to warn DSD's department heads of escalating social unrest.

None of what she's heard needs any concrete action beyond acknowledgement. It's tempting to skip the rest, but she finishes her drink and ploughs on through.

More seriously, a narcotics officer has flagged up a worrying trend – by his estimate, they're heading towards a twenty-five per cent year-on-year increase in arrests for drug dealing inside the Free Zone. Is that good news or bad? For some reason, he offers no comparable figures for the Orange Zone. Might be just an oversight.

It's late. Having reduced the pile by two-thirds, Kass sits back to massage the ache in her neck. For the first time she notices a single plug-in Rashid must have left on the other side of the desk. Beside it, there's a note telling her of his decision to take a few days leave. Despite his choice of words, she listens to his tone – what he's not saying. Once again she gets a strong intuition that something is very wrong with Rashid and it's all her fault. Listening to the message over again, her instincts like it even less.

In the morning, she intends to go down to IR10 and find out more of what Sams had told him in that interview.

Fourteen

Sleeping only fitfully, Bruno waits till morning. In the cold light of day, it's obvious Nero is in even worse shape.

He rinses the rag in cold water again and tries to balance it on Nero's forehead – not an easy task when someone keeps thrashing around. He shakes his head. This is no good; he needs to do more. If he doesn't act now it might be too late.

'It's me,' Bruno says. Remembering Nero's precautions, he adds: 'Go secure.' Thankfully, he can tell she recognises his voice. 'Is there a problem?'

'Yes. It's our friend – he's not well.'

'How serious?'

'It's bad. He's got a really high fever, keeps talking all kinds of crap. I'd say he's delirious.' Bruno lets that sink in. 'Looks to me like he might have some sort of infection.'

'Fokk,' Kass says. 'I'm on my way.'

'I won't be here,' he tells her. 'Look – I've built up the fire and done everything I can. Right now he's asleep – well sort of.' He takes a breath. 'Anyway, I've been thinking it might be best if we split up.' Bruno's tempted to say more but decides it might be better if he doesn't. 'Listen, if you have to take him to a hospital, make sure it's not the same one as before.'

'Of course,' she says. 'Don't worry, I know someone who will help.'

'There's one other thing.' Bruno steels himself for her response. 'I'm borrowing a couple of items from the collection – if you get my drift?'

It takes her a moment to guess what he's talking about. Finally, she gets it. 'Oh, right. Is that really necessary?'

'I wouldn't take them if I didn't think so,' he tells her.

'Just be careful,' she says. 'I know our friend would want you to look after yourself. This isn't a game. Keep your head down and try to stay out of trouble.'

Bruno smiles; you'd think he was one of her kids. 'I'll be in touch,' he says. 'Anyway, right now I'd better be going.'

It's been a long and exhausting hike – not helped by the extra weight of the weapons. Still it feels good to be out in the open air. The wind stirs itself; sleet particles are driven in to sting at Bruno's face like an ill omen. Though he's getting closer, it seems an impossible dream that he'll make it to the campus and then to the familiar, comforting squalor of his old bedroom.

Bruno knows his unauthorised absence from so many lectures will have been officially noted. He must also have missed a number of assignment deadlines – though there's nothing particularly new about that. He's seen a lot of footage on his stud about growing student unrest, so it's unlikely he's the only one with outstanding work. They can't discipline or expel more than half the student body.

Frozen rain is dropping straight down his neck like a thousand pinpricks. Should he have left Nero all alone like that? Anything might happen to him. What if Kass is delayed? What if they can't do anything and he dies? He has no vision of meeting up with him in the future. He hits his forehead with the heel of his hand– why is his brain refusing to help? Christ – he's waited all his life to find someone the same as him. They get along – all in all, the guy's pretty cool. They even look a bit alike.

Kass should be at the cabin by now. He stops walking to look around. The terrain ahead is particularly steep and it occurs to him that one of these old guns might accidentally go off if he slipped. He stuffs them both into the waistband at the back of his trousers – he'd rather lose part of his arse than the alternative.

Bruno's already come a long way; just one more ridge and he should be able to see the university. It's too late to turn back even if he wanted to.

Before reaching the main buildings, he can see a noticeable change to the campus. Drooping, wind-tossed banners are hanging between half the windows in the accommodation blocks. It's hard to read their slogans, but he manages to decipher a few phrases.

The tail end of one declares: RE-UNITE ELDÍSVÍK NOW. Another one starts with something that's flopped over but the tail end reads: CITY … NO LONGER. His favourite just says: HOMES NOT ZONES!

Walking through the main entrance, he's greeted by a makeshift barrier of wood and metal reinforced by dilapidated items of cheap student furniture. At first glance this blockade appears to stretch around the whole university campus.

A lit brazier stands directly in his path. Huddled around it is a small crowd of people rubbing their hands against the cold. He read about picket lines in his Social History module but this is the first time he's ever seen one for real. Despite everything, he feels a sense of excitement rising in his veins.

Most of the students have scarves or balaclavas covering parts of their faces. He senses their scrutinising eyes on him as he approaches. Bruno does his best to look nonchalant – as if he's maybe just returned from a stroll or a romantic encounter with some girl from another part of the city.

'Need to see your I.D.,' a short guy demands across a fifty-metre gap.

He keeps on walking towards them at a steady pace. 'I'm Bruno,' he says. 'Bruno Mastriano. I'm a friend of Kirk's.'

'Does that make you a student or are you some göndull from the media?'

Bruno raises both arms. 'Look at me, man. Do I look like a journo? I'm a first-year student. I'm studying History and the Environment. Old Jónsson's my personal tutor.'

A cloaked woman approaches from the far side of the brazier. 'Let him through,' she mutters with little enthusiasm. 'I know him.'

Grudgingly, a few metal posts are moved aside to give Bruno just enough of a gap to edge past the barrier.

'Thanks,' he says to the woman. Even up this close, he doesn't recognise her. Have they met?

'Think nothing of it,' she says, taking his upper arm to steer him well away from the rest of the group. To his surprise she adds: 'I've been expecting you to show up.'

Fifteen

'You're borrowing the ambulance again.' Wifrith regards Kass with a look of deep suspicion. A sedated domestic cat lies on the table behind her. Her gloves are still bloodied from the procedure just carried out. 'What if I need it?'

'Do you?'

'No – but that's not the point.' Wifrith tears off the gloves and bins them. 'Why use my ambulance when you could borrow any number of official vehicles?

And why on earth are you dressed like that? Are you going to tell me what the hell's going on?'

Too many questions. 'It's an emergency,' Kass tells her.

'Please don't treat me like an idiot. There's much more to all this.'

'There is but it's best you know nothing about it.'

She can see Wifrith is getting properly angry now, arms crossed over her chest like she's reprimanding one of their kids. 'I thought we trusted each other with everything,' she says, 'but obviously, I was wrong about that.'

Kass puts an arm around her shoulder. 'We do. I do. When this is all over, I promise I'll explain everything. The only thing I'm prepared to divulge is that a good friend of mine is in danger and I need to take the ambulance if I'm going to help him.'

Shrugging her off, Wifrith nonetheless stands aside, doesn't stop her leaving. 'This is all to do with you and Rashid, isn't it?' she shouts at her back.

Kass turns. 'This has absolutely nothing to do with him.'

The wheelchair is still in the shed – she hadn't yet been able to think of a way to take it back to the hospital without arousing suspicion. With a feeling of déjà vu, she loads it into the cage at the back.

Kass pulls up outside the cabin. She's relieved to see a curl of smoke rising from the stovepipe, tracks in the snow that come and go – reassuring signs of life.

Warm air hits her as she opens the door. Nero is stretched out on one of the bunks, muttering something that isn't a greeting as he stares in her direction, his eyes unseeing.

'A mali estremi, estremi rimedi,' he says, looking right past her to the window. He keeps repeating the same words again and again like a poem or a mantra. Her Italian is nonexistent, but she remembers him using the same phrase in conversations they'd had about a despotic regime, knows it means something along the lines that to deal with extreme evils you need to use extreme measures.

Approaching him like a horse you don't want to spook, she reaches out to touch his forehead. It's burning. It would have been better if the boy hadn't built up that fire. The familiar smell of escaping wood smoke is anything but reassuring. 'You're really sick,' she tells him. 'I have to get you to a doctor.'

'No doctors,' Nero says, getting agitated. At least he's making sense. He grabs her arm. 'Can't trust fokking doctors,' he waves an unsteady finger in her face then tries to pull himself out of bed. Limbs uncoordinated, he falls backwards onto the bunk.

Christ, she could have done with Bruno's help getting him

into the ambulance. She can see a pack of painkillers on the side table – maybe a couple of those will calm him down. On the other hand she won't be able to manage if they knock him right out completely.

'Let's sit you up, shall we?' She works on keeping her voice calm.

'Kass,' he says, suggesting he's only just recognised her.

'That's right,' she says. 'Up we come – that's it.' She props him up with pillows. 'Stay just like that for a second.'

Keeping a close eye on him, Kass wheels the disability chair over to the side of the bed.

Their destination is right on the Orange Zone border. Kass knows it will create a certain amount of attention pulling up outside in a vehicle declaring itself to be a pet ambulance.

Before getting out, she checks for patrol vehicles and any sign of security detail outside the main entrance. All clear.

Snow is coming down fast. Pulling her hood up, she gets the chair down from the back. Getting Nero into it is a struggle but one she's equal to.

There's no way to avoid the massed surveillance lenses in the entrance lobby. With any luck, no one is paying much attention to precisely who is coming and going. Nero's face is barely visible in her dad's old hunting hat. He's incapable of controlling the chair himself and so she wheels him through the entrance and up to the reception desk. The security staff pay her little attention.

'I need to speak to Dr Thorvaldsen,' she says to the dull-eyed receptionist. 'Tell Aron that my name is Arnfríður and I'm an old friend. My friend here needs urgent attention.'

Peering down at Nero, the man frowns. 'Sorry, madam, you'll have to wait: Dr Thorvaldsen is in the middle of his rounds.'

'A mali estremi,' Nero says, 'estremi rimedi.'

'As you can see,' Kass says, 'he's delirious and gravely ill.' She grabs the man's sleeve. Taking off her spectacles, she leans into his pockmarked face. 'Tell Aron this is an emergency.' Kass is careful to keep her voice low. 'I'm sure you'd rather not have to explain to a medical tribune why this man died right here in the reception area when you –' she reads his name badge, 'Kristofer, could easily have prevented it. I'm not asking for anything unreasonable. All I'm asking is that you refer my request directly to Dr Thorvaldsen.'

She lets go of the man's sleeve. 'So, Kristofer,' she says, staring at the receptionist, 'what's it to be?'

Kristofer backs away as far as the space will allow. 'If you'd care to take a seat, madam, I'll ask Dr Thorvaldsen if he can spare a moment.'

'It's okay, I'll stand right here while you make the call,' she tells him.

A couple of hours have passed since they wheeled Nero in for tests. Kass is hunched in a chair chewing what's left of her nails. What should she do next? The air's too close and she can't think straight when only a few metres away Nero's life is in the balance.

She stands up, goes to stare out through the white wall of snow at the mountains beyond; sometimes they feel like the city's guardian angels, today they seem altogether less benign.

Aron Thorvaldsen's reflection is approaching.

Kass spins round. 'Well?'

'Arnfríður,' he pats her shoulder, 'it's clear your friend sustained serious burns recently. My guess would be from photon fire. Most of the damaged areas have healed well but one is still very inflamed.'

'And?'

'Don't look so worried,' Aron says, with a smile. 'I'm delighted to say his general symptoms are not caused by sepsis as I imagine we both suspected.'

'Then what's wrong with him?'

'We've run a lot of tests, including brain scans and analysis of his cerebrospinal fluid. The results show he has meningitis.' He holds up his hand. 'Before you panic, Arnfríður, they also show it's not the deadly bacterial sort but the less serious viral variety. He's suffering from encephalitis and that's why he's talking all kinds of nonsense.'

When she starts to cry he gives her a full bear-hug. It feels so nice to relax into his shoulder and his familiar smell.

Finally pulling away, she asks: 'I don't understand – how could he get that on top of everything else?'

Aron wrinkles his nose – the exact same expression he had as a boy. 'His recent injuries must have compromised his immune system. These things happen.'

'But he is going to be okay?'

'We've already started him on targeted antivirals and antipyretics. With sufficient rehydration and so on, he should make a complete recovery.'

'If you want him to rest, I think you'd better knock him out,' she says.

Aron's face grows serious. 'So, Arnfríður, are you going to tell me what's going on? It's hard for me to guess why a police sergeant would bring an unidentified man into my hospital like this.'

'Turn your stud off. It's highly confidential.'

Kass waits for him to comply then checks again that they're alone and well away from any surveillance points.

'His name's Inspector Nero Cavallo,' she whispers close to his ear. 'Some very determined people are trying to kill him. The inspector needs to remain here incognito if he's to have any chance of staying alive.'

Aron gives her the slightest of nods.

Sixteen

Tonight, they have the house to themselves – all the makings of a romantic evening. But it isn't going to be.

Marty is getting steadily drunk, as usual. The governor thinks back to his first meeting with Dr Martin Chester – how much he'd admired his air of quiet authority; that and his outrageous charm had made the man virtually irresistible.

Since they are between housekeepers, they'd ordered out and Marty had just hoovered it up claiming he'd hardly eaten all day. Leifsson consumed very little: he's lost his appetite.

He looks into the reddened face of his lover and feels all the emptiness of betrayal. 'I had a conversation about you the other day,' he says at last.

'Oh really.' Despite the booze, he can see Marty's instincts have alerted him.

'Well, it was kind of second-hand really. It seems that one of the staff here frequents a bar that you like to use.' He keeps the tone light, for now.

'What bar?' Marty actually scoffs. You could never accuse him of lacking confidence. 'I hardly visit any bars these days,' he says. 'Would that I had the time.'

'I believe this bar has the subtle name of "The Jolly Roger", and, surprise, surprise – it's a gay bar.'

'Honestly? I can't believe you're cross-examining me about

whether I might have had a drink in a particular bar with friends. I thought we respected each other a little more than that.' Marty's face is all indignation as he gets unsteadily to his feet.

'I'm not talking about you enjoying a little fun with some young gun. I don't give a damn if you're poking the pooch into some tight little crevice.'

'Oh, for Christ's sake, what the hell is this all about?' Despite the bravado, Marty is now looking a little less certain of himself.

'Does the name Dave James mean anything to you?'

'You've been spending too much time in the police department.'

'Answer the question, damnit!' Leifsson tries to steady his racing pulse. He needs to take this more slowly, control his anger.

'No, it means nothing to me. If I've ever banged anyone of that name, I sure don't remember.'

'Is that what you think this is about – petty jealousy? I wish it were.' A look of uncertainty returns to his lover's eyes. 'For Christ's sake, Marty, I know you've been using that name for yourself. That your handyman –' He pauses to control his breathing. 'He told the police all about it.'

'What, that doddery old geezer? He must be seventy at least! With those cataracts, I doubt he'd recognise me in the street.'

'Not him, I'm referring to the other one – that stray Italian boy you persuaded me to give a job to. Don't insult my intelligence by telling me he's slipped your mind already.'

He sees the flash of full recognition in Marty's eyes – that train of thought that now sets off down the track.

'Blóðug hálfviti! I would have thought you'd have more sense at your age,' Leifsson says. 'The boy's only gone and told my interrogators about your little sideline. What were you thinking of, exposing all your dirty little secrets to some fly-by-night?' He punches his own chest. 'If it weren't for me, Narcotics would have picked you up by now. Do you realise the trouble you'd be in if I hadn't leant hard to keep you out of it?'

Marty crumbles, drops back into his seat. 'Oh shit! Oh fokk!'

Such easy capitulation only incenses Leifsson further. 'I need to know exactly what your involvement was with the break-in. You need to be totally upfront and honest with me right now or I swear I'll do nothing to save your ass. Do you understand me, Marty?'

They're already strangers. Leifsson feels sickened by the thought of any weakness he's ever revealed to this man.

'I really don't think it can have anything to do with that damn decoy leaving you that note,' Marty says. 'I swear on my life, no one from that bar aside from Salvatore knows about my connection with you – I made certain of that.' The man even has tears in his eyes – a weak and pathetic appeal for clemency.

The governor's fists are curling again. He has to turn right away. He walks into the next-door bathroom and opens the cabinet. This time he goes for the prescription stuff and swallows no more than the prescribed dose.

When he returns, Marty is still slumped in the same position. He looks across at the man and feels nothing but disgust at his red-tinged eyes. The dignified doctor has already left the building.

'I never even saw their main contact,' Marty snivels. 'I couldn't help you find anyone except for a few of their street vendors; they were too smart for that. I had to keep supplying them – they had proof of certain things I'd done in the past. They threatened me and everything I've worked for; everything I've achieved. You don't understand, they knew it all. They had proof of all the drugs I'd signed off on and showed me all the evidence; knowing I'd do their bidding after that, and I did.'

He's quietly crying, tears rolling down his cheeks and out of his nostrils like snot – not a dignified sight. 'I had no choice.'

'You had one choice, Marty – you could have come to me. Did you have so little faith in me – in my ability to help you against that scum? Or did you think you didn't mean enough to me? God damn you Marty.'

'I'm so sorry. I was wrong – I screwed up. Let me make it up to you.'

'You made your choice Marty, now I'm making mine.' He steps forward to look directly at him, eyeball to eyeball. 'Now get out!'

Leifsson finds he's enjoying the melodrama of uttering those words; that a part of him is calmly appreciating the excitement – this dramatic and definite ending to an already enfeebled relationship. They're playing out a scene of love and betrayal that seems far nobler than the pathetic petering out of his previous relationships.

The governor walks over to the nearest door and pulls it open with something of a flourish.

Though Marty looks shocked, he pulls himself together, stands up, stiffens himself with what remains of his pride and walks out with his head almost high.

'I never knew you,' Leifsson tells the man to his back. The phrase might be from some movie he can't recall now – in any case, it has a pretty good ring to it.

Seventeen

Bruno can't see the cloaked woman's entire face, only her eyes above the scarf; the brazier's red flames dance in the dark pupils. He holds her gaze for a second longer and it comes to him at once that she is Reyndis Sigurðardóttir – Krista's sister.

His obsessive interest in Krista meant that he'd learnt everything he could about her life, but he's never even spoken to Reyndis. He'd seen her often enough on campus hanging out with the other post-grads. She won't know that.

When her grip on his arm tightens, he stands his ground. 'Wait a minute – where exactly are you taking me?'

She looks up at him, softening her voice. 'To meet someone who's really keen to see you again. Don't worry – all will be revealed soon enough.' Her eyes crinkle at the edges to suggest she's smiling and he hears it in her voice: 'You'll find it's a nice surprise.'

So this someone could be her sister. He hesitates for a moment – picturing Krista all fit and well again and greeting him like they've just shared a little adventure together. He'd like to ask if she's fully recovered but, like a coward, he's not ready to face the answer yet.

And besides, logic and instinct take over; hadn't he nearly killed Krista – this woman's beloved sister. What's more, he'd smashed up their father's classic car, which, aside from his family, was the man's most prized possession. No, Reyndis must want to settle that particular score now that he's popped up again.

Bruno's tempted to reveal that he knows her identity. Then he reconsiders, not wanting to explain how that might be or lose the possible advantage of playing dumb. There could be a reception committee waiting to beat the shit out of him. He can't say he'd blame them. Bruno tries to take his mind into the future but, once again, it doesn't work. What's the matter with him?

He needs to play for time – enough to ask around and find out how Krista is. 'Okay,' he says, 'Well, I really can't wait to join you and this mystery person but, the uncomfortable truth is, I'm really dying for a piss. We're talking an emergency need here.'

'No problem,' she says, still clinging to his arm. 'We'll make a detour via block C. As you know, that's directly ahead of us.'

Reyndis only lets go of his arm when they reach the university's main entrance. Inside the building, all appears to be deserted. Harsh overhead lights flicker on ahead of them as they stride down the corridor towards the toilet block. Bruno can hear her footsteps hard on his heels.

The sign on the door makes it clear this is exclusively men's territory. She doesn't try to follow him in.

Bruno really does need to piss and makes a point of doing so as loudly as he can in case she's listening at the door. The room has no windows and the only other doors belong to the three stalls. He searches each one in turn, hoping to find an emergency exit, even a service hatch, but there are none.

As he turns to face the exit door, he has a fleeting vision of a chanting gang surrounding him. He feels like an animal trapped on all sides by hunters. Bruno transfers one of the guns to his right-hand pocket. In the end, doesn't it all come down to one choice – flight or fight?

His heartbeat increases as his body responds to the threat.

Whatever the consequences, he knows it's time for him to act. Right now he can see nothing beyond that hostile circle.

Bruno expects to find Reyndis waiting for him outside in the corridor but she isn't there. The corridor is empty in both directions. Something's wrong – this is too easy.

He looks right and left, recalling how this leads straight on past a couple of recreation rooms to a back entrance. There's definitely something he's not getting here and it's bad. Right now, despite all his abilities, his fokking brain still isn't letting him see what it is.

In the absence of any sensible alternative, he breaks into a run then slows his pace as he nears the rear exit. Again, he questions the fluke that's got him this far without a challenge. Outside, no one appears to be waiting for him and no shadowy figures are hiding in the bushes ready to pounce.

The cold air hits his face and he drinks it in. A couple of students saunter by, their boots crunching on the new snow. They're deep in conversation, paying him not the slightest heed.

Off to one side and about eighty metres away, there's an unguarded section of barrier made up chiefly of badly stacked chairs. It would be easy enough to clamber over or through that lot. Where would he go after that? In a place like this, you can't hide for long. Though he definitely won't like the tune, is it better he stays here to face this particular music?

He follows the building around and then goes over to the people manning the barrier; there may not be safety in numbers but there could be valuable information. The smell of roasting meat is carried towards him on the breeze and, realising the extent of his hunger, he wonders if they might be persuaded to give him a small portion.

As he nears the hastily built encampment, a whole line of people emerge from the shadows to block his way. There must be a dozen of them.

'Well, well, look who it is again.' Reyndis is standing off to one side. 'Expect you thought you'd given me the slip.'

Most of the others have scarves around their mouths or hoodies pulled down so their faces are lost in shadow. They advance towards him in an unhurried, almost casual, way.

'I don't want any trouble,' Bruno says. 'What happened to your sister wasn't my fault. It was an accident; I swerved to avoid a fox.'

She doesn't react.

They keep on coming. A couple of them have sticks they're tapping against the palms of their other hands. 'Save it,' the thick-necked one in the centre says. His woollen hat allows a clear view of his ugly face. Has to be their pack leader. 'You've really got it coming to you, Dago.'

'Can I suggest we refrain from using racial slurs,' a figure to his left says.

'So, let me get this right, you're happy to beat the crap out of this bastard but you're sensitive about how we address him while we're doing it?' Thick-Neck shakes his head. 'Unbelievable.'

Bruno looks along the line-up. There's no need to be clairvoyant to know what's going to happen next. Left with no choice, he pulls out the gun. With a less than steady hand he points the barrel at Thick-Neck.

'Do you think we can't see that's just a toy,' Reyndis scoffs from the sidelines. 'This is no game, Bruno. You're going to suffer for what you did to my little sister. She almost died because of you.'

Though he's grateful to hear Krista is okay, it doesn't alter his situation right now.

He remembers Dirty Harry. 'This here is a Glock 19, 9 millimetre automatic pistol,' he says. 'Currently, it holds a total of 33 rounds.'

They've stopped moving, their laughter much less certain. Still aiming at Thick-Neck's broad chest, he clicks off the safety. 'Let me ask you this one question,' he says, keeping his voice low, 'Who's feeling lucky?'

Eighteen

Leifsson looks away from the prompt-screen to address his audience. 'On behalf of the Eldísvík Government, I would like to say that we utterly condemn the barbaric murder of Mrs Andrea North. This was a cowardly and totally unprovoked killing of an innocent, law-abiding citizen. I'm pleased to announce we've already made a series of arrests and a number of individuals have been charged with this poor woman's murder.'

There's a clamour for more, which he calms with a raised hand. 'That's all I can tell you right now. As you can imagine, I have no desire to say anything that could, in any way, compromise the rightful process of the law.'

Leifsson's heavy sigh tells the wider audience it's unreasonable to ask for more. 'With regards to the other incidents – these so-called Decoy Slayings – police and security personnel are making rapid progress in their investigations. We have every expectation of imminent arrests. I have nothing further to add at this point in time.'

He pauses, to raise his hand palm outwards. Now for the tricky part. 'As a precaution, the security council considers it prudent to *temporarily* suspend the entire Decoy Programme.'

The same calmly raised hand is up and appealing for reason and order. 'Let me be crystal clear – this is simply for the time being. The decoys will continue their important work as soon we are confident the service can be reinstated.'

Leifsson turns square on to give a couple of sage and reassuring nods. 'We expect to be able to reinstate normal decoy patrols within days rather than weeks.' Damnit, Eivin had made him go over this announcement too many times for it not to sound rehearsed.

The governor clears his throat to give time for a quick check on the feedback monitor. He's been told to maintain that avuncular look – though he's not sure how he can sustain it for much longer without looking like a goddam stiff.

His eyes scan across the assembled, handpicked correspondents as he extends his index finger. 'Don't think that means we are going to tolerate more crime. Far from it; we've stepped up patrols within the Orange Zone and here in the Free Zone.'

It's time for that second gesture as practiced: both arms turn upwards and with loose open hands. Damnit – that felt so unnatural; like someone counted him in on it.

A half-smile and that slight turn of his head. 'Rest assured, you folks are only going to be disturbed in your beds by your partner's snoring.'

They oblige him with a ripple of laughter.

Kim Hart's smile is too wide. 'Showing your age, Governor. Some of us are disturbed for more pleasurable reasons.'

'Good to know you're enjoying life, Kim.' Yes – that was straight back with a light touch.

Tom Bryant is the solitary, stony face. 'Governor Leifsson – rumour has it the decoy even paid *you* a visit recently.'

'I should have thought you'd know better than to pay attention to rumours, Tom.'

Time for a short pause. 'I'm not in the habit of revealing the identity of my nocturnal visitors but rest assured all of them are expected. As for the suggestion I should provide a list of names for the media – any gentleman would never confirm or deny such matters. In any case, my lovely wife Liljan may be watching.' A wide grin. 'Only joking, *sæta*.'

Despite the general laughter, Bryant won't be diverted.

'Governor, do you categorically deny she broke into your home last week?'

He leans on his left foot. The monitor screen brightens just enough to counter any dilatation of his pupils. He's learnt to control his brow, eyes and hand movements. 'Of course I deny it. There's absolutely no truth to this story. You should know better than to give credence to cyber chitchat.'

He looks away from Bryant to make it clear he's done with him. 'I have a couple more minutes for any other *relevant* questions.'

'Won't the suspension of the decoy patrols be seen as a sign of weakness on your part, Governor?' Bryant shouts above the rest of them.

Leifsson is forced to answer. 'No; I think our increased presence on the streets will assure all our citizens of our continued strength and resolve.'

He'll be asking Hagalín exactly how this damned pest was selected to attend the briefing. 'We stand united in support of our security forces, our way of life and our freedom.' Leifsson raises his fist for emphasis.

Next, he opens his hand again. 'Any other questions?'

'Governor – on that other matter; have you tried singing exercises before you go to bed? My friend Tariq says it opens up your airways and swears he hasn't snored since.'

There's a ripple of laughter that Leifsson is thankful for.

'Well thank you for that, Joe.' A wide, relaxed smile. 'I'll pass on your advice to *my wife*.' More laughter. He looks across at Hagalín. 'Sadly, I'm being told that's all we have time for this morning folks. Thank you for your attention.'

Don't overdo it – let them see the serious expression in the eyes. 'Enjoy the rest of your evening, ladies and gentlemen. Goodnight.'

A final wave and he's out of there.

Nineteen

Bruno still can't see most of their faces, though now that they're closer, he can see their eyes.

'The idiot's got a handgun – so what?' Reyndis is addressing Thick-Neck. 'I mean, look at it, Baltasar. There's a good reason they don't make those ridiculous things anymore.'

'This is a polymer, striker-fired, locked-breech, short-recoil operated semi-automatic pistol chambered for nine millimetre,' Bruno says. 'It's got a ten centimetre barrel and the whole thing's only thirty millimetres wide. That makes it incredibly lightweight and absurdly easy to shoot.'

The men are all peering down at his gun with interest. 'These things were standard police issue worldwide for years,' Bruno says, 'and that's because they're the best all-purpose handgun ever made. Even a modern-day photon gun won't outperform this baby at short range – not for overall reliability and accuracy.'

'Is that right?' the lanky one on the left of Baltasar says. 'It's very compact, I'll say that much.'

'Someone just grab the damned thing,' Reyndis tells them. 'Go on! Look how his hand's shaking – he's no match for any of you.'

'You may not have noticed but he's the only one holding a weapon,' Baltasar tells her. His shoulders have dropped a little.

'Besides, I don't see you stepping forward to disarm him. So much for gender equality, eh?'

'With the Glock, it's dead easy to hit the bullseyes and get consistent groupings within five metres,' Bruno says. 'As you can see, you're all well within that range.'

'Look, man,' Baltasar holds up his hand like he's stopping traffic. 'None of us wants any kind of trouble here.'

'Is that so?' Reyndis has her hands on her hips. 'Don't tell me you're capitulating just like that. What about what he did to my baby sister? She could have died. What's more, my dad's classic car was unsalvageable.'

'Your sister survived, didn't she?' Lanky speaks up at last. 'And your dad probably claimed on his insurance for the car.' He turns to the others. 'I say we've got better things to do than help you settle old scores.'

Baltasar reaches across to stroke her arm with the familiarity of a boyfriend. 'And he did say it was an accident.'

'Yeah, the boy only swerved to avoid a fox,' someone else pipes up.

Lanky appeals to his fellow men. 'The sole purpose of us gathering here is to direct our righteous fury at this city's corrupt governance – this shame of a democracy that pretends to listen to its people but carries on doing the unquestioning bidding of the military's commanders.'

'I don't believe this,' Reyndis says, looking up at the sky as if appealing to the gods. 'So now you're all mates together, is that it? Power to the fokking people and all that shit.'

Baltasar goes for her arm again but she shrugs him off. 'Don't touch me, you bloody Judas.'

Reyndis walks right up to Bruno, so close he's forced to take a small step back. He worries the gun might go off accidentally. Christ, that would mean he'd have murdered Krista's sister on top of everything else he's done to that family.

'Don't imagine for one minute that you've heard the last of this, Bruno Mastriano,' she says. 'I promise you now, my uncles will be paying you a visit and, when they do, that little gun of yours is not going to save you.' Her well-aimed spit lands right in his eyes before she turns and stalks off towards the opening in the barricade.

'Our young friend here's not the only one in the doghouse now,' Lanky says.

Baltasar shrugs. 'She's highly strung. I expect she'll calm down, eventually. Besides, we're not here to dance to her tune.'

'Damned right,' someone else mutters.

'I agree with what you all said just now,' Bruno says. 'It's about time this city saw some real democracy.'

He finally risks lowering his gun. 'The trouble is, the general population, including some of our fellow students, is apathetic. They need to be mobilised, politicised. What's that line? It's something about having nothing to lose but our chains.'

'Was that Martin Luther King?' Lanky asks.

Though it's hard to tell, the others look blanker than before. 'I think it was that singer,' someone else says. 'John Lemon.'

'His name was Lennon, you fokking moron,' Baltasar tells him.

'They've already tried to placate us with their fake committees and all that other crap they gave us, but really they have no intention of listening to a word we say,' the one with the yellow scarf to his right says.

'They must think we're morons or something,' Baltasar says.

'That's an offensive term referring to a person with an IQ between 50 and 70,' Yellow Scarf says. 'I don't think you should use it.'

'Look, people, for starters we need to persuade the rest of the student body to get off their fat backsides and join us. And don't censure me for using the fokking word fat, alright.'

His raised voice has drawn the attention of a couple more students – though they could be just heading for the library.

Bruno slips the gun back into the waistband of his trousers. 'What's the point in electing a governor like Leifsson?'

Baltasar aims for the wider audience. 'That man is nothing more than a puppet on a string.'

'Just a figurehead,' Lanky adds.

Yellow Scarf nudges Bruno. 'Give us a look at that gun of yours then.' The other men all move in closer.

'Not here.' Bruno drops his voice. 'Gentlemen, it seems we've established some common ground here this evening.' He looks across the campus to where a distant brazier is sending sparks up into the darkening sky. Reaching behind, he pulls the other gun – a Browning Hi-Power Mk I. That really gets their attention. 'I can't give you too many details right now,' he says, 'but I happen to know where we might get our hands on a small arsenal.'

Twenty

Kass takes off her spectacles to clear them. She looks around at the newly softened edges of the incident room. Maxwell and Chan appear to be merged together as they work side by side with their heads down.

She breathes on the glass and then rubs away the blemishes before putting them back on her nose. Testing their clarity, she reads again what Nero had written on the board and what she herself had added. They've made little progress beyond filling in the straightforward timings. The remaining questions are still there in unforgiving black on white.

Directing her gaze at the box marked *Lime Street Bank*, she follows the arrow along to *Jacobs – Narcotics;* then on past that to *Informant – Nathan Sams*. An arrow takes her eye on to another question she'd underlined: *Source of Information*?

Earlier, she'd gone down to I.R.10 to watch the recording of Rashid's interview with Sams. From his body language and the tone of his voice, it looked as if Rashid's anger towards the prisoner might spill over into physical violence. The sound on the later part of the interview was inaudible. She'd tried to lip read but the angles were all wrong.

After the interview, it seems Rashid had come back up here and added the words *DEAD END* next to *Source of Information?* in disproportionately large letters.

His official report is equally dismissive. He'd apparently concluded that Sams was a fantasist simply making the most of rumours he'd overheard and then fabricating two unlikely informants – all in an attempt to reduce his sentence. Kass has now watched the interview twice over and studied the biofeedback – enough to question such an assessment.

Her eyes come to rest on the two words written in strong and certain capitals: *DEAD END*. Was Rashid merely showing a decisiveness that she lacked? Indecision had never been a problem for her before.

Granted, her attention has been less than focused since the attempt on Nero's life. At least he is now safely back in hospital and, by all accounts, recovering remarkably well.

Then there was Wifrith – she hates keeping secrets from her and now the atmosphere at home is anything but conducive.

But there's nothing she can do about any of that right now – better to concentrate on what keeps nagging away at her about that interview.

Had Rashid's blunt analysis been due to his exhaustion? That might explain why he'd taken this leave period right in the middle of their investigation. Maybe she should re-interview Sams? It might give her more certainty.

God, what she'd give for a long break when this whole thing is over. She walks over to the whiteboard. Rashid had squeezed in another heading: Kidnap of Nero – Murder of Nurse. From that an arrow leads to a question – Who is holding him? Alongside that he'd written in big letters WHY???

Kass has to admit she still can't answer that last question. She has no idea why someone – most likely a professional assassin – would want Nero dead and the man himself hasn't exactly been forthcoming about that. He'd insisted his attacker was a woman but she can't write that on the board without some corroborating evidence.

'I think we may have found something rather interesting, Inspector,' Maxwell says.

Kass turns to find the two constables right behind her. She makes an effort to focus. 'Okay, what is it?'

'I remembered something about the second decoy murders in Orange: District Fourteen.' Maxwell's voice rises in uncertainty at the end of each phrase. All the same, Kass notes the way she's trying to stay calm, hiding her excitement at a potential lead. 'The patrol that called it in said they were directed to the scene by an anonymous call. A call made directly to the patrol unit, which didn't go through DSD or Surveillance. We couldn't manage to trace it at the time.'

Kass smiles. 'As I remember, it ping-ponged faster than an S.T.I. in a brothel.'

'I put in a special enquiry and I've just had the results. Turns out they eventually managed to narrow that call down. Look at this schematic.'

'*Play,*' Maxwell says, starting the projection. 'It was made from the boundary between sections Fourteen and Five. Right inside this area here.'

The painted tips of her fingers draw a circle in the air across the schematic. 'We've just cross referenced that location with the new decoy patrol details and we've discovered an anomen –'

Maxwell reddens slightly. 'Damnit, I can never say that word right, an-om-a-ly. Anyway, that particular stretch of border is within the areas assigned to five separate decoy agents.'

She's talking just ahead of Kass's processing speed. 'I got Chan to check them out with the Human Resources data they gave us and, guess what? Okay, you won't guess so I'll tell you. Two of them have failed to log their monthly shifts with Remunerations.'

'You know their names?'

'No, not yet. But we do know their code numbers.'

Chan finally takes her turn. 'I've searched through all those Q.files they gave us and each time they're referred to only by their code numbers. The Commanders' Secretariat finally swamped us with all this data, but nowhere do they include the key to the decoys' IDs.'

Kass is furious. 'If I didn't know better I'd say they're stalling yet again.' She looks from one to the other and remembers to smile. 'You seem to be onto something. Well done both of you.'

At last she can feel the beginnings of belief, of a possible way forward out of all this. 'We need to go carefully,' she says. 'Inspector Ashram should be back from his leave tomorrow. I think we need his input before we take this further.'

She stands up suddenly re-energised. 'In the meantime, Maxwell, you go back to the Secretariat and point out their mistake. Don't accuse, but make sure you ask very directly for that information. Chan, you'd better go with her. No doubt they'll get very protective so make it crystal clear that we cannot proceed with this investigation without that information.'

'Yes, Inspector,' they answer in unison.

Her new rank still makes Kass wince.

Twenty-One

Rashid hasn't showered in several days. He hates the reek of his own sweat and the damp ripeness of his coat. What he wouldn't give for a good wash and a change of clothes.

The stubble on his face is begging to be scratched; resistance is a constant challenge. The way he sees it, Mikal – his new alter ego – is used to not shaving and wouldn't rub his chin raw.

Aside from all the physical irritations, he's adjusted reasonably well to being Mikal Mohammad. Whenever someone says his new name, he's learnt to instantly look up. By far the worst part is forcing himself to drink alcohol. He remembers how much Lúter liked those few beers after work. Each time he raises a glass to his lips, Mikal relishes it in the way Lúter would have; he's doing this for his friend after all.

They're in yet another dive. The late morning light is barely infiltrating the windows. Rashid is thankful his new drinking companion, Quentin, isn't much of a talker. It seems bizarre that after sharing a few beers with the man, he's already being treated like a friend.

Aside from the four men playing pool, there are no other customers in the place. Music is playing at a volume no one can hear above the noise of the game going on in the far corner.

'Gotta get me some of that.' Flouting several laws at once,

smoke pours from Quentin's nostrils as he continues to watch the action on the massive screen above the bar. Movie would be too good a word for what is being shown up there.

Katrina, the bartender, glances up at the action. 'The tits on that tart would smother a little whippet-dog like you.' She sneers at Quentin. It's clear this woman's English has been picked up on the meaner streets of the city. 'She poke your busy eyes out with that nipple ring.'

'Yeah, then maybe I'd take her from behind.'

Katrina does her best to ignore him as she vigorously wipes the surface in front of her. Rashid can't help but admire this woman's diligence, her determination to keep the bar area spotless like it might make a difference in a dive like this.

'From behind,' Quentin repeats. 'I guess a big girl like you ought to know all about that, eh?'

'Is not a problem which way, old man,' she tells him without looking up from her work. 'My girlfriends and me, we like to shut our eyes when we do it in big heap.'

Rashid snorts into his drink.

Though he's trying not to show it, he can see Quentin is taken aback. 'Do all Russian women have your dirty mouth?'

'Not all of them, but I am good; I persuade most to try it.' She wiggles the tip of her tongue in the air, then sashays her ample hips as she walks over to collect the empty glasses from around the pool table. Without missing a beat, Katrina grabs the hand of one of the men before he can slap her backside and leaves him rubbing at his sore wrist.

Quentin follows her every movement. 'I think I'm in love,' he says.

'Any man would die trying,' Rashid assures him.

'What a way to go though, eh?' Quentin runs his hands through his straggly, white hair. 'What a way to go!'

The room brightens for a moment and a rush of cold air comes in. They both look across at the open door. A tall, fat man is standing in the doorway as if trying to make up his mind whether to come in or not.

'What do'ya reckon then, Charlie?' Quentin calls across. Rashid tries to look nonchalant, wills his too-fast heart to slow down.

Finally, the door swings shut behind the man. His shiny, real leather shoes walk towards them on feet that look too small to carry such a burden. 'How's it going?' he rasps.

Rashid looks away as Charlie's gaze sweeps the room, assessing the situation. He chuckles. 'Not still bothering that fat dike behind the bar, are you?'

'I'm surprised you're still here,' Quentin says. 'Thought you'd left already.'

Charlie sighs. 'A temporary change of plan.' He turns his eyes on Rashid. 'I don't believe I've had the honour.'

Quentin grins. 'This is Mikal. Good customer of mine. Mikal this is Charlie.'

Rashid as Mikal hesitates before giving him a slight nod. Careful to keep an amiable expression on his face, he says, 'Good to meet you, mate.'

'Not so fast.' Charlie's face is serious as he turns to Quentin: 'You and me need to have a talk.' The man looks right on past him to the bar. 'Eh Katrina, give me a glass of something that doesn't taste like it's been through ten sets of kidneys already.'

Without a word, she puts down her cloth and sets the machine in motion. A few seconds elapse before a full glass emerges. 'There you go,' she says, setting it down in front of him. Charlie isn't looking at his drink. Rashid concentrates his gaze on the icy rivulets already running down the outside of the glass, the way it's pooling on the counter.

When he looks up, Katrina's smile shows a set of perfect teeth. 'House speciality,' she says. 'Has been through only two kidneys – I pissed it out myself last night.'

Charlie takes a sip. 'Yep. I'm inclined to believe you, Kat. Ah well, needs must.' He takes a longer gulp. 'I think we need a toast, gentlemen.' He holds his glass up and waits for them to copy. 'Here's to my friend Quentin here and his blushing, Russian bride.'

'Pheff. He needs to go look for his krakkmella someplace else.' Katrina walks away into the backroom.

'Now that, mate, is what you'd call a challenge,' Rashid declares with his glass still raised.

'Yeah, but not one any of us is likely to win.' Charlie's eyes stray up to the silent movie. 'That dark-haired one would do me.' He continues to watch for a few seconds then frowns. 'Eh – do I recognise that flat? Is this one of Kevin's artistic offerings?'

'We agreed on an exchange of products,' Quentin says. 'What do you think?'

'I think I'll ask for an introduction to that dirty little bitch.'

Rashid looks at the voluptuous body of the young and beautiful girl on the screen. Her eyes are dead, her lovely face as blank as an unseeing mask. He will seriously relish arresting these two scumbags when the time comes.

Twenty-Two

'You're serious – this intruder got past the mansion's high security and made it into the governor's bedroom?' Nero is sitting up in bed. Aside from a residual headache, he's feeling better than he has done for a long time. 'Why didn't you tell me this before?'

'You were hardly in a fit state. Besides, I'm telling you now,' Kass says. 'The note and the plastic duck were left on his bedside table.'

Nero frowns. After all that's happened to him of late, his brain isn't functioning as normal. Still, something about this isn't ringing true. Damnit, what is it he can't remember?

'Of course, he could have just picked someone up in a bar,' Kass says. 'And maybe he's too embarrassed to admit it.'

'Yeah – I can see that. A honey trap. Good-looking woman – Leifsson thought his luck was in. Could be one of our suspects or possibly an altogether different sort of decoy.'

Kass's eyebrows appear over the frame of her spectacles. 'I thought everyone knew the governor's into men these days.'

'Actually, he's more bisexual than anything else,' Nero tells her without thinking it through. To preserve a professional distance, he's always avoided making physical contact with his friends and colleagues – Leifsson included – but occasionally their hands had touched by accident. He'd tried to block the connection but hadn't always succeeded.

'I didn't know you and the governor were on such intimate terms.'

Nero tries to laugh it off. 'I am a detective – we're known for our detecting powers.'

'Anyway,' Kass says, 'it was most likely an intruder. Afterwards, Leifsson made sure every one of his personal staff was given the third degree in case any of them were involved. As we were so short staffed, he shipped in Dr Young and Dr Davis from the training department.' She smiles at last. 'D'you know what they call those two?'

Nero shakes his head and, for once, it doesn't hurt.

'The Liquidators.'

'Okay – why's that?'

'Because they give everyone they interrogate – well, you know.' She pulls a disgusted face. 'Niðurgangur!'

He grins at her unexpected coyness. 'It's okay. I think I get the picture.'

'I remember being interviewed by Davis for my psycho-test and he really is pretty scary,' she says. 'I heard fourteen of Leifsson's staff resigned after they'd been put through the wringer by the two doctors.'

'You're saying that she – or possibly he – managed to do all that without leaving a single trace. What's more, they're right inside the governor's bedroom and all they do is leave a plastic duck and a note. Makes no sense.'

Nero shakes his head; this time the movement sparks a niggling pain in his neck. 'They have Leifsson exactly where they want him – alone and, presumably, unarmed. Why not finish the job?'

'Maybe he, or she, only intended to scare him. There's that expression in English, isn't there – about putting the wind up someone.' Her chuckle is throaty. 'Not sure what type of wind they're referring to.'

'I think it's from hunting or stalking prey. My grandmother took me hunting when I was a boy. Don't laugh. I remember her telling me you should always approach your quarry – let's say it's a deer – from downwind. If you come towards it from upwind, it'll catch your scent and run off before you're close enough to hit it.'

'Well, in any event, they're showing him exactly what they could have done if they'd chosen to.'

'Okay – so let's get back to our original man – I should say woman – hunt. The department's finally been given access to the entire decoy files including names and operating areas. So how are you planning to arrest the suspects?'

'That's just it. Maxwell's managed to narrow the search but we still don't have their identities.'

Nero frowns. 'What about Leifsson? After this nocturnal visit, he must be on your backs night and day.'

'Not really, which is odd in itself, don't you think?'

'I agree.' Nero's excited and frustrated in equal measure. He's been missing the thrill of the chase.

'Perhaps he's just been too busy. Did I tell you he's bowed to growing pressure and suspended all decoy operations? Some think the whole department is likely to be disbanded. The atmosphere at DSD is sort of weird at the moment, I don't know…'

Her voice trails off. She seems restless. Nero guesses her stud must have given a prompt about overstaying her planned time.

'I'm really sorry,' she says, 'but I do need to get back.'

She stands up, leans towards him and then hesitates, as if unsure whether it's appropriate to kiss him. Practically, he wonders if she might be finding it difficult to choose an undamaged spot. He can do nothing but lie back and watch as she decides.

In the end she thinks better of it; straightens up.

Kass remains where she is, her face clouded with uncertainty. 'You know it's weird,' she finally says, 'just when we've finally been given all this intel on the decoys, Rashid has gone on leave. That's not like him.'

She's twisting her scarf into a tight knot. 'You know, I really shouldn't have said anything. Forget I did. You need to rest – shouldn't be worrying about all this stuff. I wish I hadn't said anything.'

There's something not right here; he knows it. 'You're quite sure you weren't followed earlier?'

'I made damn sure I wasn't.' Her cheeks redden. 'I'm not some fokking amateur, *Sir*. And before you ask, I've blocked the location tracking on my stud and I won't turn it on until I've been in DSD for a few hours – that way it'll look like a regular glitch.'

Reaching into her pocket, she withdraws a tiny package. 'Almost forgot, this arrived back at DSD – it bounced back from the other hospital. Hope you don't mind but I took a look. It's one of those new studs; never been activated so even the most sophisticated tracking system apparently can't locate it.'

'Thanks. I'll hang onto it for a rainy day.' He stuffs the unopened package beneath his pillow. 'Better find somewhere else to hide it.'

'Well, gotta go.' Kass hesitates, then raising her hand in an almost childlike gesture that's half-wave, half-apology. 'I'm assuming you plan to surface at some point,' she says, as a parting shot. 'We'll have to think of a way to explain how you got here and why the department wasn't informed about it.'

After she's left, Nero feels the full weakness of his body. He reaches for the beaker of water at his bedside and takes a long draw. Some of it spills down the side of his mouth and stings his still-healing skin.

He crushes the paper cup and lifts it as far above his head as he's able to. It misses the recyc-bin he was aiming for.

With his half-wild hair and beard, Dr Thorvaldsen is a veritable Viking dressed incongruously in hospital scrubs. He's doing his rounds with a solitary student in tow. 'This will help deaden the pain,' he says, a derm-jet poised in his right hand.

Nero's arm swiftly deflects it. The device flies out of the doctor's hand, skids across the floor and smashes into the wall.

'Pardon me;' Thorvaldsen says, staring at the broken pieces. 'I should have explained what I was about to do.'

The doctor turns to address the student standing by the door. 'Please leave us alone for a moment.' He waits for the man to comply.

Thorvaldsen bends to speak into Nero's ear. 'Rest assured we are quite alone now, Mr Cafaro or should I say Mr Cavallo.' His hair smells of the spiced meat he'd had for supper last night. 'In order to treat you effectively, we scanned your brain when you were brought in. Later on, after the various treatments we'd started, we continued to ascertain the extent of the swelling and whether it might cause any significant or lasting damage. I'm sure you understand this was entirely necessary.'

Anxiety is tightening Nero's chest.

'Now I need to carry out a further scan, just to be on the safe side.'

'I absolutely refuse permission for you to carry out any further tests. If you need me to sign anything – to take responsibility for what might happen as a consequence, I'm more than happy to do so.'

Thorvaldsen scratches his red beard. 'I fully understand your anxiety, Mr Cavallo; but you should be aware that the exact same tests have already been carried out and fully analysed by me. I have to tell you, they've already revealed your secret.'

Panic takes over Nero's breathing while he struggles to appear calm. 'I'm afraid I don't understand what you're talking about.'

The doctor gives him a thin smile. Nero can feel his hot breath against the side of his head. 'Look, Inspector,' his voice has dropped to a whisper, 'I've seen ample evidence that you are – how should I put it? That God made you a little different to the rest of us – that you're what is crudely termed a telepatico.'

The man nods his certainty. 'However, you may be assured that, as this evidence played no part in determining your treatment regime, it has already been entirely expunged from our records.' He pats the back of Nero's undamaged hand.

Is this a test? Without moving his hand, Nero concentrates on the connection. In his weakened state, it's hard to make out the other man's thoughts. He can detect no sense of malice at least. If the doctor wants something in return for his silence, it's not at all clear what it might be. Thorvaldsen's kindly smile does little to reassure him – doesn't everyone want something?

'Along with the meningitis virus, you've also sustained several recent injuries to the side of your head,' the doctor tells him. 'I really do need to authorise further tests both for your own good and for the fact that my staff might otherwise become suspicious.'

Thorvaldsen pulls his hand away. 'I'm the senior consultant in charge and I'll be on duty for the rest of today. Once I myself have seen the results, I'll make sure anything incriminating, as it were, is once again permanently removed from our records and from your own medical log.'

Nero looks directly into the man's pale eyes. 'And why would you choose to do that?'

'Mr Cavallo, not only am I an old and trusted friend to your colleague and friend Arnfríður, I am also a doctor and, despite my appearance, most certainly not a barbarian. It is, sadly, not within my power to change the course of recent history. I'm powerless to right the dreadful wrongs done to others like you by the forces of ignorance and prejudice.'

Without breaking eye contact, the professor adds: 'I can't tell you how delighted I was to find that, despite appalling persecution and against all odds, at least one person with your remarkable abilities has survived.'

He gently squeezes an undamaged part of Nero's shoulder. 'You may be the last of your kind and, whilst I am in control of this hospital, I will do all I can to protect you.'

It's clear Nero has no choice but to trust this man with his life. It's not a position he's happy to be in. Despite all the man's fine words, he can't help but wonder if Aron Thorvaldsen will want something from him in return.

Twenty-Three

Halfway through the afternoon, and heavy weather is already beginning to usher in the night. The streets around them ring empty. Particles of sleet are catching the light as they swirl around them. Rashid can hear nothing beyond the whistling of the wind. It seems this area is being actively avoided by the locals. Curfew's nothing new in the Orange Zone, but not at this early hour. He hasn't seen a patrol – not even in the distance.

'It's just up ahead, not far.' Quentin stops walking, his breath misting the air around him. 'Remember, you need to just stay cool and leave everything to me, okay?'

Rashid, as Mikal, shrugs. 'Sure, whatever you say.'

'These guys – they don't like to be interrupted. And whatever you do don't contradict them if you can avoid it.' Quentin touches his arm. 'This is how it works: They'll lay out their stall; we'll agree terms and then I'll sanction the release of credits via our contact. After that's done, he'll give us what we've asked for and we all pack up and leave. End of. Like I said, you're only here to balance out the numbers.'

'Okay, whatever, it's not like this is my first time,' Rashid tells him. 'I'm no virgin.'

'Yeah, but to extend your own metaphor, this bloke is like the biggest hóramaster pimp around here.' Quentin must have had a decent education before he chose this particular career path.

'Look, I hear what you say,' Rashid tells him, 'and I get it.'

'Sorry, I always get a little jumpy, you know, beforehand.'

They turn to the right. In the half-light, Rashid spots a line of melt-puddles in the road. To protect their city shoes, they jump over one after another. Further along it gets even rougher forcing them to negotiate a minefield of water-filled potholes.

Rashid hears a splash. Looking down at his wet trousers, his companion utters a long stream of curses.

Twenty metres on, they turn right again to face a pair of high security gates.

'Right, here we go.' Quentin approaches the gates and the security pad attached to one side. 'Five. Eight.' It's not obvious why he's reciting the numbers instead of just pressing the buttons. 'Seven. Three. Nine.'

They wait. The gates seem to waver before deciding to open. The creaking sound they make suggests these might have been closed for some considerable time.

Quentin is checking out every shadow. The man is too jittery for his own good. 'I think we're here first,' he says. 'Can't see anybody else in here, can you?' Christ – this man's whole manner is too amateur, far more nervous than Rashid had expected. Maybe he's not such a big fish after all.

Rashid looks along the flanks of the buildings that surround them. He sees no movement, no signs of life. 'I think you're right – we're the first here,' he says, struggling to keep the unease from his voice. He's been perfecting Mikal's demeanor – knows he'll stand well back from the proceedings, almost the disinterested bystander. He'll need to look like he's seen this a thousand times before.

The sleet turns abruptly to giant hailstones that begin to hammer down on their heads and shoulders. 'God, the fokking weather in this country.' Quentin ducks underneath a corrugated tin overhang and Rashid huddles in beside him. As they wait, they listen to the drumming, the manic beating on the corrugated metal above their heads. Rashid thinks back to that recon in the Double Red, how it felt to be out there like sitting ducks. They'd gone in there as a tight team, everyone covering each other's backs. They have an expression here – one of the few he's heard often enough to memorise: Ber er hver að baki nema sér bróður eigi. Lúter had told him the literal translation was "bare is the back of a brotherless man". Looking at his companion now, he scoffs out loud then hides it with a cough.

The hail stops as abruptly as it started. They both turn to the groan of the gates as they begin to open. A vehicle steals silently through before coming to rest about fifteen metres from where they are sheltering.

It's a black, Norseman 80 – ferociously expensive because those things are built to withstand almost anything. Its recognition plates are absent.

Quentin steps out of the shelter into the glare of the headlights.

Rashid expects the vehicle's occupants to get out but they don't. After a full minute, one of the rear doors on the Norseman opens. Quentin hesitates for a second before he accepts this silent invitation to climb onboard.

The door closes, isolating Rashid on the outside. He stands with his hands in his pockets though his body has stiffened with fear. None of this is going to plan.

Time passes. The wind begins to pick up, chasing the clouds westwards and setting up an incessant creaking and groaning in the metal sheets above his head. Rashid looks around him for a possible escape route though he already knows there is none. The fierceness of the wind is making the overhead wires jangle and rotate on the support poles like skipping ropes.

Rashid's unlicensed stud has no access to police or military channels. The intermittent moon shows him all too clearly the wide expanse of ground between where he's standing and those closed security gates. He's memorised the code but those gates would take far too long to open. He has no other options but to simply stand and wait.

The same door opens and Quentin climbs out. Then another man gets out to stand directly behind him. Finally, a long, tailored leg emerges from the front and a tall figure emerges, his pale face turned towards Rashid. 'Well, well,' he says. 'If it isn't Sergeant Ashram.'

The shock of hearing his real name makes him instantly nauseous. He has to stifle the urge to scream aloud. What would Mikal do?

He steps out from underneath the sheltering roof. 'What? You seriously think I'm a cop?' He makes himself glance behind as if he might shift the blame on the non-existent person standing there. 'Really? That's funny. Hate to contradict you but that's fokking hilarious.' Rashid manages something near to a laugh.

'Save it. There's nothing to be gained by continuing this masquerade.'

'I mean it, man. I have absolutely no idea what you're talking about.'

'Just deal with him, for fokk sake.' The words are spoken from inside the car. 'No need to drag it out.' A woman's voice that seems familiar. Rashid can't quite get a handle on who it might be.

The tall man turns to the speaker. 'I think we should leave the clearing up to our friend Quentin here. After all, this is his mess. Wouldn't you agree?'

'I see your point,' the unseen woman says.

The man behind Quentin pushes him forward like he's expecting him to do it immediately.

'Look, I'll deal with it – with him.' Quentin's voice is

pissing its pants. 'Like I said already, I really am, I mean I can only apologise for my serious error of judgement.'

He holds up his hands in appeal. 'I wasn't the only one he fooled; but that's neither here or there, is it? This is absolutely my fault and I'm more than happy to deal with the consequences.'

He stares at Rashid, his face full of anger. 'In fact, it will be my fokking pleasure.'

'Okay, that concludes our business for now,' the woman inside the car says. 'Let's get out of here.'

The tall bloke isn't done. 'But what's Ashram doing here? We need to find out what he knows.'

One of the vehicle's windows glides down to reveal a shadowy face. 'Who gives a stuff?' This time it's a man. His outline looks bulky, his voice oldish – probably late forties early fifties. 'Once Quentin's popped him, it'll solve the problem.'

Rashid hears a distant rumble. 'Let's not hang around,' the woman says. 'We need to be on our way before the next patrol passes.'

The tall man retreats into the car. 'Any slip up and we will want to know why,' he says. 'You got that, Quentin?'

Though Rashid's insides are molten, he forces himself to notice the man's accent is from the north side of the city.

He sees the weapon in Quentin's hand. 'Sure. I'll take care of him.' The raised barrel is shaking a little. Could be a good sign.

The vehicle turns around and then almost soundlessly negotiates the rough track before gliding out through the gates to be swallowed up into the night.

Grateful that his odds have improved, he turns to Quentin. 'You don't believe them, do you? All that crap about mc being a policeman – I mean it's complete and utter bollocks.'

Quentin shakes his head. 'I think there are times, my friend, when it's better for a person to speak the truth.'

His weapon is now directly in line with Rashid's head.

Twenty-Four

The icy ground has gained a thick covering of fresh snow that makes walking a little easier. Carrying a heavy pack, it takes her half an hour from the nearest tunnel entrance to get to the feeding ground on foot: a place she made sure they'd become familiar with as growing cubs. She knows they'll have already sensed her approach and be waiting nearby.

She'd chosen the site with care – an area of wasteland too near to the Red Zone for development; open enough to be aware of anyone approaching and yet sheltered from view if a patrol should pass.

The night sky has cleared and the aurora is now suffusing the landscape in greens and blues like some subaquatic ballet.

Reaching the small ridge that surrounds the place, she's pleased to see most of the vixens are already there. Studded with rocks and scrub along with hundreds of hollows and gullies, the landscape offers the animals cover until they're within a few metres of this spot. As a beam of light pirouettes across the sky she can see them more clearly; the rusty red-brown of their winter coats standing out against the harsh white of the snow.

They stand their ground; their sharp muzzles held high to the wind; their ears pricked and turned in her direction.

As she descends, they follow her every movement alert

now to the smell of the food she has brought with her. Other members of the pack emerge from the shadows to surround her.

She takes off her backpack and pulls out the container with the food she's brought – a pungent mix of mostly fish, mollusks, lamb scraps and stale bread.

As usual, she lays it all out in one long strip. They gather around it, each choosing their individual feeding spot with care. There's some commotion, more barging and shoving as they wait. At her signal, they set to, growling low if another vixen should stray too close to what they consider to be their fair portion.

With full bellies their movements become slow and playful: stretching, licking as they roll onto their backs and expose their white bellies. There's some half-hearted wrestling but none of it becomes serious.

She retreats a step or two to retrieve her backpack. A few pairs of eyes idly follow what she's doing, perhaps hoping for a few treats – the sort she likes to reward them with after they've performed well.

She unzips the front compartment and in one movement pulls out the photon gun. Before they have time to fully react, against an agony of shrieks and yelps, she blasts into them one by one.

It's done. A cloud of hot gas envelops their piled-up bodies. She steps back to survey this tableau, tries to count each gory, still-smoking pelt though she can hardly bear to witness all that wild beauty reduced to so much dead meat.

Despite the freezing conditions, predators will soon be drawn here by the smell of their corpses. It's much better to think of them being eaten by native ravens or sea eagles in the noble circle of life, though she knows it's more likely they'll be consumed by rodents, feral dogs and other red foxes.

She reminds herself that regret is a pointless emotion. It had to be done – they were of no more use to her – their continued presence a hindrance to her future plans.

It's hard to bring herself to handle their soft, still-warm bodies in order to lay them out in a long line on the hard ground but she knows it's important to make sure.

'Fokk!' she screams, before counting them again. She was right the first time – they are not all there. Three of the vixens must have somehow escaped.

She scans every rock and bush between where she's standing and the distant horizon. There's no movement. What did she expect – they're masters of disguise after all. She can see no trails of blood in the snow in any direction. Their earlier paw prints only confuse the picture. Somewhere out there three sets of eyes are trained on her, fully aware of exactly what she's capable of.

She reaches into her pocket to extract the whistle she always carries; its frequency is too high for her to hear it. For the first time ever there is no response.

Her vixens have always accepted her authority, but their intelligence means they learn fast and this must have been quite a lesson.

Maybe she should come back tomorrow night and try summoning them again when they're hungry? It hardly seems likely that, with their fellow pack members still lying here dead, they would return to this place – unless it's to predate these corpses. Are they capable of fastidiousness when it comes to their own pack?

If she had the means, she'd clear up these carcasses and dump them elsewhere. As it is, she has no choice but to leave them here.

She can still sense the accusing gazes of the missing three. What must they be thinking now that their trusted pack-leader has betrayed them? How could anyone not admire these animals – such natural born killers famous for using their wits to outsmart their potential prey.

In the wild, they've even been known to play dead, going as far as to stick their tongues out in order to attract would-be carrion hunters. As the hapless bird moves in to eat them, the fox will make a grab for it – virtually the same method every decoy uses to trap their would-be attackers.

Twenty-Five

An orderly comes into his room. 'You've got a visitor, Mr Cafaro.'

Breaking off from the pointless game he's playing, Nero looks up. He's never seen this middle-aged orderly before and doesn't much like the look of him.

'Hi, Uncle,' Bruno ducks out from behind the man. 'Surprise!' The boy even does jazz hands, a bunch of grapes wedged beneath one arm.

Nero forces a smile. 'This is unexpected.' *Damnit, you should have known better than to come here like this.*

'Just thought I'd drop by to give you some news,' Bruno says. He turns round to peer at the orderly. 'Private family stuff.'

The man takes the hint though it's clear from his expression that his interest has been piqued.

Nero rolls his eyes. 'Sei uno stupido! What the hell are you thinking just waltzing in here like this?'

'Kass said you were definitely on the mend and I imagined – correct me if I'm wrong – that you might want an update on certain persons you've been trying to locate. But if you'd rather I went– ' Theatrically, he takes a step towards the door.

'Okay, okay – I was only thinking of your safety,' Nero tells him. 'You're here now and it's really good to see you.' The truth of this surprises him a little.

He smiles at the boy and then glances back at the door.

Bruno understands him. The boy opens the door abruptly. 'Boo!' He laughs out loud. 'Nobody out there – see.' He waves the door back and forward. 'The coast is definitely clear.'

After closing the door, Bruno drops into the chair by the bed, offering Nero the slightly squashed bunch of grapes.

'I can't believe you actually brought those,' Nero says.

The boy shrugs. 'You didn't seem like the cuddly toy and balloon type.'

To please him, Nero takes a couple. They taste sweetly of nothing – like they've never known sunlight.

'I kept quite a bit of stuff from you when we were in the cabin,' Bruno says.

'Go on.' The tough skins from those grapes are proving hard to swallow.

'Information I didn't think you were ready for in the state you were in. Now you're almost better, I thought it was time I came clean, *Inspector* and told you everything I know.'

'Don't say anything out loud.'

'Got it,' the boy says, touching the back of his undamaged hand. The strength of the connection overwhelms Nero.

He's walking with the boy in freezing snow; sharing his disorientation, his utter desperation as he reads a sign above a deserted factory: Sveinsson & Kjarval Ltd.

With the boy, he breaks into the abandoned building for shelter, walks through the ruined workshop then enters a small, dank room with a bed of sorts.

He wakes calm enough before the encounter with the hooded woman and those snarling vixens ready to attack him at her whim.

Finally entering her mind, he's assaulted, overwhelmed by the passionate, twisted logic that rules the woman, the full force of her dark and brutal loathing, most of all her determination to be the blunt instrument of change.

Ása Sturludóttir – the name her adoptive parents gave her. How she loathes them for that and for so much more. 'I am no one's daughter.' So many aliases but whatever she calls herself, her mind remains like no other, unique in its dogged ferocity.

He shares Bruno's relief to be leaving that damned factory at last despite the tortuous route that finally leads him to The Jolly Roger. Inside, he hears the music's incessant beat, sees those strobes circling like searchlights. At the bar, the conversation the boy has with David. In a split second, he learns everything that follows from that encounter.

'Enough.' Nero breaks the contact. The boy's palm has left an imprint on the back of his hand – red like the handprints left by long ago cave artists; a mark that will only gradually fade.

Nero's head is still throbbing with Bruno's thoughts. Rubbing at his forehead, it occurs to him that, simultaneously, the boy will have learnt every detail of their investigations including exactly what happened when they went into that bank.

Christ, this was a mistake.

'Well, I'd better be going.' Bruno stands up. 'I've got an assignment I need to work on.'

'Wait,' Nero tells him. 'I know why you came here. It's not your job to right every wrong. I don't want you taking any more risks. And throw those fokking guns into the fjord.'

'Relax, it's no big deal. I'm just hanging out with a group of students. Okay, they claim they want to lead a revolutionary uprising but really they're just a bunch of privileged idealists. You and I know from bitter experience that the real thing would scare them shitless.'

'So keep your head down and get on with your studies.'

'Okay – I get it. No need to look so anxious, what can possibly go wrong?'

'Plenty,' Nero says.

The boy returns to his bedside. In a whisper he says: 'Look, treat all this like you would an anonymous tipoff. Now you know, you can stake out that factory.' *I would have told Kass but then I'd have to explain too much. When you're back on your feet, you'll be able to commandeer half an army to raid that factory and all those tunnels they hide in.*

Bruno straightens up. 'Should be like shooting fish in a barrel.'

He winks back at Nero on his way to the door. 'See you soon, Uncle.'

So, following orders and in fear of his life, it was Bruno who managed to evade the security, distract the mansion's staff and open doors so she could slip unseen into the mansion to plant that duck on Leifsson's bedside table.

Should he tell Kass? How would he explain what he knows? There's no way he's going to mention that disused factory at this stage; he's not ready to risk his own life right now or hers. If they were to fail, what vengeance would Ása Sturludóttir bring down on Bruno's head?

Nero spends the afternoon fretting. When he checks again, it's already evening.

One thing's certain – he's been lying in bed for long enough.

All data readouts at his bedside inform him that his temperature has been hovering around normal for the last twenty-four hours. The latest blood analysis shows the antivirals have already worked their magic.

Nero pulls back the covers and swings his legs off the bed. The floor chills his bare feet. Now he's upright, the ache around his ribcage recedes a little, though his head feels contained – like he's wearing some invisible helmet.

Dressed only a thin bodywrap, he stands for a while allowing his legs to get used to bearing his weight. The bodywrap is sufficient to hide his nakedness but certainly won't protect him from the elements outside.

After the ambush, all his clothing had either melted or been cut from his body. Before they escaped from the other hospital, Bruno had purloined various items of clothing that had come from a person who was heavier built and shorter than him.

He has no memory of being admitted here but presumes he must have been wearing those same borrowed clothes when Kass brought him in. There's no locker in the room. Where might they have put them?

Taking it slowly, Nero makes it over to the door without a hitch. He looks through the glass panel and sees the corridor outside is still empty. With a sense of déjà vu, he recalls their hurried exit from the previous hospital.

He shuffles the full length of the corridor without stumbling once. The window at the end gives out on a wide view. Out there, all the artificial lights merge into a complex web binding up the whole city. Hardly anyone is out on the street. No vehicles on any of the roadways though the skyscrapers are still lit up like rockets. He pictures other faces at other windows looking out like he is.

'I see you're on your feet, Mr Cafaro.' Dr Hazim, Thorvaldsen's registrar, is standing right behind him.

'You startled me,' he says. 'You must have been good at grandmother's footsteps.'

'I'm sorry. I always wear soft-soled shoes on the evening shift; I try not to disturb anyone's beauty sleep.'

Nero smirks at her. 'In my case, it's sorely needed.'

'You must be feeling better if you're angling for compliments.'

'Yeah well, I've always been insecure about my good looks, I guess.'

Her laugh is dutiful; all the same it's a nice laugh.

'I must say, it feels pretty good to be standing upright at long last,' he says. Immediately the words are out, he worries she might think he intended a double entendre. Instead, she gives him a warning look. 'Make sure you don't go overdoing things. Remember the story about the tortoise and hare.'

Nero can't help but pull a face. 'I don't know whether I got round to thanking you for everything,' he says.

This time her smile is wide and generous. 'I don't know whether anybody ever got round to thanking you for risking your life in the line of duty.'

'I'm sorry?' he says, dumbfounded. Kass hadn't gone into a lot of detail about his cover story.

'I understand you work for the fire and rescue service. I guess we both just get on with what we're paid to do.'

'I'm mostly involved in admin these days,' he tells her.

'What, with all those burns of yours – I think you're being far too modest, Mr Cafaro.'

'The truth is, I'm not sure I always see what I've achieved; in your line of work it must be obvious every day.'

'Not really.' Her face clouds. 'We fail more often than we'd like. I've just left a young man of twenty-seven who's slowly dying of a disease we ought to be able to cure this late in the twenty-first century. What do I say to his family?'

'That must be tough. I guess you tell them you've done your best – that's all any of us can do.'

'But it's not our best. We could do so much more if only this city prioritised health care a little more.' Her frustration is clear.

'Perhaps, with all these calls for reform,' he says, 'things might improve.'

'I very much doubt any change in this city will be for the better.'

He can't disagree. For a moment they stand in silence looking out at the lights.

Dr Hazim rouses herself. 'Anyway, back to you, Mr Cafaro. It's patients like you who keep us going. The speed of your recovery has been truly remarkable – miraculous almost. You must let me know your secret.'

Nero tries not to wince. 'Maybe that makes me the hare after all?'

'You've been given a new beginning. I know all too well how pressure can get to you – how, just to let off steam, people can fall into things.'

Nero doesn't know what to say to her. Is this a confession? 'It's understandable when you are dealing with life and death issues like you are,' he says. 'I don't know if I could cope –.'

'I was referring you, Mr Cafaro, not myself.' Though she smiles, her eyes remain serious.

His head does that odd catch up thing. 'I'm sorry. I still feel a little disorientated. I'm afraid I don't understand what you're talking about.'

'We'll leave it there for now, shall we?' she says. 'You look a little faint; let me walk you back to your room.' She takes his elbow and together they go back along the corridor. Wanting to understand more, he concentrates on the connection but the bodywrap makes it impossible.

Nero's reluctant to lie down. 'I'll just sit here for a while,' he tells her though his strength is already ebbing away.

Perhaps he's done enough for today.

Twenty-Six

'Keep moving, damnit.' The weapon pressed into Rashid's ribcage emphasises his point.

'Listen, can't we discuss– '

'Shut it, Ashram. I don't want to hear it.'

They trudge past the first set of buildings further on into the compound. It's no longer sleeting and the clearer air allows Rashid to study the high fence running around the perimeter. Night is almost upon them. As far as he's able to make out, each section of wire is stapled down firmly with no discernable gaps underneath. Coils of rusting razor wire run along the top in an unbroken run. It would be impossible to climb up and over in a hurry.

Out beyond the compound, the shadows are thickening. There's nothing out there – no distant lights, no sign of any other life.

'Okay that's far enough,' Quentin says. 'Now turn around very slowly, and I do mean slowly.'

This has to be the moment.

Rashid twists his elbow round high enough to jab just below the weapon. As he makes contact, a photon beam fires high like a distress flare before the weapon skids away over the damp ground.

He grabs Quentin's arm and pulls at his jacket only to recoil as a sharp knee digs deep into his groin. The pain doubles Rashid up. Bent in two, he has to pull every breath. He scans the ground, sees the silver silhouette of the weapon off to his left.

A boot comes towards his face but he catches the man's ankle before it can make contact then raises it to force the man down. He rotates Quentin's foot, spinning him sideways until he's close enough to let go.

The shining promise of that weapon is now within his reach. Rashid launches himself on top of it. His hand finds the grip and, switching his weight to one side, he levels the barrel at his opponent.

'Okay, you got me.' He can see the pale palms of the man's hands are high in the air; there's no excuse to shoot him now.

'So, Ashram,' Quentin gives a short laugh. 'You planning on killing me right here or what?'

Rashid gets to his feet breathing heavily. 'All things considered, it seems the most sensible option.' His other hand comes up to support his wrist allowing him to hold the gun without wavering. He wills Quentin to make a move but instead the man hangs his head beaten.

'Get it over with then.' They're so far away from the light, he's barely visible – just a dark outline in front of him breathing heavily.

'You seem to be in a hurry to die.'

Quentin shrugs. 'Either way, I'm already dead.'

'That's not true – you still have choices. We can offer you witness protection if you give us what we need in return.' Rashid lets his thoughts run ahead. He wonders how much this man knows about who set them up for the bank raid. Perhaps he's close to finding out who killed Lúter.

Quentin scoffs. 'Your faith is touching.'

'I can promise you– '

'Spare me the litany. I know all about this city's justice system; that's why I'm here. It was all going just fine until you blundered in.'

'You're talking in riddles.' Rashid moves closer to the man.

'Let me spell it out to you, Sergeant Ashram. Those guys who just left, they've come to trust me. I'm so close and now you've left me no options either way. If I don't kill you, they'll kill me. Simple. I've managed to get my feet on the ladder but, now you've fokked it all up, it's back down the tail of the snake once again.'

'So, let me get this straight, are you seriously trying to convince me you're working undercover?' It's Rashid's turn to scoff. 'Am I expected to believe you're a police officer?'

'No. I'm not working for the police. If I were, I wouldn't be out in this god-awful weather, splashing around in the mud of an old army outpost with a photon gun aimed at my head. No, I'd have done my allotted shift, spent the evening with my family and be looking forward to a warm bed and giving my wife a quick one before I roll over to sleep.'

'So why are you out here?'

'Why am *I* out here?' He fakes a laugh, which slowly turns into the real thing. 'I'm doing the exact same thing you're doing but with a whole lot more success.' Quentin's silhouette shakes its head. 'I'll admit tonight was a stupid, stupid mistake on my part. To give you your due, you totally fooled me. I took you for some tag-along punk I could use to make up the numbers, not a fokking would-be hero of a cop. Did you really think you could play with the big boys and nobody would figure out who you really are? They don't operate in isolation, Sergeant, these guys make damn sure they have sources everywhere.'

For a moment, Rashid's tempted to correct his police rank but thinks better of it. 'Go on then,' he says, 'I can see you're dying to enlighten me some more.'

Quentin takes a step towards him. 'Okay. Lesson one, Sergeant: this city is divided into zones. We have the Free Zone where everyone has a jolly nice time enjoying all the benefits of a successful trading economy and effective law and order, while out in the other zones it gets a little wilder until you finally get to the Double Red where it's every man for himself – Dodge City without the horses. Is that what you idiots down at DSD really believe?'

To maintain his distance, Rashid has to take a step backwards. 'I assume you're now going to tell me otherwise.' He hopes the other man recognises the sarcasm in his voice.

'Second lesson,' Quentin says. 'Our city's elders noticed a long time ago that every time they rounded up illicit suppliers – whether it was arms, drugs or whatever – it only created a job opportunity for their rivals so that, pretty soon after that, they start killing each other all over again. As a policeman, you've surely noticed the many-headed hydra of crime can never be beaten.'

Again, he edges closer. Rashid stands his ground, holds his weapon steady. 'Go on.'

'They got smart. Decided that a deal could be struck. It took some while to negotiate, but eventually the cartels were persuaded to vacate the central part of the city in exchange for a great deal more tolerance out in the borderlands and free run in the red zones. That was the beginning of a million mutually advantageous arrangements, benefitting everyone involved so long as all parties continued to show restraint.' He thumps his chest. 'I was part of the fokking window dressing. Sent forth for the greater glory of keeping the Orange Zone free of any up-and-coming talent.'

'You're claiming you're a decoy?'

The man's loud laugh is almost ghoulish. 'Got it in one, Sergeant.' He brings his hands together in a desultory clap. 'Personally, I prefer to use the term patsy. Oh yes – convince us we are doing something for the greater good of humanity and then wind us up and watch us scurry back and forth along the firing line.' He spreads both arms out. 'Decoys – the clue's in the fokking name. We draw out what's lurking in the shadows on the borderlands while all the serious stuff goes on elsewhere.'

'So, if you're a decoy officer, what exactly are you playing at?'

'I got a little bored out here in no-honest-man's-land, so I decided to take advantage of the autonomy the job allows. Guess I'm here for the exact same reason you are. I started by studying the distribution of arms and I've been making my way slowly, bit by bit, towards some of the many heads.' The man's certainly keen on his metaphors. 'Recently, they've been moving through more shipments with impunity – getting altogether bolder because they're being protected by higher forces.'

Rashid can't really make out Quentin's features so he isn't in a position to judge whether the man is telling the truth or not. Along with his gun arm, his resolve is beginning to waver. 'If you're a decoy, as you claim to be, then where's your vixen pack, eh?'

'I had to deal with them. It was unavoidable.' His cough sounds forced. 'It wasn't an easy decision.'

'If you're telling the truth, how come you didn't just come to us at DSD and tell us everything you've found out?'

'You've got to be kidding me.' The outline of the man's head turns from side to side. 'Let me tell you something else. A few months back, I learnt about a consignment containing certain exto-suits way more sophisticated than the ones issued to regular decoys. Some of us began to speculate that certain parties were tooling up, as it were, in preparation for their next move.'

'And what would that be?'

Quentin falls silent. Finally, he says: 'Who can say for sure? This city is like an oyster, they only need to insert a knife at the right point and boomf!'

The man's hands mime an explosion that seems more apt for a hand grenade than an opened-up oyster.

'That's all I've got so far,' Quentin says. 'I'm not working alone, there are others I'm in contact with.'

'What others?'

‘That’s all I’m prepared to tell you. Right now you’d better go ahead and shoot me.’

‘How do I know you’re telling me the truth?’

‘You don’t – so shoot me.’

Rashid feels the full weight of the weapon in his hands. ‘Can you prove any of this?’

‘No – I mean what proof could you reasonably expect me to offer?’

‘I need more details. Let’s start with what you know about the raid on that Silver Street bank – the one where one of our team was killed.’

The man’s contemptuous laugh tempts Rashid to fire at his legs. ‘Ah, so that’s what brought you into the Orange Zone. Your mate was he, your best pal? And now you’re here to avenge his death. All very noble, I’m sure.’

Quentin’s too close now, his chest almost in contact with the barrel of the weapon between them. ‘Or maybe you’re trying to assuage your own guilt?’

‘Look, you need to tell me what you know or so help me I’ll –’ Rashid is ready for him. He can smell the stale alcohol on the man’s breath.

‘You’ll what? Going to kill me twice over, are you? In any case, what the hell makes you think that *I* know anything about that bank?’

‘Nathan Sams told me you were the one who gave him the information about the bank. He knew we were looking for the decoy who killed all those people in the Double Red and Sams claimed it was you who told him that bank was her headquarters.’

Quentin snorts. ‘The little weasel may have told you that, but it didn’t come from me. I said nothing to him about that decoy and before you ask, I’m not prepared to say anything now.’

He leans over the gun, his face right in Rashid’s. ‘I didn’t give any such information to Sams, so now the question is,

Sergeant Ashram, who else helped him set you up? As for that particular decoy – she's chosen her own path, who am I to interfere?'

'Surely you don't think every decoy has the right to act in whatever way they choose?'

'Isn't that precisely what they ask of us? The Commanders permit us the freedom to roam here and there within our own territories. We're even allowed to play the part of God to our vixen packs. Now Leifsson's suspended the whole programme, do they expect us to sit around and wait for them to implement their usual retirement plans for us – blasting us to kingdom come like they did to Harris?'

Though hard to believe, this last revelation has a ring of truth about it. 'Some of us plan to use this opportunity to winkle out the true criminals,' Quentin says.

Rashid frees the supporting hand to rub at his stubble while he tries to think. 'Besides,' Quentin says, 'Correct me if I'm wrong but haven't you yourself gone more than a bit rogue? I doubt anyone at DSD knows where you are tonight. Showing that sort of initiative in this city is likely to get you killed sooner or later.'

Rashid steadies his grip on the weapon. 'Why not come with me now to DSD? You and me, we're on the same side, we should be working together.'

'Oh dear, Sergeant, still not getting the picture here, are you?' Quentin raises his hands to the sky as if appealing for Godly understanding.

Rashid swears under his breath. 'I need you to shut the fokk up for a minute. Will you do that?'

'Or you'll what?'

'I really don't know what to think.' Rashid brings the gun up until it's in line with the man's skull, then lets it drop. 'I can't shoot you,' he says. 'Not like this. There are no other choices. He turns the gun around, offers Quentin the grip. 'Here, take it. If you're lying, I guess I'll know about it soon enough.'

Quentin seizes the weapon. After a moment, he places it on the ground and kicks it away. 'So, what do we do now, Sergeant?'

'Inspector,' Rashid tells him. His own laugh is all bitterness. 'I recently got promoted to Acting Inspector, with the emphasis on acting.'

While Quentin remains where he is, Rashid backs away from the confrontation, goes over to sit down on anything that feels solid enough – in this case a discarded oil drum.

Far above him the last clouds part to reveal the beauty of the stars arrayed across the night sky. He'd forgotten all that majesty was up there once you got away from the dazzle of all those lights.

A sound makes them both turn. Rashid hears splashing, gravel scattering. A vehicle is approaching the gates. From what he can see of its shape, it looks like the same Norseman 80. Perhaps that stray photon fire had alerted them and that's why they're back. Could even be someone else arriving. The answer to that question is one of the many things he'll never know.

He looks over at Quentin. 'I think you'd better pick that weapon up and shoot me right now,' he says.

'Are you serious?'

'You can calculate the odds as well as I can,' Rashid says. 'It's more or less guaranteed we'll both die if you don't. What other choice is left?'

He gets to his feet. 'Go ahead. I'm ready.'

Twenty-Seven

Kass is trembling; she wills herself to stay calm though her legs are barely holding her upright. As the most senior homicide officer present, it's her duty to treat this with the same professionalism she would any other investigation – though this is hardly *any other* murder.

Those members of staff who were first on the scene have already been escorted to the examination suite. Maxwell and Chan are in the process of shepherding everyone who'd been on duty at the time into one of the function rooms. Kass had made it clear they should be offered basic refreshments but, without exception, no one can be allowed to leave until they've been interviewed.

Opening her kitbag, she removes a SOC suit and pulls it up over her clothing and then her head, carefully tucking every strand of hair inside. She then covers her boots with plastic socks before positioning the mask and goggles to cover most of her face. Finally, she isolates her hands from anything she might touch by pulling on nitrile gloves.

Like it's a test she might give a rookie, she runs through the standard steps in her mind. Her first concern had been to preserve the primary scene and cordon off a wider area beyond. Inevitably, there's already been some contamination but Kass is confident she's done all she can to prevent any more occurring.

Her next task is to conduct a thorough search of the murder scene itself. Everything found or observed must be meticulously recorded. Once that's done, she'll be forced to turn the whole thing over to the forensics team. They'll begin the methodical preservation of all the physical evidence; this is her one chance to examine the undisturbed scene before any of that happens.

Kass reminds herself that anything she picks up must first be recorded in situ and returned to precisely where she found it without being contaminated in any way.

She checks the building's schematic and takes a few deep breaths as she nods to the officer on guard and steps across the tape.

It's the first time she's seen the place up close. Treading with care, she walks in through the impressive main entrance. Her wrist monitor scans the walls and floor while she progresses further into the building.

At first sight everything appears orderly with no sign of anything amiss. Checking for any significant marks or scratches on the treads or balustrade, she climbs the stairs and then continues along the corridor towards the master suite.

Through the open door, she can already see the bathroom floor and two bare legs protruding from a blackened pool of blood.

Steeling herself, Kass steps over the vomit on the bedroom's threshold. Preliminary reports suggest this isn't from the victim but the security guard who discovered the body.

She notes the intermittent trail of blood along the pale, plush-piled carpet. Taking care to circumvent a set of crimson prints, she makes her way over to the doorway of the bathroom itself.

She keeps close to the edges, noticing how the blood is lighter where it's flowed away from the body and out along the gridlines of the floor tiles.

Here more bloody footprints are coming and going. Along

with the ones in the bedroom, these will be compared to those from the members of staff known to have had contact with the body – including the security guard who'd knelt right here to check his vital signs.

State Governor Leifsson is slumped against the back wall. Despite his bulk, given the room's stately proportions he's taking up surprisingly little space. The usual ruddiness to his cheeks has been replaced by a washed-out mask, which seems to bear only a passing resemblance to the man he was.

Kass curses the way various people had blundered about. Forensics will be arriving inside five minutes but for now this scene is hers and hers alone; she'd better not waste this time.

Turning towards a sound, she sees a suited-up figure standing in the doorway. 'It's me,' Maxwell says, pulling down her mask for a moment.

Buoyed by Maxwell's presence, Kass stares down at the tanned and muscled torso and then the obscenity of the black and silver handle protruding from his chest. Looks like someone was aiming for his heart.

Christ! The whole thing is in almost to the hilt. Not an assassin's specialist weapon but something you might use for butchery. It would have taken a great deal of upper body strength to plunge that knife in so deeply.

The spectacle holds her mesmerised. 'Where do I start?' she says out loud. She looks at the poor man's wet and thinning hair, the way his mouth is wide open as if in ironic laughter.

The lower portion of Leifsson's body is splayed across the hard tiles. Kass follows the line of one leg to the shrivelled penis tucked in below the swell of his belly. Along with everything else, this mountain of a man has been robbed of his dignity.

She's tempted to take down one of those fluffy white towels and cover him up for decency's sake. His vacant blue eyes offer her no clues, those enormous, empty hands seem to implore but, at first glance, they hold nothing to incriminate the perpetrator of this hideous act.

'Even though I'm looking at his body, I can't believe he's really gone,' she says. 'It's never been someone I know before.'

She feels a light pressure on her upper arm, looks down to see Maxwell's gloved hand squeezing it. 'I was talking to him only a matter of hours ago.' Kass is determined not to cry. 'He made some crack – the usual jibe about my glasses.'

'I know what you mean. In a strange way, I was quite fond of the big man.' Maxwell sighs. Cocking her head to one side, she says, 'He looks sort of more than dead; like this body lying here in front of us was never actually alive.'

'I wish I felt the same.' Kass has to look away for a moment – across the room to the fancy toiletries arrayed along the glass shelves, the brush still holding a fine skein of dyed-black hair. 'And fokking forensics will be here any minute.'

'You can do this, Inspector.' Maxwell's voice is soft, full of understanding. 'Take it one step at a time. Why don't we start with the recordings?'

Kass pulls herself upright. 'Thanks for the offer, but I can handle this by myself.' Her words are braver than she feels. Right now, her hands seem too clumsy to set the equipment at the precise angles required. Then again, hadn't she watched Nero work a murder scene so many times before? In truth, she already knows exactly what needs to be done here.

'Maxwell, I think you'd better – um.' She pulls back her shoulders. 'Once the swabs have been taken, you and Chan should begin the preliminary interviews. Start with the patrol personnel who were first on the scene. When I'm finished here, we can interview the governor's personal staff together.'

'Yes, boss.' Maxwell's SOC suit rustles as she leaves the governor's suite.

Left alone with the body, Kass takes the first imager from her bag and sets it up on one axis, then does the same with all the others.

'*Begin recordings.*' The machines start their sequence. In a series of clicks that are almost inaudible, they scan and simultaneously record everything necessary to reconstruct a full 360-degree holo of the murder scene.

A soft bleep tells her they've completed the task. She steps inside the circle. Voicing her precise observations, Kass studies the poor man's corpse in minute detail, her voice level and clear with no hint of the emotions running through her.

It comes to her that if you could ignore all the gore, with marble covering every surface and those touches of gold, this room might be taken for a mausoleum designed to contain the dead body of the late state governor of Eldísvík.

Twenty-Eight

A man in green overalls bursts into Nero's room. 'My stud just went totally dead. I mean completely! Is yours working?'

He's never seen this person before, can't guess at his precise role in the hospital. 'Sorry, but I can't help you.' Nero holds both hands up. 'My stud was destroyed in the accident that got me in here in the first place. Haven't got round to getting a replacement yet.'

'Fokk!' The man gives him a look of disbelief. On his chest, his ID tag declares he's called Viktor and he's a grade three maintenance operative. It looks genuine enough. 'That's just terrible – how the hell you been managing?'

Nero shrugs. 'Tell you the truth, I'm rather enjoying the peace.'

The man detaches his stud and holds it out in his open palm. 'This thing's almost new. I ran a diagnostic and all functions are green-lighted but nothing's coming through. Not even the fokking weather report.'

'Then my guess is the whole network must be down.' Does this man have an ulterior motive for being in here?

The man's eyebrows come together in a desperate peak. 'How is that even possible?' He looks around the room as if seeking someone or something to blame. 'Maybe there's been one of those solar flares. Or else some kind of massive power surge that's blown everything.'

'Who knows?' Nero says, pulling himself higher in the bed. A spasm of pain makes him hold his breath. The new binding on his back makes the gesture look more like a nervous tic.

The man's shoulders sag. 'Everything seems to be going tits up in this city. What's next – that's what I want to know.' He turns to go, pauses on the threshold and then rushes out leaving the door wide open. 'Fokk this!' The man's cri de coeur echoes on down the corridor.

Nero takes his time getting out of bed. When he's finally upright, his muscles feel like they've run a marathon – not that he's ever been tempted to expend energy on anything as pointless. He walks slowly over to the door and looks both ways along the empty corridor before he shuts it. Sadly, there's no locking mechanism.

Reaching up to the room's air outlet, Nero retrieves the package from behind the air-con grill. He blows away some dust before unwrapping the stud Kass had brought in. Strange how quickly he's adjusted to not wearing one of these things.

He steers it to the implant in his ear and the device snaps into place. 'Turn off location tracker,' he says. The maintenance man was right about the public network being down. It takes Nero a second or two to remember the override code. 'Seven, five, three, three, eight, four, two. gamma, epsilon.'

After a slight delay he hears, '*you are successfully connected to the emergency police network.*' An all-personnel message is looping.

'*...be resumed once evacuation has been satisfactorily completed. Full emergency procedures have been implemented. All police and security personnel must report immediately to their section commanders. I repeat, Governor Hagalín will make an all-citizens broadcast at noon today.*

'*Curfew conditions remain in operation in all controlled zones. Public access to subway systems and outer tram networks is temporarily suspended. Citizens are being directed to vacate all outside areas. The search for possible terrorists, along with any suspicious devices that may have been planted, is ongoing. Normal stud and network coverage will only resume once these have been completed and the threat level reduced. Officers not directly...'*

Shock radiates through Nero's body. The announcement would have said *Acting* Governor Hagalín if Leifsson was still alive.

'Quel povero bastardo!' His mouth dries on the words. He'd never liked Leifsson much but that's beside the point. As his nonna used to say: chi cambia la vecchia via per la nuova sa quel che lascia – and Leifsson was the devil he knew.

What or who could have killed him? The governor's high blood pressure and heart condition was an open secret. The events around the decoy murders had certainly added more than the usual stress to his job. It would hardly be a surprise if the autopsy found a cocktail of illegal substances competing in the man's bloodstream. However, the emergency measures in place would seem to rule out natural causes.

All things considered, Hagalín certainly had the most to gain from the man's death. He must be delighted to have achieved the pinnacle of his ill-disguised ambition. Rumour has it Leifsson only tolerated him as his deputy because he appeared to be less of a threat than any of the other candidates. Maybe it was a question of keeping his enemy closer. It's nothing short of frightening that someone with such obvious personal flaws now holds the reins of power in Eldísvík.

He recalls how Lúter and Rashid had perfected a double act mimicking the way Hagalín's practiced, oleaginous voice gave way under questioning to a high-pitched whine. They'd take turns contorting their faces to the sharp awkwardness of the man's features, the way his voice appeared to emanate from the side of his mouth.

Nero's smile drops as tears roll down to his chin. With the heel of his hand he smears them across his face. How often people bandy about phrases like *time's a great healer* or more pretentiously: *this too will pass.* In his experience, grief is a tag-along – there for the duration. There's never much respite.

Exhausted, he sits back down on the bed. His stud gives a soft bleep to indicate an information download. Nero sniffs hard and then accepts the distraction.

The information's hardly reassuring. Can he get through to anyone in Homicide? It's unlikely. In any case what value could he add to the situation from here in his damn hospital prison.

The door swings back to admit Lianna, the Senior Therapy Nurse – a big woman with a handsome face. Today she's carrying something under one arm. 'How's it going, Mr Cafaro?'

Lianna puts the package on the end of the bed. 'I got to tell you,' she says, checking the burn dressing on his arm, 'you've no idea how lucky you are up here out of the way of things. The whole hospital's gone nuts and that's no exaggeration.'

Her hands move gently from one wound to the next. 'Security's everywhere, no admissions allowed unless it's life or death. Guards on every entrance and not just the regular ones.' She shakes her head. 'The Porcupines are out in force – full-body shells, photons bristling from everywhere. You'd better not sneeze down there or you might get fried.

'Okay, now,' she leans forward. 'Doctor Hazim tells me you're back on your feet. Congratulations, just remember there is no rush. If you wouldn't mind lying down for a second.'

She goes to the bottom of the bed. 'Feel any pain – just yell.' A short laugh. 'But maybe try to keep it down a little – we don't want Security rushing in here.'

Nero looks down at his body. The bodywrap he's encased in has a pale sheen that's making him look like a pupa or a freshly disturbed maggot. 'I'd like to go for a short walk,' he tells her. 'I'm really going to need some clothes.'

'Well then, it's lucky I've brought you some.' She gives him a wide smile that makes her look younger, more carefree. 'Somebody – I'm not naming names – must have got your clothes mixed up with someone else's. All of it was way too small. I went through lost property – as we euphemistically like to call it – and found some more your size.'

'You want me to walk around in dead men's clothes?'

'They're just clothes – no need to get squeamish about it.' She unwraps the bundle to produce underpants, a decent looking pair of trousers, a shirt and a thick jumper. He's disappointed to see there's no topcoat. Lianna notices his expression 'Besides, everything's been through the sterilizer.'

Nero sits up. This time it's easier to swing his legs off the bed and onto the floor. Being back on his feet makes him less light-headed than he was yesterday.

'Okay,' Lianna says, 'remember to take it easy, Mr Cafaro. There's plenty of time. Let's face it, no one's going anyplace in this city for a while.'

Twenty-Nine

Hagalín stalks the room. A mere four hours had elapsed since the Committee of the Commander had conducted his perfunctory swearing in. His official appointment will need to be ratified by the full parliament in due course; however, with the constitution of Eldísvík firmly on his side, that is merely a formality – a bit of pageantry for a later date to please the good citizens and give them something to cheer about.

The new governor walks over to the window of his new office and stares down on the emptied-out city. Even the cranes – those ever-present sentinels around the docks – are static. He can see no workers, no shoppers, no dog-walkers; no queues around the entrance to the subway. The curfew seems complete and absolute. The only movement is a line of swaying trees moving in sync with a few redundant overhead cables.

It really isn't good enough – he's been waiting for ten minutes for a simple sandwich and a mineral water. He's the governor now and the people around here need to understand that when he asks for something he expects them to fokking jump to it.

Closing his eyes, Hagalín attempts to remain calm and in control. The Commanders had seen fit to remind him how necessary that was – as if he didn't understand that better than anyone.

He's rehearsed the announcement until it sounds like it's coming from the heart. Eivin's words tick every box. They run through shock, sadness, regret, respect, resolve, determination, competence, faith, hope and finally strength. He'll start with wiping away what they'll assume is a single tear and he'll end it with a raised fist.

He's trying hard not to get annoyed about that sandwich – it's an inconvenience, nothing more. Knowing Leifsson as he did, it seems pretty unlikely the catering staff have dissolved in floods of tears. Heads will roll if there's a repeat of this. Yes, under his administration things are going to be a bit different around here.

It's now eleven o'clock. At precisely eleven-fifty he'll enter the main briefing room by himself. There's no way anyone, except the technicians, will be able to tell the announcement isn't coming out live.

Amie is still sniffing as she moves around the outer office filling up boxes that a military courier is standing by to take away. He idly wonders if Liljan or Marty will be the recipient. That's the sort of thing he can leave to Amie to decide. Will those small relics from Leifsson's life – the family photos, the signed rugby balls, various framed degrees – be treasured, or will they lie in some cupboard for a year or two until someone gets round to throwing them away? One thing is certain: Leifsson will leave no legacy here.

The new governor goes back to the window appraising the view it affords. It really is far better than the one from his old office. If you didn't know, you'd swear it was a warm spring day out there. They have a word for that here – Gluggaveður or window weather – the illusion that everything is fair until you step outside into the real world.

Amie comes in. 'What did you want me to do with these?' She has a pile of random folders in her hands. 'This is the governor's personal correspondence with members of the public.' Her eye make-up has run into black lines down her face. Not a pretty sight.

He pretends to consider for a moment. 'I think they should be incinerated. I expect you to use your judgement, Amie. Anything that isn't confidential can be shredded ready for recycling.'

Hagalín summons up a kindly smile. 'Is there anything else you're not sure about?'

She shakes her head, turning away to pile the folders onto a chair just outside the door.

He moves over to the desk and sits back into the soft, beige leather chair. When Amie comes back, he follows her shapely backside as she works her way along the shelves he's told her to clear.

Leifsson had given her the job despite that big booty; he'll probably keep her on because of it. Well, that and the fact that she knows more about how to do this job than anyone else, dead or alive.

The door opens and a spotty young man with a tray appears. 'You took your time,' Hagalín says, as he motions him to put it down on the desk. 'The chef had a problem getting butter because of the curfew. It took a while for the frozen stuff to–'

He shuts him up with a gesture and then shoos him away.

The tray is reflected in the desktop's polished wood. Hagalín takes a moment to admire the run of the grain with its whorls aligned in perfect symmetry. He's always envied the governor this desk.

Despite the wait, the sandwich is good. Someone's already unscrewed the top of the water for him. He'll instruct them not to open it next time. Besides, he always likes to hear that hiss as the bubbles escape.

Hagalín looks around him. Already, the room works better without all that crap. Minimalism is always the answer. Leave others to do all the plodding stuff while you stick with the big picture. Leifsson got himself bogged down in too much detail – one of the man's many inadequacies. As head of state, your role is to oversee; you have the end vision – leave others to execute things for you.

That's how he plans to proceed and, now he's in charge, that's certainly how it's going to be from now on.

Thirty

Initial forensic reports confirm that Leifsson had died at approximately 3.30 a.m. as a direct result of the injuries inflicted by the knife wound.

'No surprises there,' Kass says out loud. Looking over the preliminary tox report, she's intrigued by the fact that they'd found high levels of a specific poison called saxotoxin in his blood. Jue Hai promises to let her have more details once the autopsy has been completed.

It's likely Leifsson was already in a weakened state when the attack occurred. Looks like a sort of belts and braces murder – crude, old-fashioned even, but undeniably effective.

With an unknown assailant, they always have to consider who might have held a grudge against the victim. In Leifsson's case, it's hard to know where to begin.

Maxwell has already finished interviewing the security guard – a thick-set man named Gunnar Einarsson – who had first discovered the body. After finding Leifsson in the bathroom, he'd gone to fetch a first-aider – Dorotea Lundin. Dorotea had double-checked the governor's vital signs even though she could see he was dead. Dorotea was holding up okay but couldn't tell them anything they didn't already know. Despite his size, Gunnar was in severe shock and hadn't been able to give them any help.

'The note left on Leifsson's bedside table said *you are next.*' Maxwell holds up both hands. 'A clear enough threat from whoever left it there.'

'You're right,' Kass says. 'Before we do anything else, I think we should go through all those interviews Young and Davis did on Leifsson's staff after the intruder broke into his bedroom. *If* the murderer is the same person who left the plastic duck and that note, we'll be able to prove it was premeditated.'

Kass starts to pace the room. 'Everything would seem to point to this being the work of one of the decoys we're looking for but, in this case, the M O seems to me to be very different.'

'From what Dorotea told me, those interviews by the two doctors were full-on interrogations,' Maxwell says. 'She reckoned they really shook things up around here. His personal cook stormed out even though she'd been with him for seven years. Then one of his drivers upped and left. The cook was replaced only two days ago by a Mrs Bianca De Morenos and, um –' Maxwell scans her log. 'The driver was replaced by a man called Alyn Keane. A couple of additional guards were assigned to the house: Haas and Flannery. Background checks on all new personnel were rated triple A, as you might expect.'

'Mm, I see it was Dr Young who conducted the majority of the interviews they all objected to,' Kass says. Her stud bleeps with yet another report. The analysis on the newly installed Hi-Sec system shows no breaches or malfunction. The whole system being state-of-the-art and even better than DSD's. Staff movements show no obvious irregularities. There'd been no outside visitors in the twenty-four hours before his death. Leifsson's wife and kids remain at the grandma's house. The governor's lover, Dr Chester, hasn't been back to the mansion in a while.

They've been warned by the techs to keep the load on this stud frequency to a minimum. She's as brief as she can be: *'Message: Dr Silas Young, DSD Training. Please meet me at the governor's mansion a s a p. Inspector Kassöndrudóttir.'*

After a couple of minutes, Kass changes her mind. Maxwell and Chan should stay here to conduct the bulk of the interviews. '*Replacement message*,' she says. '*Recipient: Dr Silas Young. Meet me, DSD room I.R.10 in ten minutes. Homicide Inspector Kassöndrudóttir.*'

This was, after all, the city's highest profile murder case in fifty years; it was no fokking Cluedo game.

Young takes fifteen minutes to arrive. Tall, dark-haired; he's overconfident, cocky even, and dressed far too casually. Kass gives him the names of the four they are about to interview.

He looks disappointed. 'It's not my job to criticise, Inspector, but you might want to widen the net a tad.'

'I'm open to suggestions.' Resentment clips her words.

'I think we should bring in Dr Marty Chester: he's a special friend of Leifsson's.'

'I know about Dr Chester,' she says, 'But he seems to have moved out recently and he definitely wasn't there last night.'

'Even more reason to suspect he might have a motive – a man scorned and all that. Oh, and then there's Salvatore Machelotti – a good-looking young man who worked in the grounds. We found him very helpful: he's observant and loves to gossip. However, he's simply vanished into thin air. Then there's the ex-driver and the ex-cook. It's far from easy to find alternative work these days. Who wouldn't be mad about losing their job?'

'But none of the people you mention has been near the mansion recently. Directly after you'd questioned the staff, several were pissed enough to resign.' She gives him a long look. 'That doesn't make them suspects for Leifsson's murder.'

Young raises both eyebrows. 'You may be right but in my considered opinion, as an expert, I'd say such defensiveness is excessive. In the cook's case, it might be partly explained by the fact that she'd fled the extremes of the Delgado Regime. But ex-asylum seekers are hardly thin on the ground in this city.'

Kass finds his unwavering gaze is becoming uncomfortable. She imagines he was a Birgir-no-mates until he found his vocation scaring people. Still, the guy's success is legendary.

'As for the driver,' Young looks away at last, 'we exposed a long-term drug habit that was utterly incompatible with the responsibility of chauffeuring our head of state. I don't know how it was overlooked. The man didn't resign – Leifsson had to fire him.'

Kass grins. 'If either of them has homicidal tendencies, I would have thought their targets ought really to be you.'

Young holds up both hands. 'The assignment of guilt by individuals is never straightforward, Inspector. You're right – we all need to watch *our* backs right now.'

'In my opinion, as an experienced homicide officer, I'd say it makes sense to start with the people we know to have been at the mansion when the murder occurred.'

He shrugs. 'Let's agree to leave the four of them out of it for the time being, Inspector.' It's a very small concession.

'Call me Kass.' She isn't sure why she said that, it wasn't as if there's any chance of them becoming friends.

'Can we have Mrs De Morenos first?' she tells the screen.

A middle-aged woman shuffles into the room. Kass motions the guard behind her away. The cook's gaze remains on the floor. Her reddened hands show a lifetime of hard work. They are visibly shaking; she can't seem to hold them still.

'Do take a seat, Mrs De Morenos.' Kass tries to sound unintimidating, but the bulk of that chair makes its purpose all too apparent.

The woman's knees seem to be about to buckle. Kass fights an instinct to grab her before she collapses onto the seat.

When the cook finally raises her head, she stares at the blank wall behind them. The skin across her forehead lies in deep, worrying furrows. There are dark circles around her eyes. The eyes themselves are deep brown and shining with unshed tears. In her lap, her hands claw together for safety.

Both of them are experienced enough to know that, despite all competing theories, they've discovered Leifsson's killer.

Thirty-One

So far Mrs De Morenos has only answered to confirm her name, and then, after several more minutes, her occupation. She's almost catatonic with fear.

Kass signals to Young that they should leave the room. She's quite certain of the woman's guilt but perhaps this was not the vicious attack the scene had suggested. The cook seems timid, aside from her well-developed arm muscles, she appears too insubstantial to have plunged that knife up to its hilt in the centre of Leifsson's chest.

Could this be another case of an interrogation triggering a response associated with earlier traumas? IR10, with its forensic lights and array of electronic feedback equipment would induce fear into any normal person. They need to be sensitive, to remember how this city is full of refugees who've fled war or devastation; all of them carry so many unseen scars.

In the corridor, Young turns on her. 'Why call a halt to the proceedings at this point? We have her. You've seen the state she's in.' He leans in. 'It'll take me less than five minutes to get it out of her.'

'But I don't want to be party to that kind of confession.' Kass stands her ground, out-stares the starer.

'Exactly what are you trying to imply, Inspector?'

'Last time I checked, we still had a justice system in this city.

The woman's clearly traumatised – we can agree on that. I'm going to ask Maxwell and Chan to take over the questioning.'

'What, for the feminine approach? A little woman to woman chat – is that your idea?' He narrows his eyes. 'We're talking about the murder of our head of state.'

'I believe we'll get far more out of her if she feels less intimidated. In the state she's in, a good lawyer will argue any confession was elicited under duress.'

'It seems to me, *Acting* Inspector Kassöndrudóttir, you have little idea of how to conduct a professional interrogation.' The veins in his forehead look like they're about to pop. 'Or perhaps the real truth is you don't have the balls for the job?'

She meets the full force of his hostility with a thin smile. 'Like it or not, Dr Young, *I* am in charge of this investigation. I officially note your opinion, but we are going to do things my way.'

'You're making a big mistake, woman. Perhaps you don't understand the gravity of the current situation or your own precarious status. We are not investigating the slaying of some little punk on a street corner; there's a state emergency and we need a result right now. We haven't got time to start making hot drinks and offering back rubs.'

'You're right, this is a pressing case, and that's why we need to be certain we don't try to solve it at the cost of the truth.'

'Oh for fokk sake grow up! In the real world, there's nothing so noble.'

Young marches off towards the door and then hesitates. 'As you can imagine, Inspector, I'll be taking this matter up with our new governor.'

'Go right ahead.' Kass doesn't waver. *'Maxwell and Chan to IR10 immediately,'* she orders, aloud for Young to hear. Unfortunately, the bastard's already well out of earshot.

The guard outside the interview room stands to attention. 'Move the suspect to IR 2,' she tells him.

Kass ushers the two constables into an anteroom. 'I want you to take the lead on this, Maxwell. Chan you're in the second seat.' They both look bemused.

She turns back to Maxwell. 'I'm relying on you to take a softly softly on this. Mrs De Morenos is clearly in some kind of traumatic state, ready to admit to anything – so don't go leading her.'

Her gaze crosses to Chan: 'I don't want either of you to put words in her mouth. The equipment's a bit dated in there, so make sure none of it is on the blink. We want a full and true record and I want a simultaneous stud relay. What I definitely don't want is a false confession that won't stand up under scrutiny.'

'Any kind of confession is gonna stand up right now.' Maxwell's words hold a lifetime's cynicism.

Chan gives her a long look. 'But Inspector Kassöndrudóttir wants the truth.'

Maxwell rolls her eyes. 'Does that mean there are unicorns too?'

Kass fights back her anger. 'Look, Maxwell, I trust I can rely on your professionalism. If you're not up to doing things properly, I'll make Chan the lead. You got me?'

She maintains eye contact until Maxwell looks uncomfortable. 'I want this done by the book,' Kass tells her. 'Ask open questions. Allow her to take her time. Don't make it up for her. She's got something she wants – no, *needs* – to tell us. The woman's not a natural killer, she needs to confess. So let her tell it her way and in her own time; up to a point that is.'

Maxwell moves a little closer. 'So why aren't you doing this yourself, Inspector?'

'Because I interviewed her earlier with Dr Young and that will have tainted me, by association, in her eyes. It was my mistake to bring him in on this and now he's off to bleat to Hagalín along with his boss – Dr Arthur. Meanwhile, we'll get her legal representation. I believe Mrs De Morenos will find the two of you far less threatening. Though in your case now, Maxwell, I hope I'm not going to be proven wrong.'

'We won't let you down, ma'am,' Maxwell tells her.

'Seems to me the real issue here is how that woman was given a triple A security rating in the first place,' Kass says. 'And that's what I'm going to find out.'

Thirty-Two

They're obliged to wait for the woman's lawyer to arrive – a seasoned public defender by the name of Jasmine Lundy.

'Kass seems to have really grown a pair,' Maxwell says, sipping a coffee from the machine. 'I hope they're big and heavy enough to take on Hagalín along with Dr Arthur and his infamous liquidators.'

'You make them sound like a jazz band,' Chan says.

Ms Lundy arrives looking harassed. Once she's had a few minutes to confer with her new client, the two of them enter the room and sit down opposite the suspect.

'Mrs De Morenos, I'm Senior Constable Maxwell and this is Constable Chan. We're here to take a statement from you concerning your movements from sixteen hundred hours yesterday when you were seen entering the governor's residence and four-twenty this morning when the police arrived. Do you understand?'

'Yes,' the woman says, not lifting her head.

'I'm sure Ms Lundy has explained your rights.'

Nodding, the lawyer says, 'I've informed Mrs Morenos that she's under no obligation to make a statement and certainly not one that could incriminate her in any way.'

'Mrs Morenos.' Maxwell attempts to make eye contact

with her. 'We just need to know where you went and what you did during those hours.' When there's no response, Maxwell adds, 'In your own time, Mrs Morenos.'

They wait. The silence is disquieting. Chan wonders how long Maxwell can keep this up.

Twelve more minutes drag by with no response from the suspect. Chan sees the lawyer's eyes go up to the clock above their heads but she remains silent. They all understand what's at stake here.

Across the table, Mrs De Morenos has now sagged down into her chair. Her bent shoulders speak of a lifetime of heavy work. Her hair must once have been jet black, now it's peppered with white especially around the temples. Chan thinks how easy it is to pass a hundred women who look like this on the street every day and never really see them.

They're approaching half an hour when the woman's gaze finally lifts from the floor and she looks directly at them. Her eyes keep coming back to the same spot – she seems fascinated by Maxwell's name badge.

She begins to mumble under her breath then at last she speaks up: 'Senior Constable Masswell,' she reads aloud. 'Do you, Senora Masswell, have children?'

Maxwell's taken aback, defensive. 'No, as a matter of fact I don't.'

The woman's gaze moves to Chan. 'And you?'

'No, but I would like to have them one day.' Hoping this was the right answer, Chan smiles.

'When I am,' the woman's voice is almost inaudible. She clears her throat. 'When I *was* little, my mother she take me to see the, um, the gitanos.' A sad, wistful look has replaced the blank expression in her eyes. 'She say they know to tell you the future. We go into tent that is very, very dark, and, and my mother she lead me up to where the woman, la gitana, sit. She is not so old but, oh – such old eyes. Very dark, yes, but also bright like the flame.'

Mrs De Morenos' face is luminous, transformed by her memories. 'She tell me I live long. Then she say I will marry a man with black hair. Then nothing. My mother she ask about the children I have and la gitana she say to me that I will give this man one son and one daughter.'

The woman remains silent for a while. When she speaks again, her voice is stronger. 'My mother say la bola de cristal is magic, it never lies to la gitana.' She waves a finger in the air. 'She does know it tell only half of the truth.'

Her eyes go back to her lap where her fingers seek out the rings on her left hand. 'My son, he is small, so, so small when he born. He live for only one day outside of me. On the piece of paper it say he have one day of life. This is not true, in la matriz; el utero he is every day with me for eight months.'

The woman leans forward to grasp the edge of the table. Chan can feel the vibration in her own hands. 'At the funeral for him they all say in the time we have more sons, we are both still so young – '

Maxwell hands her a tissue and waits.

'Alejo, he not understand how a mother feel. How could he? For him I cry over and over every month when my bleeding start again.'

She blows her nose. 'We wait and we pray and pray but there is no baby. Alejo say that God decide he not give us another son. We wait ten years – '

She gives a strange kind of snort and then shakes her head. 'I do not believe is true when the doctor he tell me that after so long we are waiting, Alejo and me we will have another baby.'

The weariness leaves her face. 'Alejo say is miracle that happen to us. When she born I am so afraid. I pray to La Virgen please to let her have this life.' A wan smile settles on her lips. 'Anjelita – our gift. She is so beautiful. Alejo he want a boy, but when he see her I know he love her more than any son.'

After five minutes of silence Maxwell intervenes. 'Did something happen to little Anjelita?'

'When she go to school they say she very clever. And when she only twelve years old the boys they see she is already so beautiful. They all are wanting to be her querido – her boyfriend.'

'What happened to her, Mrs De Morenos?'

'So clever.' She turns to her lawyer. 'She want to study the law like you. We are so proud. She make the highest mark, except for one other, when she graduate from the university. Alejo, he say to her, you can choose to do anything. He should not tell her this.'

Chan leans forward: 'Why is that, Bianca?'

'Because she say she want to work here, at the DSD.'

Maxwell sits up. 'But you were against her working here?'

'Everything change when she come to this place. They tell Anjelita that she so clever that she perfect for special job. And then she come and tell me: Mama this what I want. I asked her: why not be lawyer or teacher? But she say this work is more important.'

'What job did Anjelita do at DSD?'

'At first she is like you, in police.' She looks at Chan. 'A badge like you – just the same. She put it on my shirt one day and then she step back and laugh. But then she have different badge – *Senior Constable Morenos*. She don't talk about job so much. She don't tell us, but Alejo he guess that she is to be the Senuelo.'

Chan leans forward. 'Are you saying your daughter became a decoy?'

Mrs Morenos nods. 'We do not know this, not for certain. But then she tell us she need to go away; she cannot talk on her stud any more. Just for little time, she promise.'

'So you killed Leifsson,' Maxwell says, 'because your daughter became a decoy.'

The woman turns on Maxwell, her face transformed by

rage. 'No, I kill him because he is all smile on that big city screen when he tell everybody that these decoys do good job, is all maravilloso they make this city safe. And he is the person who do this. The person to vote Governor. But is big lie. My Anjelita, she is not safe.'

Her anger spent, Mrs Morenos looks down at the floor. Chan has to strain to hear her words.

'They tell us we no see her body. For our good, they say. But Alejo go to the young man in the deposito de cadavers and he say no until he offer him the credits and then he say okay but only for minute he will let us see her so we tell her goodbye.

'He ask us if we are sure and then he pull out drawer – just like you pull tray from oven.'

A tear finally wanders down the woman's lined cheek. 'He take off the cover.' Her hand goes to her mouth. 'Her beautiful face it is piece of meat. We see terrible things all over her and then between the legs–'

She genuflects and then bows her head. 'My Alejo from that moment he is dead too. Just one month after funeral he have attack to the heart. But his heart already broken when he see su hija Anjelita.' She holds the tissue up to cover her eyes like a shield.

They wait.

'But me I not die.' Her chuckle is low and bitter. 'I know is because I see him, the Governor Leifsson, with beautiful wife, beautiful family, when I have now nothing, nothing because of him. I hate him in my heart.' She thumps her chest. 'Is sin but it not me who is the sinner. Already my life is infierno already, every day; every day...'

In the silence all they hear is her quiet weeping. Maxwell touches her hand. 'Mrs De Morenos, how did you get a job as Governor Leifsson's cook? Did someone help you?'

'Yes, I have the help.' She looks at them both in turn. Chan sees the strength return to her face as she pulls her hand away from Maxwell's and points her finger upwards. 'It is the Lord my God who help me.'

Chan walks just behind Mrs De Morenos as they take her up to Processing. She notices the way the woman's wide ankles spill over the edges of her shoes making it difficult for her to keep up with Maxwell's pace.

They've done their jobs well – extracting and recording more or less everything the prosecution will need to argue that the murder had been premeditated, brutal enough for a category one conviction. The defence team will certainly struggle to get diminished responsibility, under the tight new guidelines on mental health pleas. It's likely they won't even consider mitigating circumstances.

There was no doubt the city will breathe more easily with someone to officially blame for the murder of their head of state, especially with the prospects of the public trial to come. The media pack will pounce on the evil nature of Governor Leifsson's killer. No doubt efforts are already being made to construct a narrative around the act – how it was random and could not have been foreseen; carried out by an unhinged middle-aged woman who poses no threat to anyone else. The news briefing will declare something along the lines of: "Governor Slain by Menopausal Maniac".

As for punishment: an ancient law still prescribes a public execution for treason; but Hagalín's likely to take the opportunity to show his more sensitive side and send her to a high security mental hospital for life. Chan grimaces – she'd opt for an execution over that any day.

The processing sergeant takes over. He walks with legs half splayed behind Mrs De Morenos, ready to block any escape route. The sad, defeated woman continues to stumble along at the same pace, as she walks through the double doors into Remand Holding.

During her training, Chan had watched the processing officer's unflinching stare as naked prisoners were further stripped of any remaining personal items – including the surgical removal of their stud base; to be directed along a white tiled tunnel and assaulted by jets of water, then detergent, then water and then hot air.

At the other end there's a shivering wait for that itchy blue shirt and elastic-waisted trousers. Whatever happens, Mrs De Morenos will now be wearing the same outfit for the rest of her life. Chan turns away.

They walk back to Homicide in silence.

In the incident room, Maxwell sits down in front of the giant whiteboard with all its unanswered questions. Chan watches her rub her eyes and then yawn. After a while she begins to stab and jab at the edge of the desk with her log stylus until the whole thing is pockmarked.

A soft orange light glows as the main console announces: *Full autopsy report available.* The report shows that the saxotoxin had come from seafood Leifsson had eaten approximately four and a half hours before his death, inducing a condition known as PSP, Paralytic Shellfish Poisoning.

It seems algae had contaminated the shellfish in the harbour during a bloom they called a red tide. The PSP poisoning could have been accidental, but the city had in place strict regulations that obliged all suppliers to test shellfish for such toxins before sale.

'If Mrs De Morenos doesn't testify, this report might help to suggest a reduced length of premeditation. She must have been aware Leifsson was in a weakened state and then attacked him more or less spontaneous,' Maxwell says.

'The jury might just buy it,' Chan says, with little hope.

Maxwell doesn't reply.

Chan wishes she could go home, but there are still formalities to be gone through. 'I'll go get us both a drink, shall I?'

'I need something stronger than that piss awful coffee sub.'

‘When we’re done,’ Chan says, ‘we could go round the corner to the Bay Club.’

Maxwell pulls a face: ‘That might be the final straw.’ She carries on rubbing the back of her neck. ‘Really, I just want to go home and get some sleep, but I know we need to do the intels.’ She picks up the machine. ‘God, I’ve really fucked up the end of this stylus; better get another from supplies.’

‘You’ll have to run the gauntlet of Norm ’n’ Gorm.’

Maxwell turns at the door. ‘I quite like those two geeks – at least they really love what they do. Sometimes I wish I had a job where I just dealt with machines and not people. Life would be far less complicated.’

Left alone, Chan notices that the Secretariat has now finally supplied the last of the information they’d requested. She transfers the data to her personal log with a triple encryption.

Her stud buzzes – it’s a warning from Maxwell that, although they’ve documented the initial confession, other interrogators could be brought in to iron out the details using their usual methods.

They’re required to hand in reports. Chan stresses that she and Maxwell, having gained Mrs De Morenos’ trust and are best placed to conduct all further department interviews with her. This is vital, Chan argues, if they’re to obtain sufficient details concerning both the poisoning and the fatal wounding. She’s prompted to describe the aims of any future interview sessions – *to pinpoint exact timings and movements in order to ensure a detailed account of the suspect’s actions and motives can be presented accurately to the court.*

Half an hour later, she’s completed her first ever All Officers Intel Report – its futility almost overwhelms her.

Maxwell hasn’t returned. Having completed all that could be required of her, Chan decides it’s time to leave. The curfew regulations mean she will have to sign out and then join a queue for official transportation to her apartment building.

As she waits in line, she wonders just how many of the Free Zone's freedoms will be buried along with the late Governor Leifsson.

Thirty-Three

Nero is walking through the entrance lobby of the hospital when everyone stops moving at the same time as if they're caught in a movie freeze-frame. A message cuts in over all media. Nero hears the new governor's voice in his ear. Simultaneously, *Hagalín*'s head is projected into the space in the centre of the area. The man's hair has been brought under control and he's lifting his chin in a statesman-like manner.

'Good morning, everyone. This is State Governor Hagalín speaking.'

One or two children and a few adults actually greet him back. The mouth on the giant face falls into a serious smile before it opens again.

'I am pleased to announce we have arrested a suspect – an individual whom we have subsequently charged with the murder of State Governor Leifsson. The prisoner we are holding has made a full and detailed confession. It seems our poor late leader met his death at the hands of a lone, deranged individual.'

A short pause before he adds: *'Homicide officers are not looking for anyone else in connection with his murder.'*

There's lots of muttering around Nero – mostly expressions of relief.

The new governor waits a few seconds to allow this information to sink in.

'No further details can be released at this early stage. As governor of Eldísvík, and as a long-time friend and colleague of Mr Leifsson, I assure you I will make it my primary duty to ensure that we proceed to the trial of this individual as quickly as possible. Further statements on this matter will be issued in due course.'

Hagalín nods sagely. His mouth breaks into a benevolent smile.

'As a result of this person's successful and speedy arrest, I am pleased to announce that the emergency curfew has now been lifted. You are all free to go about your daily lives as usual.'

His upper body now visible, he opens both arms wide – the benevolent god. *'Finally, folks, let me assure you all that the rule of law will always prevail in Eldísvík. I hope today every one of you will enjoy the many freedoms this city offers its citizens. As you resume your regular routines, I hope all of you will rejoice and give thanks for that freedom.'*

There's a round of spontaneous applause as if Superman Hagalín had just saved Gotham City.

Shaking his head, Nero steps outside into the chill of the street. As he takes in a lungful of freezing air, it seems extraordinary and unexpected that he should have regained his own freedom at last.

It's a brand new morning and the streets are all impeccably clean and calm. Right now he could be a traveller walking through a city he'd left behind a lifetime ago, hoping that in his absence everything had remained unchanged. In reality, Nero knows he'll never experience these familiar streets in the same way. Things will never be as they were before the ambush, before Lúter met with such a brutal and undeserved death.

He can sense the residual fear and mistrust in the people he passes despite the lifting of the curfew. To be sure he's not projecting his own feelings, he tries to analyse what he's seeing around him. Though the observations are fleeting – it's there in the muted cries of street vendors, in the worried glance of the man approaching him – how he's pretending to look straight on past Nero to avoid noticing anything or being noticed.

On the next corner, half a dozen people are greeting each other. The restrained nature of their words and gestures suggest to Nero a fresh awareness that they are all being watched.

Without a jacket or topcoat, he's exposed to the elements. He turns into a wind that's burdened with frozen grains and they dodge into his eyes and scratch at his naked hands.

Perhaps he's being fanciful. Already, life seems to be going on pretty much as before. The shops are opening up for business. Despite the daylight, the lights are on and its business as usual inside every high-rise building.

Along the horizon, the grey sky sags. The daylight has a dimness to it that promises another invasion of snow. Soon a thin white line will sparkle along every horizontal, though most will melt as soon as they touch the geo-thermally warmed streets. As their new governor, Hagalín may well seize the opportunity to pose against a picture-postcard backdrop like some benign Papa Christmas.

Having walked about a kilometre, his whole body is wearying to the point of exhaustion. He heads back to his apartment.

It's a relief to see the expressway system is running normally. Every pod is overcrowded but he manages to wedge himself into a gap near the emergency exit. When one of his fellow passengers leans against his bruised back, a hot pain shoots through him. He grips the grab rail and waits for the worst of it to subside. His new trousers are too tight around his thighs and the shirt collar is rubbing the back of his neck sore. Nero moves the small package he's carrying to the front of his chest, holding it like a shield to ward off any further assaults.

His apartment looks more or less how he must have left it. Everything smells fresh – suspiciously so. Someone – maybe Kass – must have been in to clear away the stale food that would otherwise have announced itself.

Nero casts an expert eye around and notices that several small things – the toiletries inside the bathroom cabinet, the crockery in the cupboard – appear to have been moved. He suspects that, in his unexplained absence, his apartment has been thoroughly searched.

He puts the package on a chair before going to flop down on his own bed at long last. There are things he'd planned to do but the journey here has drained him so thoroughly he can only close his eyes and let sleep overtake him.

Nero is disorientated when he wakes. He looks at the blank ceiling above him and remembers how things had altered since the last time he'd lain here; how, back then, the future still held the vague promise of something better to come.

Unlike the hospital, this apartment has no windows to look out from. Even in the daylight hours, there's only ever a steely glow spinning down through that long central tube to illuminate a portion of this room.

Still, sleep has done its work and he feels refreshed. He asks for more light and climbs carefully off the bed. In the kitchen area, the store cupboard offers enough to make a meal though his appetite is already waning.

He drinks a full glass of water while casting an appraising eye over his home. Looking around, a visitor might think he'd only just moved in. Why hadn't he made more of an effort with this place?

His gaze comes to rest on the curves of the old espresso machine; it never fails to speak to him of a time when such functional beauty had been unremarkable and real coffee an everyday luxury. How much had he paid for that last precious packet from Gianni's friend at the docks? A sleight of hand and conscience that, along with everyone else, he'd so easily dismissed as harmless.

No one he knows, no matter how ethical or public-spirited

they consider themselves to be, could swear hand on heart that they always obey the letter of the law and never turn a blind eye when it suits them. All those little individual deals add up to a whole other economy running in parallel with the official one.

As his years in the police department had so often illustrated, no matter what the law decrees, it can be a struggle to identify sinner from saint. All is relative – there can be no absolutes.

Just who is he trying to fool with this line of thought? If he's honest, he's searching for an argument that might excuse Chan for what she'd done to him – for whatever she might have been playing at when she slipped that sedative into his wine glass that night. How many times had he thought about her, damn near obsessed about her, since then?

If she'd spiked his drink, was it to hack into his stud? Worse still, could it really be a coincidence that she was called away for an assessment just before they set out on that doomed raid on the bank? All things considered, he should keep a wary distance from the woman from now on.

Once again, Nero is aware of the things he could and should be doing but he's unable to summon up the necessary will to begin.

'Enable location tracker.' He waits a moment. 'Hi, yes it's me,' Nero tells her. 'I thought a call might scare you less than if you saw me in the flesh. I'm still quite a sight. People have been crossing the street to avoid me.'

'Thank God you're okay, Inspector,' Chan says. The warmth in her voice almost convinces him. 'Kass just told us you've been suffering from amnesia all this time.'

Christ, this pretense isn't going to be easy to maintain. 'Yes, that's right,' he says.

'She said you've recovered some of your memory but don't

remember being abducted or how you got to the other hospital.'

'That's right. Whole thing's a total blank, I'm afraid. I've been told my memory of it might return over time.'

'So how are you feeling, you know, in yourself?'

'Much better,' he says. That expression she'd used – in yourself – suggested his body had a life of its own, like he might be his own avatar. 'They discharged me from hospital this morning,' he tells her.

'That's great news.'

'Yeah, though it still feels really strange to be out.' He rubs at his forehead. 'Don't get me wrong – it's a good sort of strange. Seems so odd to be home again – to be here all by myself in my own apartment.'

Chan says nothing. He hears her take a breath before she speaks. 'I'm just finishing my shift. Would you like me to come over?'

'You must be really busy,' he says, playing for time.

'I'd still like to see you – if that's alright?'

'Of course – but I mean I can order something in for myself. There's no real need. I can manage just fine by myself. These days, I don't just do lying down; I've progressed to standing up and walking around – the whole dizzying gamut of life.'

He can hear someone else talking in the background and then, not to him, she says: 'That might take a little while.' A pause. 'Yes, okay – I will.'

'Look, I'm sure you're up against it right now. I won't disturb you any longer.' Before she can reply, he breaks off. There's only the slight buzz as his stud disconnects.

Nero finds he has to consciously exhale. As he slumps down onto the couch, a sharper pain encircles his ribs. His head is heavy – like he's trying to hold up a lead weight. He wills his muscles to relax, tells himself the emotions overwhelming him are all to do with those damned painkillers wearing off.

He's tempted to reach for the pills but, little by little, the ache in his chest begins to subside. Without the physical discomfort to focus on, he only feels worse. How did everything get so totally fokked up?

The room around him blurs and Nero realises his eyes are streaming. Lying in that hospital bed, he'd wept for the first time in years. Since then, it keeps on happening.

He shakes himself free. This is no time for self-indulgence, for crying like a child over some impossible dream.

He gets up. This time his limbs move easily as he walks across the room to study the panels just above his bed. From the middle of the headboard, he counts along to the fourth one on the right. The surface of it looks identical to all the others. Judging the dead centre, his fingertips go through a sequence of movements as if playing an invisible keyboard. He gets it right first time. The panel needs only the lightest pressure before it comes away.

Feeling inside the narrow gap, his fingers close on the weapon. Whoever it was who'd searched this apartment, can't have found this hidden space. He pulls the gun out first, unwraps the rag he'd covered it with all those years ago. A streak of light runs the length of its newly exposed barrel as Nero weighs it in his hand.

Thirty-Four

The abandoned farmhouse seemed a good choice back in the summer but now the wind is slicing through it from every direction. At least the ground outside is still clear. She'd selected this particular area because, though you wouldn't know it by the temperature, the earth's natural heat is warm enough to melt all but the heaviest of snowfall.

The firewood is damp – hissing out little more than smoke. Breakfast is a can of something gloopy and beige; these things taste so indistinguishable she doesn't even bother to check the labels these days. Her water carrier is already two-thirds empty – the minimum she needs if this is going to work. Last night's visitor had supplied the final piece of information. Now, at last, it's time to act.

She undresses. Shivering, half holding her breath, she runs a wet cloth across her bare skin until patches of red and blue mottle every inch.

Once she's dry enough, she pulls on underwear and then her clean, blue top. Its tightness should stretch the creases out. Her black trousers cling to her still-damp flesh as she drags them up. Bending over the old sink, she wets her hair, rubs in the minimum amount of shampoo and then leans forward to pour the last of the water over her head.

With her already damp towel, she dries her hair sufficiently to comb it into something that might pass for a style. Make-up soon hides the winter pallor of her face. Her still-trembling fingers take up the kohl pencil; she draws a sweeping line along each of her eyelids.

She stows the rest of the food along with the torch and her bedding in the cupboard beneath the rusting metal staircase before putting on her jacket. It's a bit thin for the season, but it will pass.

With luck, there will be time to check on her vixens tomorrow. Today they'll again have to fend for themselves. This will bring them into conflict with the territory's competing predators, but it can't be helped. During yesterday's visit to the feeding area, she'd repeatedly signalled, had waited over an hour but still two of her vixens hadn't shown up. There's no way of knowing what's happened to them but she can easily guess.

Outside, a bank of cloud is approaching from the east. As she watches, it takes on the same blue-black colour as the old gravel track. In her city-style boots, she'll need to avoid the worst of the melt-puddles.

Pleased with her progress, she jogs on past the derelict filling station, and then takes the left fork that meanders on southwards. Her boots are less than ideal for running in. Fat raindrops are peppering her jacket and the wind is tugging at her damp hair, melding her clothing to her body.

Finally, she reaches the sheep track. The going becomes slower but she knows this is a good shortcut and will, despite all its crazy twists and turns, eventually bring her out onto the old highway with its relatively smooth surface. Then she'll be able to pick up speed. Once she's over the crest and into the next valley, she should get a clear sight of the first – or should that be last – stop on the expressway.

This is by far the safest route in. She knows the secure-a

beam system is faulty on the eastern side. Provided there are no hitches, she'll soon be lost in the morning throng and riding straight into the Free Zone.

Within her pocket, her fingers continue to work on the telltale crispness of her most recent ID card. The prospect of a hot shower spurs her on.

Bruno is in the wrong faculty block, but no one has bothered to check his ID. With the curfew lifted, security guards are gone from the exits and lectures have resumed. The protest leaders are talking strategy and yet they're quietly attending their classes in case they fall too far behind with their studies.

The layout of this labyrinthine building is unfamiliar and so, with his mind full of so many other things, he's forced to keep checking the schematic. Though he's not really religious, he prays he's right about this.

As he draws nearer to Zhender's office, he goes over his cover story in case he needs it. He needs to believe it, or he'll never convince the professor. Shouldn't he be encouraged by the fact that, since he started his degree, several of his fellow students have drastically changed their minds about what they're planning to do once they've graduated. The way things stand, someone like himself might easily be considering a future master's degree in the psychology of serial killers. It's a sexy subject – one that would appeal to any young person with an active imagination. On campus, Zhender is considered a quite a rock star.

As he approaches the professor's office, Bruno's delighted to see a conversation going on in the open doorway – all of it exactly as he'd foreseen. There's quite a contrast between the hirsute vitality of the professor and his visitor: a short, thin-framed man.

People come and go while Bruno hangs back, giving them time to conclude their conversation. He lingers by a notice-board as they say their goodbyes with a friendly handshake. So far – so good.

The visitor turns and begins to head down the corridor towards him. Their eyes meet and Bruno can see he was right about everything. There's no one else around, no observation cameras in the vicinity. The man has moved over to the left, ready to walk on past him. The harsh lighting gives his bald head an unnatural shine like a helmet.

'Excuse me,' Bruno says. 'But don't I recognise you? Aren't you Dr Arthur?'

The man looks surprised and a bit suspicious.

'Oh my God – it really is you!' Bruno hooks both hands behind his neck and spins on his heels like he can't believe his luck. 'I just need to tell you I'm such a big fan of your books. I must have read *The Deep Humanity of Animals* a dozen times – I'm not even kidding.'

He touches the man's sleeve. 'But my personal, all-time favourite book of yours is *The Animal Inside Every Man*. So fokking insightful! Excuse my language – it's just that it's no exaggeration to say that book has changed my life.'

He's blocking the corridor, there's no way the psychologist can get past him without pushing.

A smile crosses Arthur's face. It doesn't suit him. 'Extremely kind of you to say so, young man.'

'This is amazing.' Bruno beams back. 'Would you mind letting me shake your hand?'

'By all means.' Dr Arthur holds out his bare hand allowing Bruno to shake it with gusto. More like a priest than a student, he puts his other hand on top to seal the full contact.

'Are you alright, son?' Dr Arthur pulls his hand away.

'Sorry. Yes, I'm fine. Just felt a bit dizzy for a minute there. Must have been the excitement of bumping into you like this. I mean, what are the odds?'

The psychologist peers at him. 'You haven't told me your name, young man.'

'Bruno,' he says, mastering his breathing again. 'Bruno Mastriano.'

'Well, it was nice to meet you, but if you wouldn't mind stepping aside, I'm afraid I have a pressing matter to attend to.'

'It's been such an honour to meet you at last.' Bruno makes a show of reluctance but nonetheless complies.

As he walks on past him, Dr Arthur says: 'I'll be sure to remember your name for the future.'

The highlight of her visit to the gym was that longed-for shower. She's stowed her day clothes and, courtesy of the contents of a stranger's locker, is sporting the latest line in running gear.

An hour ago the thunderclouds had made their way slowly inland leaving a light drizzle that makes her training run less suspicious. She'll need to work up the requisite speed.

She spots her quarry. Behind him, ribbons of light are escaping from the inky shadow of a tanker to dance ashore. She can see him quite clearly; though the brim of his hat is hiding his eyes, it's easy to spot those familiar features. In the flesh, he's somewhat shorter than she'd imagined. Despite his age, his shoulders are broad and square beneath a tapering body. It's impossible not to admire his dog; straining to be off after the seabirds lining the walls of the jetty. A wolf-dog, grey with light patches either side of its face and on its flanks. Probably a German Shepherd cross. Not a Husky, for sure.

'Heel, Tundra, for Christ's sake.' He jerks the lead until the bitch comes back.

From this angle and this distance, she can't make out the person he's deep in conversation with. She waits for him to conclude his business and then begin the walk back to the waiting Norseman 80. Her plan relies on calculating the precise distance as she passes.

Running flat out, she emerges from the shadows. The dog sees her first and shows its teeth, its snarl alerting the man at the end of the tether. The man's head turns towards her. His wolf-dog, hackles raised, teeth bared, springs at her. Its teeth pierce the thin material and sink into the flesh of her thigh. For a second she feels no pain.

'Get down! Tundra! Down damn you!'

The dog releases its grip. The man's visibly shocked. 'You stupid bloody bitch!' He shortens the lead until the animal is near to choking.

Flinching from the pain, she holds her bleeding thigh while the dog remains at the man's side, its eyes still fixed on her. The pain intensifies drawing genuine tears to her eyes.

'Are you alright?' He holds the dog behind him. 'I'm so sorry. What can I say?' He goes off to tie the animal to the harbour rail some distance away then walks back towards her. 'Please accept my heart-felt apologies. I can't imagine what came over the animal. She's never done anything like this before. How badly are you hurt?'

'I'm okay. I don't think it's too bad, although – ' Blood has soaked through the torn material – a startlingly red stain that's spreading wider by the second. 'I guess I might need a few shots,' she says.

'Please, let me help you. I have a private physician who can take care of this. My car's right over there.'

'I'm – No thanks.' She doesn't imagine a lone, female runner would readily get into a strange man's car. 'Really. I think maybe I'd better go to a hospital'

'It's quite safe, my dear. My driver is actually a police officer. I'm sure he'll verify the fact that I can be trusted.' He turns her towards the Norseman. His chauffeur is already on his way over. 'Show this lady your ID, Williams.'

The badge reads Sergeant Gavin Williams.

'Well, um, okay then.' She gives him a strained smile. 'Something to stop the bleeding would be good.'

'Williams, get the first-aid kit.' He touches her shoulder. 'We'll have you right as rain in no time, my dear.' His hand is now supporting her other arm. 'Let me help you over to my car.'

'Thank you.' Her sudden floppiness makes him take most of her weight. She feels the softness of his jacket against her cheek; smells expensive cologne on his neck. 'I must have startled your dog. He was probably just trying to protect you.'

'Tundra's a bitch. Stupid animal should have known the difference between a jogger and an attacker. I'm not sure I'll ever be able to trust her again.'

'Oh, please don't punish her on my behalf,' she says. 'Really, I'm sure this wound's not serious.'

'You're very brave, my dear. I'm Tom by the way. And your name is?'

'Alison.' She smiles as she looks into the face of Commander Thomas Rockingham.

Thirty-Five

On his way to meet his friends, Bruno takes one of the walkways. Turning a corner, a sizable man barges straight into him. 'Sorry,' he says, though he doubts he was at fault and must have come off worst in the collision. The other man doesn't apologise.

In the light from a nearby window he glimpses the man's face – that distinctive bushy beard.

The recognition is mutual. Bruno is furious. 'Oh for fokk sake – not you again.'

'Now, now. Have to say that's no way to greet an old friend, is it Salvo?' Kleiner steps back to survey him from head to foot. 'So, I see we've smartened ourselves up. Hanging out at the university these days, are we? You pretending to be a student this time?' He scoffs into Bruno's face, his breath stinking of stale whisky. 'Well, I'm sure my friends will be pleased to hear of your whereabouts at long last.'

Bruno straightens up to the big man. 'You know Ása won't be pleased if you go bandying that knowledge about and blow my cover.'

'Exactly who are you trying to kid with this bullshit?'

'I'm just saying she won't appreciate you barging into the situation. Things are on a knife-edge up here. As you know, if she's not pleased, she won't be tossing her tame bulldog his usual treat.'

'Trying to wind me up, are you, pretty boy?' He steps forward, sizes up to Bruno to make it clear how unevenly matched they are. 'Would you believe it's working.'

The boy jabs his finger into the hard wall of Kleiner's chest. 'Woof!' He spits the word into the man's face. 'Woof!'

Kleiner grabs him by the throat, his windpipe is restricted to the point where he can hardly breathe. While he's squeezing Bruno's neck with this hand, the other brandishes an ugly-looking knife, which he deliberately holds up to Bruno's eyeline. A hunting knife, the blade dulled along the edge by dried blood.

Kleiner lays the blade against Bruno's throat. He feels the sting as it digs into his neck. They're standing chest to chest, Kleiner breathing hard in his face.

The contact brings the knowledge that this man wants to kill him here and now, but he's worried how Ása will react. He's reluctantly deciding not to slit Bruno's throat before getting her approval.

Stepping back, Kleiner withdraws the blade. 'Give me an excuse, pretty boy.' Releasing his hold, he shoves him up against the wall, the knife a quick lunge away. He's about to contact Ása when his head flicks round at the sound of approaching voices.

With his attention elsewhere, Bruno reaches behind, pulls the Glock from his waistband, releases the safety catch and aims it at the big man's chest.

Kleiner's eyes register surprise. They stand frozen in this stance, both hoping the people they can hear decide to go in another direction.

Laughter. Singing that trails off into shouts and jeers – sounds that grow louder then very slowly fade away to nothing.

In the silence, Kleiner throws his head back and laughs. 'You seriously threatening me with that thing, you little shit?' He peers down at the barrel that's less than half a metre from his chest. 'Been years since I've seen one of them. How did a little loser like you get hold of a Glock 19, 9 millimetre automatic?'

Bruno stands his ground. Supporting the gun with his other hand, he holds the barrel level and steady just as Nero had taught him, though he's not sure he'll be able to shoot this man if it comes down to it.

'Go on then,' Kleiner says. Sensing his weakness, the big man leans in. 'Too scared to pull the fokking trigger, eh?' He forces his full weight onto the gun. 'Seems to me you don't have what it takes to drop a man.'

Images fill Bruno's head: that blood on the blade, the murdered girl. He knows Kleiner is about to knock his gun from his hands and sink that same blade into his gut. Reeling in agony, his liver punctured, he'll fall onto the asphalt, his blood pooling on the frosty ground around him as he finally loses all consciousness.

Present and future coalesce. Weighing the odds, Bruno squeezes the trigger. He hears the gun's muffled crack and then there's just the stench of cordite and burning flesh.

His hand shaking uncontrollably, Bruno drops the warm gun and steps back to watch the man slump to his knees. Kleiner sways a little as if undecided about whether to accept this version of his fate before he falls, face-first, onto the icy ground. Though the soft thud of his body falling was barely audible, the sound of the gunshot was only partly deadened by Kleiner's bulk; it must have echoed a long way out into the campus. Any number of people could have heard it.

Christ, he's done it – he's really gone and shot someone. Bruno expects to hear running footsteps, almost wills them to appear and accuse him after what he's done.

When no one comes, he rouses himself, checks to see if anyone might have witnessed what just happened. As far as he can tell, no additional lights have come on; the pathway remains empty in both directions.

Retrieving the Glock, Bruno crouches down until he's

level with Kleiner's ear. He keeps telling himself this act was entirely justified. 'That was for Linda Jakobsdóttir,' he says.

Kleiner's eyes are beginning to glaze over. 'That was the name of the innocent girl you murdered in cold blood tonight. That's right, you moron – a case of mistaken identity. You brought this on yourself. I just hope you burn in hell.'

The big man's eyes continue to stare unseeing. To be quite certain, Bruno checks his pulse points – the wrist first and then the side of the neck just below the chin. He can't detect the faintest heartbeat.

'I'm rather fond of this particular claret.' Rockingham pours two glasses from the same decanter and carries them across the room to where she's sitting.

'This wine is probably older than you are, my dear. As you might imagine, it's no longer possible to acquire more.'

He runs one of the glasses under his nose. 'Without wishing to sound like a sommelier the precise balance of merlot and cabernet sauvignon gives it those subtle notes of blackberry or plum. From the terroir, the grapes acquire a certain smokiness which underpins all those earthy tannins.'

His smile quickly fades. 'Forgive me, I should allow you to decide for yourself.'

The glass he hands her is cut into a hundred facets to slice up the blood red liquid inside. As she raises the drink to her lips, she smells the mustiness of it. She takes a careful sip. Its taste reminds her of underground things.

'I'd quite forgotten what the real thing is like,' she says. Her smile would sicken her if she could see her reflection. 'It's delicious but I'm not sure I should re-educate my palate. I could become too discerning and then where would I be?'

Commander Rockingham is quietly studying her reactions. The claret he's sipping is the same purple-red as the thread veins on either side of his nose. Still on his feet, he comes closer. The smell of the wine mixes with his recently refreshed, cologne.

'Thirty-three years ago, I had my man lay down a quantity of this particular vintage,' he says. 'I try to ration myself, of course. It would be a travesty not to savour these things in the way their quality demands.' The expression on his face produces a sickening jolt in her stomach. 'I like to think I'm rather good at recognising quality when it's before me.' Again, that briefest of smiles; when it drops, it leaves no creases behind.

'It's very good of you to treat me with such kindness.' She looks down at the bandage on her bare leg. 'I'm sure this little scratch will heal in no time.'

She feels confined, pinned-down even, in this plush chair and decides to stand up. Meeting his height, she sidesteps him to gain the centre of the room. 'I hope you won't punish your poor dog on my account,' she says. The drawn curtains are blocking what must be an impressive view. 'She was only protecting you, after all.'

'You're very brave, my dear. However, I learnt a long time ago not to overlook indiscipline. Once an animal, or a person for that matter, has shown its teeth, I've found it's less reluctant to do so a second time.'

'But she was only acting on instincts and in your best interests.'

'Nonetheless, I can never fully trust her again. Don't worry, the bitch will be found a new home. I am not a cruel man, just one who expects absolute loyalty. Always.'

The expression in his eyes is far from kind. 'Please – won't you take a seat by the fire.' He holds one arm out like an impresario. 'Let's make ourselves comfortable, shall we?'

With no choice, she complies. Flickers from the extravagant open fire give Rockingham's pupils a yellow glow. The blaze itself looks genuine but she notices that the logs on it haven't burnt down since the manservant lit it.

She shivers. 'I really ought to be getting back.' She puts her half empty glass on the table.

He retrieves the decanter and holds it the above her glass. 'There's no hurry, surely. And you'll need a change of clothes; we can't have you wandering around in those torn joggers.'

He signals to the servant. A second later her wine is topped up. 'I trust there isn't a burly husband waiting to question your lateness.'

She shakes her head, knowing he will have already checked her legend.

'Besides,' he continues, 'It's not often I find the opportunity, or should I say the occasion, to broach such a fine vintage.' He pours far less into his own glass. 'Every drop deserves to be savoured. I'm sure you'd agree?'

'I take your point; it is quite delicious and far too good to be hurried.'

'Indeed. Then let us savour the moment, shall we?'

With his pale eyes directly on hers, she experiences a tiny sliver of fear. He's been a little too generous with the wine. She considers the taste she's been asked to appreciate. Could it contain something she hadn't suspected? Certainly the effects are seeping into her body, willing her tired muscles to relax. If she takes tiny sips to his larger ones, perhaps he will lower his guard like a lizard in the sun.

Her throat contracts. She needs to distract him, needs to tell her skin not to react on instinct. Not yet anyway.

The candlelight is held in all the glass and silverware on the table. Another servant is on duty – this time a uniformed one, for God's sake. The man bustles to and fro in the shadows before presenting their food on antique plates.

Nothing is artificial, at least as far as she can tell. Her taste buds respond with treacherous enthusiasm.

A brown, irregular slab lies diagonally across the centre of the next new plate – the main course. Its texture and aroma suggest it might be real, though she can't tell what creature might have died in order to be served up covered in mushroom and wine sauce. Slicing into it produces watery blood that mingles with the ruby depths of the sauce. The taste is disquietingly pleasurable.

'I hope you like the venison.' He notices her confusion.

'This is deer meat?'

'There are far too many in the grounds.' He looks up from his plate. 'It's just not sustainable, you understand?'

'Yes, of course.'

'Culling can be an act of kindness.' He's watching her intently. 'A few need to be sacrificed to secure the future of the many.'

She swallows. 'I agree completely, Tom.' She lets him see the sincerity of her expression. 'And, I must say, I can't imagine a more delicious sacrifice.'

'I'm glad you concur, Alison.' His attention returns to the food on his plate. Though his long thin fingers are controlling the cutlery with ease, only the smallest amount of food rises to his lips. She notices the odd way he chews and it comes to her that he might not have a full set of teeth.

Thoughts of what might transpire later create a spasm of revulsion inside her. She hopes her shiver hadn't been visible; covers the possibility by raising her glass. 'To the deer, who died to save all the little darlings.' Her awkward pun is served up to him with a wide smile.

'This is a hind. I shot her myself. We marked her out but she proved very skittish; seemed to have a sixth sense whenever I raised the barrel. Had me lying in wait for almost half a day, but it was worth it in the end.'

She slices off a large chunk from the meat. 'I really can't remember anything I've enjoyed as much.'

Rockingham gestures to the servant and the man bends to hear his master's words. She carries on eating, determined to make a show of savouring the dish.

It's as if she imagines the music before it's audible. The notes are so soft and yet the melody rises until it's insistent and undeniable. She recalls an afternoon when her bored keyboard teacher took over and began to play the piece himself. Something had seized him and he took the simple tune away in a direction she would never have thought possible. She'd been shocked by his transformation from a fat, unremarkable instructor into a man gripped and transported by rapture.

Looking across at Rockingham, she notices how his right hand is describing the music in the air as he enjoys the rhythm and beauty of the tune. Even so, she doubts he could ever be a man swept away by emotion.

When he moves his cutlery together his food has barely been touched. Both plates are whisked away in an effort to hide the evidence.

'Mendelssohn, Lieder ohne Worte, I believe.' She remembers struggling with an easier part of this piece before a high school performance.

'Very good.' His surprise is clear. 'Yes: *Songs without Words*. Garben is a fine interpreter of the work.' The sides of his mouth twitch into a thin smile. 'What a pleasure to have a fellow enthusiast as a dining companion.'

His gaze hasn't softened one iota. It will be no easy matter to catch him in an unguarded moment. He's right about one thing – the wait will make her final satisfaction that much greater.

Thirty-Six

It happens sooner than Nero expected. Before answering the door, he looks around for somewhere to hide the weapon. Stuffing it under his pillow is far from ideal but it's all he can think of.

Chan's extraordinary beauty catches him out all over again. She smiles up at him. He wonders if she's about to embrace him but instead, like an apparition he might have conjured up in a fever, she drifts on past him into the apartment.

'Kass gave me the evening off,' she announces. 'She said to say hi. Maxwell too. Unfortunately, Rashid's still AWOL so everybody's relieved that you're out of hospital at last.'

She holds up a carton of food. 'I've brought agnello con patate – this is your homecoming, after all.' The gaiety in her voice sounds more than a little forced. 'And red wine to go with it, though I wasn't sure if you're allowed to drink just yet.'

Nero remembers his nonna sending him out into the garden to pick rosemary and bay leaves when she was making this same lamb dish, how the taste of those sunbaked herbs would bring out the flavour of all the other ingredients.

'This is really very kind of you,' he says, taking the bottle and the food from her. The foil seal on the wine bottle is still intact.

Chan takes off her jacket, stuffing her gloves into the pockets. Underneath she's wearing a dark purple sweater and black trousers – not the outfit of a seductress but practical enough for an assassin.

Nero takes her jacket. Hanging it up, he feels a stab of pain between his ribs and has to hold his breath while it passes.

He stands well back from her – tries to keep his distance both literally and figuratively. However, after only a few minutes, he's gravitating towards her – understandable given the confined space.

'It's really freezing out there,' she says, rubbing her hands together. 'Makes me – well, you know. Is it alright if I use your facilities?'

In her absence from the room, Nero quickly unwraps the package he'd brought with him from the hospital, cursing himself for not doing it sooner. Every item in it had had to be officially released by Kass from the hospital room where Nelson was murdered. The bulk of the parcel contains the clean underwear and toiletries Jue Hai had brought in when he lay injured after their ill-fated bank raid. Kass has also given him back his father's watch and, for some reason, his old, blackened stud.

He remembers showing this same watch to Nelson and the conversation they'd had about old timepieces. Though he'd said nothing to Kass, it grieves him that, with no physical or surveillance evidence to go on, the department has made no progress in the hunt for whoever killed the nurse. For that reason alone, he needs to get back to work.

The last item in the parcel is a tiny box containing the micro-tracker. Kass had assured him it was state-of-the-art and absolutely couldn't be detected or blocked. He'd refused to tell her why he needed it.

Nero checks to make sure Chan hasn't yet reappeared. With his hands still less than steady, it's difficult to pick up the tiny speck though easy enough to attach it under the collar of her jacket. He's relieved at the way it completely blends into the material.

A second later, he hears the bathroom door unlock and then there she is again, walking back into the room. She comes over, is close enough for him to smell her perfume – jasmine with a deeper note he can't quite place. Has she just reapplied it?

Taking a step back, he says: 'We should celebrate your role in catching Leifsson's killer.' It's hard to keep the edge from his voice. 'Who would have thought our state governor would be murdered in his bathroom by his cook, of all people? Anyway, we should raise a glass to you catching her.'

Chan pulls a face. 'It's hard to feel happy about it when that poor woman will be spending the rest of her life in prison.'

'She's a killer all the same,' he says. 'There can never be an excuse for murdering someone in cold blood.'

Chan doesn't argue. Instead, she walks into the kitchen area. 'Are you okay to drink wine with your meds?'

'It'll be fine. I've always been impervious to that sort of thing.' His eyes search hers for any sign of a reaction. Nothing. 'Besides, the doctors aren't here now, are they?' he says. 'No one's watching us. They won't know I've disobeyed orders – not unless you inform on me.'

Chan holds the unopened bottle away from his grasp. 'I don't want to be responsible for a relapse.'

He's overwhelmed by the extraordinary smoothness of her skin; has to fight the urge to reach out and trace that perfect line around her chin. In the low light, her pupils are enormous. 'In the end we're only responsible for ourselves,' he says, unsure what it is he's trying to say.

She puts down the bottle to take off her scarf – a long unravelling. Turning back to him, she says: 'I don't think you believe that about responsibility. You're a senior policeman – you take on the responsibility for investigating the actions of others. When someone is murdered you try to find out who's to blame – who's responsible. You deal all the time in responsibility; we both do.'

He needs a distraction. Picking up the food package, he walks over to the heating unit. She follows him, close at heel.

He busies himself with heating their meal. 'You know, this sort of dish used to be called cucina povera in the old days – the food of the poor made from whatever they could find,' he says. 'Nonna told me her own grandmother used to cook this exact dish on an open fire with a pre-heated lid on top. Fire from below and fire from above.' He smiles across at her. 'The poor lamb didn't stand a chance.'

He's caught her studying him. She breaks their mutual awkwardness with a heavy sigh. 'You know when Maxwell and I interviewed that cook, Mrs De Morenos, yesterday – ' Chan appears to be on the verge of tears.

'Kass sent me through some updates earlier. I read your report,' he says. 'The interview was well conducted – very thorough, very professional. Neither of you led the witness.'

'Yes, but neither of us felt happy about it afterwards. What will happen to that poor woman – how's she going to survive banged up like that? In the end, she was just a grieving mother looking for someone to blame for her beloved daughter's death.'

'Maybe she was right about that.' He takes down a couple of glasses. Reaching up makes his muscles catch and his head spin a little.

'Tell me, what do you think of Hagalín our new governor?' she asks – her face poker-blank, offering no clues to her own opinion.

He snorts. 'I think he's what we've all been asking for. I'd say the man is absolutely perfect for the job.'

'Hagalín? You really think that? What about his personal qualities? I hear he's not exactly an inspiring leader.'

'They're right about that – the man's a complete fool and almost certainly morally bankrupt. That makes him ideal leadership material, at least in this city.'

Her expression turns to concern. 'It's been a long day for

you. You need to give yourself some time to adjust, to being back home. You're not planning to return to DSD any time soon, are you?'

'Honestly – I just don't know what I'm going to do from one minute to the next.' Reaching up for the plates, he tries not to flinch.

Chan opens the hot containers and takes over serving the food. She's standing in front of the drawer that holds the cutlery. 'Sorry, I just need to get round you,' he says.

She stays where she is. 'Let *me* get whatever it is you need.'

'There's no need.' He hates that she's treating him like he's still infirm and useless. 'I'm quite capable of doing it.'

'Of course.' She stands aside. 'I'm sorry.'

The woman can still do that trick on his defences. 'No, forgive me – I'm being petulant,' he says. 'I've had enough of being treated like an invalid.'

'I can imagine.' She picks up her plate and takes it over to the small table.

Damn, he can't carry his own plate plus the glasses. Balancing a heavy tray would be impossible. He'll have to start with the food and then come back.

Reaching the table, he stumbles and she has to grab his plate before the floor gets it. 'I'm sorry,' she says again. It's not clear what she's apologising for this time.

'It's alright,' he shakes his head. 'I'll admit I'm pretty useless right now. Perhaps you could go and get those glasses. I can't carry it all.'

She gives him a wide smile, her teeth so ridiculously even. 'Sure thing,' she says.

'Sure thing – now there's an attractive turn of phrase.' He hadn't meant to say that out loud.

'Are you flirting with me, Inspector Cavallo?' She laughs, this time with her head tilted back – on safe territory dealing with one more flirtatious man.

'Sorry, I was quoting someone else.' He doesn't mention Rashid by name.

'Don't worry, I've heard far worse.'

'I'm sure you have,' Nero says. 'You must be pretty sick of the way we men keep throwing ourselves at your feet.'

'I don't always object.' When she smiles, the creases at the corners of her eyes fall into lines that are perfectly symmetrical. Her hand comes towards him but then tucks a stray strand of her hair behind her ear.

Nero searches her eyes for guile, some sign of pretence. A simple touch might tell him for sure – but would it tell him too much? Does he even want his delicious delusions snatched away again? In any case, they must have made a mistake about the drugs they claimed were in his system – had to be some mix up at the hospital.

In the ensuing silence, he turns his attention to the food on his plate. The lamb is perfectly tender and the potatoes soft with a crispy coating of what could be genuine Parmesan. 'This is really good,' he says between mouthfuls. He hadn't realised how hungry he was.

She pours wine for herself and then tilts her head towards him in a wordless question.

The memory of that other time, that other drink, comes back to him with perfect clarity. 'Just a small glass – can't do me any harm, can it?' When she hands him a glass, he stares down into its blood-red depths before raising the glass – a soft clink against hers. 'Saluti,' he says, taking a sip then pausing for a moment before he swallows.

After they've eaten, she puts a gentle hand on his shoulder to stop him from getting up and he sits back to watch her clear away.

When she comes over to join him on the small couch, her face seems softer – more relaxed. 'Does that old coffee machine actually work or is it just there for show?' she asks.

'It may be old, but it's in perfect working order.' Chuckling, he gets to his feet. 'Bit of an art to it though – if you'll let me show you.'

She looks on while he goes through the familiar ritual. The machine's noise takes over the whole room. While the coffee is dribbling into the two small cups, she comes up behind him. He's much too aware of her closeness.

'A real man's machine,' she says. 'So much sound and fury for such a small outcome.'

He laughs out loud then winces with the pain this creates. She touches his face so suddenly he has no time to block the connection; yet, despite their physical contact, he finds he can't even begin to read her thoughts. He's only found this to be the case with a handful of other people and can't decide if he's relieved or disappointed. How can this one woman, of all people, remain an enigma to him?

Her hand strokes his brow. 'Still so handsome, though now you look like a real tough guy.'

'Yeah, look at me: practically a cripple but with looks that could kill.'

Her fingers trail along his hand as she gives him the espresso cup. Sipping her own coffee, she leans in and he smells jasmine all over again. 'This tastes delicious,' she says. 'Well worth the fuss, after all.'

She puts down her cup and leans right in, her soft lips begin to brush his. His response is immediate. Opening her mouth to his tongue, she tastes of coffee and something a whole lot sweeter. Chan hangs both arms around his neck then springs back when he winces. 'I'm so sorry,' she says. One hand goes up to cover her mouth. 'I forgot about your injuries.'

Nero takes hold of her hands and guides them back to where they were. Kissing her again, he's overwhelmed by too many competing emotions.

She breaks off but only to plant more kisses down his neck. Her delicate fingers open his shirt buttons one at a time and then begin working their way down his bruised chest. He holds his breath when she takes hold of his wrist and places his hand on one of her breasts.

With no sign of shyness, she undresses very slowly in front of him. So many sensations engulf him as he steps forward to explore her naked body. It's hard for him to distinguish pleasure from pain. When his exposed back brushes against the bedroom wall, he cries out loud.

She jumps back from him. 'Oh fokk. I'm so sorry. This is a really bad idea – it's causing you too much pain.'

He pulls her back towards him. In her ear he whispers: 'Nothing can hurt me nearly as much as it would if we were to stop now.'

Thirty-Seven

An urgent report comes through in the small hours. Kass shares a look with Maxwell. They listen in shocked disbelief. With the situation so volatile, it takes some time before they can speak directly to the man who called it in – a rooky patrolman name of Benedickt Þórsson.

With all the chanting and shrieking in the background, Kass struggles to make out what the man's saying. 'Can you tell us more about the circumstances,' she asks. 'How were the bodies discovered?'

'Like I said in my initial report, Inspector, the body of the young woman was found in the postgraduate accommodation block – Block F, room 509. Her throat had been slit more or less from ear to ear. Due to the lack of blood at the scene, my partner reckons the murder must have taken place elsewhere and then her body was moved. Fully clothed; no sign she'd been raped – nothing to suggest a sexual motive as far as we could tell.'

Kass hears someone shout the order to raise visors – a tactic often used to deescalate tension by reminding adversaries of their common humanity.

'Whole scene looked odd, ma'am.' Þórsson sounds breathless, like he's walking fast. 'Everything had been arranged to make it look like she was sleeping. Her friend and fellow post-grad – Anja Muller – couldn't get an answer and thought at first she might have gone away. Then she got worried because it was unlike her not to say anything about it to anyone. Anja finally persuaded the janitor to unlock the girl's door.'

He pauses then clears his throat several times before he speaks. 'Anja eventually calmed down enough to identify the deceased as a Linda Jakobsdóttir. She was only twenty-three. The two of them were studying bio-genetics. Looked like her friend had been dead for a little while.'

'So tell me about the other body?' Kass says. 'Who found him?'

'Patrol officer 248 Blythe. We were looking for the murder weapon and thought it might have been thrown into one of the dumpsters. He was in the middle bin of a line of three behind Block C – an undergraduate student block. The corpse was partly frozen. Looks to have been shot by an old-style handgun. It's possible both of them died around the same time though we won't know until the forensics team have had a chance to examine their bodies. There was no ID on him. No bio or facial match to any registered citizen. Not even a stud or the implant.'

Þórsson breaks off. Kass hears firing followed by some kind of explosion. 'Are you alright officer?' she shouts.

'Yes, ma'am – improvised incendiary; missed us by a mile. What was I saying? Ah yes, the implant had been cut right out of the man's earlobe. From the lack of blood from the wound, probably done after death. He looks to be Caucasian, early to late forties we thought, tall and well-muscled; dressed all in black. Clothes fit perfectly. Students were all hanging out of their windows, so they got a ringside view when we discovered his body. Word must have spread and they started to gather in considerable numbers around the taped-off cordon. We overheard one or two saying the dead bloke looked of some kind of assassin. Must admit it's hard to disagree with that.'

'You're breaking up.'

'I'm sorry but we haven't been able to extricate the bodies. We did our best to secure the scene before everything started kicking off. I expect you can hear the racket behind me. We were still examining the dead man when the students started swarming around us. There was quite a bit of shouting and pushing. They seem to believe the girl's murder was political and we represented that same system – which, to their minds, makes us the enemy. Some dark-haired young lad with a scarf hiding his face reckoned she'd uncovered something in her research they – whoever *they* are – want hushed up. We haven't been able to identify him yet. Obviously a conspiracy junkie, but from the way the others took his word for it, I'd say he's one of their main leaders.'

'Sjitt! Look, we should be there shortly.'

'With all due respect, you'd be wasting your time; right now it's impossible to get anywhere near the crime scenes, ma'am.'

The patrolman breaks off again. Kass can hear chanting. It sounds like "*Who killed Linda?*" or possibly "*They killed Linda!*" There's a high-pitched shriek followed by lots of yelling and cursing.

'Sorry about that. Like I was saying earlier, we decided not to wait for forensics and attempted to load the bodies into our vehicle. They started throwing all kinds of missiles at us and then a group of them crossed the cordon, which unfortunately will have completely contaminated the scene. More then poured in behind them. As you can probably hear, they're occupying the whole area.'

'And no one's been able to reason with them?'

'We tried but it was just the six of us against tens possibly even hundreds of them. Several were brandishing weapons though mostly the old-fashioned type – handguns, shotguns along with one or two rifles. I don't mind telling you, we were shit-scared.'

Kass is beginning to have her suspicions about this ringleader and the small arsenal these students have managed to get their hands on.

'When the first Sentinel escort arrived, a few of their own incendiaries bounced straight off and back into the crowd. They all went ballistic – acted like we were the ones that had thrown those firebombs at them. Then military arrived and took over. They ordered us to retreat.'

Kass shakes her head in disbelief. 'So where exactly are you now, Officer?'

'Right out on the perimeter of the campus – about fifty metres downhill and well outside the students' own barriers. Another military unit arrived a few minutes ago but they're still struggling to contain the situation.'

Kass hears two loud explosions. 'I'm sorry, ma'am, looks like we might have to withdraw to a safer distance.'

'Before you go, do you know the name of the person who issued the order for you to retreat?'

'Ma'am, look, I'm sorry but we've just been ordered to withdraw completely and leave the situation to the military.' Speaking to someone else he says: 'Okay, understood. Yes, right now.'

They hear nothing for a moment and then Þórsson's voice breaks in again: 'We're on the move again, ma'am. You asked about the order to retreat. All I can tell you is we were assured it was a direct order from Governor Hagalín and –'

His voice fades out. The connection goes dead.

Maxwell gives her a long look then shrugs her shoulders to show she's at a total loss. Dropping her head into her hands, Kass has absolutely no idea what to do next.

In desperation, she tries Nero's stud. On the fourth attempt he acknowledges. 'Inspector,' she says. 'I'm sorry to disturb you, but –'

'It's okay, Kass, I wasn't asleep.'

Before she can utter another word, Maxwell comes up to her, vigorously shaking her head to make her disapproval quite clear.

Kass knows she's right – she really shouldn't be bothering

Nero with all this and certainly not in the middle of the night. Chan might still be there with him, though it would be inappropriate to ask. Besides there's no point in calling Chan back in when there's nothing she'd be able to contribute to the situation.

'What's happened?' Nero demands 'What's wrong?'

She should end this call but not so abruptly that he'll get suspicious. 'Sorry, I had no idea it was so late,' she says.

'Forget all that – tell me what the problem is.'

Kass curses Nero's perceptiveness under her breath. Why the fuck couldn't he play along for a once? 'Nothing really, everything's okay here. I was just wondering how you are, what it feels like to be out of hospital at last and, you know, back in the free world?'

'Are we in a free world? Depends on your definition of free.'

'Well, in any case, I only wanted to say hi. Better go. I'll talk to you again soon.'

'You're right,' he says.

She's unsure what he means but leaves it. Time she wrapped this up. 'Wifrith sends her love,' she says.

Nero's quiet for a moment and Kass wonders if he's fallen asleep. 'You two are so lucky to have found each other,' he says. 'I hope you'll always remember that.'

'Well, you take care.' Why would he say this to her just out of the blue? 'And don't go overdoing things – give yourself time.'

'Always make sure you look after your family– '

Their communication is cut. The lights flicker and then go out. In total darkness, the two of them wait for the emergency generator to kick in.

A low rumbling and then the lights are back but the main console is still blank. In disbelief, Kass and Maxwell stare at its screen. A few seconds elapse and then it glows an icy blue. An announcement occupies the entire interface.

EFFECTIVE FROM 01:30 THURSDAY 5TH MARCH 2068.

FOR THE PROTECTION OF ALL CITIZENS OF ELDÍSVÍK AND, BY THE ORDER OF STATE GOVERNOR HAGALÍN, A MARTIAL LAW ORDER HAS BEEN DECLARED AND RATIFIED BY THE EMERGENCY COMMITTEE WITH IMMEDIATE EFFECT.

ANY PERSON NOT ALREADY AT THEIR REGISTERED HOME, HOTEL, HOSTEL OR WORKPLACE MUST IMMEDIATELY PROCEED TO THE NEAREST DESIGNATED PLACE OF SAFETY AND REMAIN THERE UNTIL FURTHER NOTICE.

ALL CITIZENS HAVE UNTIL 02:30 TO COMPLY WITH THIS ORDER.

YOU MUST REMAIN INDOORS UNTIL INSTRUCTED OTHERWISE. ALL WORKPLACES, SCHOOLS AND COLLEGES WILL REMAIN CLOSED UNTIL THIS EMERGENCY ORDER HAS BEEN LIFTED.

THERE IS NO NEED FOR ALARM. ALL VITAL SERVICES INCLUDING FOOD AND MEDICAL SUPPLIES WILL BE MAINTAINED AND SAFEGUARDED.

FOR YOUR OWN PROTECTION, POLICE AND MILITARY UNITS WILL BE PATROLLING THE CITY. ANY CITIZEN WHO VIOLATES THIS ORDER WILL BE DETAINED.

IN COMPLIANCE WITH THE PROVISIONS CONTAINED IN THE EMERGENCY POWERS ACT 2066, ANY PERSONS ACTIVELY ENGAGING IN RIOTING, LOOTING OR BEHAVING IN ANY MANNER

INCOMPATIBLE WITH THE MAINTENANCE OF PUBLIC ORDER WILL BE SHOT ON SIGHT.

Kass is on her feet. 'Oh, for Christ's sake!'

'I don't fokking believe it,' Maxwell kicks at the desk. 'Okay so there's a disturbance going on around the university but this has to be one hell of an overreaction.'

Thirty-Eight

Nero had been lying awake before he spoke to Kass. A few minutes earlier, he'd reached out to find her gone, the covers on the bed pulled back into position as if Chan had never lain there. He'd known for certain he wouldn't find her anywhere in his apartment.

It's an awakening in every sense. After his communication with Kass is cut short he waits in anticipation for that official message, read in a neutral tone that would make it all the more unnerving. A full martial law order – it doesn't shock him as much as it ought to.

It seems the fragile equilibrium operating in Eldísvík might be about to tip into something a whole lot uglier. He wishes he didn't know exactly what it was like to live through the bloody turmoil that follows the breakdown of democracy. A terrifying prospect but what can he as a mere individual do to stop that from happening here?

Staring up into the darkness, Nero lies utterly still, concentrating. He always starts any investigation by going right back to the beginning. For him, this had started with a dream – that startling vision of a lone woman walking down an alleyway about to encounter the men she would kill. He can still see her outline, the vague shape of her, but not her face. There's something he's missed and he knows it was right there at the very beginning.

He conjures her up again, slows her pace so he can focus in on every movement. There's definitely something about her shape, about the exact *way* she's walking. It's tantalizingly – just at the edge of his consciousness.

The woman Bruno had encountered in the disused factory had a name – Ása Sturludóttir. Are these two women one and the same?

The boy had talked to Ása and even seen her face up close. Nero shuts his eyes and tries to see her exactly as Bruno had. Once again, all he gets is the boy's own reaction – the overwhelming fear she'd elicited in him.

Sitting up, Nero asks for lights. He has only a name to go on and that could easily be an alias. The security encryptions protecting the newly-acquired and highly confidential data on the serving decoys are quite rightly impenetrable to anyone outside the DSD building. He could ask Kass for help but how would he explain this new lead to her? In any case, he'd be amazed if the name Ása Sturludóttir appears anywhere in those records.

Nero gets out of bed more easily this time – a welcome sign his strength is returning. It doesn't take him long to verify that every trace of Chan has disappeared except for her scarf. Was that symbolic? Only a few hours ago, her slight, warm body had lain across his, her long hair isolating their faces inside its silken walls: 'There's no rush, we've got all night' – words kissed along his cheeks like an oath.

A pulse begins in his ears – a whooshing sound. He slumps down onto the couch and lets the dizziness subside into pain. What the hell is Chan playing at? Had she calculated that, after their lovemaking and the wine mixed with his pills he'd be out cold until she could sneak back in? His search for a good reason for her to leave comes up empty. Is he her alibi for the night and, if so, an alibi for what?

The pack of painkillers is sitting next to the cold remnants of their meal. He swallows a couple of pills with a glass of water then sees a folded note propped up against the espresso machine. It holds all the promise of a courtroom exhibit. Oddly enough, the paper isn't his. He unfolds it to read:

I'm sorry to leave so abruptly. There's something I have to finish. Sorry too for a lot of things that I'd do differently if I could go back in time. I expect you're now thinking last night meant nothing to me – that couldn't be further from the truth.

With love

Jie Ning.

His fist thumps the counter causing a satisfying jolt of pain. What the fokk is she up to? He begins to pace in an effort to calm down. Isn't his outrage hard to justify; when it comes to deceit, is he any better? Like some spook in a movie, he'd taken her jacket when she arrived knowing he would place that speck-sized tracker under the collar.

As a serving homicide officer, he should be able to access DSD's intelligence channels. Nero gives the code to his console. The interface lights up. '*Track Hunter 250,*' he says.

An aerial topographic model is projected into the centre of the room, and then rotates 90% to align to his eye level. The woman he's obsessed with is now reduced to nothing more than a pulsating red dot. If he hadn't planted that device, he'd be able to fool himself she'd responded to the emergency and is now at her desk in DSD.

As he watches, that dot turns northward. Her speed of travel suggests she's taking one hell of a risk running out in the open.

A few adjustments and the projection shows him all the roadblocks, street surveillance points and current security patrols in place. Chan has access to the same data; so far she's deftly avoided all these obstacles. Despite the necessary detours, she continues to head due north for a couple of kilometres and then veers off towards the north-west apparently heading for the Free Zone border. The route projection line suggests she's making her way to the Orange Zone – most probably Section Five. This can't be a coincidence. He remembers his last visit to that particular section, the painful discussions while under the boot of the second decoy agent – the woman responsible for those copycat killings.

Nero stands back to watch that red dot, hoping it's going to deviate from its path and prove his growing suspicions wrong. It does no such thing.

There's no way he can physically catch her. Any verbal communication, however secure, to a location this far out of the main conurbation is likely be picked up and red-flagged – putting Chan in real danger. His finger traces the broken orange line projected in front of that dot, willing her to change her path and turn back towards him.

As if responding to his wish, the dot abruptly stops. Holding his breath, he waits for her to turn around and head back but she simply stays put. He can see the patrols have been increased all along the border.

Another hour passes and Chan is still stationary. Anything could be happening to her out there.

Nero's stud buzzes. Not Chan, instead an unfamiliar male voice. 'Go secure,' the man instructs him. Intrigued, he complies. The caller hesitates. 'Am I speaking to Inspector Cavallo?' The accent is local.

'Who is this?'

'I need confirmation. Is that –'

'Yes. Yes, this is Cavallo – though, if you're using this channel and you've reached my stud, you must know that already.'

'I have a message from your friend Rashid.'

'You mean my officer. Where the hell is he?' A creeping sensation begins in Nero's neck and migrates to his whole scalp. 'Surely he can speak to me directly, without an intermediary.'

'No, Mr Cavallo, I'm afraid he can't.'

'What do you mean? If you've harmed him in any way I'll– '

He can hear the man's breathing. 'I'm sorry to tell you Rashid's dead.'

'You're lying, you– '

'Right before he died, he told me to get in touch with you – no one else. He said to tell you that the Bears will never be as good as the Kruger's Stars.'

The rivalry between their teams had been part of their ongoing banter. 'That proves nothing,' Nero tells him.

'Rashid is dead. I killed him.'

'You twisted fokk –'

'Listen carefully – I was forced to kill Rashid, in fact he begged me to. I can't tell you all of it right now only, believe me, I wouldn't have shot your friend if I'd had a choice. I didn't. We both knew it was the only option left. Rashid Ashram was extraordinarily brave – without a doubt the bravest man I ever met.'

Nero recognises the truth. A spasm of pain grips his chest.

'You and me, we're on the same side,' the man tells him.

While he continues to talk, Nero shuts his eyes. He can see his friend kneeling on the ground with the barrel of this man's weapon pressed against his temple. Rashid had been trying to find Lúter's killer but instead he'd walked smack into trouble. Those dark eyes of his are wide open – all seeing; feeling only a resigned serenity. "I'm ready." Then louder: "Shoot me now, damnit." A look exchanged between killer and victim to offer and receive absolution. A hero's death – but why had Rashid made such a sacrifice? What could possibly be gained to cost him his life?

'Are you still there, Inspector?'

Is he? Head spiralling, he bends double to throw up. The meal Chan had brought over is spewed up half-digested on the floor at his feet.

'Cavallo, I need you to listen carefully.'

This whole thing had happened while he'd been lying in a hospital bed unaware. All his life he'd been cursed with seeing too much and yet he'd known nothing, sensed nothing. Through this stranger's memories he can revisit Rashid's last moments, but they will never play out in different way.

'I need you to help me stop what's about to happen,' the man says. 'It's no exaggeration to say the future of this city depends on it.'

He should have been there, intervened in some way.

'Cavallo!' Quentin says.

'I hear you.' Old instincts kick in, stopping him short of using the man's name when he hasn't given it yet. 'Tell me where you want me to meet you.'

Silence. The man's uncertain now that it comes down to it, whether he can trust a person he's never even met. Then he names a precise location and a time.

Nero thinks of Harris and what all those cowards in their armoured vehicles had done to him. At least one of the Commanders is guilty of the illegal and unwarranted execution of a serving decoy. The decoy he's talking to, Quentin, has chosen to fight back.

'I'll be there,' Nero tells him.

Thirty-Nine

A knock at the door wakes her. She's unprepared, having spent most of the intervening hours speculating and, ignoring the pain in her injured leg, pacing the length of the silk rug until she'd given in to the comfort of the vast bed.

'Come in,' she says.

A man enters, his eyes averted; the same man who'd served them their meal. 'Forgive the ungodly hour, I've been instructed to wake you. Can I offer you some refreshments, *madam*?' The tone injected into the last word betrays all of the man's contempt. She's beginning to warm to him.

'Coffee would be nice.'

Left alone again, she's in no doubt that she's being watched. Why have they woken her at this hour? She glances around, pretending to admire the ornate ceiling, the heavy furniture and panelled walls. Her trained eye spots a small anomaly halfway along the plaster cornice and then another a bit further along. She knows there will be many more.

The drink arrives; the authentic aroma of coffee is overpowering even before the tray is placed on the bedside table.

'If you're sure that's all you require, madam.'

'Quite sure.'

'Breakfast is laid out in the morning room,' he says withdrawing. Not exactly an invitation.

Out of bed and aware of those unseen eyes, a rush of cold air comes under the door to her bare ankles. On the chair are the clothes he'd lent her. She wonders if they'd been left behind by some eager to depart ex. She strains to hear footsteps in the corridor outside. Has Rockingham returned? As casually as she can, she walks over to the door, but all is quiet.

Rockingham had warned her the house's security equipment would block her stud. With no external intelligence, she can only guess at what might have taken him away so suddenly last night. Such isolation would not normally concern her but, at this crucial stage, she hates being in the dark.

Everything had been going according to plan. How easy it had been to show her disappointment at such an abrupt end to their evening together. 'It would be most unsafe for you to leave at this hour,' he'd said. Playing the gentleman, he'd insisted, had more or less ordered her, to stay the night, stroking her arm in a slow, possessive manner before he left; as if she were a gift he planned to unwrap later.

The room's adjoining washroom has a genuine tub but she chooses the shower. Inspecting the dog bite on her leg she's pleased to see it's no worse than before. Water jets assault her from every angle and yet fail to make her feel any cleaner.

Once dressed, she goes downstairs. From a shadowy alcove in the hallway, a woman comes forward to show her into the morning room.

The room is far too big to be comfortable. Most of the furniture is early last century and artfully sparse: a dark stained bookcase along the end wall, a table in the centre surrounded by six well-stuffed chairs and a lone side table displaying a vase full of showy flowers. From the window, artfully placed lights illuminate the shrubs on a sloping lawn and the banks of a small lake.

Again, for those unseen eyes, she selects a book and pretends to read the contents. The only sound is the quiet tick of the effete-looking clock on the mantelpiece; its thin hands confirm the absurd hour. There's an array of food on the table but she has no appetite yet. The quantity on offer suggests there could be other guests in the house but no one comes in to take an early breakfast. If Rockingham doesn't put in an appearance soon, she'll have no option but to try to leave.

She hears voices in the hallway – two people talking too quietly for her to catch what they might be discussing. She waits for the door to open but instead the footsteps continue on down the hallway. Further along, another door opens and then firmly closes. Someone begins to climb the grand staircase.

She opens the door. 'Tom, is that you?'

Rockingham pauses on the first landing to peer down at her. 'There you are, my dear,' he says, the same false note as before. 'I presumed you were still sleeping.'

She's caught him off guard, forcing him into such an unconvincing lie. He's standing his ground, isn't about to come down to her. 'I was sorry our evening was interrupted.' He looks away, distracted. 'How's the leg? I trust you're not in too much pain.'

Forced to mount the stairs, she says, 'I'll survive.' She smiles up at him. 'It was a lovely evening and so kind of you to let me stay.' His expression remains unreadable while he watches her approach, step by step. 'I wanted to thank you properly, personally,' she says, almost on a level with him now.

His smile might fall away at any moment. When he doesn't move, she's forced to take the final step towards him. She leans in like a conspirator. 'Such a shame you had to go.' Her body language is unequivocal.

He's forced to make a choice; she sees the tiny movements that reveal his deliberations. When his left hand extends towards her, she looks directly into his eyes.

'You must have been told many times how beautiful you are,' he says, his voice a little softer than before. 'Ravishing.' He breathes out slowly while his hand moves down to stroke her neck, then her shoulders, and then, though they're exposed to anyone passing, he paws the material above her left breast. His thin, dry lips come forward to graze the side of her face and on down to her neck, like an old dance routine he's remembering.

It occurs to her that he might be impotent; however, his hot breath on her skin suggests otherwise. She catches his free hand and moves it to her other breast. This time he squeezes hard as if she might be offering him sustenance.

'Shall we retire to the bedroom, my dear?' His voice is uneven. At last she has him under her power.

He takes her elbow and leads her along the corridor into the room where she'd slept. Someone has already been in to straighten the covers, though they haven't stripped the sheets.

She lets go of his hand to climb onto the vast bed and lie back among the newly arranged cushions. He remains where he is at the foot of the bed, studying her every move.

She props herself up. Checking his face for reactions, she begins to work her way down the many small fastenings on her blouse. He gives an audible sigh as she finally pulls the material aside. Should she begin to caress her nipples, or would that be too blatant for his tastes? No – she simply lies quite still, allowing his greedy eyes to travel back and forth over her exposed flesh.

'Such perfection.' He seems enthralled, as he lowers himself onto the bed. His hands take possession of her bare breasts. She's quick to disguise her shiver of revulsion when his tongue traces a wet line around her navel, moves up her sternum and then across to feather her nipple. His weight shifts onto her while his mouth fastens to her breast.

A hand comes up hard between her legs and a moment later begins to fumble at the fastenings of her trousers. He's quick to lose patience. 'Take them off.' Not a lover's request but an order. He moves aside, waiting for her to comply.

'I'm not sure,' she says, looking up at the ceiling. 'I'm really not comfortable with the idea of other people watching us.'

He struggles to stifle his annoyance. 'It would seem a pity to turn out the lights.'

'In any case, wouldn't your surveillance system simply switch to infrared?' She moves her knee rhythmically against his trousers at the groin. 'Couldn't you just ask them to turn the system off, just for a while?'

He sighs. 'Not without speaking personally to the head of my security detail.'

'If you wouldn't mind, Tom,' she says. Sliding off the bed, she undoes the fastenings on her trousers and they pool on the floor. 'I promise I'll make it worth your while,' she says, stepping out of the material's circle.

Suddenly distracted, his head turns away. It's clear he's listening – that his stud operates in here despite hers being blocked.

'I'm afraid I must call a temporary halt to proceedings,' he says, getting to his feet with surprising agility. 'Unfortunately, there's a most pressing matter I need to attend to.' He gives her a hard, assessing look. 'It seems events have again conspired against us. Another time, it would be most enjoyable to get to know you better, my dear.' He looks away, brushing an imaginary hair from his trousers.

'I quite understand.' She feigns disappointment. Not too much or she'd just look petulant. 'It must be time I left.'

'You're quite welcome to stay.'

She pulls her blouse together. 'No, I'd better get back.'

'As you wish.' Instead of leaving, he continues to watch as she buttons up her blouse. 'Meeting you has been such an unexpected delight.' His hand comes up to cup her arse cheek, squeezing her flesh with some force. 'A little more time and I'm sure it would have been an exquisite pleasure.' He touches the marks on her thigh where his dog had bitten her, tracing the line over her skin.

She flinches when his other hand runs up the inside of her thigh. 'So soft.' His searching fingers find the edge of her panties.

She squirms at his touch but stops short of pulling away. 'I really should go home,' she says.

His groping hand is withdrawn. 'Let me give you a lift. It won't be light for hours yet; a lone woman is hardly safe on the streets. My chauffeur can drive you home once he's dropped me off.'

'Thank you, but there's no need to go that far,' she says. 'He can let me out at the nearest expressway stop.'

'I insist,' the commander says, 'and I'm afraid I do like to get my way.'

Forty

The mirrored sides of the vehicle must make it hard to pick out at night especially when it's stationary. 'Why the devil have we stopped, man?' Rockingham's voice is calm as he speaks into the link with his driver.

There's no reply.

She watches him begin to comprehend the reality of the situation. He doesn't open the door but simply sits back and makes himself comfortable. Is he feigning this apparent composure? 'I think it's safe to assume my driver has been overpowered.' He clears his throat. 'But I can assure you that is all that's going to happen.'

He turns to her, his features emblazoned with triumph. 'You see, this vehicle is totally impenetrable. A distress signal will already have been triggered by our unscheduled stop. In a matter of minutes, the security forces will arrive in force.'

He opens a small compartment containing all the paraphernalia of a bar. 'A regrettable situation, my dear, nothing more.' He lays down two heavy glasses side by side. 'Perhaps you'd like a stiffener while we wait?' He pours two large shots of the amber liquid.

'How reassuring, Tom.' She accepts the one he offers her though with no intention of drinking it. 'You're quite sure we're not in any danger?'

'Absolutely certain, my dear; my protection has been ensured in every possible way. This vehicle has no vulnerable fuel source; the outside panels can repel any explosive device you care to name, short of nuclear that is. I think it safe to assume any would-be kidnappers are unlikely to possess such a device.'

He gives her a winner's smile as he raises his glass to touches hers. The chink is barely audible. Rockingham appears to be enjoying this diversion.

She pretends to take a sip. 'How long do you think it will be before the police get here?'

He snorts. 'We're not talking about a few flatfoots – my safety falls under the military's jurisdiction. Fortunately, there's no need for us to speculate about their arrival time.' He leans forward, touching a panel that lights up. 'This security breach has been fully verified. Security forces will arrive in precisely nine minutes and thirty-eight seconds.'

'Then, cheers,' she says. 'That gives us just enough time.' She gives him a mischievous smile.

'Your sangfroid is most agreeable, Alison.' He takes a sip of his drink. 'Tell me, had you anything particular in mind?'

She puts her glass down before touching his knee, then trails her hand up his thigh to stroke his groin. 'I certainly do. I'm sure a discerning man like you enjoys a show.' Her hand travels across to her own thigh and then up to her waist. 'I have a little surprise for you.'

One movement has the blade at his throat. The glass falls from his hand as age pours into his face, popping out the veins at his temple and blanching his cheeks.

She holds the knife steady.

Taking considerable care, he swallows. 'I'm disappointed in you, my dear. So much potential wasted. Your presumed intention is to take me as your hostage.'

She scores a shallow line across his turkey-like neck. A finger on her other hand traces the cut and she holds it up to his bulging eyes. 'If we prick you, do you not bleed?' She runs the same finger across her tongue. 'I think we have a positive on that.'

He arches his back, tries to pull away from the knife. 'This will be a somewhat hollow victory,' he says. She can feel the pulse in his throat under her hand. 'You and your accomplices will be overpowered in a matter of moments.'

She laughs into his face. 'You still believe they'll arrive in time to save you?'

Freezing air rushes in as the door is unsealed. For the first time Rockingham looks shocked. A uniformed man is standing there in the dark.

Rockingham's words escape like bubbles beneath her hand. 'Careful, Williams, remember this woman has a knife at my throat.'

Williams steps aside as she half-drags half-pushes Rockingham out of the vehicle. 'Six minutes, forty-two,' the chauffeur says.

She nods at him. 'Agreed.'

Withdrawing the knife, she allows Williams to wave his employer sideways with the barrel of his weapon.

Holding up both hands, Rockingham stares at his chauffeur, 'Why are you doing this, man? What can you hope to gain? Whatever it is, whatever she's paying you, I'm sure the two of us can reach an agreement.'

'Quiet!' Williams shouts. With the barrel of the photon, he gestures for the commander to walk on into the conifer plantation.

Rockingham shakes his head, remains where he is, legs braced apart. 'I'm going nowhere. If you fire that photon it'll bring them here even quicker. You can't escape; our drones can and will follow you everywhere. Your only hope is to come to your senses and turn that weapon on this cheap little whore here.'

Williams turns to her. 'We need to go, right now. Dogs won't be able to track us if we follow the river.' She tosses the chauffeur one of the packages from the driver's compartment and then steps in front of him. The point of her blade comes to rest just above Rockingham's heart. Behind them both, she hears Williams shake the garment out and then the uniquely unpleasant clawing sound as he forces his body into it.

'Well now, Tom, I can see in your eyes that you've recognised your chauffeur's new attire. Shh now! Don't be modest. I have it on very good authority that the acquisition of these suits was one of *your* pet projects. Bravo! What a vision! A suit that confers invincibility, or something remarkably close to it, on its wearer – like a gift from the gods. And yet– '

She rotates the tip of the knife, delights in his stifled cry of pain. 'You decided they'd be wasted on the police or your own security forces – including us lowly decoy officers.'

Rockingham's expression shows a new understanding, though he doesn't dare speak. 'They say waste is simply bad economics. So, with what some might consider impressive lateral thinking, you chose to think big – opt for far greater returns from the wider marketplace. I wonder if you wrestled with your conscience even for a moment about that?'

She increases the pressure but not enough to do real damage. 'You set about identifying those individuals who'd naturally appreciate the value of such secrecy of movement, the near-divine power these suits confer on whoever happens to be wearing them.'

Her free hand strokes his thinning hair as if he were a pet. 'So now, here we all are.' She leans in trying to detect that smell of fear; better still of bodily functions letting go – betraying the body's self-awareness that death is near.

She's disappointed that he smells of nothing except the familiar cloying stench of age and privilege. Looking into his set-hard face, she could almost admire the commander for his resignation – this small last defiance. His jaw is clenched in readiness just as hers would be if their roles were reversed.

'So you'd rather stay exactly where you are? I admire that,

Tom. But surely, you must have calculated that you'll stand a better chance if you eke this out until the military have time to close in? Am I right?'

Keeping the tip of the blade on his skin, she reaches down to cup his genitalia with her other hand. 'Let's test just how big those cajones of yours really are?'

He rears backwards away from the knife. 'For Christ's sake, Williams, this fokking woman has poisoned your thoughts. There's still time to change your mind. If you allow yourself to be complicit in my murder, they'll track you down, shoot you like a dog.'

'Tut tut, Commander – isn't that metaphor a tad unoriginal?' she says. 'Besides, there are two of us, so it should be *dogs*. Haven't you already demonstrated how severely you punish unruly behaviour in dogs?'

'There's no time for this,' Williams shouts. 'We need to go right now.'

She notes Rockingham's intake of breath as she squeezes his scrotal sack. 'How would *you, Tom*, dispatch a dog? This is something I ask myself. We already know about deer – all that culling that's not the same as killing. What is the accepted method of putting down a canine?'

She walks around behind him, pushing his head forward to prevent him following her movements. Into the back of his neck she asks, 'What did you do to that poor bitch, Tundra? What exactly was her reward for defending you so loyally?'

He remains silent. The muscles in her arm tighten. 'Shall we see how it's done?' She draws the blade from left to right, missing the jugular but severing both his carotid arteries. Blood spurts onto the sleeve of her jacket.

Rockingham falls to the ground writhing and trying to stop the flow with his own hands. 'You're bleeding out,' she tells him. 'You'll lose consciousness in two minutes and be dead inside five.'

Williams looks shocked by the sudden turn of events. 'Go!' she shouts to rouse him. 'I'll catch you up.'

Once he disappears into the trees, she blows on the near-silent whistle. Pulling on her own suit, she exhales; the white mist of her breath dissipates into the freezing air. Today really is such a beautiful day.

On the ground at her feet, Rockingham is still twitching. She bends over to take one last look at the sticky heap that had once been the Chief of all the Commanders. For a second she studies his death-pale face and half focused eyes. 'I nearly forgot to mention, Tom – my vixens are on their way. Can you hear them? Before you're quite dead, I'll leave and they'll begin to pull your body apart. Such poor table manners, they're bound to quarrel over the choicest parts of you. Then they'll carry their quarry – all those small pieces of you – into every corner of Eldísvík; the city you've helped to shape into everything that it is today.'

Rockingham issues incoherent noises. 'Come, come,' she says, 'this is no time for modesty, Tom. We both recognise your life's work.' His terrified expression confirms her words are still hitting their target. She lays a finger across his open mouth. 'Of course, the feral dogs and rats will feed on what my vixens discard. Forensics will eventually bag up your half-gnawed bones and take them somewhere out of sight. I doubt there'll be any memorials; you'll leave behind no lasting legacy. Along with everything you stand for, your remains will eventually be incinerated – the same way you removed every last trace of my friend Harris. That name ring any bells, Commander?'

The first few vixens have arrived. She catches their pungent scent as they draw nearer. Ears pricked, mouths open and panting, they close in.

Rockingham's hands fall from his wounds as his body goes limp. She leans into his ear and whispers: 'Brought down by a mere woman; in the old days they would have called that Karma.' His eyes have already stopped looking into hers.

Forty-One

In every direction there are cranes folded up like giant insects defending their territory. Nero's aware of the risk of being discovered here without reporting his intended movements to DSD. He had expected there would be security officers, backed up by the military, patrolling the harbour area but, intriguingly, there appears to be no one around.

The wind has already taken his hat, which he's still cursing about, and now the weather's plastered his hair to his head. He draws near enough to the water's edge to hear the rhythmic slap of the tide against the many craft lining the jetties. He catches the familiar whiff of decomposing seaweed.

The scream of a lone gull makes him reel around. What might have disturbed the bird? Nothing leaps out in answer. Given the weather, the night sky seems curiously clear and stars are visible in patches here and there.

At this early hour, the perimeter lighting is at a minimum with only the odd light shining from the rows of moored vessels. It's a struggle to make out berth numbers without a torch; the white markings seem to swim in front of him before he's able to make out individual letters and numbers.

Nero continues to count them down one at a time until he's finally standing opposite B58. Despite his thick coat, the cold has seeped into him and he's shivering. All he can do right now is wait. Out in the open, he's too exposed and so he retreats a short distance to stand close in to the bulk of the ancient steel-hulled vessel berthed at B59.

Such old ocean-going trawlers run solely on diesel – a commodity that for the last twenty years had been almost impossible to obtain either legally or illegally. She looks to have been fully restored by some unknown enthusiast. The smell of fresh paint and oil almost overpowers the stench of rotting kelp. Who would have spent all that time and effort unless they expected to embark on more than an occasional short sea voyage?

After a few minutes, Nero begins to make out the outline of a man approaching. As far as he can tell, he's alone. Though scale is hard to judge from a distance, he'd say this person is on the short side – certainly not an imposing figure. As he draws nearer, Nero remains where he is in the shadows.

The man comes to an abrupt halt opposite him. Without turning his head, he utters a single word: 'Revontulet' – the Finnish word for the aurora.

'Fox fire,' Nero replies, as agreed. 'Don't turn around,' he adds. 'Keep on walking down to the sea wall at the end. I want to check you haven't attracted any unwanted attention.'

The other man hesitates as if he's going to protest but then thinks better of it. Walking on, he adopts an unlikely saunter. Even without martial law in operation, anyone seeing the two of them loitering here at this time of night would figure they were up to no good. With so many towering ships moored up so close, any number of weapons might be aimed at one or both of them.

Watching the man's even-paced walk, Nero thinks of the warm bed he's given up to breathe in this dank, night air. Had this been a good or sensible decision? With hardly a moment's thought, he'd consented to meet this stranger – the same man who'd admitted to the murder of his friend and colleague. They'd agreed not to discuss Rashid, and by so doing, Nero feels complicit.

The decoy is nearing the last berths on this arm of the harbour. No one else has appeared; Nero hears no approaching footsteps above the lapping water.

When they arranged this rendezvous, he'd been curious enough about the man's choice of code words to do a little research. It seems the word *Revontulet* refers to the old Sami belief that the aurora was caused by the tails of foxes brushing the ground as they ran through the tundra and sending trails of sparks up into the sky. As far as he's aware, Quentin isn't a Finnish name – but this decoy could be a Finn by birth or extraction. Or maybe it's merely the sort of legend that would appeal to a decoy.

Nero reaches into his pocket for the pack of painkillers. When Quentin had convinced him about all this, he hadn't been thinking straight. The flaws and uncertainty of the situation are now glaringly obvious to him. Everything relies on information that, given the current circumstances, is impossible to verify.

He swallows only one pill this time. This could all be a wild goose chase or, worse still, a trap.

The man has turned and is walking back towards him. Pleased to be moving his frozen feet, Nero closes the gap between them. 'I'm fairly sure no one's following you,' he says.

'I could have told you that' The decoy shrugs. 'I'm Quentin, by the way.'

'So, Quentin, now you've got me out here against my better judgment, maybe you'd like to tell me the exact reason I'm standing here with my nuts like gelato. You claim to have information about an illegal shipment due to arrive at the berth over there tonight.'

'I'd pretty much stake my life on it.'

'It seems we've both done that,' Nero says. 'So, now the two of us are face to face like you insisted, I need to know more about your informant.'

'The party in question was outbid in the auction, as it were, and isn't too happy about it. You've heard the expression my enemy's enemy is my friend – that just about sums it up.'

'Why didn't you pass this tipoff to the port officers, or failing that, one of the patrol teams?'

'The answer to that question is going to seem a little unlikely.'

Nero laughs in his face. 'Is that so – '

Quentin holds up a hand. 'Hear me out.'

'Okay, go ahead – I'm all fokking ears.'

'It all boils down to a question of trust – or lack of it. I have no idea who is paying who around here.'

A soft sound turns both their heads. It's a bow wave running ashore; the vessel's approach hidden until now by the bulk of the various crafts moored alongside them. She's coming in almost silently using battery power alone, her dark mass becoming visible to the naked eye. There are no lights on her deck, only the dull red and green navigation lights on either side. More waves follow the displaced water, white foam lacing their edges.

They hear her engines reverse, the churning water at the stern before she drifts in towards the empty berth. She seems too large to fit the allotted space, but an unseen helmsman steers her perfectly into place.

The two of them duck behind the hull of the neighbouring ship, peering out now and then to check for any onshore party coming to receive her cargo or crew. In the far distance, Nero thinks he can see lights but perhaps they could be a trick of the waterside's many reflections.

A grating noise accompanies the deployment of the hawser. The sound echoes out across the water. Nero watches two thick metal cables protrude further and further ashore to automatically coil themselves snake-like around the fore and aft bollards.

He waits for a hatch to open, for the officials and stevedores to greet her with the usual calls issued back and forth.

Nothing happens. On the ship itself, not one single person emerges to stride the deck or let down the glinting shore ladder resting against her side.

'Doesn't seem to be a lot happening here,' he whispers.

'Maybe we just need to wait a while longer,' Quentin says.

'D'you think your informant might have made a mistake?'

The decoy shakes his head. 'No chance.'

'Could have got the wrong vessel, or the wrong time or date.'

'They won't have done. We wait, okay?'

Quentin's voice has an edge that suggests he's fighting to stay calm. 'Like I told you before, this ship is carrying a consignment that's destined for the Red Zones. You're a detective so why do *you* think there's no one leaving this ship, even though, presumably, they've just endured a long sea voyage. And where the hell are the people who'd normally oversee the berthing of a vessel?'

'You're right,' Nero says. 'Under martial law, the onshore authorities are specifically required to be extra vigilant to stop opportunists smuggling in contraband or illegal immigrants. Do you see any port security officers?' Nero moves further into the shadows.

'I say we wait for a bit,' Quentin says.

Nero nods his agreement.

Lifting both arms in exasperation, Quentin breaks the silence: 'Okay, so we've waited over half an hour and still not a single person has disembarked.'

'Something must have happened,' Nero says. 'Maybe the same thing's scared off the reception committee. Could they have got cold feet and called the whole deal off?'

Quentin's silhouette shakes its head. 'Damnit.'

'What do we do now?' Nero asks – a question as much for himself as the other man. He rubs at his upper arms to help stimulate his circulation. 'We need to find a way to board that ship to inspect her cargo. I daren't even access any DSD systems using my stud – it's too big a risk.'

'A small confession, Inspector, I've got ScramJam on mine curtesy of my revolting little friend, Charlie.' Just above a whisper, Quentin says, *'ScramJam. Main harbour area – current intel.'*

They wait.

'Nothing on any of the usual channels,' Quentin says. *'Update all intel.'*

Another wait. The decoy seems about to speak but instead he pulls on Nero's sleeve, dragging him deeper into the gap between the two vessels opposite.

He shakes the man off. 'What's going on? Tell me.'

Quentin takes a deep breath. 'This whole thing had to be arranged by someone in a position to impose a severe case of myopia on the port authorities.'

'And?'

'I may have underestimated how far this whole business goes.'

'What makes you say that?'

'According to the chatter, something big just happened. If it's true, it's likely to change everything.'

Grabbing the man's lapel, Nero pulls Quentin towards him. 'If you don't tell me right now, I'll– '

'Okay, I'll tell you, though you have to remember it's only cync-chatter.' Quentin lowers his voice until it's only just audible: 'It's Rockingham – they're saying he's just been assassinated.'

Forty-Two

Chan wakes with a start to total darkness; it takes a few moments to recall where she is. Then she remembers how the frequency of the border patrols had forced her to take refuge inside this ramshackle shepherd's hut. Her whole body is stiff from lying on its bitterly cold and dusty floor. Damnit – she'd been asleep for nearly three hours.

When she opens the outside door it nearly falls off in her hand. At first the blackness outside is intense but then her eyes adjust and she can see the shape of the frosted landscape.

She pulls on her cheap infrared goggles – they're far less sophisticated than the ones DSD use but they still do the job. The world glows green in her eyes; the Free Zone now only an emerald light in the distant horizon. No sign of any humans just a handful of grazing sheep over on the next ridge.

She walks back down the rutted track that led her here. A fierce wind has got up. Once the ground becomes more even, she breaks into a run, reminding herself how any patrols she encounters will have standing orders to arrest anyone breaking the curfew. Reservists will have been brought in to help; in their nervousness, those rookies are more than likely to fire on sight.

Her face becomes damp though it hasn't rained and there's no fresh snowfall underfoot. It's a struggle to keep up her previous pace where the roadway starts to break up but she daren't slow down until she's cleared Section Four and navigated around all its surveillance points. Swaying vegetation has swallowed up whatever has remained standing out here, exactly like seaweed colonising wrecks.

'Update, area map,' she says between breaths. Still no sign of any patrols; the schematic confirms she's entered the next quadrant and is right on course. For a run like this, she'd normally stop several times to take on liquids – tonight that isn't an option.

The fastenings of the infrareds are rubbing both sides of her cheeks; she pulls them down and allows the ambient light to guide her. Chan's throat is bone dry and her leg muscles are already burning but, given all the constraints and obstacles, she's setting a good pace.

The topography of the landscape has been gradually changing. Chan slows her pace. When she checks again, aside from a few small mammals, her infrareds can detect no heat signatures. She pulls them down to her neck and continues her run.

A little over forty minutes later, she stops to check again. Less than two kilometres to the target – so close at long last. Double-checking the time, she knows she can afford to slow to a regular jogging pace; this gives little benefit to her legs, but her heartbeat is steadier and her breathing gradually returns to something nearer normal.

The vastness of valley floor spreads out around her, utterly empty and barren wherever she looks. It's an extraordinary experience to be somewhere so devoid of buildings with no trees or scrub above knee height. She's alone in an alien world – one in which there's nowhere to hide. In such a featureless space, the abandoned mag-track stands out as stark reminder of the past. Following its snaking line will take her the rest of the way there.

Walking beside the silent rail, she stumbles over rutted and stony ground. She's tempted to stop, take a deep breath and allow herself more time to think this whole thing through.

No – it's too late for that. Everything she's lived through has been leading up to this night and this journey. She may be set on a collision course but so be it.

The infrareds show only low-level background heat in all direction though she knows better than to rely totally on that. She checks the time and her co-ordinates for final confirmation that both are right and she's currently a mere two hundred and twenty metres from the target.

Chan begins to make out the row of shacks hugging the side of the old track. These must originally have been put up to shelter the line-workers all those years back.

Drawing closer, she can see every door is ajar; they're lined up in front of her like open graves. The wind howls as it runs between them as if to have her believe there's nothing here but emptiness.

She walks on down the line. The first and second huts appear to be empty. She stops level with the third. A slight creak of weary metal, nothing more. You wouldn't otherwise know.

'Thought you might … change of heart?' The shrillness of the distortion catches her off-guard.

'It wasn't easy avoiding the patrols.' Chan can just make out a density to the shadow in front of her – nothing more. Less than five metres separates them.

'Were you followed?' The ugliness of the synthetic sound leaves her ears resonating.

'No.'

'Can you…sure?'

'I'm quite certain.'

'You told no one…here?'

'Not a living soul.'

The dense shape moves nearer, as indistinct as a swarm of bees approaching. 'Quite…risk to take.'

'I'm aware of that.'

'Well then, I can't wait to hear what you have to say... hope you're not going to disappoint.' The voice makes her wince; it has the resonance of something being scraped against a polished surface. Understanding the sense of the words, putting each sound together, reminds her of trying to piece together Mandarin when she was a little girl.

Two unseen hands begin to pat her down for weapons. 'Could you turn off the sound-effects?' Chan asks. 'I can't understand half of what you're saying.' She stands her ground though her legs are now shaking with trepidation and exhaustion. 'Communication needs to be a two-way thing.'

'… matters is, I understand you.'

Her pulse begins to pound in her ears, 'I'm sorry,' Chan says, as the featureless landscape seems to spin around her, 'I really need to sit down for a minute.' She's determined not to collapse right here on the icy ground at this decoy's feet.

'Up there.' This time, the voice is clearer, like she might actually be talking to a human being after all. A not-so-gentle shove on her back. 'Start walking, … remember I'm right behind you.'

The broken off stump stands out against the night sky. Wiping away a layer of snow, Chan sits down heavily. 'Exactly…you here?' The words emanate from a spot right in front of her. 'Don't leave anything out … I'll know.'

All the way here, Chan had been wondering what she'd say at this precise moment. 'I need to start at the beginning or it won't make sense.' When this elicits no response, she continues, 'I'm a police constable. During my training, I was sent for a preliminary psychological assessment to the head of that department – Dr Arthur. He was very kind, in an avuncular way. He told me I showed real promise and might be suitable for what he called "special assignments" in the future.'

Her throat is so dry she has to swallow several times before she can continue. 'For my final placement, I was seconded to the Homicide Team. I assumed the head of that department had been told of my aptitude – I only mean that my scores were higher than average.'

A wraith-like laugh fills her ears. 'Modesty should be…of your concern right now.'

The intense darkness before her suggests the decoy is very close – possibly only an arm's length away. 'The team were investigating those decoy murders in the Double Red and Dr Arthur asked me to hide a plastic duck at the crime scene and then to apparently find it. To plant it, I needed to wait for a moment when they were all distracted. The rest of the team assumed it was the killer's signature object.' She recalls how conflicted she'd felt about the idea of evidence planting despite Dr Arthur's reassurance.

'They were impressed by my find – my apparent thoroughness. I felt so guilty deceiving everyone because I was really enjoying working with them all. From the start, the Inspector was particularly kind and very encouraging.'

She recalls Nero sitting with her in that café, so clearly upset about the second lot of murders but still struggling to be good company.

'Doctor Arthur came in person to my apartment and told me there was a question mark over Nero – Inspector Cavallo–'

'… know who he is.'

'They suspected he was corrupt though he said he couldn't divulge anything more specific. I was told to invite Nero to my apartment for a meal. Dr Arthur handed me a small vial of liquid that I was to put in his drink to make him sleep. They needed to find out what had been deleted or doubly-encrypted on his stud in order to prove whether he'd been in touch with what he called *undesirables*.'

'And had he?'

'I don't know. My orders were to swap his stud for a duplicate and give the original one to Dr Arthur and no one else. When it came to it, Nero was already a little drunk, so I only gave him half of the dose and that knocked him out, just like that.' The snap of her fingers echoes out into the emptiness. 'He didn't regain consciousness until the next morning. Even then, he seemed quite groggy when he left. They'd called him in early. That same morning, I was ordered back to the training department for psychological testing, which they said would take a couple of days. Dr Arthur went out of his way to praise me for the special work I'd done so far.'

'Go on.' Undistorted now, the voice clearly belongs to a woman.

'While I was off being evaluated, the rest of the homicide team had received a tipoff from Narcotics, which led them to raid a former bank premises in District Sixteen. They believed it was the decoy's HQ.'

'And you missed this raid?'

'Yes.' The weight of her confession makes it hard to continue for a moment. 'They were ambushed and Sergeant Stefánsson was killed. I always liked Lúter Stefánsson; he was kind and helpful and really funny too. I asked one of the pathologists to let me see his body. It was awful to see him lying there fried black by photons and totally unrecognisable. He had a wife and children.' Her voice falters. Unable to speak, Chan turns her head, tries to see beyond that oppressive shadow.

'You felt responsible.'

She nods. 'Worse – I felt I was on the wrong side. And then there was Nero – he very nearly died. I thought he was going to be disabled and permanently scarred or maimed. Back in my apartment, he'd been perfect – so strong and handsome. After the raid, his skin looked like raw meat and he was covered in scars and enormous bruises. I told myself the decoy was the one responsible, because otherwise – '

'Otherwise it meant you might have had a hand in setting them up.'

'I began to wonder whether it was my fault. I just didn't know.' The wind stings her wet face. 'After that awful raid, they had to reform the Homicide Team; everybody got promoted. All of it so wrong. And I wanted just to hunt down that fokking decoy and find out the truth.'

That last bit might have been a step too far though the shadow in front of Chan appears not to move or react in any way. She has to finish her story. 'The Commander's Secretariat had refused at first to release the information we needed on the identities of the decoy agents. When they agreed to give us limited access, they kept delaying – like it was just the usual bureaucratic inefficiency, but it seemed more like they were doing their best to block the investigation. Without Nero, the department started to fall apart. Rashid Ashram just disappeared off God knows where and Kass still had PTS and couldn't seem to make any decisions. So everything came down to Maxwell and me. We were only junior officers.' She shakes her head. 'On such an important case, it just wasn't right.'

'Tell me more about Leifsson's murder.'

'I guess you know he was stabbed in his bathroom by the new cook, appointed after his old one left. So bizarre that our head of state could be murdered not by a trained assassin but by a middle-aged, female Latino. I mean, if you saw her – you just couldn't pick a more unlikely killer.'

She sniffs then wipes her face against the sleeve of her jacket. 'Before all that, someone had *apparently* broken in and left another plastic duck exactly like the one they got me to plant. Leifsson's previous cook was interrogated over that and she'd resigned because she was really upset by the appalling way a member of *Dr Arthur's* own team interrogated her. We then find out Mrs De Morenos had a longstanding hatred of the Governor – the poor woman blamed him personally for her only daughter's death, yet she'd passed enhanced security vetting – how could they possibly have missed something like that?'

The silence that follows is broken by the high scream of a

vixen. 'How did you find me?' Looking up, it seems to Chan that black shape is looming only inches away.

She shrugs, 'Straightforward detective work. I checked through the anonymous pay records of the decoys and noticed two of the entries hadn't received any credits for the last month. I guessed one of those had to be the decoy I'd met with the homicide team – an old guy called Harris. He told us he'd be retiring immediately afterwards. That meant he was almost certainly one of those two encrypted names. I've studied different methods of encryption – it was an add-on option – and I know how to access and use various advanced methods of analysis.'

The decoy snorts. 'You want me … believe those encryptions … that easy to break?'

'Not without a key; but I already had that with the name *Harris*. It was also a reasonable assumption we'd dropped him off in, or very near, his particular sector – so I had a key for that too.'

'This is nonsense – someone gave you my stud code, didn't they?'

'No. Let me explain: when the Secretariat finally deigned to release the list of corresponding names to our department, I suspected straight away there was something not right about the whole thing.'

Chan waits long enough for the silence to rile the decoy. 'Go on,' she commands.

'I was fairly convinced they'd deliberately tricked us – made sure the people on that list were dead ends. It turned out, the list was genuine enough but came from more than twenty years back.'

'How could you possibly know that?'

'I wasn't sure, so I asked the tech guys to help me.' Still seated, Chan's hand moves very slowly down her leg. 'There were certain unexplained anomalies to the file. They saw my point and ran various diagnostics, concentrating solely on how the information might have been altered over time. They found some vestiges – stuff that didn't match the official signature trails. After that, they were able to date the bulk of the data to a much older original which had been recently modified.'

'I really can't … where this is leading and frankly I'm beginning to … a little bored.'

Chan's searching fingers feel the reassuring bulk of her ankle holster. 'I went back to my original theory. As you know, decoys usually have short careers but there was one exception – Harris. Comparing the two lists, I was able to decipher which entry referred to him. You were the other unpaid, missing decoy.'

This woman's vixens have to be nearby. Should she make her move now or wait?

'Through trial and error I was able to solve more of the encryption and that's how, after several miscalculations,' Chan works at keeping her voice level and calm, 'I finally managed to decipher the code for your stud. Once I had, I knew curiosity would get the better of you and you'd agree to meet me.'

The decoy laughs into her face. 'I've always liked … quote from Neil Armstrong – when you get overconfident that's when something snaps up … bites you.'

Chan laughs right back at her. 'And yet I'm confident you're still dying to know who else I might have told – just how far your cover's been blown.'

Forty-Three

Quentin drops back into the galley of the small craft they've taken refuge in. 'Nothing doing out there,' he says. 'If you ask me, no one's coming to offload anything from that ship before daybreak.'

With the hatch closed, they're able to switch the bulkhead light back on. Nero looks over at the decoy and nods. 'You're probably right but we should give it a bit longer.'

Quentin is a short, wiry man – the ideal stature if your job is to look like a would-be victim. Beneath his totally white hair, his face is pale but not nearly as lined as the hair would suggest. If he's a Finn by birth, the name he's using is probably an alias. He can't tell more without touching him; the idea doesn't appeal. Nero needs to act like he trusts him, for the moment at least, but it's a struggle to hide his feelings in such close proximity. Every time their eyes meet, he can't help but picture Rashid's execution at this man's hands.

Though he'd known the security code from one touch, he'd stood back to allow Quentin to break the lock on the hatch. Part of the wooden frame had splintered in the process. When they find the evidence of their intrusion, the owner of this handsome boat is likely to assume some adolescent had broken in looking for booze or someplace to find privacy with a sexual partner.

'I'm all out of ideas.' Quentin throws up both hands then lets them fall to clap his sides. 'Any suggestions welcome, man.'

Nero hates his use of the word *man*. Instead of looking up, he continues to stare at the remnants of their pilfered, make-shift meal. To keep his energy levels up, he'd forced himself to swallow a few mouthfuls of the fish and beans mix, swilling it down with a beer. In the confined space, the lingering smell of tinned fish and alcohol threatens to turn his stomach.

Looking away to the blank space above one of the bunks, he sees Chan's face, those extraordinary eyes looking directly into his. Her mouth opens to form a smile and then broadens as she gives way to a deep, throaty laugh. The image is extraordinarily vivid; Nero's almost convinced she's down there with them when her face dissolves into nothing.

'Well?' Under the light, Quentin's blue eyes have an unnerving coldness about them. The man's already put away more than a third of a bottle of something that tasted so harsh one sip had triggered a coughing fit in Nero. Seeming no worse for it, Quentin takes another long swig before pointing the bottle in his direction. 'Got anything?'

'Maybe.' Nero shrugs. 'Though it's quite a longshot.' He hasn't exactly finessed the fine details. 'Not sure what odds I'd give it, but it definitely beats doing nothing and letting them sail back out of here on the next tide.'

'So then let's hear it.'

'For a start, I'll need to spruce myself up a bit.'

'You're not thinking of touting for trade on the dockside?' Quentin laughs – a disarmingly pleasant laugh for a self-confessed killer. 'Only, no offense, but with all those bruises and stuff you got going on, I think you might need more than a quick brush up.'

Nero's a long way from being amused. He stands up. With any luck, the owner of this boat might keep a clean shirt onboard.

'Double or quits on the next shot?'

'Yeah, okay – what the hell?' Standing just outside the open door, Nero hears the soft click of colliding balls, followed by a raucous cry of triumph.

Inside, the room smells of sweat and marijuana. Nero loudly clears his throat. Both dock officers turn abruptly. A full ashtray and a near-empty unlabelled bottle of amber-coloured liquid sit on the table just behind them.

'Good morning, gentlemen.' He holds up his ID. 'I'm Inspector Nero Cavallo – head of DSD's Homicide department. I'm here to locate a newly arrived vessel. We need to examine part of her cargo.'

He gives each of them a long, knowing look. 'We have reason to believe she may be carrying certain items linked to a *high-profile murder case*. I'm afraid any further information is classified.'

A beat passes before they scrabble for jackets and hats. The older man surreptitiously extinguishes the evidence of their dismissible offence while his colleague shields him with his back. Still buttoning his jacket, the younger man steps forward, uncertain whether to shake hands or salute; in the end he does neither. 'I'm Port Officer Svensson and this is Senior Port Officer Andersen. How can we help you, Inspector?'

'First of all, I need to check through your vessel movements log.' Nero waves a hand in the air. 'Due to the ongoing situation, some of our intelligence systems are currently down at DSD.'

Stretching his neck and regaining his composure, Andersen steps forward to make it clear he's the man Nero should be addressing. 'That shouldn't be a problem, Inspector.' From the quick glances they give each other, Nero can see they're still worried he might report them for misconduct or dereliction of duty.

'Good man.' He hopes his smile will relax them a little. 'As representatives of the port authorities, I'll need you to accompany me to the vessel in question. My officers are already in positions at various points around the harbour. They will be providing us with cover – though let me assure you that, should there be any sign of resistance from members of the crew, we will withdraw and my officers will move in and deal with the matter.'

The two men look suitably worried.

Nero addresses Andersen. 'A small team of stevedores should be on standby and ready to unload her cargo on my command.' Nero shuts his eyes as a flash of pain shoots up his back. When he opens them again, Andersen looks close to panic. 'After the declaration, our stevedores went straight home, sir. We've only got a skeleton crew of two and they're – '

'Happy to help, I'm sure,' his colleague cuts in. 'Is this connected to what's happening, Inspector – martial law and all that?' Both men look a little wild-eyed and overexcited at the prospect of being key players in such a high-level drama. He needs their cooperation but it's vital they stay calm.

'I'll be honest with you, gentlemen,' Nero says, lowering his voice, 'we can't be certain about this intelligence. This could all be a complete red herring but, let's face it, in the current circumstances we can't afford to leave any stone unturned – if you follow my meaning?'

Andersen's frown has deepened. His younger colleague looks crestfallen.

'Let's assume your movement log shows nothing out of the ordinary – I'm sure you port officers would have investigated otherwise. In any event, the crew of the vessel in question are almost certainly unaware of what they might be carrying. We'll need to remove the cargo and subject it to extensive analysis back at DSD to be certain that it complies to regulations.' He's going off piste – isn't he supposed to be investigating a death, not imposing commodity safety standards.

Both men's frowns have deepened. Svensson points to Andersen and then himself. 'So you're saying neither of us will be what you might call *in the firing line*?'

Nero shakes his head more than once, thankful that the drugs are now taking the edge off the discomfort this produces. 'We're not expecting any opposition. I can assure you that we at DSD are extremely risk averse; it's merely as a precaution that my marksmen are in position with their precision weapons trained.' What made him mention the weapons? He needs to distract them from all the nonsense he's spouting. The two men standing behind him could easily overpower him should they begin to detect this is so much bullshit.

'Let's begin with that movement log for the last sixty days,' he says, taking charge. Andersen goes to the nearest console and makes the relevant request. Nero captures the data stream and then relays it to Quentin's stud.

'Thank you, gentlemen.' He gives them a quick smile of appreciation. 'It's clear you keep a tight ship here. I can see nothing untoward in these entries.'

He lets his expression grow serious. 'And now, if you wouldn't mind alerting the two stevedores you mentioned, let us proceed to berth B58.'

They very nearly collide as Nero holds up a hand. 'Remember, it's imperative you don't mention the fact that I'm a *homicide* inspector – we don't want to alert the crew to that particular possibility at this stage. I'm sure you can appreciate my reasoning.'

He's pleased when the two men nod in unison. 'After you, gentlemen,' Nero says. As they walk out of the door, his trailing hand makes contact with Andersen's. The man's an open book. So far, he's buying the whole unlikely story. So far, so good. This nonsense may have been enough to convince these two men but what about the crew onboard? What if the captain or his officers are in on this?

Walking back towards the ship, Nero's legs are leaden – he's quite possibly just engineered his own demise.

Quentin meets them further down the quay. Aware of how dishevelled the decoy must look, he says, 'This is one of my undercover officers.' Both men raise their hands to acknowledge Quentin.

They walk on towards the vessel. Nero's pleased to see no sign of activity on the deck or anywhere else. He steps to one side and gestures to the two dock officers to approach the shoreside's address system.

'Nehalennia Star, this is the port authority officer-in-charge,' Andersen says, a slight wobble in his voice. 'We have a few routine enquiries. Please open your hatch to allow us to check your documentation is in order.' As an after-thought he adds: 'All the usual stuff.'

The request is met with silence.

'Nehalennia Star,' Andersen repeats. Various metallic sounds echo across the water. When the hatch of the ship is fully raised; a lone man is standing there. No sign of a weapon but he could hide anything inside that thick coat.

'Good day to you.' The man's voice is heavily accented – a singsong delivery of a carefully learned phrase. 'I have all the–' he shakes his head, 'pappersarbete. Dokumentering?'

Quentin moves forward: 'Er du Svensk?'

'Ja, jag er.' The man begins to nod and smile. A conversation between the two starts in earnest. Despite their names, like Nero, neither port officer appears to be following the conversation.

After a good deal of gesturing and laughing, Quentin turns to the others. 'This is Captain Elias Lindgren. He's Swedish, comes from a little village I know very well. Would you believe, I worked on his cousin's farm when I was a student? He says he would like to offer us all a little welcoming drink while we make our checks.'

The port officers are all smiles. 'Tack,' Andersen says.

'Tack så mycket,' Svensson mutters.

The captain steps aside as more of the crew appear and begin to put a gangplank into place. Quentin and Nero continue to smile like their lives depend on it.

Forty-Four

'It's just the two of us out here alone; why not satisfy my curiosity and let me see your face?' Chan keeps her eyes trained on the space in front of her while her searching hand undoes the catch on her ankle holster.

On their way back from Double Red Zone, Harris had pointed out a virtually invisible air intake under the left arm of his own ecto-suit; he'd told them it was the only weak point. This decoy may be wearing something far more sophisticated but it's possible her suit is vulnerable at that same spot. It had to be worth a shot.

'*Cloaking off*.' The darkness separates out; part of it takes on a recognisably human form. Chan's disappointed to see a hood still masking the decoy's face. Soundlessly, she slides the photon-gun free of its holster.

Chan inwardly counts to three. She jumps to her feet, swinging the weapon out to her right in an upward arc. Taken by surprise, the decoy emits a noise partway between a scream and a laugh. When her arms come forward in defence, Chan shoves the barrel under her left armpit then brings her other hand up to hold the weapon steady. 'Okay,' she says, adjusting her balance, 'I need some answers before I decide whether to kill you right here.'

'You think you've found a chink in my armour.' The decoy's

voice is now all too human – no doubt a ploy to make it harder for her to pull the trigger. 'You'd shoot me without even reading me my rights?'

Neither of them moves. 'Go on then – shoot me,' the decoy says. 'Why the hesitation? I'm at your mercy – fire away.'

To Chan's right there's movement in the shadows and then the decoy is bringing her arm across and making a grab for the weapon. Chan tightens her grip. While they wrestle, it fires; the blast shoots up to illuminate the sky above their heads like a distress beacon.

'Damn!' The decoy pulls Chan's arm into a lock while exerting pressure on a point at her wrist that makes it impossible to maintain her grip. The weapon falls to the ground and she stamps on it. Pushing Chan off balance, she flips the photon with her foot. They both watch its shiny surface spinning end to end in the air.

The decoy snatches it first. 'Seems I have the upper hand again.' She stands over Chan, pointing the weapon at her head like a trained assassin. 'That blast will have been visible to a dozen patrols; they'll have homed in on this precise location.' Her boot digs into Chan's side. 'On your feet; we need to get out of here.'

Chan stands up. The gun is pressed into her back. She's angry with herself, is tempted to stand her ground but knows the smart choice is to co-operate.

'Start walking.' Chan reluctantly complies. They head back down the hill. 'You know I once watched someone spray poison into an enormous wasp nest,' the decoy says, jabbing the weapon into her spine.

'What the hell's that got to do with anything?' It's clear they're heading back to the huts.

'It has everything to do with everything. The insecticide killed the queen at the heart of the nest, which meant all her drones – who'd been out getting her food or wood pulp – flew about not knowing what the hell to do without their leader. Some flew straight back into the nest and the deadly poison. Others frantically circled the entrance expecting their commander-in-chief to miraculously emerge. Of course they tried to sting the pest-control man again and again. With no remaining purpose, most simply flew off to die. The rest went hunting for a substitute queen.'

Chan stumbles but keeps her balance. 'And your point is?'

'The military, along with the security services, have just lost their supreme leader. Some will be plotting, many will be confused; all of them will be in a state of near panic and desperate to find someone to blame. The patrols coming our way will be trigger-happy.'

'Maybe, but going back to your wasp analogy, we already have a new state governor.'

'You don't really imagine I'm talking about Leifsson's murder?' The decoy's laugh echoes out into the night air. 'You don't know Commander Rockingham's been assassinated?'

Shock momentarily halts Chan. 'And I'm guessing you know exactly who was responsible.'

The push to her back means business. 'No comment.'

Chan struggles to keep her footing. If this decoy or her fellow conspirators have murdered Rockingham, killing a lowly police constable would be nothing to her. So why is she still alive?

Above them the sky has cleared and the moonlight is sparkling the snowy terrain in every direction. On another night, this empty landscape would seem so beautiful.

They're nearing the huts. 'You really don't understand the magnitude of what you've got yourself mixed up in,' the decoy says to her back. A bark from up ahead suggests this woman's vixens await their orders. Chan can make out several sets of eyes trained in their direction. Looking to the right and then the left, she can even pick out the white fur at their throats.

She has no choice but to walk on towards the abandoned huts and whatever this decoy intends once they reach them.

Vixens begin to pour soundlessly out from behind every rock and bush until the pack surrounds them. As the animals move closer, their feral stench catches in Chan's throat.

Kass has never seriously questioned anything Nero has asked of her before. It's crazy-o'clock and she's still at DSD working alone in the empty incident room. It seems totally unreasonable to expect her not to log her movements with the department when they're under martial law with a curfew in operation. Nero's no longer the officer-in-charge – she is. What's more, the man's only just left hospital and might not be thinking straight.

'If our intelligence is correct, this thing is huge,' Nero tells her. 'It's no exaggeration to say it could change everything.'

He'd used the word *our*. Who is he working with? Kass tries another angle: 'So what exactly is it you've found?'

'I can't go into detail – not even on a secure line.'

She hears his breathing, knows he's already impatient for her answer. She takes off her spectacles and rubs at her eyes.

'Technically speaking, I'm no longer your commanding officer,' he says. As if that helps. 'It's entirely up to you whether you meet us or not. Right now there's no security and, unlikely as it seems, no military presence here. That situation could change any minute.'

'You must think I need to be there, or you wouldn't have asked me.'

'I do. But you need to understand you could be walking into danger.'

Looking up, all the shapes in the room around her blur together. 'You have Wifrith and your kids to consider,' he says, a note of genuine concern in his voice. 'This has to be your decision. If you decide not to show, forget that we ever had this conversation.'

The mention of her family scares her more than anything else he's said. She hears someone else's voice in the background. 'Look, I've got to go now,' Nero says. 'Meet me here inside the hour if you're coming.'

Could it be Rashid who's there with him? Who else is with them? This is no fable or saga where some tiny band of heroes can defy all the odds to restore a just society – whatever that might be. He's given her a choice but how is she meant to simply forget a conversation like that?

It's an easy decision. She knows herself, knows that her sense of loyalty is such that, as long as Cavallo remains alive, he'll be calling the shots. This whole thing could be nonsense but if she doesn't go and something awful happens to him, how could she begin to live with herself?

They're nearly at the huts. Everything has gone against her expectations tonight and now fear is anchoring her feet. 'In there.' With the barrel of her own weapon, the decoy is pointing her towards a dense thicket.

'You're not serious?'

The raised photon-gun suggests otherwise. In open ground she feels safer but, right now, she has no choice.

'Okay, that's far enough.' The vixens take up positions all around them like a Pretorian Guard. The weapon disappears as the decoy kneels down and begins to scrape away at the earth. Chan can't see the photon-gun. It might be easier to grab it with the decoy distracted like this but, even if she could locate it, she doesn't fancy her odds against the whole vixen pack.

'I need your help,' the decoy says. 'This hatch is much harder to raise from this side. Remember – the patrols will have been alerted by that little light show back there. Now might be a good time to get off that fence, Constable, before the razor wire tears your arse to shreds.'

It's a straightforward calculation: dressed in that suit, the decoy's heat signature is non-existent, which means she would be the target – a sitting duck out here.

Chan gets down on her knees to help scrape away at the soil. Is this the point where she goes from being this woman's prisoner to being her willing accomplice?

In a matter of minutes, her fingers detect a metal edge to some sort of manhole.

The decoy stands up. The next minute she's above her wielding a stout piece of timber. If she had a god, Chan would be praying right now.

'Can you feel a small indentation near the edge?' she asks Chan.

'Yes. It's some a sort of handle.'

'Good, now find the one opposite. Grip hard and pull when I tell you to.'

At her second attempt, she raises the cover a few centimetres – just enough for the decoy to push the piece of wood underneath one edge for leverage. She hears the woman straining and then the hatch finally sits upright on its hinge.

Chan peers down into the featureless void that's now revealed.

'You first,' the decoy says. 'It's a short drop, no more than three metres.'

'Don't we need to shut the hatch behind us?'

'*I* do. Which means you need to go first.'

There's no ladder, no hand holes anywhere. Looking into the incalculable depth, Chan's aware she only has this mad woman's word that she won't be falling to her death.

'Call it a leap of faith,' the decoy says. 'You could, of course, wait for the first patrol to latch on to your heat signature. If you hold your hands up high enough it's even possible they won't shoot you. But then of course you'll have to explain why you're out here. If you tell them about me and they pull back this hatch, I'll be waiting for them. The chances are they'll be young rookies; you'll have their deaths on your conscience. So, Constable, what's it to be?'

She's hemmed in by foxes; breathing in their disgusting smell. Anything could be waiting for her down there in that utter darkness. Sitting there on the edge, her dangling feet meet no obstructions. She's about to launch herself into oblivion with no idea what will happen next.

Chan breathes in and then lets go.

Forty-Five

They raise several more glasses of schnapps with the Nehalennia Star's crew to endless repetitions of "*Skål*!"

Finally, Nero looks around the circle of cheerful, ruddy faces and clears his throat. 'Ursäkta.' They all look at him expectantly. His Swedish gives out. 'I have orders to inspect the cargo in hold five,' he says.

Quentin translates. No one speaks for a moment.

'Jag förstår. Inga problem,' Captain Lindgren finally says, slapping Nero on the back. The mix of alcohol and painkillers he's consumed takes the edge off the resulting pain.

Below deck, the captain leads the four of them along a labyrinth of walkways and then down a steep ladder into Hold Five. Once inside, he points to the cargo and begins to count under his breath.

There are 24 soft-wrapped bales sitting on pallets and securely bound by unbroken straps. 'Tjugofyra!' Lindgren announces.

Behind these, Nero counts off 35 sealed wooden crates. 'Trettiofem. Is correct, yes.' From Lindgren's intonation, it's hard to tell if this is a question or a challenge.

The descriptions on the manifest insist these pallets contain "fireproof clothing" and the crates are full of "fire-fighting equipment".

The outer packaging is peppered with official-looking government stamps. Unusually, the whole consignment is marked as destined for a specified warehouse. Via Quentin, Lindgren tells them the rest of the ship's cargo is bound elsewhere.

It's obvious the captain is puzzled by their sudden interest in these particular items. Quentin tries to reassure him in Swedish. From the few words Nero can identify, he seems to be telling him how the city has an urgent problem with too many flammable materials. Fortunately, being a fair few drinks ahead of them, the captain appears to be more or less happy to go along with this nonsense.

In any event, the emergency situation had caught the crew off-guard and they seem delighted with this opportunity to off-load this inconvenient cargo in order to be on their way. It's agreed that the consignment is of a modest enough size for the ship's own derricks to complete the task of unloading without the need for any of the dockside cranes.

Nero pulls Andersen aside. 'These are difficult times, I'm sure you'd agree.'

Andersen nods. 'Once we've got these goods unloaded, they'll need to be secured for the time being in one of your bonded warehouses,' Nero tells him. 'Under the current circumstances, it's the safest place for them to be stored.'

Andersen continues to nod. 'Shouldn't be a problem.'

Nero moves a step closer to the man. 'At this critical stage in our investigation, it's vital that no one divulges the whereabouts of any of this evidence – not to anyone,' he whispers, 'under any circumstances. Once we've got them safely inside the warehouse, I'd like you and Svensson to stand guard outside while we gather some samples for testing. We don't want to arouse any undue suspicion but I'd prefer to leave my officers in place around the harbour perimeter.'

Andersen looks at him with blood-shot eyes. 'I understand the need for s-secrecy, Inspector.' The word secrecy had a worrying slur to it.

'Good man.' Nero pats him on the back. 'My colleague and I will need to check through the contents of these crates.'

'You'll need a sharp knife and couple of crowbars,' Andersen says, looking marginally more alert.

Once the stevedores and crew have unloaded Hold Five, Nero allows Quentin to take charge of the warehousing process. He's exhausted both physically and mentally and, as an excuse to sit down for a few precious minutes, he goes back to the office with the port officers to complete the necessary paperwork making sure nothing would look out of the ordinary to a searching eye.

Within minutes, Quentin appears in the doorway. 'It's all ready for you now, Inspector.'

Getting to his feet, Nero turns to Andersen. 'I'm sure you appreciate our need to get this important evidence back to DSD tonight.'

'We'll keep watch outside like you asked, won't we Svensson?'

Nero smiles for the two port officers. 'DSD really appreciate all the help you've given us tonight.'

'Happy to do our duty.' Andersen's face grows redder still. 'Let's hope you catch the bastards you're looking for.'

The bonded warehouse is only half full and seems to contain mostly crates of imported alcohol. The two stevedores have carefully stacked all the pallets to the right, leaving the nearest one easily accessible. By contrast, the wooden crates are spread out so that they can randomly break open any they care to.

Nero makes sure the door is firmly shut behind them. The lighting level is less than ideal. 'Start with the pallets,' he says, sitting down on a crate of what purports to be Jamaican rum.

Quentin doesn't argue. He produces a flashlight and props it up at an angle that will shine the most light on whatever is about to be revealed. Nero watches him cut through the thick outer straps. The decoy takes more care when slicing through the various layers of plastic that protect the contents.

Both men turn at a sudden noise from outside. Nero hears several raised voices. 'Stay here,' he tells Quentin as he moves towards the door. Outside a serious sounding altercation is in progress. Nero slips a hand inside his coat to locate the weapon he'd been hiding for all those years.

Forty-Six

Bruno doesn't foresee himself running into trouble with the security forces, though, as always, he can't trust to foresight alone.

As a precaution, he hikes a couple of kilometres up into the foothills behind the university. It's rough terrain, hard to see more than a step in front of him despite the ambient light coming off the fallen snow.

He reaches an area that's too steep and inaccessible for any patrol vehicles. No more delays – this is it.

'Hæ, Ása.' Though his legs are shaking, he makes his tone light, matter-of-fact. 'It's Bruno, otherwise known as Salvatore, aka The Salvo. Remember me?'

'You,' she says. 'You're still alive then.'

He sits down at the edge of a rocky outcrop. Concentrating hard on the blank surface between his feet, he prays his AVR stud will allow him to read her thoughts again.

Where's the little shit been hiding?

Did she really think that or is he mistaking a guess on his part?

Did he manage to disappear all by himself or did he have help?

Was that her or him?

'I'm alive and kicking,' Bruno says. 'Just wanted to touch base.'

I haven't got time for whatever fokking game he's playing.

He's sure that last one was no guess. Before she can interrupt, he says, 'You might recall, this stud – the one you gave me – is pretty damned cool. My location is totally untraceable, although I'm sure you're busy testing that theory as we speak.' He tries a laugh, but it comes out too fake. 'I promise you won't find me – so I'd suggest you don't even bother looking.'

What the hell is this stupid kid playing at now? Bruno can feel her emotions in the roots of his hair. Her rising anger begins to infect his thoughts like some deadly virus colonising his brain. To get the full picture, he'll have to ratchet things up. Better brace himself.

'I expect you're wondering where that tame bulldog of yours could have got to?'

She's not slow to get the reference. Still she says, 'I really have no idea what you're blathering about or what you want.'

'I'm referring to our mutual friend Kleiner – although it's true to say he was nobody's friend. Let's agree to call him our mutual acquaintance Kleiner, shall we?'

'What about him?'

He waits ten more maddening seconds. 'Spit it out,' she finally says.

'I know for a fact that you won't be seeing his smiling features again unless you're planning to take a trip to the city morgue.'

If Kleiner is dead, how could he possibly know that? Has to be bluffing – repeating some rumour he's heard.

'I'm being a touch insensitive,' Bruno says. 'I suppose he was your colleague. I imagine you might have been fond of him in the same way you must have feelings for your vixens.'

Shit! He'd hit one hell of a nerve with that one. 'I'm sure you want to take a moment to mourn his passing,' he says, hoping to disguise his shock at what she's done. Right now he needs to distract her from that line of thought and everything it's leading back to. 'Anyway, I thought we should have a chat about it – just the two of us.'

She's about to break the connection; he needs to get her attention fast. 'I know for sure Kleiner's dead. I was the one who killed him.'

She's not buying it.

'Of course I had to improvise a little.' Bruno recalls the swaggering surety of those old movie gangsters, the way they talk when they have the upper hand. 'The thing everyone forgets about a weapon like the Glock 19 - 9 millimeter, is that it can still be surprisingly effective when it comes to putting a hole through a man's chest.'

She's beginning to believe him. His goading sends her thoughts running in every direction at once. At last he can fully enter her mind, experience every impulse as she wrestles with that primary, driving instinct of hers to extract revenge on whoever crosses her; in this case – him.

He screws up his courage and plunges deeper and it's like diving into a toxic well – his whole body begins to shake as he plumbs the mad extent of her ambition. He's drowning, his brain barely coping with the circularity when her thoughts become his. At the heart of all that anger, one overarching concern – she's about to embark on the next step of her plan and can't afford this distraction, however tempting.

'I'm wondering just how a non-entity like you might get your hands on an antique weapon like that,' she says.

Her suspicions break into his consciousness. She's calculating, speculating. She'd sent Kleiner to the university to kill that poor girl for reasons he now understands. Her next guess is that he must have been hiding out on the campus all this time. Logic takes her from that to the information she'd received about the two bodies found at the university. She's certain now that one of them must have been Kleiner.

He's overwhelmed by the knowledge of what she's already done and what she's intending to do, his head heavy with the weight of all the new information in his brain.

Ása is bringing herself under control; conquering her rage

as she makes the surprisingly sane decision that she needs to prioritise. 'If you really did kill Kleiner, why would you call me?' Her suspicions are fully aroused.

'Hard to explain.' He forces the separation, pulling himself back into his own consciousness. 'You know how it is with young men of my age. We often seek the recognition and approval of people we've come to regard as parental figures, in an odd kind of way.'

'Horse shit.' Her words are heavy with contempt. 'You're deliberately wasting my time.'

'Wait a second – I just wanted to tell you about a few plans I have of my own. I feel sure you'd like to know what they are. You're bound to be impressed by the final outcome.' The stud connection is already dead.

He needs to tell Nero – he'll know what to do.

Forty-Seven

Nero cracks open the warehouse door. Looking out, he's relieved to see Kass in the centre of the commotion. The two port officials have their guns trained on her. 'I'm a police officer, for Christ's sake,' she says, holding up her open ID badge along with her weapon. 'I assume you can read.'

'It's alright, everything's okay,' he tells them. 'This woman is one of my team.'

'As I've explained to these gentlemen several times now.' Kass glares at each of the men in turn.

Andersen and Svensson finally lower their weapons and stand down. They must have been spooked that she's dressed from head to toe in black and has no markings on her body armour to indicate she's a police officer.

'Well done and thanks for your vigilance,' Nero says, clapping Andersen on the back.

Kass waits for both men to fully holster their weapons before she lowers her hands. There's something odd about her appearance. Nero realises she's not wearing her glasses. Without them, she's less distinctive – which has to be a good thing. At the same time, she looks younger and more vulnerable. He wonders again if he was right to drag her into all of this.

She glares at him, her cheeks flushed with unspent anger and with that determined crease in her brow. Looking down, he can see the bulge at her ankle where she's strapped on that lethal hunting knife of hers. It's not like this woman can't handle herself in a fight.

The port officers continue to stand guard outside while Nero ushers her into the warehouse. 'I'd more or less given up on you,' he says, once the door is shut behind them.

'How exactly did you expect me to get here on foot in under an hour? I've had a hell of a job dodging all the extra patrols from DSD to here.'

'It's good to see you. Thank you for coming,' he says, like she might be some guest arriving at a party.

By way of further explanation, he leads her over to the lit-up area of the warehouse where Quentin is busy unwrapping the top bale. 'This is Quentin,' Nero says. 'Quentin, this is Kass, the colleague I told you about.'

The decoy nods to acknowledge Kass though, still bent on his task, he barely looks up. The stench of all that booze and worse is coming off him.

Kass gives Nero a long questioning look. 'This man's a decoy officer,' Nero says, as if that might explain everything.

'The men out there seem to think there's been a murder.' Kass looks around her. 'We're inside a bonded warehouse. Correct me if I'm wrong but I'm not seeing a corpse or any signs of anything we, as homicide officers, need to investigate with such urgency.'

'I had to pretend this was a high-profile murder investigation or they wouldn't have gone along with it,' Nero tells her.

Kass looks like she might pull her weapon on him at any minute. 'I need you to tell me right now, why at this ungodly hour and instead of being on sick leave, you're down here under false pretences without even logging your movements with the department and in the middle of a fokking curfew?' There's a pause before she adds: 'Sir.'

'Look, we're pretty certain we've intercepted an illegal shipment,' Nero says. 'If Quentin's intelligence is correct, all this lot here was destined straight for Double Red Zone.'

'An illegal shipment?' Kass keeps shaking her head. 'If that's the case, I don't see why the port authorities can't handle it. Why the hell do we need to intervene?'

Touching her arm, Nero feels the full extent of her anger run through his hand. 'It's not as simple as that,' he says.

'Perhaps you could–'

'Careful – there might be some sort of booby trap inside,' Nero shouts.

The decoy ignores him and continues to peel away the final layer of wrapping. 'Voila!' With no sign of caution, he plunges both hands inside. 'Would you take a look at this?' He lifts something clear of the bundle. 'It seems the rumours were true.' He holds it up to the beam of the flashlight. 'This is extraordinary.'

Nero still can't see what he's holding. He moves closer. Between Quentin's outstretched hands, something catches the light and then disappears again. Reaching out, Nero touches a surface that's cool and smooth. 'There's bound to be a more technical name for these,' Nero says, 'but I believe what we're looking at is essentially a whole consignment of state-of-the-art, invisibility suits.'

'Unbelievable!' Quentin says. 'And there must be dozens of them in this one bundle alone.'

Nero turns to Kass. 'You remember Dr Bjarnadóttir tried to analyse that scrap of material we found at the Double Red scene.'

'She said she'd never seen anything like it.' Kass slowly extends her fingers towards the material as if it might be red hot.

'After seeing the projection from the massacre in Section Five,' Nero tells Quentin, 'Jóra Bjarnadóttir believed the suit that perp was wearing must have been covered in sensors, each one reading the pixels of the space they occupied. The surface of the garment you're holding would appear to collect and emit light in a way that cloaks the person inside, rendering them invisible to the human eye.'

'That's not the best part,' Kass says, finally running her hand over the material. 'Those sensors must be bonded to something incredibly strong. We've seen proof that, wearing one of these, incoming fire is deflected straight back. The decoy murders will have provided the perfect demonstration of just how effective they are.'

'Unwittingly or not, they couldn't have advertised them better,' Nero says. He turns to Quentin. 'If someone makes the mistake of firing their weapon at a person wearing one of these, they're highly likely to be committing suicide.'

Quentin stands up with his arms outstretched. 'This thing's quite heavy, but then I guess that's what you'd expect.'

'And someone's ordered enough to equip a small army.' Nero tries to calculate the dimensions of the twenty-three other bundles besides this one. 'Looks like they're planning a fancy dress party to end all others.'

Forty-Eight

Keeping her body loose to take the impact, Chan lets go. She drops down into the hole, landing upright on her feet. The decoy had been telling the truth about that much at least.

The ground is softer than she'd been expecting. Though it's impossible to see anything to her left or right, a thin light is filtering down through the open hatch above her head. From the tool marks just visible on the curved walls surrounding her, it's clear she's inside a man-made tunnel. The air is stale and slightly sulphurous and she wonders if it's totally safe to breathe. Somewhere nearby water is rhythmically dripping into a pool.

Several vixens poke their muzzles over the edge to peer down at her. Their white bibs stand out in the darkness in a way that would be endearing if it weren't for the eerie glimmer of their eyes as they catch the light.

A low throaty growl issues from one; as it grows louder, the others join in; a couple begin to yelp like dogs.

'Quiet!' the decoy shouts and they shut up instantly.

Everything grows dimmer overhead. 'Are you okay down there?'

'Yes. I'm fine.'

'Good. Now stand well back.' Though she resents having orders barked at her, Chan complies.

Foxes begin to leap through the hatch, one after the other like lemmings dropping off a cliff edge. They keep coming – so many and so rapidly she gives up trying to keep track of them. Each one lands on its feet with barely a sound. Once or twice she feels a soft pelt brush up against her.

Standing in the dead centre of the whole milling pack, she feels the heat rising off their backs. Their sharp stink hits her throat – so overpowering she has to fight her gag reflex. Unease creeps up the back of her neck. Are these the same vixens that ripped apart all those bodies in the Red Zone? She stands ridged, arms tucked in, desperately wanting to put a hand to her face to block out the smell but afraid any movement might provoke them.

The rectangle of light above her narrows and she sees two legs floating before her in mid-air. 'Support me,' the decoy says. 'You came out here to find me, now make yourself useful. Come on. Don't just stand there – grab my fokking legs while I shut this thing.'

Foxes are pressing in all around her. A rumbling growl issues from the nearest vixens' throats as Chan pushes through them towards the decoy. With those dangling legs barely visible, it's not easy to decide where she should take hold of her.

The full weight of the decoy is suddenly in her arms, despite her slight figure, she's really heavy. A loud thump, then the last vestige of light disappears leaving the two of them in a strange embrace.

She lets go her grip; there's a soft thud as the decoy lands on the ground in front of her.

The woman's hot breath is on her face. 'Follow me,' she says. 'And make sure you keep up.' The foxes jostle Chan as they stream past, brushing against her as if she were merely an obstacle to be navigated around.

And then she's alone in complete darkness. Should she try to re-open the hatch? Call out? Take her chances with the patrol? No. She's taken so many risks, come so far to track this decoy down at long last. Her nerve can't fail her before she's seen this through to the end – whatever that turns out to be.

'Wait! I can't see a thing.' Her hands grope the rough walls.

'You'll get used to it.' The voice is faint – already some distance away. 'The eyes adjust.'

'Where are we going?' No reply this time. Chan remembers the infrareds still hanging round her neck. Given all the geothermic energy in the area, they ought to be able to pick up enough warmth from the surrounding earth to reveal the sides of the tunnel.

With the goggles in place, she can see the way forward. A glowing, rat-shaped silhouette crosses her path. She watches its cartoon-style form stop to sniff the air. Without breaking step, she kicks at it and the rat squeals as it scuttles out of her field of vision. Chan shudders; she's pretty certain those things live in colonies.

Round the next corner, she glimpses the pale green flank of a running vixen. Sweat now soaking her back, she sprints hard to catch up. Her stud directional readout suggests the tunnel is taking them eastwards.

Splashing through ankle deep water, she rounds another bend before finally catching sight of the pack stretched out in a line in front of her, their bodies glowing like phantoms, the ends of their brush tails hardly visible.

She can't see the decoy, but the woman is picking up the pace, each vixen bounding to keep up. Somewhere in her research she'd read that red foxes are able to run at speeds of around 38 kilometres per hour. To match their stride, Chan has to sprint. Heads down, the vixens trail out behind their pack leader.

After twenty minutes of hard running, Chan finally makes out a glimmer up ahead. Is this journey's end? This particular light at the end of the tunnel may not be a good thing.

The animals in front of her stop dead and she almost collides with the tail end of one. Its ghost-green face turns, mouth open, the dead disks of its eyes lock onto her as it gives a long, howling shriek that could almost be human – a woman calling out in distress. Amplified by the nearness of the walls, the pitch of its cry sets her ears ringing. The rest of the pack responds with answering calls, forcing Chan to block her ears.

The din stops in a single beat. Chan lowers her hands, welcoming the silence. It's broken by the sound of footsteps approaching. Despite the narrowness of the passageway, the whole pack gives way, each animal pressing itself hard against the rock-face.

The approaching shadow begins to take the shape of a person. Chan hopes it's the decoy she's been following – the devil she knows seems preferable right now.

No body heat is escaping from whoever it is. From the negative space between the vixens and the tunnel wall, Chan tries to estimate the height and build of the person coming straight for her.

She thinks back to those holo images she'd studied so closely after the second mass killings. From the slightness and height of the person bearing down on her, she guesses it's a woman. She's not sure if that's a good or a bad thing.

Chan remembers the discussion she and Nero had with Dr Zhender and how they'd agreed on the obvious differences between the two attacks. All the evidence suggested the massacres were the work of two different female decoys. The Orange Zone murders had displayed all the hallmarks of an impassioned attack that might have been an act of revenge while the first one had been far more cold and calculating – most likely carried out by someone with a fully psychopathic personality.

'Constable Chan.' A statement – the two words electronically reconstructed in that now familiar shrill pitch.

The shadow comes to a stop a few metres in front of her.

Though the woman's face is covered, Chan gets the feeling she's being surveyed from head to toe. 'Odd that we should meet at long last in such unlikely circumstances.' No distortion this time.

She's fairly certain this isn't the same decoy. 'Who are you?'

'Let's just say I'm someone who's been interested in making your acquaintance for some time.'

'Well then maybe you'd like to introduce yourself.'

'Don't worry your pretty head about that now. I guarantee you'll recognise my face when the time is right for full introductions.' She catches all the menace in her voice. The first decoy was scary enough; this one's in another league. It's not difficult to imagine the figure in front of her slaughtering all those people in the Red Zone. The dark shape comes closer, blurring Chan's vision. 'You're wearing a fokking stud.' A hand comes out of nowhere to rip the device from her ear. She hears it splinter and fragment on the floor of the tunnel and presumes it's been ground to nothing under this woman's foot.

'There was no need for that.' Chan can't disguise her anger.

'On the contrary, there was every need. From now on you'll do exactly what I tell you to. I should stress that any deviation from my instructions will be fatal.' She gives a short snarl of a laugh. 'To you, that is.'

Forty-Nine

Quentin continues to stare at the object in his hands like a man enthralled. When Kass steps forward to pull the next garment from the bundle, Nero notices a change in the decoy's body language – the way he's adjusted his stance as if he's guarding the consignment.

'Wow,' Kass says, holding another suit up to the torchlight. 'Imagine what you could do wearing one of these.'

Her enthusiasm fuels Nero's growing sense of uneasiness. 'I think we all appreciate these things are game changers.' He has to breathe through a sharp pain in his chest. 'What we need to remember is – this is no game.'

'Okay, point taken.' Quentin hasn't looked up once. 'Still, it would be fun to see exactly what these things can do.' He could be talking about taking some new vehicle for a spin.

Both Quentin and Kass are now holding the garments up against themselves, clearly eager to try them on for size. 'I'm looking for the switch that turns it on,' Kass says. 'Imagine being totally invisible.' Her face is animated in a way Nero's rarely seen. 'At the same time, wearing this thing, you have guaranteed supremacy against anyone who threatens you or happens to get in your way.'

'Kitted out in these, a militia force would be unstoppable.' Nero's mind races ahead. 'Multiply that by several factors and it would be like the Romans against the Celts or the Mongolian hordes conquering Asia all over again.'

'Or Sauron holding the One Ring,' Kass says, slipping her hand into a sleeve.

Nero rubs at his forehead. 'I'm being serious. With your militia wearing these, you'd be in complete control. Might would be right and all that Ragnar Redbeard style bilge.'

Kass withdraws her hand from the material. 'I get what you're saying.' She looks up at Nero and then across to Quentin. It's obvious she instinctively distrusts this decoy and her instincts are usually good.

As if released from a spell, Quentin claps Nero on the shoulder. Still gripping the garment with his other hand, his expression is all bonhomie. 'Forget all that philosophical crap and cheer up, will you. All this lot is ours now and we're the good guys, remember.'

A cold sensation spreads across Nero's scalp. Being under the other man's grip is far from pleasant. The hand resting on his shoulder is the same one that held the weapon to Rashid's head as he knelt on that icy ground, unarmed.

'Let's see what's in the other half of the shipment,' Nero says. Quentin's hand falls easily from his shoulder. Relieved to distance himself from the decoy, he walks over to the stacked-up crates.

The torchlight picks up the two crowbars lying on the warehouse floor, where the port officers had dropped them earlier. Looked at from one direction, Nero sees they form the shape of the Christian cross. Tilting his head another way, they could be crossed spears barring the way. With no warning, his vision becomes fragmented, his legs weaken and then his mind floods with too many images at once.

Closing his eyes against the onslaught, Nero gropes for the nearest crate and slumps down heavily on it. A hot energy floods his body, taking him past the pain threshold.

'Are you alright?' Her voice is already long way off. 'Nero!'

His inner vision sharpens on the image of Bruno. Every inch of the boy is clear – the way his skin remains tanned and freckled despite the climate here, that fringe that's always falling into his eyes like he's hoping to hide behind it.

The boy's mouth opens and he begins to speak but Nero can't grasp what he's saying. Disjointed words enter his head; he tries to piece them together like he had to when he first arrived here with only broken English. 'I can't understand you,' he tells him.

'I said, are you alright, Inspector?' Kass interrupts.

'Shh! I want to hear what he's saying.'

'Dammit, he's using his stud. I thought we weren't taking that risk.' Quentin's voice –far too close.

'Nero's not a fool. Besides, look at the way his eyelids are flickering.'

'Is he having some kind of fit? Is he epileptic?'

Concentrate, Nero. I said, we need to get there as fast as we can. You know the place – that disused factory I told you about.

'Don't be a bloody fool, boy. Go home. This whole situation is far too dangerous.'

'Who does he think he's talking to?'

You old men worry too much. Besides, I've got a handgun.

'That stupid thing's not going to get you out of trouble. For God's sake you've no fokking idea what you're up against here.'

Tut tut, Uncle Nero. Using a profanity right after taking the Lord's name in vain. I thought you were brought up a good catholic.

'This is hardly the time for jokes.'

That's where you're wrong – this is exactly when they're necessary. Besides, I know what we're up against and what they're planning next. The three of you better come *prepared. I suggest you bring a crazy amount of weapons like those guys in The Matrix.*

'This is no movie. Besides, where am I supposed to get my hands on them?'

Are you kidding me? You're sitting on a whole arsenal right now. Open that crate under your arse and you'll see what I mean.

Oh – and hold off on the moralising for a bit – those suits are going to come in handy so bring a couple of spares. You know where to meet me. Gotta go now.

'Wait dammit! Who are the other ones for?'

'Wait for what, Nero?' He opens his eyes onto Kass's concerned face. Without her glasses, her pale blue eyes seem far too exposed.

'Wait until this is over before you ask me any questions,' he says.

Quentin is staring at him, unblinking; the suspicion is mutual.

Sensation is returning to his legs and Nero finds he can stand up, though he gives himself a moment to make sure the blood has returned to his legs. Taking a few steps, he's relieved to find his body once again fully under his control.

Bruno has convinced him they have to act fast. He picks up one of the crowbars and weighs it in his hand. 'Right – let's get this crate open.' Once he's cut the bands binding the crate, he can see the top is simply nailed down in the usual fashion. He inserts the narrowest end of the bar under the first plank and levers it partway up.

'You're obviously not well; let me do that,' Kass says. 'Why don't you rest for a minute?'

'No time,' he tells her. 'Besides, I feel great.' It's true – it may just be the adrenaline but he's never felt better. 'If you want to help, there's another crowbar on the floor over there.' The wood is already beginning to split under the pressure.

'Why this sudden rush?' Quentin demands. 'What's in these crates?'

'You'll see,' Nero says. They've almost got the top off. With Kass levering along the other side, the lid finally springs free and clatters to the floor. The two of them begin to remove the layers of protective materials underneath.

'We'll need to tell Andersen and Svensson that we're taking certain items away for testing,' Nero tells Kass. 'I'll persuade them to lock this place down under maximum security.' He grabs her arm. 'Before we leave here, we have to convince them not to divulge the whereabouts of this little lot to anyone no matter how official or persistent they are. Those two stevedores are the weakest link but they're going off duty very soon.'

Quentin blocks his light. 'Hang on a minute; do you really think those two outside are up to the task?' He gestures towards the door. 'Ne ovat idiootteja.'

'I'm sure you agreed we have to stop all this stuff getting into the wrong hands,' Nero says.

'Then maybe *we* need to stay here and fokking guard it.' Quentin scowls at him. Judging by the deep lines on his forehead, it's the expression he's happiest with. 'If you two want to go chasing around, I'll stay here.'

'No; you're coming with us. We need boots on the ground.'

Nero looks up half expecting to see the decoy standing over him with a raised crowbar. Instead, he's peering into the crate. 'So what's in Pandora's box then?'

They remove the final layer of packing and Nero pulls out the first weapon he sees.

'Fokk! Is that really an RST 50?' Kass is thrilled; this unknown Secret Santa appears to have delivered everything on her wish list. 'I've never actually seen one of those – not in the flesh, as it were.'

'Holy Christ!' Quentin says. 'Someone must have been planning a small war.'

Nero turns the sleek body of the weapon over before checking its sights. 'Once the safety blocks are removed, this thing should be ready to fire,' he says. Reassuringly, the gauge on the side of the grip is at max. 'We won't be able to test them – too dangerous in a confined space.'

'You're right,' Quentin says. 'And the patrols will be onto us right away if we fire outside.' The decoy's face is lit up with excitement.

'In your line of work,' Nero says, 'I expect you've become familiar with the underground network.'

'I've never dared use any of those tunnels myself but I know where some of the entrances are. Rumour has it, there's quite a warren down there.'

'Then your help would be invaluable because that's where we're heading.' Nero looks from Kass to the decoy. 'Now would be a good time to opt out.'

'You've got to be kidding,' Kass says, shaking her head before turning her attention back to the contents of the crate.

By way of an answer, Quentin says, 'Let's see what else is in here.'

While they pull out more weapons, Nero throws off his coat and straps one of the holsters across his chest. 'You should choose whatever weapons you feel most comfortable with.' The RST fits snugly beside his heart.

Quentin smirks at him – his mouth pulled unnaturally sideways. 'If we're going down the rabbit hole, we'll need to be armed not just to the teeth but to the eyeballs and beyond.'

'Better make that the hairline then.' Kass pulls out a much smaller weapon. 'Will you look here? I believe I'm holding an Aries 12 – tiny but just as deadly. Oh yes – there's a place for this little beauty on my ankle.'

Fifty

There may be no other way to get to the factory, given the curfew; still Bruno loathes being down in these fokking tunnels again. He hates how narrow and damp they are but, more particularly, the way they smell – like the worst ever case of halitosis.

He's jogging along, pleased to be making good time. Whenever he gets to an intersection, he's forced to stop. Turning off his torch helps him to visualise the right way forward. It's unsettling to be standing there alone in such complete darkness and silence. He even welcomes the faint sound of his own breathing, the distant drip of water – anything that reminds him he might still be alive.

Though he's going the opposite way, he's remembering the route well enough, especially this particular section where he can't run and is forced to crouch down. Coming the other way, those sick bastards, Ármannsson and Kleiner, had enjoyed watching him suffer. This time, he knows exactly where to duck for the low slabs of rock.

Being down here with nothing to distract him, intensifies the images in his head. To keep everything straight in his mind, it's important that he separates the on-going reality from his visions of events that haven't yet happened. Experience has taught him that precognition is unreliable. There's one guiding principle – the more vividly he sees things, the more he can depend on them happening; if it's just a vague premonition, don't bet on it.

Well, that's a lie: he's placed a few bets on things he's foreseen – ice hockey results, pika bingo in the student bar, which raindrop will reach the windowsill first. Trouble is, the tiniest change of circumstance can alter the course of things in an instant. Perhaps it's just as well he's never made much money at it.

Right now, he's a bit out of breath, knows he's not far from the rendezvous point with Nero and the others and he'll get there some time ahead of them, which logically means he could afford to slow down. On the other hand, something may have happened to alter things in a way he hasn't foreseen and they could already be there waiting for him. All things considered, he'd better crack on.

At last, Bruno is finally approaching the point where the tunnel he's in breaks into the old expressway station. His torch beam picks out the wider space up ahead and then the shining edges of the disused rail. So, this is it, he's made it. He'd been right the first time – there's no sign of the others yet.

No train has run above these mag-tracks for years. Back in the day, this place had been a crowded thoroughfare. It's a perfect choice for a rendezvous, with four separate entrances or, looked at another way, four possible escape routes.

All those people and their journeys – he only has to touch the damp walls to reach into the past.

When the trains stopped running, every entrance to this place was barred and then quickly sealed. Within eighteen months, new, unsanctioned doors were let into all four entranceways. In each case, over a single night, the new doors were painted trompe l'oeil style to perfectly match the original blockwork.

Trompe l'oeil – he's always liked that phrase and how it translates as "deceives the eye". Despite everything, it makes Bruno smile to picture those street artists, dressed head to toe in black, employing such a bourgeois technique. You couldn't help but be impressed that their hurried work still manages to fool the eyes of passing patrol officers.

From where he's standing, provided he can crack the door code – which is hardly challenging – they'll walk up the steps to street level. After that, it's less than half a kilometre to the gates of the factory. They'll be able to make their approach from whichever direction they choose. They? Who's he kidding – Nero will be the one making the decisions.

A shudder runs through Bruno. At least he won't be wandering into the place unarmed and alone – this time, things are going to be a little different.

He jumps down onto the track and clambers over the central rail; has to fight the absurd idea a train might still hit him. Despite walking a short way down the opposite shaft, he can't hear anyone or anything approaching.

Bruno turns around and heads back to wait on the platform next to the tunnel entrance, glad to have this time to prepare for what's coming. It's pleasant to be able to stretch himself out. He could turn summersaults here, although he'd have to learn how to do them first. This is hardly the time to experiment.

If those old security cameras were still working, they'd take him for some deranged commuter who'd been down here all these years, still pacing up and down the platform waiting for a train that will never come.

Running the torch beam along to his left, Bruno picks out the adverts still clinging to the walls. How cool they'd look on his bedroom wall. With those stained patches and frayed edges, anyone could tell they were authentic – the real thing. When they were first plastered up there, provided you could afford it, you could just go out and buy that car or that Swiss watch. The old cell phones are a laugh – just imagine having to carry one of those around with you all the time.

After testing its strength, Bruno sits down on one of the benches. It's not exactly built for comfort. How many people will have sat here waiting to meet a loved one off the next train?

Bruno hears a noise, something scurrying along the tracks just below him. Better not shine a light on whatever creature might be lurking down there. Out of sight and all that.

Just how much should he tell Nero? Now he's regained his strength, it's going to be far harder to keep things from him. Certain information is likely to distract him to the point where it might endanger the rest of them. He's had no practice at keeping what's in his mind from a fellow telepatico. He has a vague memory of playing a game with his mother when he was very young – a variant on Blind Man's Bluff where he tried not to give away where he was hiding. His mother – it's been a long time since he thought of her.

He stands up and bends forward to listen. Hearing nothing, he walks to the other end of the bench and sits down again. Telepatico – how he hates what they'd done to that word, changing it into a label for people like him so they could be treated like they were only half human. The scientists were the worst – forcibly detaining dozens of innocent people in their facilities to study them like they were animals. How much easier to cross the line when you can claim you're just furthering science. Look at all those Nazi doctors – the appalling things they did.

It makes Bruno angry every time he thinks about his encounter in the corridor with Dr Arthur. The man couldn't keep that smug expression from his face as he revelled in his elevated standing – the respected senior academic. He'd lapped up Bruno's supposed hero-worship. Standing there in that corridor, the man had been completely unaware that, thanks to their handshake, his dark deeds were no longer a secret. Bruno had really struggled to hide his disgust at what Dr Arthur had got up to over the years. It's vital Nero doesn't find out any of that stuff – at least for the time being, but how can he keep those things from him?

Remembering that children's game, Bruno decides to visualise a room in his mind where he can put all that dangerous knowledge for the time being. Yes, that's exactly what he'll do – drag that stuff, and every thought he's had about it, into a room inside his head and lock the damned door. Aren't men supposed to be good at compartmentalising? How difficult can it be?

Bruno shuts his eyes and begins the process of depositing that knowledge inside a small panic room in his brain. He shuts the door and turns the key in its sturdy lock. He even pictures himself nailing a sign to the front: DON'T, UNDER ANY CIRCUMSTANCES, OPEN THIS UNTIL YOU'RE SURE IT IS SAFE TO DO SO.

Fifty-One

They make their way up to the surface at last. Chan is relieved to be above ground and breathing in pure, cold air. She fills her lungs until her head is reeling.

Caught off guard, she's stunned when her infrared goggles are pulled from her head along with some of her hair. 'You won't be needing these.' She hears them land some distance away.

'Oww! There was no fokking need for that.'

'I suggest you remember the position you're in.' She's not sure which one of them said that. 'Things will go a lot easier for you if you bear that in mind.' That time, it was definitely the one on the left. Chan swallows her outrage, reminds herself that at least one of these decoys is likely to be a fully psychopathic, serial killer.

Without her stud, she can only guess their current location. Everything from the shuttered buildings, the compacted snow and paltry street lighting suggests they're well inside the Orange Zone.

Without seeming to be told to, the trotting vixens silently disperse; she watches the last of them disappear up a side alley. It's impossible not to be impressed. Chan is certain they'll continue to shadow their decoy from a distance exactly as they're trained to.

It occurs to her that, though she hadn't been able to count the animals, their numbers certainly didn't double when the other decoy – the psycho one – arrived. So where is her pack?

They're out in the open with more light but Chan can no longer make out her two companions. They must have switched their suits to invisibility mode. To the casual viewer, she would appear to be walking alone.

Bizarrely, their footsteps are visible in the snow on either side of her. Guided by these, she can just make out a faint line of disruption, nothing more than a ripple in the air. 'This way.' She can't say which one just pushed her in the back.

They continue on through the deserted streets, passing mostly low-rise buildings. Every door is firmly shut, blinds down, no light escaping from any of the windows.

As the only one visible has become the transgressor – an obvious target for any passing patrol: not exactly a comforting thought. Looked at another way, from ground level, she's sandwiched between the two of them, protected in part by their extraordinary suits.

Where are they taking her? More importantly, why the hell is she still alive? If they'd executed her back there in one of those tunnels, it's likely her body would never be found. They know her profession; despite her junior rank, and however unlikely, they must believe she can be some sort of use to them.

They appear to be heading towards an unlit alleyway running between high walls. She's had quite enough of confined spaces tonight, is tempted to stand her ground and refuse to go in there but after another shove to her back, she decides it might be better to comply.

On both sides the walls close in. Here and there the snow has melted into shallow puddles. In the confined space, the sound of the leading decoy's footsteps rings out. Chan can see lights up ahead.

They clear the alley and are once again out in the open and nearing what appears to be an old industrial estate. The cracked concrete between the crumbling buildings has almost been reclaimed by nature.

Chan is alarmed that they're walking directly towards a row of bright lights illuminating a high security fence. Under the harsh light, if it weren't for their advancing footprints in the snow, it would be impossible to detect either of the decoys.

The fence is chain-link and way too high to climb. It's protecting a block of mostly single-storey buildings. From the brickwork on the walls, she'd say these must have been constructed a century or more ago. Most of the windows have been smashed and ungifted street artists have daubed every single wall. The rooftops are all blanketed in snow.

This fence must have been an afterthought – almost certainly put in place to prevent the building being occupied for nefarious activities, which means it's highly likely she's right about them still being in Orange Zone. In the Red Zones, no one would be concerned about such goings on and in any case, so easily visible to a passing satellite, these lights would have been turned off a long time ago.

Chan notices the snow cover is sparser over one section of buildings. Given the poor insulation standards of this old type of construction, it suggests those particular buildings are still occupied – at least on an occasional basis.

Above the entrance gate, a faded sign reads: *Sveinsson & Kjarval Ltd.* Below that, in smaller letters: *makers of.* Graffiti – the usual obscenities – obscures whatever it was this place used to manufacture.

A few more shoves to her back direct Chan around the perimeter to where a section of the fence is just a fraction looser than the rest. The wire rattles as it's pushed aside by an unseen hand. She has no choice but to squeeze through the narrow opening into the old factory yard.

Looking over her shoulder, Chan sees the fence has already been repositioned. With the next fall of snow, no one will be able to tell they were ever here.

The footsteps of the leading decoy continue in a line in front of her like some kind of conjuring trick or one of those old flea circuses she'd read about somewhere. To avoid more shoves to her back, Chan follows the trail to a door that's slightly ajar. Its hinges groan; it appears to open automatically, the gap wide enough to admit one person at a time.

They're inside a building with a very high roof. Every sound echoes. Their boots crunch over the broken glass from all those smashed windows. The place smells of mould and neglect. Further in, there's a strong whiff of urine and then stomach-turning fox shit.

'This way.' Her eyes have adjusted enough for her to pick out the tall rectangle of the doorway. Chan follows the voice through this into a dark passageway that leads them into another high-roofed building. More broken glass underfoot; the shards twinkle as they catch the fugitive light from the two rows of skylights let into the roof.

'Wait here. I'd advise you not to get any ideas, my pack have followed us into the building.' That time it sounded like the first decoy speaking; the one who would appear to be marginally more sane. She hadn't been aware of the vixens behind them, so perhaps they used another entrance.

Left alone and overcome with exhaustion, she finds a patch of floor that's free of glass and almost falls down onto it. Above her, through the broken skylight, there's just a handful of stars. So still up there and so very beautiful. It's possible this could be her last night on earth.

Fifty-Two

Nero is some distance ahead of the others. The walls of the tunnel begin to widen out and then he glimpses the old expressway station.

He steps through the jagged hole in the wall and spots Bruno sitting on one of the platform's benches. The boy doesn't move. He appears to be gazing straight ahead at the track – maybe asleep, maybe just lost in thought. Then his head jerks up and he rakes that over-long fringe of his aside and smiles. 'So, what kept you?'

Nero is glad to see him. Slapping the boy's back, he's surprised by the genuine affection passing between them. It comes to him that whatever their genetic connection turns out to be, the two of them are irrevocably family now.

Despite the warm greeting, Bruno seems reluctant to look him directly in the eye. The boy is troubled by something more than the situation they're in. Holding him at arm's length by the shoulders, he asks, 'Is everything– '

'Well, if it isn't the boy wonder.' It's impossible to see Kass with her torch beam dazzling them both. Nero holds up a hand to shade his eyes. When she lowers her flashlight, Quentin is standing there right alongside her. Together they clamber over the disused rail.

'Good; we're all here,' Nero says.

'Hi, Kass.' Bruno raises a hand to greet her. He looks them all up and down. 'How come you're not wearing the suits?'

To avert their suspicions, Nero quickly says, 'I've just been telling the boy about our find.'

He turns around to show Bruno the hefty pack he's carrying. 'We found these things were surprisingly awkward to run in.'

Kass hefts off her own pack to the ground. 'Once you begin to exert yourself, they make you sweat and I'm talking bonkers amounts. We soon realised why these backpacks were in with them.' Sniffs her own armpit, she pulls a face. 'I smell pretty ripe.'

'Let's face it, you stink like musk ox,' Bruno tells her. 'You all do. I just didn't like to say anything. Let's hope they can't smell you coming.'

Kass raises her middle finger at him. She turns from the boy to the decoy. 'You've probably guessed this little runt here is Bruno. Bruno meet Quentin – he's a decoy.'

Quentin nods an acknowledgement. 'I gather Cavallo thinks you're some sort whizz kid.'

Instead of a simple nod, Bruno strides over to shake the decoy's hand far too vigorously. It had to be a deliberate ploy to try to read the man's thoughts. Nero doubts he'll get a lot from him given they're both wearing gloves. 'Good to meet you,' Bruno says, prolonging the contact. Should have been more careful to keep that edge from his voice.

'Likewise.' The decoy drops his smile along with the boy's hand.

Bruno finally makes eye contact with Nero. *Don't trust him. He could be playing both sides.*

I have my own doubts. He doesn't seem particularly curious about where we're going so I think he's already figured that part out.

Nero puts his backpack down on the bench and unzips the main compartment. 'This is yours.' Taking the weight of the extra suit, he hands it to Bruno. 'Had to guess the size.'

'You shouldn't have.' The boy holds the whole thing up to the light with an air of reverence. 'Wow! This is subzero. Look at that – it's amazing how it's sort of there and not there at the same time.' *How can we keep tabs on each other with these on?*

You'll see.

'And that's just when it's turned off,' Kass says.

'These things may be a technological miracle, but they're not infallible,' Nero tells him. 'If you look really hard, you can see a sort of disruption in the air when the person wearing the suit moves.'

'Is it a bit like the T-Rex in that film?' Bruno says. 'You remember, when the scientist bloke says, "He can't see you if you don't move".'

'Sadly, I think they've since disproved all that stuff about the T-Rex,' Kass says.

'Someone once told me owls see mostly by movement,' Bruno says. 'Although maybe it was toads.'

'It's not a sort of now-you-see-me-now-you-don't situation,' Quentin cuts in, clearly exasperated. 'You don't need to stay still to be invisible. When you're moving around, other people get visually confused, that's all.'

Nero exchanges a look with the boy. *Tonight's not the first time he's seen these things in action.*

'Moving on,' Nero says, 'Once the hood is in place, its electronics integrate with your stud's visual systems allowing you to pick out potential targets and, crucially, other suit wearers.'

'That's handy,' Bruno says. 'Glad we're not going to have to keep saying sorry for bumping into each other.'

'Forget the banter and focus.' Nero looks at each of them in turn. 'We're only about half a kilometre away from the target location and about to go up to street level.'

Bruno starts to unbutton his jacket. 'Then let's get this bad-boy on.'

Kass holds up a hand. 'I suggest we strip to our underwear.'

'Maybe we should go the full commando.' Raising his eyebrows at her, Bruno smiles. 'I will if you will.'

'This isn't skinny-dipping in the fjord.' Suppressing a grin, Nero shakes his head at the boy. 'Kass is right – we strip to our underwear. As you'll discover soon enough, Bruno, these things aren't exactly pliable. Underpants will help with the chaffing.'

Nero averts his eyes from Kass while she undresses though he doubts she either cares or notices. He looks at the small arsenal tucked into various pockets of his rucksack. In their enthusiasm, they may have brought too many weapons. It might have been better if they'd left some of these behind.

'We'll stow our clothes and packs here,' he says. 'Consider which weapons you really need and ditch the rest. Under this bench will do.'

Looking up, Nero notices that, like him, the bare flesh of the decoy's upper body is a mass of scars. One particularly raised one snakes all the way down his side as if his attacker had been trying to fillet him.

'Let's just hope we're alive to retrieve this lot afterwards,' the decoy says, the strange material already obscuring most of his damaged flesh.

Despite the cumbersome nature of the suits, they make steady progress. 'Think I'm getting the hang of walking in this,' Bruno's electronically rendered voice tells them. 'D'you think it hurts if you fall over wearing one of these?'

'Probably. Now concentrate,' Nero tells him. His own words are fed back to him a fraction of a second later. Suit-to-suit communications are via a dedicated channel he assumes is encrypted. The audio quality is poor, reminding him of those long-distance conversations with his grandmother before she died.

The factory is already in sight. 'Our primary aim at this stage is to observe what's going on,' Nero says. 'Remember we need to find out exactly what they know about the consignment and what their next move is likely to be.'

Bruno leads the way through the damaged section of fence with Nero right behind him. When they encounter no opposition, he signals for the others to follow.

Looking at the ground, Nero curses the lying snow; under the glare of the perimeter lights, their footprints stand out like flies on a wedding cake.

With his attention elsewhere, Nero hadn't seen the decoy move across to take up the lead, matching, step for step, a previous trail of footprints. Following these takes them to a dilapidated door to one of the buildings. Improbably, it's unlocked. Through his stud he hears the groan of the hinges as it opens. He taps Bruno on the shoulder. *Quentin's been here before.*

Bruno's pixilated head nods several times. *I know he has.*

Now that her body has cooled down from their trek, Chan finds she's shivering. Sprawled out on the hard floor, she knows she's not thinking straight, must stay alert; better still, she should stand up and rub some life back into her tired limbs. If only she can avoid those vixens, there might be another way out of here.

Voices: too far away to make out. Getting closer, louder. 'Like I said, something's not right.' A man: not young, not old – definitely a local accent.

The pungent and distinctive smell of fox infiltrates her airways. Snuffling sounds, then a sustained, throaty rumble. Chan keeps her eyes shut, daren't move a millimetre in case those vixens decide she's the danger they're sensing.

'They're restless.' A woman's voice, no distortion – surprisingly normal. Sounds like the lesser-of-two-evils decoy. It's possible she's not wearing that fokking suit – a much easier target.

'See that.' The same woman. 'Look how they're all sitting up with their ears back – that means they're sensing some kind of threat.'

'No sign of hostiles on any of the monitors.' The local man again then the crunch of glass under heavy boots. 'Where the fokk is she?'

'Over there.' A sneer of a laugh. 'Look at that – our Sleeping Beauty's taking a little nap. Always cuter when they're like that, aren't they?'

'Shame to wake her.' The man sniggers. 'Funny – I wouldn't have taken Ása for the sentimental type.'

'I'm wondering if my pack can hear her prince approaching.'

Through her half-closed eyes, Chan can see the woman is a slight figure next to the man. The two are dressed in regular street clothes – dark colours, no logos or marking; nothing to help pick them out in an identity line-up.

Two sets of boots come towards her; one circles around behind until they're standing on either side of her.

A single cough-like bark. The other vixens join in, the din reverberating out in the vast space.

The barking stops in a single beat. 'That's better,' the woman says. 'Can't think with that racket going on.'

Given the noise, Chan has no choice but to sit up and pretend she's just woken. Before the end of her performance, the man grabs her under the arms and hauls her to her feet.

The woman leans in close; Chan can smell stale garlic on her breath. They're almost the same height and build. Equally matched. From what she can see of her, the woman looks fairly ordinary – she's fair-haired, pretty in a bland sort of way. It would be hard to describe her in a debriefing – the perfect decoy.

The woman pushes her towards a doorway. Chan tries to shrug her off. She doesn't see or hear the signal that tells the vixens to move aside and let them through. 'What do you want from me?' she asks. 'Where the hell are you taking me?'

'You're wanted in the office,' the woman leans into the back of her collar and laughs – her garlic breath hot on Chan's neck. 'Don't worry, we'll make sure no one comes in to disturb you.'

Fifty-Three

Moving through the building, the next door they open leads to another passageway; this one's shorter. Nero signals for the other three to wait and then walks on a few steps. On hearing raised voices, he stops to listen.

A woman is speaking. 'Williams and I have checked the system over twice and everything's working perfectly. There's no sign of any intruders either outside or inside any of the other buildings. The only footsteps out there are ours. Got that.'

Bruno's voice in his head: *definitely Ása Sturludóttir – the sadistic bitch who kept me locked up here. I'd recognise her voice anywhere.*

'But you're a decoy yourself.' A second voice – also a woman.

Don't know who she is.

'An ex-decoy, remember.'

'Okay, granted,' the woman says, 'but surely you'd trust your own pack, like I'd trust mine anytime over mere technology. What's happened to your pack, by the way – where are they?'

So there's another female decoy here.

Yes and I'd lay odds the two of us have met before. Last time she had me pinned down under her boot.

Lucky you.

'There could be all sorts of reasons why those vixens are acting up,' a man cuts in.

That's Ármannsson. Viking type. Built like a barn door.

'I really don't give a rat's arse how those vixens are behaving,' Ármannsson says.

'Yeah – maybe they've all come on heat at the same time.' Another man – which makes four so far.

He's a long streak of piss called Bresson.

Nero holds four fingers up for Kass and Quentin's benefit, though he's not sure his image will be clear enough for them to read his signal from behind.

'We have an expression,' the mystery woman says. 'If someone's a little slow on the uptake we say: hann gengur ekki heill til skógar – he doesn't walk whole to the forest. That about sums you up, Bresson.'

His laugh is a challenge thrown down. Nero hears the unmistakable sound of a blade being pulled from its sheath. 'I'm tempted to cut your stupid head off right now,' the woman says, 'though I imagine the rest of your body is used to functioning without a brain.'

'For Christ's sake, simmer down and put that thing away.' Ása again – clearly the one giving the orders. There's a familiar quality to her voice. Perhaps they've already met somewhere.

Nero signals for the other three to stay where they are as he walks on down the passageway. He's met by a volley of single, short barks, almost like the vixens have something stuck in their throats.

'And now they're off again, for fokk sake,' Bresson says. 'If you ask me, they're probably just hungry. Have you fed the poor bastards recently?'

'Would you like to know what I enjoyed most about cutting Rockingham's throat?' The mystery woman asks. 'No? Well then let me tell you, it was the look on his face as he bled out; the shock that I – a mere woman – had outwitted him in the end. You'd do well to remember that.' A pause before she adds, 'Isn't that right, Williams?'

So now that makes five. Nero turns to the others and holds

up his whole hand. He's aware the sign might be misinterpreted.

Before Williams can answer, Ása says: 'No one's denying the two of you did a brilliant job back there, but remember the rest of the commanders are still alive and kicking. If Rockingham was the index case – our patient zero – they'll all be riddled with the same disease. As for Hagalín, I doubt they would have been so keen to endorse him as State Governor if it hadn't furthered their purpose. We need to make sure none of them are left breathing – and that includes Hagalín; that way they can't infect anyone else.'

'Security will be more of a problem now even with the suits,' the unknown woman says.

'Losing our nerve, are we? I'd offer to do the job for you, Freyja, if there was any way I could squeeze into that suit of yours,' Ármannsson says.

The mystery woman now has a name but it doesn't help much – there are too many women called Freyja in Eldísvík.

'In any case, I think we all recognise finesse isn't part of your particular skill set,' Freyja tells him.

'That's enough. Simmer down. Let's not fight amongst ourselves,' Ása says. 'Remember, we've got the military and the security forces all running around like headless chickens. With two suits between us, we can divide our attacks. I've already figured out a way to get to Commander Grímsson.'

'I learnt a lot working for Rockingham.' A new man speaks – has to be the one she called Williams. 'He and Commander Avraham were as thick as thieves. If anyone was in on the deals with the cartels, it was Avraham.'

'If it's all the same to you,' Freyja says. 'I'd like to pay a visit to Avraham next.'

Nero feels pressure against his back.

What are we waiting for? You've heard their plans – imagine the chaos it'll cause. We're wearing invincibility suits, for fokk sake. Don't know about you but I'm not just going to stand here.

Out manoeuvred in his cumbersome suit, Nero fails to stop the boy pushing past him. All he can do is follow behind him into an open area of the factory that's cavernous and derelict. He turns to see Quentin and Kass are right behind.

Responding to the intrusion, some of the vixens stand their ground, giving short barks before crouching down, ears forward, ready to spring. Others, like the wild wolves back in Italy, rush at them before crouching, lips curled to bare their teeth. A few begin to circle around behind them, teeth snapping together as they rehearse the bites they're dying to inflict. The whole pack surrounds the four of them, eyes flashing as they wait for their leader's signal to attack.

The conspirators are some distance away. They've already drawn their weapons – an impressive array that, under normal circumstances, would be enough to fell ten times their number.

A wall of a man comes toward them one slow step at a time; his long, unkempt hair framing a face that's been left heavily pockmarked by a disease that should have been eradicated a long time ago.

That's Ármannsson.

I guessed as much.

Time to even the score, I think.

'What the fokk do we have here?' Ármannsson is squinting as if that might make them visible.

No. Let me handle this.

The vixens snap their jaws behind Nero's back as he steps out in front of the boy. 'Sorry to gatecrash your little get-together,' he says. 'In another breach of etiquette, it seems we've all come to the party wearing the exact same outfits.'

Although it's pointless, he holds up a hand. 'I really would advise you all not to fire or the guest list on your side is likely to be depleted before we can have a civilised conversation.'

'Didn't I tell you, my pack never makes a mistake?' The speaker must be Freya. She's come forward behind Ármannsson and is now standing to his right. She looks no more than thirty. In different circumstances, Nero would describe her as very attractive. There's nothing remotely attractive about the expression on her face. 'Inspector Cavallo,' she says. 'I'd recognise your voice anywhere. The last time we met, you were wearing a balaclava. I have to say your current disguise is a bit of a step up. Perhaps you'd like to tell me the name of your dressmaker.'

That's definitely not Ása.

So, this is the same decoy – Harris's embittered friend. Her fair complexion ties in with her being Nordic, probably native born. There's just a chance they could still end this without bloodshed.

He can't talk to these people dressed like this. Though it makes him instantly vulnerable to their weapons, he retracts the hood of his suit. The cold air hits his face. 'Seems you decoys have given up on upholding law,' he says.

'The last time we met, you promised to arrest the person responsible for murdering Harris,' Freyja says.

Nero shakes his head. 'I told you I'd investigate his murder and try to find whoever was responsible. I did my best before–'

'Newsflash, Inspector, I did much better.' She peers around him. 'From the way my pack are behaving, I'm guessing you're not alone. Aren't you going to introduce us to your friends?'

'Why would I do that?'

'Talking of introductions,' she says, without breaking eye contact, 'I think it's time the Inspector here met our other guest. Williams – perhaps you'd like to go and fetch her?'

'I've heard of this bastard.' The speaker, a tall, thin man, appears on Ármannsson's left side.

That one's Bresson.

Some distance behind him, a shortish man with his weapon raised, is backing out of the door – Williams.

'Let the man go,' Nero says.

'But I've got a clear line of sight, sir.' Kass's voice in his ear. 'There could be a whole load of others in the building. He could be off fetching them.'

'You heard her – they're holding some woman hostage. Let him go and get her. That's an order.'

'What's to stop me shooting your head off?' the skinny man says, muscling up as best he can.

'Well now, you must be Mr Bresson,' Nero says. 'A pleasure to meet you at last.'

The man's taken aback at being identified but he's trying to hide it. 'Think you're pretty clever, eh? Well let me tell you, Inspector who-ever-the-fokk-you-are, you've just signed your own death warrant.'

'You don't seem to have grasped the fact that more of my officers are standing right behind me heavily armed and wearing impenetrable suits. Go ahead, fire away. We'll soon see who's responsible for their own death.'

Out of the corner of his eye, Nero sees the hood retract on Quentin's suit.

The look in Freya's eyes, tells him the two know each other.

'Where do you think we got these?' Quentin asks. 'I helped Cavallo intercept the consignment before it reached the Double Red. With their long-awaited deal suddenly off the table, you can guess how the brotherhood will react. They always settle the score with anyone who fails to hold up their end of the bargain; doesn't matter who they're dealing with.

'If we don't stop them in time, they'll indiscriminately wipe out the commanders before you can,' Nero says. 'Which means I'll have no chance of bringing any of them to trial for corruption. If all of them are slaughtered, the rule of law will have demonstrably failed. It will leave a power vacuum in this city and, with or without Hagalín, who knows what will be unleashed after that?'

Freyja comes forward to laugh in his face. 'You really are so fokking naïve, Inspector. It would almost be endearing if it wasn't so tragic.'

'Look, we know where the consignment is right now,' Quentin says. 'Through my contacts, I can reactivate the deal and flush the cartel out into the open. If we work together, we can take down the whole lot of them.'

Nero turns to him. 'That would be far too risky. These damned things need to be destroyed.'

'Not if we can stop them getting into the wrong hands,' Quentin says.

'Now who's being naïve?' Nero asks. 'They're always going to be in the wrong hands. Invincibility is too powerful a weapon to confer on anyone.'

The vixens around them are beginning to stir. Nero can see their attention is being drawn off to one side. Following their gaze, he notices a trio of foxes have appeared. He can sense they're not part of this pack. The three spread out into a lip-curling line.

'Stay back.' Nero recognises Ása's voice.

That's her just behind Ármannsson.

'Well now, isn't this nice, we're all together at last,' she says, stepping out of the big man's shadow. 'Surprise!'

Nero almost drops his weapon as shock runs through him. It's Chan! Christ, how wrong he's been all along.

'I see you recognise me, Inspector,' she says, her voice bright with vitriol. As she comes closer, he can pick out the same line of three moles beneath her right eye – the ones he'd lovingly traced with his finger – and yet all the warmth, all the humanity has gone from her face. What the hell could have made her like this?

'You should see the look on your face! Bit of a shocker, eh? Reminds me of that time when that stupid nurse got in between us.'

She prowls in front of him – such a slight figure. Knowing she was the one who injected Nelson with that lethal poison, it would be easy to strike her down if he hadn't got to know the other side of her.

'You know,' Ása says, 'I'm reminded of a story my mother – my far-from- loving *adopted* mother – used to tell. It was all about naughty old Loki, who hung around with the old gods – though he wasn't actually a god himself. I know you're an Italian, Cavallo, but surely you've heard of him. Either way, I'll spare you the details. The way my so-called mother told the story, Loki was the one responsible for the downfall of the most powerful gods and that set in motion Ragnarök – which, roughly speaking, translates as the end of the world. The moral of the tale being that nothing, not even the gods themselves, will remain the same forever. And after Ragnarök a new world will rise from the ruins of the old.'

The smile on her face mutates to an unpleasant grimace. 'Not much of a bedtime story, I'll grant you, but a valuable lesson in times such as these.'

'Tell us where the shipment is hidden.' Freyja is looking only at Quentin. 'You're one of us – you know the reality of what it's like out there on the streets every night.'

'My friend here is right,' Ása says, looking for a fleeting moment more like the Chan he knows. 'We decoys should join forces. What say we shake up this god-forsaken city once and for all.'

Fifty-Four

Struggling to control his anger, Bruno decides he's heard more than enough. 'Don't listen to the bitch,' he says to Quentin, 'she's pure evil.'

Ása cocks her head on one side. 'Well now, this is quite the reunion. Ármannsson, I believe our old friend Bruno is here with us tonight.'

The big man takes a step forward to stare into the space behind Nero. 'Couldn't keep away then, pretty boy.'

'That's far enough,' Nero says.

Bruno, whatever she says, keep your hood down. Don't let her goad you into retracting it.

'For those of you who don't know,' Ása says, 'our invisible friend here is, in actual fact, one of the last surviving telepaticos. Which makes him quite a catch for any girl.' She turns to Freyja. 'Strange how you wait years for one of them to come along and then two come at once. Not many people know that Inspector Cavallo here is also a telepatico. Okay they're both Italian, but still what are the odds?'

'Ása Sturludóttir,' Nero has turned his weapon on her, 'I'm arresting you for the murder of the medic, Nelson Tarone Wood. Other charges will no doubt follow. You are entitled to legal– '

'What, you seriously think I'm just going to simply lay this weapon down and raise my hands in surrender? And there I was believing you freaks of nature are able to read other people's minds. I wouldn't have tried to kill you, Cavallo, if I'd known how useless you were at it. No wait – that's a lie. I knew you'd keep on poking your nose into things you shouldn't. I see I was right about that.'

'Sod this,' Kass says. 'Let's get this party started.'

'Legal representation,' Nero continues. 'Any statements you make from this point on may be used in court to assist the prosecution.'

'If anyone's a freak of nature, it's you.' Bruno retracts his hood.

Oh, for Christ's sake, I warned you not to rise to her bait.

'It's about time you learned the truth about your own origins.' The boy's grin is genuine; he's enjoying himself at last. 'Maybe I should try to put this a little delicately.' He shakes his head. 'Na, sod that, Dr Arthur –'

'Don't you dare quote that fokking man to me!' Ása shouts. 'You can't believe anything that duplicitous bastard says.'

'Duplicitous or not, the truth is he made you. When I say made, I mean he literally created you using the preserved DNA of an unfortunate Chinese woman – a notable beauty who snuffed off her mortal coil more than seventy years ago. You are her clone.'

Ása scoffs 'You don't expect me to believe that nonsense,' she says, though Bruno can see she's visibly shaken.

'It might be a weird and maybe not especially glamorous way to come into this world,' Bruno says, 'but that's not the worst part. You see over there at the IBR they really do love tinkering around with nature. For years they've been adding a little bit of this to a little bit of that to alter the genetic mix of the creatures they breed. Must be a bit like making cocktails. And don't forget, they had all that stuff lying around from their experiments on wolves and foxes.

'I can tell you're beginning to cotton on, Ása.' He looks at

Freyja. 'By the way, I gather your friend here didn't tell you that she executed her own vixens.'

'It had to be done,' Ása says. 'I had little choice.'

'Trouble is,' Bruno says, 'despite your very best efforts, those three just behind you escaped. I'm no animal behaviourist but even I can see they're seriously pissed at you right now. To anthropomorphise for a moment – just imagine watching your trusted pack leader callously murder your mates. I suppose it's not entirely her fault, ladies and gentlemen, because, as beautiful as she is in some people's eyes,' he looks over at Nero, 'I'm afraid Ása here has never been fully human.'

She raises her weapon, is about to aim for his head. Reading her mind, he fires first and Ármannsson collapses onto the floor holding his chest. Sprawled out and not moving, the man appears to be dead.

Shit! Before Bresson can fire at him, he raises his arm to shield his face. The blast hits the wall, just behind Kass, grazing one of the foxes as it's deflected to smash a hole in the floor. The yelping vixen retreats.

Bresson's next shot bruises Bruno's arm before ricocheting into the man's own thigh.

'Down!' Ása shouts. While the other animals have withdrawn from the firing line, her three vixens have crept forward to surround her, snarling and snapping their teeth. She takes aim at the nearest and its body flies through the air and lands limply at Quentin's feet.

One of the surviving two sinks its teeth into her arm causing her to drop the photon just as the other one launches itself at her chest. Off balance, she falls to the floor. The animal goes straight for her throat.

Switching to a less powerful weapon, Nero blasts one of the foxes. Its body skids across the floor as he runs forward to shoot the other one in the head at point blank range. The vixen collapses onto Ása and he struggles to push its body aside. 'Chan.'

Bruno can see Ása's windpipe has been half torn out. Nero is pressing his gloved hand to the wound trying to staunch the blood flow, but he can't keep enough pressure on it without choking her. 'Oh God, Jie Ning,' he says. A hideous gurgling and spluttering comes up from her throat. It stops abruptly as her eyes glaze over.

Beside Nero, Kass has retracted her own hood and is checking Ása for any sign of life. She shakes her head 'I'm sorry, Nero, she's gone.'

'Hold your fire!' They all turn to see Williams holding a photon to a woman's head. 'Lay down your weapons, all of you or so help me I'll shoot her.'

'That's Chan,' Kass says. 'What the fokk's going on?'

Bruno looks at the hostage. She's the double of Ása. He turns to Nero.

Okay, so your girlfriend's the clone of a psychopathic killer; nobody's perfect.

Fifty-Five

At first, Chan had felt relieved when the door opened and a short, thin man in regular clothing had walked in. Getting to her feet, she'd looked into his calm, rather pleasant face and assumed he might be about to release her.

His smile had relaxed her, caught her off guard. She hadn't expected him to grab her arm and twist it behind her until her shoulder joint burned with pain. The arm-lock was swift and professionally executed.

Chan had considered hooking her foot behind his leg before leaning forward to force him off balance. The manoeuvre would risk dislocating her shoulder joint. Before she could act, something hard – clearly a weapon of some kind – had been pressed into her back. She'd had no choice but to let him march her towards the main factory. Once through the door, he'd moved the gun from her back to press it up against her temple.

The room hadn't looked the same. She'd assumed the power was no longer connected but a small pendant light was on near the empty centre of the room. The light was swaying to and fro.

Vixens were spread out around the edge of the room; they had to walk right through them. So close to those bared teeth; she knew they could be on her in a second. The man kept shoving her in the back every time she hesitated. They'd continued their awkward progress half hidden by the shadows.

On the edge of the illuminated circle, she could see a woman crouching down beside a man. He was slumped against a support beam, pressing his hand against a wound on his thigh, his clothing stained bright red from the bleeding he was trying desperately to stop.

The woman had pushed his hand away to assess his wound. If he'd severed an artery, he wouldn't survive for long.

There appeared to be a body lying on the floor to the right of the injured man with several dead foxes strewn around it. Chan had seen movement on the other side of the room. Squinting against the light, she could make out four heads visible from the neck up. Was she hallucinating? No – they had to be wearing those suits.

And then she'd looked down at the corpse. A woman. Like a nightmare, she saw her own face, white and lifeless, staring back up at her. Shock weakened her legs causing the pressure on her bent arm to intensify until she almost screamed out from the pain. She couldn't decide if the body was real or some sort of effigy that had been made to look exactly like her. Why would anyone do that? What the hell was going on here?

The man pushed her on. She saw another man lying on the ground. Turning her gaze to the disembodied heads, Chan recognised Nero and then, just behind him, Kass.

'Hold your fire! Lay down your weapons, all of you,' the man at her back shouted. He yanked her arm to force her face up to the light. 'Or so help me I'll shoot her.'

'That's Chan,' Kass said. 'What the fokk's going on here?'

The man holding her half pushes, half drags her forward a few more metres. 'All of you need to drop your weapons or this woman dies.'

He fires a shot that screams past Nero's head and slams into the wall behind. Masonry crashes to the ground. A massive black hole emerges out of the dust.

She hears a lot of clattering as Nero throws down an array of weapons. Kass offloads a couple more and the two heads-only men standing behind her do the same. An impressive arsenal is scattered along the concrete floor at her feet.

'So far so good,' the man behind her says.

He turns on the woman. 'You as well.' He increases the pressure on Chan's skull.

'You've got to be kidding me,' the woman says. 'Ása didn't want her harmed but you can blow her fokking brains out for all I care.' She folds her arms, stands her ground.

Chan's relieved when he removes the barrel from her head to switch his aim to the woman. 'Make no mistake, I won't hesitate.'

The vixens become vocal, giving out short barks, they creep forward baring their teeth. 'Back,' the woman says. Once they've retreated, she places a weapon on the floor.

'And now the knives,' he says. 'All three.'

'Ever get the impression someone knows you too well?' She throws the knives one at a time onto the ground, only just missing his feet.

'Look, Williams, I've no idea what your plan is,' Nero says, 'but it seems pretty obvious the wheels have come off the wagon and the whole thing's heading toward the fiord.'

'Maybe a cliff edge would be a better analogy,' one of the men behind Nero says.

'Shut the fokk up for once, Bruno,' Nero says, not for a second taking his eye off the man just behind her. 'Why don't we talk this thing through like civilised human beings? Put down that weapon, Williams, before someone else gets hurt.'

'What and pass up the chance of making a fortune out of those things you're wearing. I don't think so, do you?'

'I thought you were better than this,' the woman says with what sounds like genuine disappointment. Chan recognises her voice – she's one of the two decoys who brought her here.

'Look around you.' Nero's head floats nearer. 'Look what happens when people come up against these suits in a fight. For better or worse, Ása was an impressive warrior and she's lying over there dead. Bresson here won't last much longer if we don't get him to a hospital. These damned suits need to be destroyed.'

'I'm sure you think you're smart and all that, Inspector,' the woman scoffs. 'But I'm not exactly sure how you go about destroying the indestructible.'

'You've seen for yourselves tonight, these things are too divisive. They confer too much power to the wearer,' Nero says. 'They can never be a force for good.'

'But they can be a source of wealth.' Out of the corner of her eye, she sees the barrel of the man's weapon is now trained on Nero. 'We've met before,' he says. 'I should have killed you in that bank when I had the chance.'

Nero's face contorts with emotion. 'So it was you Williams – you're the bastard who killed Lúter.'

'That's right, Cavallo. I can see from your face how you're itching to kill me. Am I right? Still as keen to negotiate?'

'We can work something out.' There's a new harshness to Nero's voice.

Williams pulls on Chan's hair, jolting her head backwards. 'Skip all the sanctimony and start undressing.'

The boy laughs out loud. 'As the bishop said to the nun.'

An explosion of noise and heat inside her head. Ears ringing, Chan feels herself falling. A dark tide of blood creeps into her vision, warm against her skin. She feels nothing except the hard floor beneath her. Don't they say your brain doesn't feel pain? So this is it then; lying here on broken glass looking up into that still swinging light, this is how her life comes to an end.

Fifty-Six

Chan's eyelids quiver and then close. Bent on one knee, Nero checks her pulse then touches her forehead. She's cold. 'It's only a superficial graze but she's in deep shock,' he says, straightening up.

'That was a sweet shot, Kass.' Bruno hi-fives her. 'If a bit off-centre.'

That loud laugh of hers echoes in the vast space. 'Got the little runt almost between the eyes – what more do you want?' Kass checks the weapon. 'I just knew this Aries 12 would come in handy.'

'You want to be careful, saying things like that,' Nero tells her. 'People might accuse you of being a telepatico.'

She gives him a curious look. 'I've been called worse things.'

Quentin has moved and is now standing next to the decoy woman – almost shoulder to shoulder. Are the two of them about to make a move? Nero senses the man's continuing ambivalence – it could go either way.

Keeping an eye on him, Nero bends to check Chan's forehead. She still feels clammy. 'You're going to be okay,' he tells her. Her breathing's shallow. Holding up her wrist, it feels so insubstantial; her pulse is hardly there.

'We need to keep her warm.' He can see Bresson's in a bad way. 'Better ask DSD to send some medics out here fast.' Nero looks at Quentin. 'Can you call it in anonymously?'

The decoy hesitates before he complies. When he speaks he sounds like a very old man – the innocent bystander he's pretending to be.

Kass starts to undress Williams. 'It's not like he needs any of this now,' she says, pulling off the dead man's jacket and throwing it over to Nero. Next his sweatshirt flies through the air to land on the floor beside him. 'Roll that up and put it under her head,' Kass tells him.

Nero does as he's told then spreads Williams' jacket over Chan's upper body, tucking it in at her sides with care. She hardly responds to his touch. 'You're okay,' he tells her again. 'This is just shock – you'll recover, I promise.' Without meaning to, he looks from her over to Ása. The two of them are lying almost side by side, their faces at the exact same angle. Physically, they're indistinguishable.

He looks up at Bruno. *They could just be identical twins*

The boy shakes his head. *Dr Arthur was an open book and very proud of his achievements. In fact, he desperately wants the world to know how clever he's been but knows the International Ethics Committee would crucify him. Under his instructions, Magnúsdóttir grew ten of the cloned embryos – he forgot to mention how he'd genetically altered some of them. Only three reached the stage where they could be implanted. The third one failed to develop in the surrogate's womb. So that just left these two.*

Nero doesn't like the boy's attitude – the way he's already dehumanising the women.

'Were you lying when you said all that stuff about Ása having animal genes?' Freyja asks Bruno.

'They actually came from a wolf and, yes, it's true. Chan's adoption worked out okay. When Ása was less than eighteen months old, her birth mother began to smell a rat.'

'A choice of words that's a bit indelicate even for you,' Nero says.

'Okay– point taken. Anyway, Ása's parents confronted the hospital consultant with their suspicions. Seems they were both convinced there was something unnatural about her. They were highly religious so there was a lot of talk about moral evil. They'd even considered an exorcism. In the end the couple decided they wanted nothing more to do with Ása. Dr Arthur had a go at reprogramming her, so to speak. He had the perfect control subjects and so he experimented with techniques of implanting false memories; did it with both girls.'

Nero remembers what Rashid had told him about Chan's memory of the Shanghai Uprising. All of that must have been an illusion – a false memory.

'Eventually, another couple adopted Ása,' Bruno tells them. 'Though they only did it for the money Dr Arthur paid them. The family lived way out in the Orange Zone. Whole thing was more of a convenient arrangement that allowed him to study Ása and Chan's responses to their different situations.'

Freyja sighs. 'What a start in life. Though I have to say she was a world-class bitch – no pun intended – you can't help but feel sorry for her.'

'Seems you've got a heart after all, Freyja,' Bruno says. 'I'm Bruno by the way, in case you didn't catch that. How's the leg? Bites can be nasty.'

If we ignore the fact that she's a cold-blooded killer, I'd say Freyja's pretty hot.

'So how come you know all this stuff?' Quentin says, narrowing his eyes on Bruno.

'Keep up, Quentin,' Freyja tells him. 'You heard Ása – this boy and Cavallo are both telepaticos – if that's the plural. They read people's minds.'

Nero winces. He can't be sure how much Chan overheard but these two decoys plus Kass and Bresson – assuming he survives – all know their secret. By anyone's calculation that's too many for comfort.

Nero can do nothing more for Chan. When he looks at her, he's aware that his perception has already altered. A chill runs through him when he thinks of her and that mad decoy being one and the same. If Chan is a clone, could that be why he's never been able to read her mind?

He looks up to Bruno for an answer. The boy shrugs. *Unfortunately, I didn't have a problem reading Ása's mind. Could be that you're just a bit crap at it.*

Or perhaps, despite being clones, they were different in some way.

Maybe. In any case, who are we to judge – aren't we freaks of nature in most people's eyes?

When Nero checks again, the vixens have moved considerably closer and the two decoys seem to be almost on top of him. 'I don't know whether you consider aggression to be a desirable trait in a leader,' he says, addressing Freyja. 'For my money, humanity is the most important prerequisite.'

It's hard to judge but Quentin seems to be leaning towards the woman. Nero can sense that the two of them were close at one time, possibly still are. 'Wearing these suits, as you know, is pretty awe-inspiring,' Quentin says. 'Doesn't every kid dream of being invincible?'

Quentin's certainly an impressive operator. Bruno's voice is too loud in his head, he checks to see if the boy's lips are moving. *Remember he led you to these things in the first place – you wouldn't have found them without him. Freyja was never sold on Ása's way of doing things – that much I do know.*

'You could control the whole city just with the quantity we've intercepted,' Nero says. 'Add a ruthless, preferably charismatic leader and it's hello servitude.'

'You paint an ugly picture,' Freyja says.

'Awesome or not, these things are ridiculously hot.' Kass begins to undo the top fastenings on her suit. 'According to my stud's schematic, the medics will be arriving in six and a half minutes.'

Nero looks at the three corpses in their various attitudes on the floor. 'The patrol officers will make a preliminary assessment of the scene. God alone knows what they'll make of those dead vixens over there.'

Freyja stares at each of the bodies in turn before she looks at Nero. 'It's hard to take in what just happened here; and there's still the rest of that consignment to fight over,' she says. 'It pains me to say this, but I think you're right, Cavallo; the sooner we're rid of them, the better.'

Quentin keeps shaking his head. 'That may be a laudable aim but I can't see how you hope to destroy them. The whole point is that they're more or less indestructible.'

'He's going to dump them out at sea,' Bruno says, 'Isn't that right?'

Dammit – I hadn't planned to tell them that part yet.

'Okay, less than four minutes now,' Kass says. 'It's getting light. If we want to get out of here, we need to move it.'

Nero turns to Freyja. 'Get your vixens to back down.' He doesn't hear or see the signal but in one beat the animals begin to slink away as if they were never present. No doubt they'll remain close by.

Freyja walks over to where Bresson is slumped half upright. The injured man's eyes are staring straight ahead, unseeing. She kneels down, puts her hand to the pulse point at his wrist and then searches his neck. 'It's too late for him, in any case,' she says.

She strides over to Ása's body, pulls her photon and blasts Ása's face until it begins to melt.

'Stop!' Nero shouts.

Satisfied, Freyja sheaths her weapon before he can grab it.

'Madonna! Dio santo!' The stench of burning flesh is overpowering; Nero can taste it in his own throat. 'Why the fokk did you do that?'

'Why do you think?' Freyja says, looking across at Chan who's still lying there insensible. Did he only imagine her scream?

The act they've just witnessed has silenced the others. At last Kass removes her hand from her mouth. 'It pains me to say it, but the woman is right. Now, with any luck, they won't connect the two of them.'

She nods to the array of weapons scattered across the floor. 'We need to go and we can't leave this lot lying around. Where to begin...'

Nero averts his gaze from the hellish, blackened corpse of the woman who, for all her faults, had been the bravest of warriors. 'Leave them their own weapons,' he says, 'along with the ones that killed them. With luck, the patrol will read this as some kind of gang shoot out. Once Chan's recovered enough to be interviewed, I just hope she doesn't mention these damned suits.'

Bruno has grabbed more than he can sensibly carry. 'That's enough,' Nero tells him, putting his hand where he judges his shoulder to be. If this is what it's like being a parent, he's glad he doesn't have children. 'You need to leave this to the professionals. I think you should go back to the university and try to calm things down a bit. They'll listen to you.'

'That's all very well, but you'll need me,' Bruno says. 'I'm the one who predicts stuff – remember? No offence Nero, but you're a bit useless by yourself. For a start, I bet you don't know Dr Arthur has an ocean-going yacht to match his ocean-going ego. Bought it years ago with a load of inherited money. Once he gets wind you're planning to arrest him, he'll try to do a runner. Well, not a runner. If it's in a boat, it should be a cast off or a–'

'Stop talking,' Nero tells him. 'We're wasting time.' *This boat – what's it called?*

Naglfar. Just that, no the in front of it. Get this: he named it after some ship that was supposed to be made from the nails of the dead – human fingernails that is.

'If you want my opinion,' Kass says, 'and I know you don't, but you're getting it anyway. I think we should take Bruno along with us.'

Quentin nods his agreement. 'The boy's likely to be useful.'

'In a democracy, he'd get my vote too,' Freyja says. 'Aren't you all about consensus, Cavallo?'

'And I'm wearing a fokking invincibility suit,' Bruno says. 'What can possibly go wrong?'

'Then you have to agree to keep the hood deployed at all times.' Nero looks him straight in the eyes.

'Yeah, okay. I won't reveal this handsome face unless you tell me I can.' Like a conjurer, the boy's head disappears in front of his eyes. 'Talk about over-protective.'

'Good,' Nero says, 'now I can fade out your jabbering whenever I want.'

The story concludes in:
Within Each Other's Shadow -
volume three of Eldísvík trilogy.

Dear reader.

I really hope you've enjoyed 'No God for a Warrior'. Thank you so much for buying or borrowing it.

Please look out for Volume Three of the Eldísvík trilogy.

This series of books really means a lot to me. If you would like to help more readers discover them, please think about leaving a review on Amazon, Goodreads, or anywhere else readers visit.

This book's success depends a great deal on how many positive reviews it gains. If you could spare a few minutes to write one, I would be very grateful.

Thanks in advance to anyone who does.

If you would like to find out more about this book or any of the Eldísvík novels, please visit my website: janturkpetrie.com

Contact Pintail Press at: pintailpress.com

Acknowledgements

Once again, I'd first of all like to thank John, my wonderful husband, for reading and commenting on 'No God for a Warrior' and for giving me the encouragement I needed to finish this volume of the story. Thanks also go to the rest of my family – in particular my lovely daughters Laila and Natalie – for all their support.

I'm once again grateful for all the feedback and encouragement from my fellow writers. In no particular order, they are:

Dr Rona Laycock, John Morrish, Lise Leroux, Wilkie Martin, Meg Davis Berry, Gill Garrett, Richard Hensley, Pam Keevil, Liz Carew, Derek Healy, Pam Orr, Mary Flood, Lianna Pike, Colin Waterman, Rod Griffiths and everyone else at the Cheltenham Fiction Writing Groups. John Holland – of Stroud Short Stories, Radhika Swarup, Debbie Young, and everyone at the Alliance of Independent Authors in Cheltenham.

Special thanks go to Dr Edward Dewhirst – my delightful son-in-law – for his advice on some of the medical details. To Dr Alaric Hall from the University of Leeds for his advice on Icelandic matters – any mistakes are entirely mine – and to the extraordinary Magnús Skarphédinsson of the Elfschool in Reykjavík,

Lastly, I'm very grateful to my editor, Johnny Hudspith, and to my cover designer, Jessica Reed, for their excellent work.

47941561R00193

Printed in Poland
by Amazon Fulfillment
Poland Sp. z o.o., Wrocław